PRAISE FOR MALL

"With stunning prose, Pearson draws ~~readers into the~~ characters and weaves a horror-esque fantasy tale."

—*Library Journal*

"The two storylines wind and twist and eventually connect in this leisurely paced, lyrically written paean to the power of friendship and chosen family."

—*Booklist*

"*We Ate the Dark* is a gripping tale of friendship and grief and the real and imagined ghosts from the past that come to haunt us. Deliciously queer and wildly Southern, this book had me turning pages fast, lost in its poetic language, immersed in the lush landscape, holding my breath in anticipation. Mallory Pearson has written a stunning debut filled with sentences that continued to surprise me with their beauty and generosity until the very last page."

—Genevieve Hudson, author of *Boys of Alabama* and *Pretend We Live Here*

"Written with gorgeous, hypnotic prose, *We Ate the Dark* is a piece of uncategorizable beauty and a masterclass in suspense: a ghost story inside a mystery inside a story of queer love, friendship, and family. Pearson has added to the queer horror canon with a deeply felt, deeply human masterpiece about grief, magic, connection, and all the things that keep us coming back to one another. Spooky, tender, and heartbreaking, it'll have you turning the pages like an incantation."

—Marisa Crane, author of *I Keep My Exoskeletons to Myself*

VOICE LIKE A HYACINTH

ALSO BY MALLORY PEARSON

We Ate the Dark

VOICE LIKE A HYACINTH

A novel

MALLORY PEARSON

47N●RTH

Text copyright © 2025 by Mallory Pearson
All rights reserved.

Published by 47North, Seattle

www.apub.com, Amazon, the Amazon logo, and 47North are trademarks of Amazon.com, Inc., or its affiliates.

ISBN-13: 9781662515422 (paperback)
ISBN-13: 9781662515415 (digital)

Cover design by Caroline Teagle Johnson
Cover image: © Sabine Bungert / Plainpicture; © MirageC, © Nisian Hughes / Getty

Printed in the United States of America

For my friends.
Wherever you are, that's where my heart is.

I

Like the sweet apple which reddens upon the
topmost bough,
Atop on the topmost twig, —which the pluckers
forgot, somehow, —
Forget it not, nay; but got it not, for none could get
it till now.

II

Like the wild hyacinth flower which on the hills is
found,
Which the passing feet of the shepherds for ever tear
and wound,
Until the purple blossom is trodden in the ground.

One Girl, Sappho

Why you treating me like
someone that you never loved?

party 4 u, Charli XCX

Fall

Possession

1

WE WHO DRANK FROM THE GLASS

We'd go anywhere if it meant we'd be together. We talked about ourselves by saying *we, our, ours.* Our favorite song. Our spot outside of town. Our parties, our birthdays, our dinners. We went to the woods. We built a fire. We were together. We got too drunk. We picked each other up. We slept in the same bed a hundred times—when it snowed, when we were scared, when we were excited. We had dreams about each other. We danced in dorm rooms, egged each other on. We took night walks. We ate fries on the grass of Main Lawn and warned skateboarders about the crack in the path before it could send them sprawling. We walked that huge fallen tree until it finally snapped over the creek, dropped us ankle-deep in wildlife and algae. We braided each other's hair. We told each other how beautiful we looked. We talked about loving each other, and loving other people, and loving all the ways we showed it. We got too drunk again. We picked each other up. We picked apples. We picked flowers. We watched TV together. We fell asleep together. We drove together. We hung out of the sunroof and the windows. We cooked meals, together, all our favorites at once, and we ate and we laughed and we promised to do it again, the next day and the next, until "together" was an assumption instead of a hope.

Back then, no one ever liked to spend much time with the five of us because there was always a sixth entity taking up any empty space—a shape crafted by our embodied history, all the inside jokes and references and memories and characters we built out of years of friendship become sentient. We filled every room until we made it our room. We named it together and we left it too crowded. No one else could squeeze in. No one else could speak the language.

We created a lexicon worth living in.

Japanese Breakfast and Solange, dating apps projected on the television screen, Ouija boards, jam jars decorated with nail polish, fingernails slick with oil paint, Richard Siken poems, Carmen Maria Machado essays, Exquisite Corpse drawn in Finch's sketchbook, Club Penguin and Phase 10, Strawberitas and girl blunts packed with lavender and rose petals, zines about queer horror movies, boy drag crafted with mascara mustaches, the time Amrita accidentally did the splits on Main Lawn, the time we got kicked off the swing set by the police, the time Saz fell asleep on top of a half-eaten bar of chocolate and woke up with it smeared in her hair. Rhinestones stuck to our cheeks with lash glue. The mouse in the kitchen Caroline caught with a bag of tortillas. Finch's fire escape and the way morning smelled in the winter and the cling of cold metal through denim. Waxing moons and tarot decks. Saz's locket with Fiona Apple on one side of the heart and Kate Bush on the other, the kissing sound she made when she snapped it shut. Green eyeshadow, hand-me-downs, *Jennifer's Body*, cinnamon brooms bundled with ribbon. Sauvignon blanc and the trip to the shore where we had to pull over and let Caroline throw up outside of a Taco Bell. Amrita's broken watch. Finch's lack of rhythm, Saz's lack of tune. Wearing each other's clothes, sharing toothpaste, splitting everything we ate. The time I scraped my knees on a hike and we laughed for hours, Caroline telling me I looked butch like that, with the stripped hem of her T-shirt bandaging each bloody knee.

The thrifted denim jacket hanging in Amrita's closet with our initials embroidered inside of its sleeve. My bed smelling like Caroline.

Caroline smelling like Saz. Saz smelling like her incessantly burning incense, the rich, herb-y cling of it in her hair. "Short Skirt Long Jacket" by Cake, turned up as loud as it could go in Saz's car. *Over the Garden Wall* every Halloween. *But I'm a Cheerleader* and *Big Fish* and *Stand by Me* and all the *Hunger Games* movies. *The Nightmare* by Henry Fuseli and the field trip we took to see it. Cy Twombly's *Leda and the Swan*. Kiki Smith, Louise Bourgeois, Ana Mendieta, Ruby Onyinyechi Amanze, Artemisia Gentileschi, Helen Frankenthaler, Jenna Gribbon, Zanele Muholi, Catherine Opie, Faith Ringgold, Gluck, Mickalene Thomas, Sally Mann, Amy Sherald. The quiet night we ate dinner together with the back door open and watched the sun set over our studio. *Plastic Beach* and that one pink Devendra Banhart album. The best champagne Saz's parents' credit card could buy. Sappho's fragments, and the way Maggie Nelson wrote about blue. A pile of Doc Martens by the door. The way Caroline's voice changed when her grandma called. The photo of Saz as a kid with a stuffed Winnie the Pooh in her arms that I kept pinned to a board above my desk—how small and hopeful she looked there, black hair cut to her chin and her smile smeared with ice cream. Finch's love for card games, and the time she bought us visors for a poker game that barely lasted thirty minutes. The visor so cute atop Amrita's head as she shotgunned a beer, casting her foamy smile with a green glow. The way Saz cried each summer when classes ended, when we left each other behind, when I lost part of myself until the fall gave it back to me again. The spring break none of us left. That last good thing we promised one another.

All the things that made us an *us*. All the things that made us real to each other. All the things that made it impossible to forget and move on, even after we lost it, even when we knew the end to come.

◆ ◆ ◆

Against our insistence, there was an expiration date attached to our obsession that came assigned on the day we met.

Regardless, I treated our time at Rotham like it would continue forever, the coming months and days and minutes cupped like water in my hands in a never-ending faucet flow. Still—reality was inevitable. We made a pact not to lose ourselves. We promised to find each other in any future. *Friends drift apart,* my dad liked to remind me. *Plans change, and people move on.*

It was our senior thesis year. I was living in a delusion that did not yet have the capability to embarrass me.

If I closed my eyes hard enough to coax stars, I could summon it, that piece of Indiana where plains gave way to ceaseless woods that gave way to town, the wasteland of our hearts where Rotham burned alive. Summer's end meant the days were still hot, but the ground was carpeted with sycamore leaves. Campus glowed, morning sun bright on the Chapel's spire. I could see it all from the steps of the Manor: Lysander Gate and the path that led to the garden and the pond, Tuck House, Banemast, Slatter Hall, and Main Lawn. Eleanor Ohmend Grainer Arts Hall, Grainer to the rest of us, rose mythic at the end of the promenade. It was taller than the other buildings—its shadow shrouded them into silhouettes, and the windows lining our thesis studio were black. Asters and hydrangeas bloomed along the edges of brick paths. Pawpaw trees dropped wet fruit to the grass. Light beamed on the pond and cooked algae into a fetid mess. The world smelled like awakening.

I'd grown up somewhere I once thought lusher, where the mountains were old and knowing. Indiana seemed like such a dead world— before I came to Rotham, I imagined it to be an expanse of overgrown wheatgrass, the beige of a parched death. Tractors and town halls and minivans and maize. And it was, but it was also ours. That distinction alone had the power to make it beautiful.

My parents didn't understand what the draw was, and high school counselors gave my application a wide berth. They didn't know what to do with *The Rotham School* printed across the header and the black-and-white crest punctuating it—a medieval lantern surrounded by a laurel wreath and speckled with stars, murky where the printer's ink smeared. But extensive

Google searches and a Reddit deep dive had promised me that Rotham was where every *real* artist went to hone their craft. I didn't have to funnel my money into a precocious city and entrench myself in that culture. I could go to a place where art was revered as sacred. Where we sequestered ourselves like monastics in search of elevated belief. Where ritual still held meaning, and self-betterment could bloom out of sacrifice.

Campus hummed with the energy of our final move-in. Sticky heat clung to my upper lip and the hair along my forearms. My dad held one end of an air conditioner, and I struggled beneath the other, teeth clenched at the weight as we tried to shuffle toward the Manor's door without one of us being crushed.

"Jo!" Saz called from the entryway. The massive doorframe dwarfed her beaming face. "It's amazing!"

She looked gauzy as a flower after rain in her frothy pink dress. Her hair fell in dark sheets around her shoulders, longer than the last time I'd seen her. I wanted to hug her to me, but my arms were already occupied, so as we crab-crawled through the open door, I pressed my sweaty cheek against hers and felt her kiss the air beside my ear. She shut the door behind us, talking the whole way about the house.

"You won't believe it," she chattered. "There are three fucking floors. I mean, sorry, Mr. Kozak."

We shuffled through the kitchen and up a flight of stairs, Saz shouting from below to direct us to my room on the third floor. We were only halfway down the hall when I heard the moment Amrita spotted me, her bare feet pattering against wood. I had to twist to find her. Humidity turned her hair into a cloud. She was wearing a shirt that had been mine a few years ago, until we both decided it looked better on her. Amrita wound an arm around my waist and squeezed until I laughed. I could feel my dad's impatience in fevered puffs of air across the AC unit.

"Mmm, missed you so much," Amrita sighed against my shoulder. "You smell like coffee."

"A little help, Joanna," my dad said, strained. Sweat made red tracks along his hairline. Amrita's grasp fell away and we climbed again.

At the apex of the Manor, my room was a box with a sloped ceiling. It was barely big enough to spread my arms out and spin in a circle. But across the undressed bed and past the windowpane I could see greenery. Students milled along the promenade. Grainer sat perfect at the end of it all.

My dad set the air conditioner on my desk with a huff and pressed the back of his hand to his forehead. "Go find your mom," he ordered, pulling the instruction manual from his pants pocket. "I'll take care of this."

I obeyed and slipped back into the hall. Crumbling brick lined the walls, cool to the touch and pale with age, like the house had been built out of the ruins of some legendary castle.

The Manor was a privilege—every year groups of seniors applied and hoped to be picked. It was an old Colonial made to house four students, so we'd deemed it impossible for our five until right before the end of junior year, when Finch decided she wanted her own place. She claimed the rest of us would only be *a house full of distractions with too many dishes to do.* So we'd applied: me, Amrita, Saz, and Caroline, expecting the worst, awaiting an email that would tell us we'd be fractured across campus housing. But our names had been drawn. Proof that maybe our chosen family meant something, after all.

I padded down the stairs, the banister beneath my hand shining oily and rich. Voices rose and fell, Saz's glittery posh accent and Amrita's vibratory lull. I paused and waited for Caroline. A small part of me still expected to hear Finch too. But she had always been the kind of girl to place the ocean between us, with only her hands and her will to hold the water in place.

On the second floor, Saz's room was a wreck. Her tarot deck had fallen to the floor, and cards fluttered everywhere. The Wheel of Fortune lay beside my foot. Her bedspread sat in a heap on the floor among teetering piles of clothes, pink against yellow against orange against blue. Along with the vibrant abstract paintings that characterized Saz covering every available surface, it was like looking at the sun. They were massive displays of frenzied brushwork and half-formed words; there were snippets from conversations we'd had, lines from her favorite poems, whole pages of books painstakingly copied by hand and overlaid with fat strokes of paint. Each one layered color on color on color with the same frenetic energy I'd come to associate with Saz.

I looked for her among the chaos and came up empty, but found Amrita crouching in the doorway of the room to the right. She glanced up and brightened in that warm, private way of hers. She'd swept her hair back with a claw clip. Loose dark waves hung in her eyes.

"You're down here with Saz?" I craned over her head, resting my fingertips on her shoulder as I looked around the room. She'd already made the crisp bed—white sheets and white duvet and white pillows.

She leaned into my thigh as she undid the zipper on a suitcase and said, "Weird, right?" Her clothes hung neatly in the wardrobe; dark dresses lined up beside tailored shirts in a stream of blacks and whites and pale blues. Amrita had always been that way—muted, subtle, the same since the first day we'd been placed together in our freshman dorm by Rotham admissions. She was such a contrast to the art she made that people were always surprised to learn that her paintings belonged to her; they were watercolors rich with folkloric imagery, like pages torn from an illuminated manuscript. A folder of them sat on her desk. Each meticulously sized and trimmed piece of watercolor paper had its own perfectly ordered arrangement.

"Does that mean Caroline is upstairs with me?" I asked.

"Yeah, her name was assigned on the door when we got here," Amrita answered. We'd shared a room for three years before now. I knew Amrita better than anyone I'd ever met, closer than a sister, half of myself. The thought of living even a floor above her felt like moving to another country.

"Weird," I said, echoing her earlier statement.

Downstairs sat the kitchen—this would be my life now, step after step after step—and beside it a living area completed by the tattered couch that Amrita and I had in our room last year. Saz had already covered it with throw blankets and perched beside my mom.

"Unpacked?" Mom asked, smiling tersely.

I returned her smile weakly, and felt more than saw Saz scan my expression, her eyes hot on my cheek. Sometimes I regretted letting them all know me so well—it made concealing feelings nearly impossible.

My mom rose from the sofa and hooked her bag over her shoulder. "I'm going to find your dad," she said. "It was good to see you again, Sarah."

"Likewise, Mrs. Kozak," Saz answered brightly. She patted the seat beside her, and I sank into it as my mom disappeared up the stairs. Saz leaned close as she whispered, "She always calls me *Sarah*, with an accent and everything. Oh, and she asked again if you were dating any of us."

I laughed and thumped her knee with mine. "Yeah right, welcome to Orgy Manor."

Saz grinned. "I kind of like the sound of that."

"We can charge for admission," I suggested.

"Phones confiscated at the door and no photos allowed," she added, nodding.

"What aren't we photographing?" Amrita asked, sidestepping a box of vinyl records.

"The house-wide orgy we're planning on having," Saz said, right as the front door swung open and let Caroline in.

If I could look back on that moment now, even knowing all the ways that we might suffer, I'd still light up at the sight of her. I'd still be in awe of her, of all of them, of how they brightened every room they entered and made it somewhere I thought I could spend the rest of my life in.

Caroline elbowed the door all the way open, arms heavy with her bags and a smile brilliant on her face. "I love to see all my women in one place," she said.

Saz leapt off the couch and swept her close. We flocked and crowded. When it was my turn for a hug, I breathed in her perfume—spicy and familiar.

Unlike Amrita, Caroline Aster was the kind of girl who matched her paintings. She was golden. Her hair fell straight and smooth down her back, the color of sun-bleached grain, her waist pinching into long legs, eyes bright like jewels set in her white face. She looked like her mother—though the similarities stopped there, as her beautiful mother was neither clever nor funny—but Caroline would have killed me if I'd compared the two of them. She had more than a few inches on me—I loved to look up into the halo of her.

She emanated the same luminant quality that her artwork did—consumed by glow and shine like the warm-toned metallic pigments she favored, with an erratic nature to match the often dreamy, surreal, and abstracted landscapes she'd taken to in the past year. Looking at her was like looking at a Hilma af Klint. All symbol and shape and symmetry.

"Anyone want to give me a hand?" Caroline asked.

I bent to grab one of her bags as Saz got the other.

"You're on the third floor," Saz said to Caroline. "It's a workout."

"It's not so bad," I tried.

Saz heaved a dramatic sigh and put on a high, nasally voice. "I'm Jo Kozak, and nothing bothers me. You could stick a palette knife in my hand and I wouldn't even flinch. I climb twenty flights of stairs every day, and I do it all with a bag of rocks tied to each ankle. Let me play a sad song for you on the world's smallest—"

Immediately offended, I said, "That's not what I sound like. Is it?"

"Nah, you have a sexy voice," Caroline declared, looping her arm through mine and kissing the top of my head. "You sound like you're a member of a carpenter's union."

My face went hot. "I still don't think that's a compliment."

"We're heading out, Joanna," my dad called from the top of the stairs. I yanked my arm from Caroline's too quickly, cheeks flushing deeper as I fought not to acknowledge her confused stare.

11

I followed my parents out of the Manor's front door and closed it behind me. The three of us waited on the curb beside my dad's truck.

"Don't forget to wish Caleb a happy birthday," my mom said as we puttered around goodbyes. "Your brother is driving home for the weekend, and he'll want to hear from you."

"I know, I'll call," I said.

They shared a look. I shifted uneasily. My mom turned back to me, eyes landing on my chin. My dad gave me a tight hug. "I'll be in the truck," he said.

"Thanks for moving me in," I continued when my mom made no move to leave.

"Listen, Joanna," she said. She had that squinty expression she usually got when she thought she was giving me sage advice, a wrinkle forming between her brows. It was one I'd noticed myself occasionally adopting when I felt scrutinized. "You know that we only want the best for you."

"Cool," I said, "me too."

"Are you sure you're making the right decisions? You're already on a risky career path, and living in this house seems like it's going to be . . . full of distractions."

Sweat prickled along my hairline. I hated that she'd used the same word Finch had.

"They're my friends, and they're painters too. We learn from each other," I said.

Her frown deepened. "What about when this year ends? What are you going to do with your future?"

"We need to head out if we're going to beat traffic," my dad called from the window.

I nodded thankfully in his direction. "I'll be fine. Thanks again for moving me in."

She started to protest, but I gave her a quick, tight hug and stepped back. "I'll call. Don't worry about it."

Her expression was drawn and doubtful. I watched as she climbed into the passenger seat and shut the door hard behind her. The truck pulled away, and I kept waving until they could no longer see me.

I paused before the Manor and tried to untwist the knot she'd put in my stomach, waving to a few other fine arts majors as they walked by. Past the Manor stood Grainer and the tall iron fence that wrapped around campus. Past the fence waited the woods. Past the woods there were only occasional farmhouses and fields of corn. Rotham isolated you from all other aspects of life. You created nothing but your body of work. You gave it everything you had, your blood and life and the salt your body left behind in the aftermath.

And if you were lucky, you came home to people doing the exact same thing—like I did at the Manor, stepping in the front door again to find candles already lit in the living room and tea steeping beside the stove—and you knew that there was never anything else you could have needed. It was all waiting right in front of you.

"Hi again," Amrita said, smile haloed with joy. She sat at the dining table with a cardigan pulled around her shoulders despite the heat pushing past the windows. With her knees drawn to her chin, she looked as small as a child. "Welcome home."

I took the hand she offered, and I joined her at the table to wait for the others.

2

Self-Portrait as Water Nymph

Everyone did it, that first night back. It was tradition.

In the dark we were prowling animals, conjoined by linked elbows and a shared cigarette. We left the Manor and its mess just after eleven o'clock. My things still sat in their boxes, the kitchen light burning on as proof of our staked claim. Outside, the air smelled clean and wet and sharp. Caroline led the way with a bottle of wine in her hand. She drank from it as we walked, signet ring tapping against the glass. Rivulets ran down her jaw. I caught one with my thumb and wiped her chin clean before it could dribble onto her shirt. She gave me a smile that warmed me all the way down to my feet.

It was so natural to be together again. We fell into place as if no time had passed at all. To be fair, it had been barely two months since I last saw the four of them, though it had felt like a slow-crawling decade. In our absence a group chat kept us tethered, where we passed the same ten memes and screenshots back and forth, and we had all gathered at Caroline's parents' place in Michigan in mid-June for a week of heavy drinking, tarot readings, and skinny-dipping in the lake. It'd been Finch's feet bare on the gas pedal as she drove us to the grocery store. The five of us oversaturated with wine and Saz's pesto pasta. Sleeping in an ornate bed that had once belonged to Caroline's grandmother, the pillows full and soft, borrowing Amrita's sweatshirt and sitting by the fire until it was weighed down with the scent of smoke and her body wash. I'd never been so at peace.

Still, every time I left them for the regressive isolation of my parents' house, I was reborn with the fear that I'd return to find that it was all false—that they would remember my faults and inch away from me.

Saz's hand bumped mine. Our pinkies linked and banished my worries back to where they'd been manifested.

Lysander Gate marked the beginning of the garden. At night the path beyond it was a black snake lined with rosebushes slithering beyond the boundaries of campus. There was a Rotham story about an old woman who had wandered out into the woods and gone missing that we often used to terrify each other. We called her Mother Crone, rumored her into something Blair Witch–esque—lurking, invisible, hungry. Some iterations of Rotham mythology claimed she was a student who had drowned in the pond, mostly intended to keep us away from the water. In truth she was likely a forgetful Indiana local who'd ended up miles from her family, warped into something more sinister. But the fear remained. I avoided looking into the dark pockets of trees at all costs, where a gruesome face might peer back at me.

Instead, I kept my eyes focused forward and walked in the center of the walkway out of habit—once, drunkenly, Saz had fallen into one of those prickly roses, and it had taken an hour to pull all the thorns from her palms. My body remembered the hurt.

The moon seemed to sink as we walked—but it was just the path tipping down, the rising heads of trees obscuring the pale glow. Hedges framed the gate's entrance. Beyond it, morning glories climbed rotten trellises and benches. The garden was something out of a storybook with its fountain and its sculptures and its lush greenery, but the dark made it a labyrinth. Caroline passed the wine bottle to Saz, then lit a blunt pinned between her lips with her free hand as Saz took a gulp. Caroline tilted her head back when she exhaled. She passed it to Amrita, who considered it without taking a drag and handed it to me instead. I

15

inhaled, felt it sear my throat and lungs, and passed it back to Caroline, who gave me a knowing smile.

"Eleven eleven," Saz said, her phone a white-hot light against her face. Her hand went up to her chest and squeezed, illuminated screen muffled against pink chiffon. "I wish I had bigger tits."

Caroline, to my left: "You're not supposed to say your wish out loud. That's what they teach you on day one of wish school."

I could hear voices in the distance, tidal and swelling.

"I don't get why eleven eleven is supposed to be so lucky," Saz continued, as if Caroline hadn't spoken at all. "Seven thirty-seven is where it's at. It's such a good fucking time, you know? It feels so solid. Satisfying."

"There's something seriously wrong with you," Amrita said, laughing.

Caroline rolled her eyes. "Is that a British thing? You know you're obligated to tell us when it's a British thing."

The air was muggy. Fireflies darted between us. Humming crickets warred with pop music and the echoing splash of pond water. The party had already started. We were fashionably late.

People scattered throughout the garden. The fountain in the center burbled with sleepy life. Shoes piled around the stone lip where bare feet plunged into the water. The cherry ends of cigarettes illuminated like a new species of insect among the dark. Caroline called hellos and paused to stub her blunt against stone. The path kept warping past the gathered groups, through the stone arch that marked the end of the greenery and the beginning of the pond. The water reflected a hundred scleral moons back at us.

It happened like this, every First Night. The tradition traced back through a hundred and fifty years of Rotham students, and I assumed it had always had the same origins—though I lacked enough evidence to say if those past pupils spent their First Night exactly like we did, drunk and high and rowdy and nearly loud enough to get the whole thing shut down before it could really start, couples disappearing into the woods to get lost in each other, crickets thumping out a folk song. Freshman Jo had been so scared of it. I'd only met Amrita hours before. What I'd wanted most was to stay at Direpoint House where the two of us had been assigned that morning, our things still divisively half-unpacked on either half of the dorm room, her back to me as she did her makeup at her desk and I perched on my bed to watch. The hum of her then unfamiliar music. The vanilla cling of her perfume. Black hair falling down her back, eyeliner flicked and catty, the single bump in the bridge of her nose sloping to the septum ring that pierced it, the beauty mark high on her cheekbone accented by highlighter and purple blush. She was effortlessly beautiful in her black minidress, though maybe I just wasn't aware of what effort looked like, in my jean shorts and oversized button-down.

I'd never been drunk, and the only makeup I owned was a four-color eyeshadow palette that I dipped my fingers into. Still—I wanted Amrita to like me, to think I was cool, to want to keep wanting to know me. She'd pushed away from her desk and stood confidently on the heels of her boots, brown skin shimmering with gold eyeshadow.

She smiled when she met my eyes in the mirror hanging on the back of our bedroom door and straightened her skirt with one hand. "Come with me," she said. I hesitated.

"I don't know about you," she continued when she saw me freeze, "but I spent all of high school studying and going to bed early and depriving myself of anything remotely close to fun just so I could make it to this exact moment. Now I would love to get very drunk and very reckless."

"I'm not sure . . . ," I said, laughing, flushing red.

Amrita cocked her head as her smile spread wide, coaxing. "Friends don't let other friends go to parties alone. We're friends now, aren't we?"

I could have never said no. I was always such a sucker for a pretty girl.

So I went that year, clinging to Amrita's side and cementing ourselves as a pair—and then the next when we'd found the rest of them and become a unit. It got easier each time. It was just drinking and music, just the open air and a roster of Rotham voices. As we came closer, I recognized the other seniors I'd known since our early days: printmakers and ceramicists and sculptors and jewelers. Fellow painters Phoebe, Yejun, and Veda bent over a jug of indeterminate liquor as they leveled their pours into plastic cups. Cameron De Luca's hand sat on Mars Jackson's thigh—a relationship we'd predicted since we first saw the two of them sitting next to each other in a sophomore critique.

I knew Finch by her back—the narrow taper of rib cage to hips, tawny hair pulled away from her face and a white T-shirt stretched across the shoulders, smoke framing her like an apparition. The fine hairs frizzing out around her head glowed in the lantern light. The final painting major in our conglomeration, Thea Russell, sat beside her. They were deep in a conversation, heads tipped nearly temple to temple. Something pinched in my gut at the sight as Finch turned from the conversation to glance behind her. That same lantern light ignited her profile; her sharp nose, the circles under her heavy-lidded eyes, the satisfied curve of her mouth. My heart sang at that turn. It was like she had sensed us, like she'd know our footsteps anywhere. But my eyes rose and met the faces of the others, who had raised their hands in greeting as we stepped up. She'd likely just followed their welcome.

Thea angled toward us too. I wondered what made her think that Finch was hers to speak to. Then I wondered what made me think I had any hold over Finch at all.

"Finchard," Caroline called, and now Finch fully faced us. The recognition in her smile was worth the wait—she never looked at anyone else like that. Like she wanted to hear what they had to say.

Finch hugged me first. I still think about that, the way one arm circled around my neck and her palm pressed into the small of my back, hooking me into her. It made my heartbeat glitter along every inch of my skin. The smell of her was overwhelming this close, the bite of apple in her cologne, like digging my teeth into just-picked fruit.

18

She moved down the line, saying hello to everyone else with a brief and tight hug, as if we'd all only been apart for a few hours rather than over a month. I didn't know why I felt so anxious when she looked at me again. Some part of me was still afraid that I was standing on my own, waiting for permission to belong.

"Hey, Joanna," Thea said as I hovered, because she always called Jodie Finchard my designated "Jo" instead of by the name we'd chosen for her and left me with the mouthful of syllables. She inhaled around something charred and small—a habit that, in combination with the time she stomped on a bug in the junior studio, earned her the title "Roach Crusher" from Caroline behind closed doors until Finch asked her to stop. Thea's face was half-obscured past hanks of red hair and opaque smoke.

"Yeah, hey, Joanna," Finch said mockingly, touching my wrist. She gave me an unbothered smile. It wasn't meant to be wide, but I could see a hint of her teeth anyway.

Our unity lent itself to performance. Being in their circle made me want to lean into the evidence. Caroline's lithe elegance. Amrita's imposing ardor. Saz's vivid energy. And Finch's understated glow of charisma. Their attention gave my presence a little more reason.

"Which one of us do you think will be the last one standing? By the time Moody is done with us, at least."

Phoebe Arnett hadn't made a sound as she came up behind us. She was smiling, blond hair bobbed around her pinched face. I always found it impossible to discern if she actually wanted an answer to what she said—she spoke rhetorically, like her questions were posed for an invisible entity struggling to catch up.

Mars looked up from Cameron's hand on their knee. "Come on, it's First Night, Phoebe. Don't make us go to war yet."

Caroline smiled thinly. "Haven't we been on the front lines since day one?"

"You looked thirsty," Finch whispered as she nudged my side. There was a new beer in her hand when I glanced down. She shook it a little in offering. When I reached to take it, she pulled away with a tsk and balled her shirt up in her fist to twist the cap off.

"Pretty girls don't open their own beers," she scolded playfully as she pressed the bottle into my hand and closed my fingers around it. Cold glass battled with the warmth of her touch. I fought not to shiver.

I was grateful for the first swallow settling in my stomach despite its sour cling and touched that she'd approached me like that—like we belonged to each other, even if circumstances wanted to pit us against one another. Somehow there could be nothing worse than imagining the year to come and what kind of threat it held over us. I'd been trying to push it from my mind since I met them in the early days, since I understood what we'd be forced to do.

"Wasn't talking to you, Mars," Phoebe said, slinging an arm around me. I watched Finch's eyes catch on the place where Phoebe's hand squeezed my shoulder. "I was asking my friend here"—another squeeze, harder this time—"who she thinks will Solo."

Friend was a fickle word. Yes, I wanted these people to like me. I'd spent nearly every class with the same painting majors since I was a sophomore, after our freshman prerequisite year ended and funneled us into concentrations. We became collaborators. We went for coffee runs together. We hovered next to each other's easels and let easy compliments slip from our mouths—an olive branch extended across the inevitable threat that was Solo.

Of course, I knew what Solo entailed before I even signed the papers to attend Rotham. We all did. Throughout our final year, every student was expected to create a body of thesis work. From this work, most of us would have one or two pieces selected for the senior exhibition, where they'd fill the Grainer Gallery with a representation of our class's capabilities. But one person, whose skill and promise went beyond the rest, would earn a Solo Show. Their entire body of work would be showcased with a public reception that typically resulted in offers of representation from gallerists around the country. It was a guaranteed start to a career as a fine artist. And it would be taken from all of us, save for one lucky student.

"Come on," Phoebe stage-whispered beside my ear. "We alllll know it's gonna be Finchard."

"Shut up," Finch said around the mouth of her bottle. She'd tucked loose strands of hair behind her ears, lashes long and low, spidery shadows cast over her cheekbones. I couldn't tell if she was blushing or if the light was making her rosy.

Cameron rolled his eyes and turned back to Mars, intent on letting Phoebe's words die. Some of the other painters had tuned in now, the contempt on their faces barely disguised—I caught Yejun and Veda watching and went stiff under Phoebe's hand. The beer was hot and foamy in my mouth when I took another swig, but I swallowed it again and again. I needed to be drunk.

As if reading my mind, Saz spoke up and said, "I'm not having this conversation now. I came to get trashed."

She handed me her can of something sickly sweet and wriggled her dress over her head. It landed in the grass as she blew me a kiss and took the drink back and ran at the water with an echoing whoop. The pond stretched from tree line to tree line, water bugs skidding the surface and leaving ripples, everything so blue in the dark that the world glowed like a jewel. Saz crashed past its surface. The spray arced behind her, and she disappeared under the water, can held over her head like a buoy in the dark.

"She just got eight new diseases," Amrita said.

Saz came up again, water running over the bright blue cotton of her bra. Her hair slicked and stuck against her forehead and jaw. The moon lit her up—all pale skin and jewelry glinting, teeth bared in a grin, dark eyes taunting us. She looked like something yanked from myth. A water nymph awakened from an endless sleep. Rich with life and promise and allure.

"Don't make me swim alone!" she sang, leaning back into the water, arms spreading wide until she was making angels among the pond scum.

A breeze shook the cattails. Music coiled crass and loud between us, and laughter flickered down the crowd. Other students started stripping down to join. Caroline muttered a curse—something along the lines of *that's so fucking nasty*—and then yanked her shirt over her head.

I stepped out of Phoebe's grasp and started to unbutton my own shirt. "Seriously?" Amrita teased, but I ignored her in favor of shedding my shorts and toeing off my sneakers. I left my things in a pile and started down to the shore, Finch already following me, stripping to her underwear and laughing as she stumbled. I loved that sound, loved that we had caused it.

"You all suck so much," Amrita called, but there was laughter in her voice, too, a barely disguised pleasure.

Together we crashed into the pond, the five of us half-naked and half-drunk under the moon's spotlight, the water thin and cool. Amrita threw her arms around me. Finch went under and slicked her hair back as she came up again, water dripping around her smile. Caroline wrapped her arms around herself to keep from shivering, and Saz tackled her, pulling her back to the rest of us where we could splash and dunk each other.

"Enjoy this while it lasts," Caroline said, laughing with her head barely poking above the water. "When it's time for Solo, you'll wish you'd drowned me."

Saz pushed herself skyward with her hands on Caroline's shoulders. "Don't tempt me, Aster. I have all the power right now."

"You're drunk," Amrita said. She twisted her long hair into a coil and wrung water from it. Finch stood dripping beside her, backlit by the bonfire. She slipped a hair tie from her wrist and held it between her teeth before beckoning to Amrita, who went smiling, eyes slitting shut with contentment as Finch braided the wet hair away from her face.

Saz released Caroline at last. In the dark, her grin was radiant. "No, I'm a witch. The moon is charging me up." She threw her head back, arms flung wide. "I'm going to cast a spell and sacrifice our enemies and make us the best artists that ever lived."

Finch let out a sound past the hair tie pinned between her lips, half grunt and half laugh. She plucked it free and twisted it around the end of Amrita's braid as she said, "Right, let me know when you're done with that."

Saz held up her can in a toast. "Give me two to three business days, and I'll incant five Solo spots. Nobody loses. The whole family wins."

It was such an indulgent dream, one that instantly made me sink lower into the water where no one could see the flash of want wash over me. Right now, it was a joke. The funny, far-off inevitability of Solo, the teasing insinuations that it would be Finch or Caroline in the number one spot. What other choice did we have? We joked because we wanted it desperately. *I* wanted it desperately. But could I bear being the one to Solo if they couldn't? Could I watch them succeed without even the tiniest hint of resentment?

"Yeah, good luck with that," Caroline said to Saz as she tackled her back into the water, the two of them splashing each other until Saz started to whine, scolding Caroline for getting pond water in her drink.

Tradition was a thing hard won—by the end of the night most of Rotham's senior body was in the water, all of us screaming and singing and floating and swimming and beaming. It was my last First Night. It was a temporary perfection.

3

Exodus of the Exquisite

As thesis painters, we had the whole sixth floor of Grainer to use as our classroom and workspace. That was where we gathered officially four days out of the week, though I found within the first few days of our senior year that most of the painting majors ended up there every night—the motion lights stayed on all the time, and no one ever locked up.

The sixth floor was the highest point on campus, rivaled only by the Chapel's steeple. Most of the buildings dated back to the 1880s when Rotham first sprung to life as a trade school for agricultural engineers. Grainer was no exception—inside it was warm and rich, everything made of oiled wood and veined stone. There was no air-conditioning, and the freight elevator only worked half of the time, so climbing to the sixth floor left me sweaty and heaving each time. But the ceilings were tall and crosshatched by wooden beams dotted with industrial fans. Arched windows lined the wall and cut the grid of our studios into rectangles of light. Viewed from above, it was a maze—fifteen blank rooms with walls that rose over our heads and met open air, with a worktable, an easel, and a stool waiting for each student's use. At the center of the room, near the doorway where the stairwell descended, a white wall waited with a half circle of foldable metal chairs dragged up to it, a designated space where we would hang our work for critique.

To the right of that sat three sinks and a vat for excess oil paint and dirty rags. The lesson had been drilled into us since our first painting class—proper disposal was important. We were children playing with chemicals, trying to make something beautiful out of the mess before it had a chance to wreak havoc on our internal organs. Rotham did not want to be responsible for killing us.

I toured the studio with my parents the spring I turned eighteen. I'd loved it with fearful immediacy, self-consciously adoring as I peered into each student's space to witness the alchemy they had made of them. Canvases spanned each one from corner to corner, the floorboards littered with scraps and worktables piled with curled tubes of half-consumed paint. Sheets of fabric were pinned to plaster and the windows made trapezoids across them, highlighting wet brush strokes down to the frayed edges where scissors had snipped them into pieces. Everything smelled of linseed oil and the funk of wet plaster. A sink dripped, always, forever, echoed by the scuffling of something mammalian in the rafters. My parents hadn't been impressed. They thought the room was dirty and not worth the exorbitant price tag. But I was enamored. I thought that if I could spend a year in that room—a month, a day, a minute—I could become a smarter version of myself. I could make something impressive. Something worthy of hanging on a wall and drinking in.

I signed the papers—admissions and loans, clauses and acceptances, a lifetime of debt and the chance to make something worthwhile. I committed myself to possibility.

When it came to the reality of being a Rotham student, none of us loved the institution of school itself. Well, I guess *I* did a little—in a private way I admitted to few people other than Amrita. Rotham could be money hungry and disorganized. Our studios were cramped boxes with a mouse problem. Indiana was a droll cornfield where the only options for fun had to be swallowed or smoked, and the train took three hours to ferry us into the heart of Chicago. Still, we showed up to class every day, mostly on time. Because we had a common goal. And because we all adored Moody.

There were eleven painting majors in total. The five of us were a unified and insular near-half of that student body. Some of them we admired; some of them we hated; and the ones that fell beyond those black-and-white boundaries became characters instead, typically designated by nicknames sprouting out of some odd incident that mattered to no one but our group, like Cameron, who Caroline dubbed "Big Shoes" after he wore a ridiculous pair of boots every day of our freshman year. Of course, this language and cast of characters existed only to our audience of five. And to everyone else, we were probably incredibly annoying. But we loved to bask in that shared awareness, understood only by one another, conversations held with silent flickers of a gaze and the slightest twitch of lips. If you got it, then you got it. We weren't sharing.

Rotham wasn't a same-sex college, but its student population was overwhelmingly female, and that demographic made itself apparent. So it made sense that we all admired Jennifer Mooden. There was something unnervingly alluring about our senior mentor that made me want to be *more*. More engaging or desirable, more intelligent or conscious of the space I commanded. Capable of commanding space at all.

Moody, as we affectionately called her, stood at nearly six feet in her heeled boots. Her hair had gone prematurely gray—Saz once scoured her Facebook for hours to find proof of its beginning in her midtwenties—and it fell to her waist in a great cloud unless she clipped it up and revealed the dangling earring on her right ear. When we first met Moody, Seminar professor in our junior year, I used to spend the full three hours of our class's discussion staring at the simple silver chain and the black stone hanging from it. Amrita had once stopped Moody in the hall to tell her she was missing an earring. We never let her live that one down. Women like Moody didn't need the adornment of two—a single jewel was a statement of its own.

She was just as elegant the morning of our first class of senior year, perched on a stool before our waning moon of metal chairs with the critique wall behind her. The studio burned hellfire hot despite the overhead fans. As a result, her hair was up in its clip, leaving the shoulders of her dress bare. Past the cuffed sleeves, fine line tattoos unfurled down to where her hands clutched a hot coffee. Everything smelled peaty and overwarm, in a way that made my mouth cottony. I looked at Moody's paper cup and sweated.

I was hungover. The pond water left my hair feeling like straw even after a still-drunk early-morning shower, and just over two hours of sleep hadn't been enough to bring me to life. The rest of the group didn't seem to be faring much better than I was—I had no clue when the festivities of First Night finally tapered off, but Saz, Caroline, Amrita, and I had left around three, when I was pleasantly drunk enough to barely keep Saz's wasted form upright. Finch stayed, claiming she wanted to talk to Thea about something. I tried to pretend that part had disappeared to the fuzziest inebriated corner of my mind. I should have been even drunker. I should have sloughed the thoughts off and let them sink somewhere syrupy and black.

Now Finch slouched in the chair to my right, and Amrita sat rigidly upright to my left. I was acutely aware of the heat and how sticky it left my bare arms, and what it might feel like if I shuffled an inch closer and pressed my elbow to Finch's.

Condensation ran off my coffee and left a ring where my denim shorts met my thigh. I dragged a thumb through it absentmindedly until Amrita touched my arm. Amrita looked fine, though she always did. Her hair was braided away from her face again, and her gauzy button-down sat open over a black dress. Caroline stood behind Finch with her arms crossed over her chest, blond hair a glossy sheet under the glow pouring in from the windows. She hated to sit if she didn't have to. I envied the defined line of her calves.

"It looks like we're still missing one," Moody said, thumbing through the packet on her lap and dragging her finger down a list of names. The bodies in the room fidgeted as if marionetted by her hand. My gaze passed over the faces that had been obscured by shadow during the First Night swim, the remainder of our motley eleven—Veda, Phoebe, Cameron, Mars, Thea, and Yejun. Some of them I knew better than others. Some of them probably hated me for my proximity to Finch and Caroline, the polarizing and enigmatic kingpins of our class. But that was the only threat I posed—I didn't think any of them thought of me as a good enough artist to have a shot at Solo, and for the most part I shared their assumptions. It was seductive to hover in someone else's shadow and allow myself to remain obscured, especially if it was an outline I adored.

"Well, you all paid for my time. I suppose I won't waste any more of it." Moody slapped the papers against her thigh and stood to face the critique wall. Its fresh coat of paint turned it into a blank canvas. I wanted to stand beside Moody and drag a brush over it. Wanted to leave a lasting mark.

I felt Finch prepare to whisper before I heard her voice—warm breath against my already hot ear, sweat prickling along my hairline. "Where the fuck is Saz?"

I shrugged and spared a quick glance at the door. Moody dragged a hand across the wall in an arc, like marking a half circle in the plaster with her touch.

"Creation," Moody said, "is a window cut into the head."

A curious chorus of *hmm*s echoed around the room, as if we were at a slam poetry performance. I expected someone to start snapping.

"It sounds violent, and it is. You came here for violence. You came here to push your creativity to its limits. You've spent years honing the ideas that you want to express to your audience, and you've learned the techniques to make them possible. In that process, you've pried open a window and invited us to peer inside."

Still staring at that blank wall, Moody tapped her temple once. I wanted to close my eyes and picture it—a chasm carved into the veneer of my skull, my interior on display. Instead, I fidgeted with the ring on my thumb.

Finch wouldn't give up. Her whisper was even closer this time. "Didn't she come with you guys? Or did she oversleep?"

Saz was always oversleeping. But Caroline had been the one to wake her up that morning, our first as a household, one foot prodding the edge of Saz's stiff Rotham-issued mattress as she yelled, "*You have five minutes before we leave without you!*"

"She wanted coffee, and the line was long," I finally whispered back.

Moody faced us again. I straightened. I could feel someone staring at Finch and me, and the discomfiting awareness was nearly all-consuming enough for the whine in my ears to tune Moody out.

"I am not an overlord. I am barely even a teacher. Those of you who have attended one of my classes before know this," she said as she yanked her stool closer with a shriek of metal and sat again. "Trying to create something because you expect it will satisfy me or help you pass this class is not a goal. It's an excuse. I'm an artist, like I expect you to have grown into, and we are sharing a creative space with the intention of building a thesis. You're showing me your reason for sitting in this room. You want me to engage with it. You want me to believe it so wholeheartedly that I"—she paused to run her finger down the list of names—"make a mark on this page and signal you as a standout. As an artist worthy of being witnessed *en Solo*."

Chills prickled along my arms and the nape of my neck. Sometimes, when it was just us, Caroline would make fun of the way Moody talked—she'd put on a haughty voice that sounded nothing like Moody's true crisp consonants and parade around with her arms crossed over her chest saying things like "Think about the *bodily experience* of the canvas, Ms. Aster," and "Can a tube of paint *have a narrative of its own*, Ms. Aster?" And we'd obediently howl with laughter. But I was afraid to tell the rest of them that I liked the way Moody spoke. I liked her weird inflections and her ferocious pretentiousness and her eerie omniscience. I thought if I could be a fraction closer to her orbit, maybe

I could understand what I was doing among those talented painters, why I thought I had any right to claim the same Solo title they did when I could barely figure out what I was meant to paint half the time. Up until this point, I'd mostly focused on detailed landscapes from my childhood. Sometimes I sketched my women, but I hesitated to commit to putting them down in paint. I just thought they were beautiful. I wanted Moody to think they were beautiful too.

Footsteps on the stairs announced her before the rest of us swiveled to look. Saz entered with a tote bag hanging from the ditch of her elbow, aforementioned coffee in the hand connected to it, ribbons hanging from two tiny black braids and her shorts frayed at the ends where they clung to her thighs.

"Sorry, sorry, carry on, please!" she said in a too-loud attempt at a whisper. Moody's gaze trailed Saz from the door to the seat that she claimed behind me. Saz gave me a pat on the head as a hello, and I sank in my chair, embarrassed to have been singled out.

"The time you spend in this studio is directly correlated to your effort," Moody continued, thumb pressing into a spot on the paper where I imagined *Sarah "Saz" Murphy-Choi* was listed. "I'm not here to pass judgment on your character or grade your homework. We're sharing a collaborative space. I expect you to show up on time and stay late and forfeit your weekends if you need to. Because if you aren't doing those things, you are performing a disservice to yourself and your peers when you show up to our group critiques. Lackluster effort will leave you with a painting vying for attention in a crowded group show, while your classmate's entire body of work hangs *en Solo*." Moody leaned forward, elbows propped on her knees, hair akimbo in its clip. "Got it?"

A sea of fervent nods, my own included. Finch's hand rested on her knee, her anxiety apparent in her thumb's grazing back and forth across her jeans. The floor creaked as Caroline shifted her weight. Amrita's pen scratched across a notepad as she took notes and Saz leaned forward to read over her shoulder.

"I'm sure many of you have understood how this year will go since you stepped onto campus. In fact, I'd be disappointed if you didn't." For the first time that day, Moody smiled. "But as the course requires, we'll walk through the timeline together."

She rolled the packet in her hand until it was a thin tube and gestured to the rest of the room behind us. "We'll begin by establishing studios, setting up your materials, and personalizing your spaces. You are free to do anything in your cubicle that does not cause irreversible damage to school property. If it can be cleaned up or painted over, you're free to go wild. Oh—and you can't sleep here. Pay your rent and get out of my hair."

That got a few laughs. Her smile widened, but her eyes remained serious. "You will create a body of work composed of at least twenty pieces of art. This is, of course, up to interpretation in your practice, but you should work with the expectation of filling the atrium's Solo Gallery. Those of you who are not selected will be expected to choose one to two pieces from your portfolio to hang in our Senior Show at the end of the year."

Uncomfortable silence. I shifted, one foot starting to fall asleep. "Mandatory class occurs Monday through Friday, ten a.m. to four p.m., though I expect you will find yourself in this room outside of those hours on most days. On Wednesday mornings you will attend your Fine Arts Seminar with Professor Kolesnik, where you'll craft thesis papers and learn how to market the work you're creating. These first couple months, I will have one-on-one visits with each of you to discuss your progress. After that, we will have voluntary critiques. If you don't sign up, you don't get a critique. If you don't get a critique, then deal with the consequences."

My stomach fluttered at the thought of Moody evaluating whatever I had created, then curdled when I realized that meant the rest of them would scrutinize my paintings too.

"When you all return from Thanksgiving break, we will hold Survey. This is an open critique with fellow professors, alumni, and art professionals invited into the Grainer Gallery to view the progress on your thesis work and give you direction. Directly after Survey, your class will be narrowed down to the top five students who can expect to have a chance at Soloing. You will take their feedback and apply it to your work throughout the spring, until it is time for a panel of Rotham professors and guest artists to select the Soloist. Unselected students will choose their best piece to be presented in Grainer Gallery's group show. Any questions?"

This time we all shook our heads. If I hadn't had my hands knotted together, they would have been shaking.

"Alright. Now that that's settled. You've each been randomly assigned a number that designates your individual studio space." Moody's gaze returned to the unrolled packet. "When I call your name and number, you may go find your studio. Fill out the card beside your doorway with your name, and then we'll gather again to discuss how the next week is going to kick off."

I straightened, heart pounding, and tried not to look at the others—I wanted to be close to them and also wanted to get as far away as I possibly could so I couldn't spend the entirety of my time comparing myself to them, afraid of always being the one who would fall flat.

"Phoebe Arnett, Studio 6," Moody began. "Caroline Aster, Studio 4. Amrita Balakrishnan, Studio 7. Veda Chaudhry, Studio 1. Cameron De Luca, Studio 2."

People started to move. Amrita touched my shoulder as she stood and followed Caroline, already stalking through the maze of rooms and scanning the labels on the exterior walls with a determined frown. Moody continued to list off names.

"Jodie Finchard, Studio 10." Finch's chair groaned when she rose. I kept my eyes on my hands. "Mars Jackson, Studio 3. Yejun Kim, Studio 8. Joanna Kozak, Studio 11. Sarah Murphy-Choi, Studio 9. Thea Russell, Studio 5."

Finch had already disappeared by the time I started to weave down the halls. The studios closest to the critique wall were 1 and 15—that meant the path followed in a spiral, with the center cubicles falling between 6 and 9 and the other studios containing the rest of us—which also meant that I was beside Finch. The two of us were tucked away in a corner of that murine conglomeration.

"Hey, neighbor," Saz greeted when I reached my studio, poking her head out of 9 with a grin.

There was no door, just a cutout that served as an entryway. Inside my cubicle were three blank plaster walls that met a brick one with an enormous window stretching high overhead. Before the window sat a worktable. Beneath the table was a cabinet of drawers for supplies, and across from it stood a metal easel and a stool. The walls were freshly painted, the floor stained in places, dust gathered in the corners. Beyond the lower panes of the glass where the elements caked a fine film, Rotham unfolded like a pop-up book, the Chapel perforating the clouds. I could see myself sitting there before it, could imagine that table piled high with materials: my glass palette with its mountain range of dried paints in shades of cadmium and titanium and ultramarine and phthalo, brushes still slick with safflower oil no matter how many times I scrubbed them in the sink, the chemical waft of turpentine and the tang of linseed forever dried into my rags and my apron and my skin. There would be no delineation between work and body. This room would become an extension of me until the work the two of us produced could transmogrify into something worthy of standing on its own. Or, as Moody liked to say, of performing *en Solo*.

It wasn't necessarily a healthy thought. But I hadn't come to Rotham to live wisely.

"It's a nice view, right?"

Finch stood behind me in the doorway, smiling the kind of tight-lipped grin that told me she was thrilled and she didn't want anyone else to know it. Up close I could see where her eyeliner had smudged and sweat dampened her cheeks. "I can't believe we share a wall," she continued. "Everyone else is going to be so jealous."

Moody's voice carried throughout the room as she called, "After you find your studio, report back to me for further discussion . . ."

"Jo," Finch said, the sudden sensation of her fingers encircling one of my wrists and squeezing, searing me all the way down to my feet. I blinked back at her, shaken awake. "I *said*, are you excited to get to work?"

"Sure," I answered immediately. "Of course I am."

It was the truth. But beneath the excitement lived a pit-dark hunger—dread that coiled and waited for my joy to wear off, and contention to encroach in its stead.

4

THE BURDEN OF BURNING

I had no fucking idea what I was doing.

This was the doubt that became my mantra in our first few days back at Rotham. I was supposed to have come to our final year with a plan for my thesis, but I was afraid I'd forgotten how to paint anything at all. Instead of answers, I sought routine.

Those days moved like this: I'd wake up around eight. By eight thirty we'd all gather around the kitchen table, save for Saz, who made it down by nine about 70 percent of the time. Breakfast was one of my favorite things about living with them. Caroline made the coffee, and Amrita made the tea. We usually fended for ourselves when it came to eating, settling on a granola bar or a cup of yogurt. If we cooked, it was me or Amrita feeding everyone else. Amrita was the best at making eggs, but I liked to fry up potatoes and whatever vegetables would otherwise eventually rot in our shared fridge. In some ways, it was a part of our language. I wanted to show them I cared. So I fed them.

We'd meet Finch in Banemast by nine fifteen for another round of coffee. Then it was the hike up the stairs to the top of Grainer. The heat rose as we climbed, panting the whole way and dreaming of the coming winter. Moody was always there before us, no matter how early we tried to arrive.

"Do you think she ever leaves?" Caroline asked once as we hauled ourselves up the marble flights. The climb never seemed to affect her. Her breathing always remained steady. "I have a feeling that when the room empties out and the lights go off, she keeps sitting on her stool, staring at the critique wall and waiting for us to come back."

"That's just a wet dream of yours," Finch called behind us, and dissolved into laughter when Caroline told her to *go fuck yourself.*

Amrita gestured at the cameras in the high corners of the stairwell. "She can probably hear everything you're saying."

Finch shook her head. "Remember when someone stole my phone last year out of Wolitz's class on the fifth floor? I asked them to check the security footage, and administration told me they're just props meant to discourage theft. What's the fucking point?"

The first two mornings in the studio started with Moody's announcements about whose studios she planned to visit for chats that day, and then we'd split up with the intention of making a masterpiece or twenty.

There was an immense, unbridled pleasure in filling the space with pieces of myself. I hauled all my materials from the Manor and started to fill my studio—paint tubes in the cabinet drawers, a cheery yellow coffee can full of brushes, color-caked glass palette on the worktable, a roll of unstretched and unprimed canvas worth more than most of my possessions combined propped up against a wall. Palette knives and box cutters and spackling trowels. A stack of books leaned against a tub of primer: *Hold Still* by Sally Mann, a retrospective of Cy Twombly's work, *The Artist's Way* by Julia Cameron, dog-eared essays about Jenna Gribbon, a thrifted volume on medieval beasts in art.

Moody came to me on Tuesday with a knock on my studio. "Ready for a chat?" she asked, leaning against the doorframe in a sleek A-line dress, wrists rimmed in bracelets and her hair heavy around her shoulders. She had a pair of glasses pushed up on her head, pinning loose strands away from her eyes and revealing that one stone earring, swinging on its chain.

"Of course," I answered. I gestured to the stool and she smiled as she took it, sitting on her hands. I felt like a child beside her in a dirty pair of jeans. There was a certain elegance to her that I would never be able to emulate.

My progress so far was two yards of canvas unrolled and pinned to a blank wall. It hung there from a row of nails beside a few charcoal sketches that I'd spent the first day making.

"Unstretched?" Moody asked, nodding at the fabric.

She meant my canvas—traditionally, a painter would construct a frame of four wooden bars and cut a length of canvas to fit it. Then they'd staple it into place and apply layers of a thick white primer called *gesso*, sanding between each to smooth down the surface, until it was a substrate that paints could be applied to. Over my years at Rotham, I'd taken the more tactile route of leaving the canvas naked and loose like a scroll and painting directly on the wall. The process was satisfyingly physical. But I was always doubting myself. I would get halfway through a painting and fear that I had made the wrong decision from the start.

Moody leaned in to get a closer look at the sketches. Several showed depictions of the same moment—my women around our dining table in the Manor, silhouetted by the faint glow of a lamp, heads thrown back in laughter or knees pulled up beneath their chins. Below those was a sketch of the four of them sitting on the beach in Michigan, Caroline's head in Saz's lap and her eyes locked on the viewer.

"Portraiture," Moody said thoughtfully. "This is a little different from how you described your previous work to me. Tell me more about it."

I wanted to say something that might impress her. Wanted to express the way I felt when I made the sketches, which was akin to coming home, like their lives could melt into mine until no lines remained.

"I'm always trying to depict family," I said, talking with my hands, face already heating up as I fumbled over the words, "you know, like, old photos, and artifacts, and traditions. But I've been thinking about

37

doing it with scenes of my friends from my life and how we've crafted a family here, together."

She hummed. I couldn't tell what that meant. Finally, she said, "I think it's a nice time capsule. It's rare to have friendships like those later in life, and they don't last forever."

I stood in resolute silence. *Not me*, I wanted to say, *not us*. We might change, but if we did, we'd change for the better—because we chose each other, because we made each other more interesting, because I felt most myself when they witnessed me.

"I want you to push the boundaries. I don't want idyllic scenes forever—I want to see every fraction of the good and bad in these relationships depicted through your figurations. Give me something to work with, Joanna."

As if summoned by our conversation, Finch passed my studio door with an empty canvas frame hooked over her shoulder and a staple gun in one hand. Her gaze hesitated on Moody, then flickered up to me. She shared a conspiratorial smile and wriggled her empty hand at me before she disappeared.

Heat in my cheeks again. A sudden prickling of emotion behind my eyes. I lacked the words for the way it made me feel when she looked at me like that, as if she were so pleased to see me. Such a wordless feeling. Like learning to speak all over again.

If I could convey it with paint, then maybe Moody would be able to feel it too.

Wednesday was our first class with Professor Kolesnik. It was a three-hour morning seminar, with the afternoon available for either an additional elective class or an open time block that could be spent at the studio. Most of us chose extra studio time, though Amrita surprised us all by signing up for some obscure class called Theory of Craft: How

Visual Artists Interpret Practical Work, and Saz selected Professor Williams's The Art of the Book.

Rotham's idea of a "lecture hall" was a room filled with enough seats for our class of eleven and a podium and desk for Kolesnik at the front. He was a burly man, tall and solid and mostly bald. He wore his shirtsleeves cuffed up to the elbows to reveal copious amounts of the hair missing from his head. This was what I focused on every time he gestured to the syllabus for the semester on the board.

Seminar had been a part of our curriculum every year since we started attending Rotham. It was a discussion intended to help us better navigate the professional art world and shape our theses, though Seminars in the past had usually ended up as lectures where professors talked at us for three hours about the importance of different painters throughout history. Kolesnik, however, quickly let us know that we would not get away with silence. If he asked a question, we were expected to answer it—with enthusiasm.

The warring animals inside me begged to please him and resented his attention. Kolesnik was notoriously hard on all students, and receiving his approval felt like hard-earned validation. As a working artist with gallery representation for the past forty-six years, he was one of Rotham's most revered staff members, and it was considered a privilege to take his class throughout our senior year. But there was another facet to his status as a tenured professor at Rotham—plenty of reviews on his Rate My Professors profile claimed that his lingering eyes and wandering hands made him uncomfortable to interact with. It wasn't a problem I had endured, but my boyish gawkiness typically gave me a kind of invisibility when it came to men, unless it was a slur slung at me on the street. Caroline, however, took his Art and Activism in the '80s course our junior year and dubbed him "Professor Perv" within the first week. And Moody always got a look in her eyes when he was mentioned; one that I read as a deep, unhurried resentment.

Still—he was a resource we were expected to take advantage of if we had plans of Soloing. He had established himself as an admirable and frustrating leader. Kolesnik's roots in Abstract Expressionism were evident in his work, which consisted of the Jackson Pollock-y drips we were all more than familiar with by now in bruised hues that gave his paintings the pinkened bodily tones of a Philip Guston piece. Beyond his individual practice, he was also instrumental in implementing traditions that were now commonplace at Rotham, like the annual Masquerade Grotesque that took place every Halloween, where students designed their own masked apparel and Kolesnik led the party in an exquisitely crafted boar costume that earned him the bristly and accurate title of Boar King.

Even without the fur coat and its tusked hood, he was imposing. Mars shifted in their seat in front of me as Cameron slouched down in his. Veda sat between Phoebe and Yejun. Finch had arrived before the rest of us to claim the seat beside Thea—a sight that managed to unnerve me just as much as Kolesnik's presence.

"Painting isn't even half the work," Kolesnik announced. "Maybe a fourth of it, if that. Beyond Rotham's confines, you'll find that your art is a by-product of the process of being a working artist. Sure, you're painting for you, because you want to. But when you leave your Grainer studio, your work happens alone. The real meat of a community—of the community you're trying to stake a claim in—is the way you're able to talk to others. You need to be capable of selling yourself to someone who doesn't give a shit about you. And the only way you're going to accomplish that is by knowing what you stand for and how to make someone else believe in it, too."

Kolesnik smiled beneath his beard. The expression might have looked like joy on anyone else, but on him it was scrutiny. Amrita took notes beside me, clicking away on her laptop keys.

"Over the course of the year, you'll complete a ten-page thesis paper as an exploration of your thesis. This paper is intended to help you learn how to talk about your work commercially until you feel prepared to market yourself with gallerists, curators, and buyers. At the end of the year, you will condense this paper into an artist statement that can be shown with your work. This will either exist as a sheet that accompanies your biography and a price list at your Solo Show, or it will be a printout pinned to the wall beside the piece or two you get to display in Grainer. I don't think I need to tell you which option holds more weight, do I?"

We all shook our heads, except for Cameron, who raised one hand and kept the other crossed over his chest. The air conditioner ruffled the black hair at the nape of his neck where it curled with sweat. "What's the point of the thesis paper then, if we're boiling down the same concept to one digestible page?"

"Could you give me that page right now?" Kolesnik asked. "Could you summarize your work in a succinct passage that would make me look at you and think, yes, this kid should Solo?"

I stared at the back of Cameron's head, at the way the muscles in his neck strained as his jaw worked.

"See," Kolesnik continued. "I don't think you could. I don't think any of you could. I'm sure that you think you might be capable of it, and I'd bet that you could write a few paragraphs down and hand them over, hell, by the end of the day. But it wouldn't mean anything to me. It would be the musings of a kid trying to talk their way to a reward. And that's not what we're doing here, is it? You want to be an artist. Okay, I'm listening. But you came to Rotham because it promised to shape you into an artist that innovates. You invested yourself and expected to glean results, so you're going to do it the way I tell you to, and you'll understand why when you finish this paper and see what it has taught you about yourself."

Kolesnik's hands gripped the edge of his desk as he leaned against it. Together they made a hulking being—all dark wood and massive shoulders. I could smell solvent clinging to someone's clothes. Maybe even my own.

"Any more questions?"

Another round of shaking heads. Cameron remained silent. Kolesnik clapped his hands together, and I jumped with the sound.

"Good. Let's talk about timelines. If you pull up the email you received last week with the syllabus, you'll see that—"

He paused and sniffled hard, then pressed a knuckle beneath his nose. When he pulled it away, his hand was smeared with red. "Damn. Nosebleed. Alright, pull up that email and give me a moment." He yanked a few tissues out of the box and stepped into the hall, noisily blowing his nose, and I watched Caroline's face crease with repulsion.

A text window from our group chat popped up over the notes on Amrita's screen and snared my eyes. The blue bubble of Caroline's text read: bro he's such a dick.

Saz sent a GIF of a gorilla beating its fists on its chest.

Then Finch: he's subjecting us to a three-hour jerk off session. Anyone want to get lunch after this?

She was right. But nothing could have killed the part of myself that rose to meet him—that wanted to work hard and prove myself. That wanted him to read what I produced and tell me that I had impressed him.

Did that make me terrible too?

Working at the library was the perfect job because it had given me *my* Finch. The Finch that unfolded in our privacy, unconcerned with being the top of the class or fitting into the mechanics of our group, her casual, warm, cocky self, the one that seized my heart, the one that fostered a festering crush that had clung to me since we started the job halfway through our freshman year.

We walked to our shift together down the promenade. Campus boomed with late-summer thunder as it tapered off from an afternoon storm. We'd hidden from the rain in Grainer after Kolesnik's class, where I was unable to accomplish anything other than perch on my stool, staring at the tentative brushstrokes I'd made on my first painting and spiraling into stagnancy.

"I don't know how we're going to last a full year with that guy," Finch sighed, one hand hooked in the strap of her tote bag and the other swinging by her side as she walked. My pinky brushed hers: once, twice. I tried to focus on sidestepping puddles in the brick path.

"Could be worse," I said. "He could be Aysel."

Aysel Polat was the printmaking professor our junior year who told Finch and me we were too pretty to be gay after Finch spent a semester crafting a poster that read BIKINI KRILL in blocky letterpress type under a crude illustration of two shrimp kissing. It had taken months of complaining to the Fine Arts Department to drum up some accountability for his actions and a reminder from Caroline of the hefty donations her family provided before Rotham finally fired him.

"I think Kolesnik is the type to give Aysel a run for his money. During last year's Junior Survey, he told me that my paintings made him want to prescribe me fresh air by the sea for my obvious hysteria," Finch said.

I laughed. Finch shoved me, fingertips circling my bicep for a beat of time that made me shiver.

"Ignore him," I said. "He's senile. He doesn't understand what you're going for."

She held the library door for me and gestured for me to enter, tilting her head with a wry smile. "And what is it that I'm going for, Jo?"

"Nightmare fuel," I answered, and her laughter trailed behind me all the way down to the library's basement. Rotham's subterranean level consisted of a massive archive—shelves and shelves of library-exclusive material that wasn't allowed to leave the building. We waved to Kirsten, the lead researcher who handled most of the acquisitions in the library's collection, and headed down the hall leading to the equipment office where Finch and I worked. The walk was interspersed with a glass display case, illuminated by hundreds of tiny bulbs. Inside it was Kolesnik's Boar King costume with some of the other famous masks from Masquerade Grotesques in the past. Eyeless structures watched us pass by—rabbits with long and patterned teeth, hulking hides wrapped around the shoulders, clown faces painted on plaster, narrow beaks with bursting plumage that turned the whole display into a burlesque performance. I hated that case—it always made me feel as if someone's eyes were on me, no matter what path I walked.

Finch unlocked the office and flopped into her rolling chair. Our shared L-shaped desk was a bulky antique much like Kolesnik's, with a computer for each of us to work on. I sifted through papers and pulled out the log for the evening. Our primary task was to help students rent photo and film equipment, so sometimes we spent whole hours with nothing to do, mostly dicking around and sending vapid videos back and forth to each other and trying not to laugh loud enough for Kirsten to hear us.

I took so much pleasure in the quiet contentment of my own private Finch. It'd been that way since we met in the equipment room, eager scholarship students up to our ears in debt trying to make enough extra cash to splurge on good oil paints and something other than the garbage they served in Banemast. Up until that point, Amrita was my best and only friend; we woke together, walked side by side to every class, ate every meal across from each other in Bane. And while that was enough—more than enough really, the first time I'd ever felt entirely unencumbered by a friendship to that degree—upon first sight, I was immediately enamored with and intimidated by Jodie Finchard.

Pretty was the wrong word for her, but it was a repeating thought I couldn't banish. Charming was a better fit. Irreplicable. Entrancing. She was only an inch taller than me, but I always pictured her bigger, louder, gave her more space in my head than she truly took up. She was always fidgeting, warm no matter who was on the other end of a greeting. Attention from Finch made me feel cooler than I actually was, like some of her magnetism rubbed off with a hello. She was enigmatic. Unassuming and flawed—faint spots suggesting teenage acne on her cheeks, a scar in her eyebrow from an old piercing, the skin around her knuckles red where they dried and cracked every winter. Her hair was overgrown in a forgetful, masculine way, fine and dark and swept behind the ears as if she wanted to pretend it wasn't present. Sometimes while working, she would knot it at the nape of her neck with a rubber band, thin strands framing the lines of her face. She made it easy to understand why everyone said Rotham was such a competitive school. I looked at her and instantly *wanted* to be prettier, smarter, clever enough to make her laugh. And when I did for the first time—in such an inane way, by holding a stapler up beside my mouth and clicking it together to make it talk in an imitation of Kirsten's voice—her resulting grin made my heart pound with obsessive delight.

"Thank god you work here," she'd said when the laughter had finally died down and I was blushing with the pleasure of having put that smile on her face. "I can't imagine wanting to sit in this room with anyone else."

I thought there could be nothing in the world more wonderful than loving someone and wanting to share that adoration. I knew Amrita would love Finch because I loved Finch, and I knew Finch would love Amrita because a rock would have loved Amrita if I could have made it animate.

That night, in the bed beside Amrita's with the lights shut off and her slow breathing the only sound left, I'd said, "Wanna meet my work friend?"

Now it felt like such a spoiled pleasure to sit with Finch, to know her mannerisms and moods, to anticipate all the quiet moments where she'd take the opportunity to prod at me. She pulled her knees up to her chest and propped her boots on the edge of her seat as I took the chair next to her. I could feel her eyes burning against the side of my head.

"What do you think about all of this?" she asked finally, resting her cheek against a fist propped on the armrest. She spun slowly, back and forth, back and forth. "You know, Solo and Moody and Kolesnik and everything."

I shrugged. "I mean, I don't know. It will take a bit to get into the swing of things, but we'll figure it out. I think talking with Moody will help me shape up the direction of my thesis."

She nodded, but I could tell by her slight frown that she had something else on her mind.

"How are you and Caroline?" I said before she could ask me anything else, pretending to be fascinated by the spreadsheet of returns.

Finch hesitated. "What do you mean?"

"We all know the two of you are at the top of Moody's list for Solo. She raved about your work in Junior Survey, and she chose you as her first one-on-one of the year."

"Speculation."

"Don't be humble, it's the truth. And . . . I know that Caroline can be competitive if she feels threatened."

Finch frowned. "She has no reason to feel threatened. She's good, I'm good, we're all good or we wouldn't be here in the first place. Caroline just can't bear to have her ego bruised. If she spent more time painting and less time worrying about the whims of Moody's Solo list, she might be able to chill out. Besides, with the amount of money the Asters funnel into Rotham, there's no way she won't Solo. It would be a fuckin' crime."

"Rotham wouldn't be *that* sleazy," I stressed. "You're both incredible. They'll have to choose on merit, or the rest of us will riot."

"Stop discounting yourself." Finch turned back to her computer. "Besides, whoever Solos can expect a riot regardless. I have a feeling that none of us will go down without a fight."

"True," I said. "But Caroline—"

"We're fine, Jo. Don't cause problems where there aren't any."

The scolding hushed me. We worked the rest of the evening in near silence. A few people stopped by to borrow equipment: a boom mic, a camcorder, a cable for connecting a portable hard drive to the computer. But most of the evening passed with my glazed-over eyes lingering on the screen, my mind drifting far from work and landing in the anxiety that was becoming commonplace. What the hell was I trying to accomplish with my paintings? How could I ever beat out anyone else when they were all so inventive, when Finch and Caroline could create something masterful in the time it took me to drum up my most futile ideas? Why did I think my art was anything more important than the others—let alone significant enough to be shown as a Soloist? And how did I ever think I could reach that accolade if I couldn't even be proud of what I was making?

The thump of a cardboard box on the desk shook me back into my body. I looked up from the computer into Finch's face with guilty urgency, like she'd caught me in the middle of a spiral.

"It's almost ten; we can lock up in a few. Also, I sorted through that box of materials someone donated and set these aside," she said, tapping the lid of a box with her blunt nails. "Thought you and Sazzy might like them."

I stared at the box, someone's blocky handwriting spelling out FREE on the side in black marker. Finch reached out and squeezed my fingers, and the pen I was holding clattered to the table. I hadn't realized that I'd been fidgeting until she stopped me. "You sure you're alright?" she asked. "You seem like you're really on edge."

"Just tired," I said, and most of me meant it. The rest of me would figure it out.

She nodded and started to shut down the computers as I gathered the box in my arms. Inside was a stack of a few books. I pushed them around and peered at the titles: a Wassily Kandinsky catalog, a few copies of *Artforum*, and a book called *Ninth Street Women*. Beneath them was a massive tome with a rough, leathery cover and an embossed word stamped into the material that read *ANTHROPOMANCY*. I dragged a thumb over the letters, feeling their ridges and valleys, and gave Finch a smile before shutting the flaps of the box.

"Cool?" she asked, her eyes soft.

"Cool," I said. "Thanks."

5

We Lit All the Candles

Saz loved *The Craft*, so we usually watched it at least twice every fall, when Finch's list of gory horror hits was too much for the group to sit through. She kept it taped beside the TV with a fat red marker crossing off everything we'd already watched and marked a few of our favorites with a smiling star sticker: *It Follows, The House of the Devil, Suspiria, The Descent.* Saz adored them, could never watch enough, but sometimes Amrita got scared—she'd always been weird about sleeping in total darkness. When we were freshmen, there were nights I'd return late from the library and find her already in bed with the lamp on her desk aglow.

"You can turn it off. I was just waiting for you to come home," she'd admit, comforter pulled up to her chin and exposing only her eyes, muffling her voice and making her so little that I wanted to crawl into bed beside her. I often did. I'd kick my shoes off by the door and change into my pajamas. She'd lift the comforter and I'd curl up beside her, her hair tickling my throat and fingertips circling my wrist like she needed something grounding to hold on to.

Now the September breeze made everything smell like wet leaves past the living room's cracked window. Our first week back at Rotham had passed in a long drag of forming habits—arriving at the studio early and staying late, manifesting answers to Moody's questions that might make me appear like I knew what I was doing, trying to take Kolesnik's words and burn them into my own perception of my work.

Saturday morning held the promise of first freedom. I could hear distant laughter, a smattering of footsteps, wind in the trees, the TV playing Siouxsie and the Banshees. Saz and I lay across the sofa with her head at one end and mine at the other. The blanket over our legs was too warm, but I was unwilling to disrupt the comfortable cradle we had created.

"You guys look like the grandparents from *Willy Wonka*," Amrita said, dropping her bag in the doorway and plopping down next to Finch on the rug, shuffling until her head was pillowed on Finch's shoulder. Finch threw an arm around her and stoked a tiny, jealous flame in me.

I had brought the box of books home from the library and showed them to Saz. Now she had *ANTHROPOMANCY* open across her lap. Daylight made slats through the blinds across the pages and blanket over her knees as lightning flashed on the screen with an echoing scream. She pushed her feet into my ribs and I jumped.

"That makes you Grandpa Jo," she declared, and while they laughed, I snared her ankle and tugged, sliding her down the cushions and closer to me. Saz writhed, giggling, until she abandoned the book and launched herself up on top of me, fingers digging down into my sides until I pleaded for her to let me go. We wrestled like that, movie nearly forgotten, until she hushed me with her fingers over my mouth. "Wait! This is one of my favorite parts."

We watched dutifully. Sometimes I thought I enjoyed these movies because I loved what they taught me about my friends, unfiltered access to their adoration. I could feel Saz's heartbeat thumping in her fingertips against my lips. When I was sure she wouldn't catch me, I flicked my eyes back to her face, to take in the entrancement there.

Saz and I had always bonded over movies. It was how we'd met. The two of us sitting side by side in a sophomore Philosophy of Film class, one I'd taken to fulfill a liberal arts credit after every other interesting class filled up for the semester. I spent a lot of classes trying to sketch her without getting caught—she was always wearing something bright and improbable and dyeing strips of bleached hair in an array of colors. Sophomore year had been her blue period. The ends of her bob curled neat and ultramarine just above her shoulders, legs crossed and terminating in platformed black boots beneath a calf-length periwinkle dress. Her knuckles were laden with rings. She flicked a pen between each finger as she kept her eyes on Barry Jenkins's *Moonlight* beaming from the projector, her every movement clicking metallically. I tried to copy the outline of her profile in the corner of my notebook.

She surprised me by turning to face me near the end of the movie, her eyes silver with tears, ringed hands pressing a tissue to her nose as she sucked in a deep, trembling breath. I immediately slid a hand over my sketch and tried to pretend I hadn't been staring.

But she just spoke as if we'd known each other all our lives, too-loudly declaring, "Why the fuck would they make us watch this in class? Don't get me wrong, it's incredible, but I would have worn waterproof mascara if I'd known this was on the syllabus."

I blinked back at her, stunned, and my hand slipped away from the drawing. Her eyes glazed over it, and her frown quirked up at the corners. "Hey, that's pretty good," she sniffled, prodding my arm with the end of her pen. "Aren't you a painter, too?"

It had been ridiculously easy to pull Saz into our budding group. She brought a light to our dim corner.

Now Saz was a soothing weight atop me as she called "What's taking so long?" down the hall, where Caroline killed the screeching kettle and poured water into a French press. She yelled back something scathing about being ungrateful. Amrita guiltily hopped up to help her carry mugs, and then we were all in the room again. Something about it was nearly right enough to lull me to sleep.

But weekends were no longer a comfort. We'd spent half our Saturday like this, and it left me full of impenetrable anxiety, the lizard part of my brain insisting that we should be in the studio. Every moment I wasn't working felt like a waste, and every moment I *was* working felt like some other girl's life taking the place of my own. Sometimes I wondered if I would have the same drive without them at my side. If Rotham fed me only isolation, would I still find it worth it to work as hard as we did? I thought I wanted to be good—a good artist, a good friend. But I was a little afraid that I just wanted to be good enough to impress them, and no one else.

"That's the kind of spell I'm talking about," Saz said vaguely, her eyes trained on the film as she sat back and pulled *ANTHROPOMANCY* into her lap again.

"What do you mean?" Finch asked. She plucked at the frayed edges of her shorts. Her hair was pulled back sloppily, and the strands that grazed her cheek made me soft. I wanted to twist one around my finger.

Saz gestured to the screen. "They knew the importance of power. And like, sacrifice to a higher being. *That's* what I want. Something momentous and earth-shattering and delicious. Something that could give us all a chance to reach our highest potential."

"Don't tell me you're on this spell idea again," Caroline said from the doorway. Her fingers spidered around the rim of her mug, eyes downcast. "You should accept the inevitable now, Saz—it's called Solo for a reason. The sooner you realize we're all going to duke it out, the better chance you have of not getting knocked on your ass."

We fell quiet. I wanted to blame my anxiety on an empty stomach. There was a part of me that found it easier to resign myself to likelihoods—that Finch and Caroline were some of the most talented students in our year, that they would end up at the top of Moody's list, that the rest of us would cheer them on from the Grainer Gallery. But beside that lived a deliriously fatuous hope, one that felt capable of killing. The idea—the *dream*—that I could have a chance of Soloing. What would I do for that kind of power?

I couldn't think about the end. I was already terrified of all the ways it might tear us apart.

We ended up in Grainer by late afternoon. If one of us went to work, the rest of us followed—it was a forced accountability that I adored and resented all at once. Saturday turned into Sunday before we gave up and returned home to sleep, Finch splitting away to go to her apartment in Tuck House. Later in the morning, we repeated the process. Fucking around and watching something brain-meltingly insipid on the TV, cooking each other breakfast, prolonging our laziness until finally one of us got dressed and made the rest of us feel guilty. Then it was back to Grainer to spend the rest of our evening.

A life could pass like this, I thought. *A life could walk right by me.*

We weren't the only ones there. I passed Mars at the sinks scrubbing spray paint from beneath their nails, and Cameron crouched on the floor shooting staples into a canvas. Quiet music poured from the direction of Studio 1, where Veda must have been hard at work.

In my studio I put on headphones and started a playlist Caroline made me consisting mostly of sad folk songs, offensively titled JO'S TORTURED LESBIAN TUNES, and tried to focus on the project at hand. Moody sparked fresh anxiety in me—I wanted to prove her wrong and show her I could make us interesting. I'd taken the sketches of the four of them at our dining table and transferred the same image onto a canvas. Right now, they were still an underpainting—a technique we'd learned in our sophomore year where the artist laid all the shapes and tones out in a burnt-umber oil paint that would later be layered over with full color. It gave the rest of the painting a lively heat. But in its current state, my women were ghoulish apparitions illustrated in terracotta hues.

Darkness fell across campus without my realization. By the time Caroline poked her head into my cubicle, I had sketched out the first shadows of the painting with a wide brush—sweeping greens so dark they were nearly black surrounded our group, illuminated by the orange glow of the table lamp. Their hands were blocky shapes atop the table, each overlapping where I planned to add a linked pinky or an inter-locked elbow.

Caroline's mouth mimed out a silent proposal as she rapped on the wall beside my painting.

I slid my headphones off. "What was that?"

"I said, let's get pizza tonight. I'd rather swallow my own tongue than cook something. Wait, this is looking good!"

"Don't sound so surprised," I answered as she leaned closer to the painting.

"You made me so sexy," she continued. "I look like an ancient depiction of Lilith."

"Come on, it's just the first layer."

"I'm serious, it's a compliment!"

Caroline turned to me, smiling. There was yellow paint on one side of her nose where she must have scratched it. I thumbed it off for her, and her eyes shut in content.

I met Caroline in a Chemistry of Pigments class our sophomore year. It was the type of course that my dad had laughed at when I first registered for Rotham, saying that it was funny none of us had the chops to take a real science class. But that was part of what made Rotham so alluring to me. It was the kind of place that made our curiosities corporeal.

Caroline's first words to me, "I want to crush them between my teeth," were a perfect example. She had been talking about the fine granules of mustardy pigment sifted into a small container on the table in front of us. Professor Bervoets paired us up for the first in-class trial. We ground color down with a glass muller that was made for turning the powder into smooth paint when combined with oil. We spun the muller into the mixture for what felt like hours. Caroline had swiped a finger through it, turned to me, and pretended to lick her skin clean. I'd been too surprised to laugh. Instead, my eyes traced the spiraling motion of her tongue, the little curl it made in its playacting.

"Does it look delicious to you, or is that fucked up to say?" Caroline asked. "It's like what I imagine would come out if you pressed a thumb into an overripe apricot. Like you were separating the color from the object."

"It's not fucked up," I said quickly, taken aback that she would ask me, that she would want to hear what I had to say. The curse sounded wrong in my mouth, overly formal. "It looks divine."

She laughed and pointed the ochre-covered finger at me. "Divine, that's right. What a perfect word."

She was our final missing piece.

Was there a term for learning you hadn't been as complete as you might have once imagined? For discovering shards of yourself? For seeing these people and knowing it at once, like the slow acknowledgment of a finger falling asleep. For learning the things that constructed their desires and their personalities and all the ways they fit with you, like interlocking fragments of a machine.

Now I wanted to tell Caroline the truth—that even after three years at Rotham, I felt entirely aimless. That I didn't think there was a point to anything I was painting, that I was foolish for trying to depict the ways we were special to one another as if it might mean anything to anyone outside of our five. But Caroline hated it when I was self-pitying, and I was trying to become the kind of person that didn't expect my friends to carry my insecurities on their backs. So I just slid off my stool and scrubbed my brush in a jar full of solvent. Color swirled into chemical as I kept my question casual. "Did you already ask the others?"

"Yeah, I thought we should drive into town, but Amrita wants to save money, so I think we're just going to eat some of the nasty Bane pizza. We're supposed to meet by the sinks in fifteen. Clean up so we can go find them."

By the time we gathered at our usual table in Banemast, the dining hall was overcrowded and overwarm.

"We should have just taken our food home," Amrita said, cutting her eyes at the table next to us as someone tossed a rolled-up napkin through the air. We watched it fly. "This place is a zoo."

Saz leaned back in her seat. "I don't know. We could probably benefit from friendships outside of the ones at this table. Maybe we should join like, a kickball league or something. Get some camaraderie going."

Finch rolled her eyes. "Do you have to be such a dyke all the time?"

Saz gasped. "That's rich coming from you, varsity softball player. You eat carabiners for breakfast."

That shut Finch up, until their prodding dissolved into a unanimous roast of the new photo the admins displayed on the wall in Banemast. It was a portrait of Rotham's deans lined up with the rest of the administration, alongside a fair chunk of the full-time professors on campus.

Finch squinted at Kolesnik's grim smile. "When are they going to put that guy down and give us someone new? It's sad. He's like a rheumatic dog."

Caroline snorted.

"You're going to hell. You're probably first in line," Saz said. "Isn't he only like, sixty or something?"

"Sixty-eight," Amrita corrected.

"Exactly," Finch clarified. "Geriatric. Let's get someone in here who's less of a ghoulish bastard. That first class was a slog."

That got a round of thoughtful nods and the conversation devolved into commiseration about our progress. Finch was cagey about the painting she was working on, and Caroline kept checking her phone. Amrita picked at her margherita piece, leaving slices of pale tomato behind on the plate, and bemoaned the advice Moody had given her on how to limit the color palettes in her folkloric watercolors. She didn't want to limit anything, Amrita told us, tearing her crust into hunks. If anything, she wanted to expand until the paintings were rich with hues and contrast. It was so funny to hear her talk about color while exclusively wearing black, her sweater sleeves pushed up to her elbows. Saz thoughtfully chewed on her salad as she listened. The greens had seen better days.

"Okay," Saz said, interrupting the end of Amrita's rant. "I have a proposal, but you have to promise to hear me out before you argue."

"I already hate where this is going," Amrita sighed.

Saz ignored that. "We're all struggling to figure out where we want to go with our theses, correct? Am I wrong to say that?"

She waited. We shook our heads. No, she wasn't wrong. Over the past three years, I had built a recognizable style for myself: earthy, muted rooms and landscapes with poses from family photos transferred within them. But the portraits always ended up a little soulless. They needed something *more*—and I hoped that painting the five of us might bring that necessary sentience to each piece. I felt like a freshman all over again; completely insecure in everything that I created, self-deprecating, resentful, uninspired.

Saz drummed her fingers on the table beside the copy of *ANTHROPOMANCY*. It went back and forth between Grainer and the Manor with her often, and she had brought it into my room the other night. Her knee had nearly whacked me in the stomach as she threw herself down beside me and splayed the book open to a saved page. It revealed a gruesome print of an old Greek painting, a man splayed across a stone slab and surrounded by figures digging around in his exposed entrails. "Look," she'd whispered, awestruck. "It's a kind of divination with intestines of a dying body. How fucked is that?"

Gore never bothered me much. But I had found that illustration unbearable to look at. I nudged the book shut with the back of my hand and told her it was cool, but it was about to make me spew my dinner.

Now her voice was firm as her eyes darted around the table. "We all want a shot at Solo, don't we? If it can't be all of us, then it's one of us or bust, that's what we agreed on?"

I didn't like to think about it. Those five spots at the top of Moody's list were my worst fear. In the pit of my heart, I prayed it would be our group who would advance, and that the Solo spot would belong to Finch or Caroline. If the rest of them could move forward, I could still be proud.

But also—I wanted it. And the thought was annihilating.

"Get on with it," Caroline coaxed. "What's your big idea?"

Saz stabbed her fork into the salad until it stood up straight. Her smile was wickedly pleased. "There's this . . . ritual that I found. To amplify creativity. It's supposed to unlock your deepest inner path and allow you to create to your fullest extent."

Finch laughed. "Sounds like someone's fucked-up ayahuasca trip."

But Caroline's eyes were bright. She flipped her phone face down to where she couldn't see the screen as Saz scoffed at Finch. "Not at all. Everyone who tried it said that it led to their making the best work they've ever created, and their career really took off afterward. Gallery representation, whole retrospectives, sales on their crafts and artwork that earned them enough cash to quit their full-time jobs. Awards and grants, postgrad travel around Europe and Asia, adjunct professor positions in some of the New York schools. This is the real deal."

Caroline swallowed a mouthful before she spoke. "What do we have to do?"

Saz prodded at her wilting lettuce again. Amrita leaned back in her chair as Finch crossed her arms over her chest. "Well, we have to like, sacrifice someone."

My reflex was to laugh. It was a high, nervous sound, a weak attempt at easing over an argument that hadn't yet begun. I darted a glance around Bane, searching for an eavesdropper, but the dull roar of conversations seemed to block out our voices.

"Come on," Amrita said. "I thought you were being serious."

"You never let me explain before you get mad! We're not killing anyone. We're basically . . . cursing them, or hexing them, or like, fixing the evil eye on them. We pick someone that really deserves it, and we toss them the misfortune that would have stuck to us instead. We're left with all the good stuff."

"How?" Caroline pushed.

Saz shrugged. "I don't know how it works; it's the fucking universe or something. It's intuition or karmic retribution or the High Priestess or all three at once."

"No," Caroline said, "I mean how the hell do we do it?"

Now Saz smiled again. The shape of it lit up her eyes. She had Caroline snared, and we all knew it.

"Like I said, we have to make a sacrifice. It's not enough to give up something physical of our own. It's more like . . . we need to be able to live with giving that misfortune to someone else. You gotta be willing to steal someone else's joy."

"Easy. I only have two settings," Finch said around a full mouth. "Bitch and cunt."

Amrita nodded solemnly. "Truest thing you've ever said."

"You have someone in mind," I said to Saz. It wasn't a question. I could tell by the cagey way Saz was presenting herself—she knew more than we were privy to, and she was delighted to lay it out for us.

"Well, yeah. Kolesnik."

His name summoned the image of the man standing at the front of our lecture to mind, along with that creepy Boar King costume suspended in the library's glass Grotesque display. I could feel the weight of him—not in physical stature but in his status at Rotham, in the domineering way he dismissed our words, the unnerving closeness of his gaze on us in class, or a heavy hand on the shoulder as he passed our seats. Years of rumors about Kolesnik himself: that he made his female students increasingly uncomfortable, that he was crude and cruel, that he thought himself above reprimand after everything he'd given to Rotham's institution. If there was anyone who deserved to bear a curse, it was Kolesnik. But the idea still gave my stomach a twist. Saz's idea sounded like something I would have believed in as a kid. Berries smashed in the palm and smeared all over the body. Stick dolls bound with grass and smashed underfoot. Pagan and animal and close to the heart. It was probably all nonsense, the kind of ridiculous game we might have played late at night after getting too high and reading each other's tarot cards, Caroline lying on the rug with our fingertips grazing her arms and thighs. *Light as a feather, stiff as a board, light as a feather, stiff as a board.*

But if it was real—if even a fraction of it could come true—who were we to use the stain of Kolesnik to advance our own work? Weren't we meant to better ourselves by putting in the hours, by channeling something within ourselves rather than bargaining for it from the world? If the talent wasn't there, then that was that. I didn't feel that I deserved to win if I hadn't somehow earned it myself.

Still, I watched the interested downward tilt to Caroline's brow as it deepened with satisfaction, the kind that formed when she was listening extra close. She absentmindedly drew patterns in the condensation her water cup left on the table. "So what, we burn a picture of him? Stick it with pins? Spit in his water bottle?"

"We have to use bodily material to craft a likeness of him," Saz answered immediately, as if she'd been waiting for one of us to ask. "So we actually need *his* spit—or hair, or snot, or blood, or urine. I'm sure you can think of a few more options."

Amrita shoved the remnants of her food away from her. "I was still eating, thanks."

"All we do is gather that stuff and mix it with something of ours in the form of a handcrafted Kolesnik model, where it can live forever and ever, unless we decide to destroy it." Saz splayed her fingers and wiggled them, as if finishing a magic trick. "Abracadabra and all that jazz."

"It sounds like you've been reading that nasty book too much," I said loftily, gesturing at *ANTHROPOMANCY*. "Where did you say you found this idea again?"

Now Saz flushed pink. Her palm rested on top of the book. "Um . . . Reddit."

Finch pushed away from the table and piled her trash onto her plate. "Well, you guys can have fun with that. Personally, I don't think we need a hex or a ritual from the depths of 4chan. As much as I think he's a prick, I'm not making a Kolesnik doll, and I'm not collecting his piss, and I'm not sacrificing him to the devil. I'm going back to the studio to do my work."

"All you bitches do is complain," Saz said, shrugging. "Don't jump down my throat just because I tried to help."

Caroline's slowly blooming smile could have powered the electricity in all of Grainer. "I love you and your beautiful brain, Saz, and I think it's a great idea."

"Still not doing it!" Finch called over her shoulder as Amrita stood to join her.

"She's right, you know. There's no point in wasting time on a ritual when we should just be directing all that effort toward Solo. Jo, you coming?"

I felt caught between them—Amrita's waiting gaze as she hovered at the edge of the table, Saz tugging on my wrist as she heaved a devastated sigh and said, "No more studio, you said we could watch *The Ring* tonight!"

Amrita's dark eyes were questioning. She touched my shoulder lightly, and I could feel the coaxing in it.

"I really should get some work done," I said finally, standing to join Amrita and Finch. "Tomorrow. I promise. We'll all watch it tomorrow."

"No, fuck you lot, I'll watch it by myself and wake you up at three in the morning when I have a nightmare." Saz slung her bag over her shoulder and waved us away. "Go, go, have fun selling your soul to Moody."

We split like that, Caroline deciding she was too tired to join and Saz leading her home. I followed Amrita up the stairs after Finch, past the empty classrooms and buildings along the promenade to the glowing tower of Grainer, to the studio and its buzzing fluorescents, to the overhead fans ruffling papers around the room and the windows cracked open to let some of the night air inside.

We worked until midnight. Until my headphones finally died and I had to sit in silence, dragging my brush across the canvas and marking out the outline of Caroline's legs. Until I thought I heard someone behind me in that studio—peering over my shoulder and watching me work—and I turned to find the space empty. Until Amrita came to fetch and ferry me home. Until we left Finch there, her light burning on, her studio covered in sketches and sketches and sketches, all depicting the same gauzy black outline of a profile with hyperrealized eyes staring back at us.

6

Symptomatic of the Wild Heart

"Rough day?" Amrita asked as she pulled out the chair to my right and settled into it. Her bracelets clinked when she moved, and the sound echoed throughout the dining hall. Banemast was nearly empty save for us. The lunch rush had ended long ago, but I hadn't been able to summon the energy to go back upstairs.

I looked up. "How could you tell?"

"Your coffee's black, you only drink it like that when you're irritated about something. And you didn't show up for Moody's afternoon check-in. You'd only skip that if your appendix burst or something equally nasty. Your appendix hasn't burst, has it?"

My grasp tightened around the paper cup. Tears burned high in my nose. I wanted to lean forward and lie in her lap. Instead, I rested my forehead on my arms and stared at the table, feeling it stick to me in places. Amrita's hand came up and stroked my hair.

It had been a horrible day and a horrible week. Day after day of useless time spent in the studio, all of us incapable of making anything worthy of hanging up for critique, with the only reprieve being the moments in between when we came together in the Manor to complain about our lack of progress. My greatest and only joy was in our mundane routines. Coffee and lunch, Finch's deck of cards, Saz's clay face masks, dinner on the table and in a pot on the stove. Beyond that familiarity, my hands no longer felt like a part of me—everything I painted had the disjointed quality of someone else's brain piloting the mechanics. The ideas wouldn't translate from my head to canvas. Sketches were no better. I wasted a forest of pages trying to put an interesting image down on paper.

"You alright?" Amrita prodded again. Her hand was still stroking, fingers hot against my scalp. "You seem so . . . tired."

I shrugged, forehead digging into ulna and radius. "I'm pitiful. Everything I make looks like garbage. I feel like an imitation of myself. A really shitty imitation."

She waved her free hand under the table and above my knees, where I could see it. I finally lifted my head and she smiled as she smoothed her thumb across my brow. "You've got a red spot," she murmured.

"Great. Ugly *and* pitiful."

"Oh, shut up. You think any of us know what we're doing? Moody told me my horse painting looked like a starving dog, and I still don't know if it was an insult or a compliment. Come on, let's go up together. The others would never forgive me if I left you down here to wallow like this."

I followed her because I knew she was right. Amrita linked her arm through mine, and together we went back to the studio. Moody barely looked up when we entered, but the frown on her face told me she was annoyed. "You're late, Jo," she called. "Don't make it a habit."

I saluted her, and then despised myself for it. Amrita snickered.

"Come on," she said. "You can do your sketches right here." In her cubicle, she shoved aside the papers on her desk and cleared a space for me. "If I see you pull out your phone or get distracted, I'm going to pinch you."

We stayed long past the end of class, Amrita scraping paint across the sheet of paper taped up to her studio wall while I sketched at her desk. I drew her side profile, the way her hair fell down her back, the long flutter of her lashes, the swell of her bottom lip held between her teeth, the beauty mark on her cheek just below her right eye. She looked like a hundred women I'd never meet—I could see her face and imagine her mother in it, and her mother's mother, and a million mothers before her. My sketch immortalized her there among the others as I thumbed through the pages.

There was Amrita again, in her bed. I'd drawn her as I watched her crochet—it was a foreshortened portrait, with her socked foot large and primary as it led to her bent knee and her face half-obscured in the background. Then Caroline in the bathroom, putting her hair up in the mirror with a scrunchie held in her mouth, half-lidded blue eyes staring at me in the glass. Saz sitting on the kitchen counter and eating out of a bag of carrots in her pajama shorts, the newly dyed strands of pink at her temples held back with star-shaped clips. Finally, Finch—sitting on the steps of Grainer and smoking a cigarette she had bummed from Mars, the smoke shadowing her in a gray haze, shoulders stooped forward and a smile on her face.

In a perfect world, this would be my thesis: my women and the record I made of them. It didn't have to be any bigger than that. There would be no expectations of Soloing, no pressure to perform, no need to impress Rotham and the world beyond it. It would be enough to hear their footsteps on the stairs, to smell Caroline brewing coffee and see Amrita's hair tie on the edge of the sink. I could eat fruit from the fridge and read books on the shelves and hear music coming down the hall, Saz's, something round and electric. I could be happy like that, content with their immeasurable simplicity.

"You always make me look so pretty," Amrita said softly, her voice beside my ear. I turned to her and she rested her chin on my shoulder, smiling again, that beaming expression that made my heart ache with love for her. *That's just what you look like*, I wanted to say, but I didn't want her to dismiss me and ruin the moment. I watched her go back to fretting over her painting again, her brush making hesitant strokes.

At least I wasn't alone in my spiraling descent.

I started to dread Kolesnik's class even more than studio. He was a physical reminder of our looming deadlines. He liked to start every class with two countdowns: one for our end of semester Survey—a measly 52 days to go—and one for the Solo Show, coming in at a whopping 171. Those days felt like minutes. I was hurtling toward an inevitable end. In between these reminders, he'd spout off long lectures about the state of the contemporary art world and all his resentment for current trends. Those self-indulgent rants typically led to him turning on us and asking how our thesis papers were going. Every time he questioned me, I floundered and began to spout off nonsense about family and effervescence until he'd finally give up on me, turning to Veda or Cameron. Sometimes, if I was lucky, he'd be interrupted by one of his frequent nosebleeds before he had the chance to reprimand me. He'd pinch his nose closed with a tissue and nasally complain about Rotham's dry air.

This was my routine. Go to class, stumble into inadequacy, float from room to room and building to building with the hopes that one of my steps might lead me somewhere more meaningfully defined. I was still waiting, still finding no results. There was a permeating doubt at the back of my head wriggling in my mother's voice: *What are you going to do with your future?*

It was finally starting to cool down on Wednesday when we left Kolesnik's class early. He'd declared that he had a board meeting that afternoon and let us out by eleven. Outside on the promenade, the world had that earthy scent of decaying leaves. We walked in unison—all of us except for Caroline, who we'd lost somewhere along the way.

"Do you think she went back to the Manor?" Saz asked, scrolling through her texts in search of one from Caroline.

Amrita shrugged, looking back at Slatter Hall where we'd just left Kolesnik's class behind. "She would have said."

I reached for my phone and patted an empty pocket. A jolt of anxiety halted me in place. "Fuck, I think I left my phone in Kolesnik's. I'm gonna go grab it before he leaves."

"Meet us in the studio!" Finch called, and I gave her an acknowledging wave as I jogged back in the direction we'd just come from.

The building was nearly silent, everyone either still in class or heading to Banemast for lunch. Kolesnik's class was on the first floor down the west wing. I retraced my footsteps back to his room. The door sat ajar, the lights still on, but my relief at the sight only lasted a moment.

Past the opening, Caroline stood with her back to me beside Kolesnik in his desk chair. Her voice spilled into the hall—it was the tone she used every time she spoke to a professor, that clipped, clean resonance she'd been raised with, the one that reminded me she came from the kind of family who had given her particular tools and would always operate in the world differently from the way I could.

"Would it help if I came to your office hours? Time is not an issue for me. I'm willing to put the work in."

"I'm glad to hear it," Kolesnik said, his voice a rough timbre beneath hers. "Of course I welcome your company, Miss Aster. But I don't know if just showing up is enough to set your work apart from the rest of this group."

There was a certain low warmth to the way he said *company* that made my nose wrinkle.

Caroline tucked a strand of hair behind her ear and turned to meet his upturned face. Kolesnik's desk lamp lit up the outline of her profile. There was a placating smile on her lips and a flat glaze over her eyes, an expression I recognized as her pretended interest. It was the same look she adopted whenever Saz talked about astrology.

"Whatever you recommend, I'll do," she declared, and her eyes lit up with the fire that had drawn me to her since we met.

It kind of broke my heart, to listen to her like that. To witness the pressure she put on herself that the rest of us weren't permitted to see and to know that she meant it. Caroline's parents weighed expectations on her that made me feel ridiculous for thinking I had it bad—the Asters had spent a lifetime donating to Rotham, hosting charity events, attending annual galas. They were patrons of the arts. They expected Caroline to be their link to the payoff, her success a physical representation of the culture they cultivated in their lives.

I took the smallest step back from the door. Just behind Caroline, I could see my phone face down on a desk. They couldn't talk for long. I would just wait until they were done, and then I would slip in before he locked up for the day.

But before I could turn away, my eyes snagged on Kolesnik's hand rising and landing on the back of Caroline's thigh, his face tilted up to hers, knees splayed wide in the leather chair. His fingers encircled and pressed down. I watched in frozen horror as he yanked her into the space between his spread knees, Caroline rocking forward and her face falling in surprise.

"It takes a certain dedication to be worthy of Soloing," he said roughly, the words unfurling like a lick of flame. "Will you devote yourself?"

Heat in my cheeks, the kind of immediate fury I hadn't known myself capable of. His knuckles strained as he squeezed—his thumb digging into her skin just below the thin fabric of her cotton dress, the hem brushing against the tops of her long thighs, her eyes widening for a split second before they hardened over again.

Caroline stepped out of his reach and crossed her arms over her chest, as if pulling her exoskeleton back over exposed organs. Frenzied, I pushed the door fully open and entered with the announcing creak of old wood.

Both heads swiveled to face me. Kolesnik straightened in his chair and cleared his throat, his hand falling to his lap again.

"Office hours are over," he snapped, turning back to his desk.

I was already halfway across the room, phone snatched in one hand and the other reaching for Caroline's, pulling her with me into the hall as I said, "Sorry, forgot something." The door slammed hard enough to rattle the paintings on the wall.

"Jo, stop," Caroline finally said, tugging her hand out of mine when we finally reached the main doors of Slatter. She folded her arms again, that armor between me and her heart.

Campus was busier now, but I didn't care who might hear—I just hissed, "What the hell was that?"

"What are you talking about?"

"Caroline," I said sharply. "He grabbed you."

Her frown deepened. "It was hardly a grab. I handled it."

"I'm not saying—I know you did, but—" I kept sputtering. I wanted to cut his fucking hand off at the wrist. "He can't just *do* that."

"Drop it." Caroline's face was a mask.

Impossible. I flared with anger. The branches of my rushing fear kept opening new avenues for me to consider—Caroline had visited him in years before as an advisor, had taken that Art and Activism in the '80s class. Had named him Professor Perv for a reason. But I hadn't imagined that reason could be so physical. "Has he done something like this before?"

"I said fucking drop it."

She started toward Banemast, her back to me again, an unreadable solidity to her gait.

I hurried to follow. "Would you drop it if you were me? You don't even have to answer that, I know you wouldn't."

"Jo, please, just stop. We can talk about it later, okay?"

She was walking too fast for me to keep up. I beelined after her into the rush of the dining hall, scanning the crowd for the others, trying to swallow past the stone in my throat. She beat me to the table and sank into a seat with a grate of chair legs on linoleum.

"There you are," Finch called. "Find your phone, Jo?"

"What? Oh, yeah, I did." I pulled out the chair across from Caroline, between Finch and Amrita. Amrita pushed her plate in my direction and gestured toward an uneaten half of a sandwich. The sight of it made my stomach turn.

"We were just talking about thesis papers and Creep-lesnik," Saz said.

Caroline stiffened but kept her head down, scrolling through something on her phone. I obediently started to eat when Amrita nudged me again, but everything tasted mealy between my teeth.

"Can we change the subject?" I asked. The bread caught in my throat. I could feel it cling as I tried to force it down with a gulp of water.

"Ignoring the fact that we have to write these papers won't make them go away," Saz sang, poking my arm across the table.

"I just want to talk about something else right now."

There was a beat of silence. Caroline fixed me with a hard, irritated look. "Go ahead, Jo. You can say what you really want."

Saz's eyes flickered between us. "What's going on here?"

"Nothing," Caroline snapped. She shot me a glare that told me to shut the fuck up.

"Caroline—" I started, and she interrupted with an exasperated sigh.

"Jo saw Kolesnik being a creep, as per usual. It's fine. He was just getting handsy. I got him off me, and that was that."

"Are you fucking kidding?" Finch said, sitting up straighter in her chair at the same time Saz started to ideate in a rush.

"Caroline. We'll report him to the dean. Or we'll kick his ass. Or we'll do both."

"Keep your voice down, oh my god. I said it's fine. I don't want to deal with any of this right now. I have plenty of other shit on my mind. Can we please just go home and chill before I need to deal with work again?"

There was such a ragged, desperate quality to her voice, in the way she said *home*, like she was begging, like she couldn't bear one more second of this. We went silent. We could hear what she needed from us, even if it wasn't what we wanted to give.

"'Course," Amrita said quietly. "Let's go home."

We never went to the studio that afternoon. Instead, Finch came home with us, and we took a break for the first time in what felt like weeks by curling up in the living room under a pile of blankets, Caroline rigid and quiet with her knees pulled to her chest on the couch. I had to fight to keep myself from continuously turning to look at her. *Hellraiser* played on the TV as the sun set beyond the windows. Saz and Finch picked up a pizza—real pizza this time from the spot in town that we loved unanimously, an enormous thing smothered in shallots and arugula and honey and salami.

I still had no appetite. I left my piece half-finished. All I could think about was Caroline in that room—and how if I hadn't seen her, she might have kept that moment all to herself. I wanted to know what else she contained. I wanted her to know that she could give those worries to me, that she didn't need to isolate herself, that Solo wasn't the defining moment of her life no matter how absolute it seemed, that it wasn't worth a fraction of suffering if it meant subjecting herself to the power trip of a man like Kolesnik.

Because that was what this had to be about, right? Kolesnik's influence held such magnificent sway over the final Solo decision. He was half of Moody's erudite team. He was meant to be a guiding force for us. Caroline, whose drive toward the insurmountable mountain of Solo could not be discouraged, would always take the initiative, even if that put her in Kolesnik's direct path. Of course, we had all thought he was unsettling. Instinct couldn't be argued with. But he was still a beacon of success on the track we hoped to ascend—someone whose approval we craved as validation for the work we were creating. Caroline, under the pressure of her family's investment and her mother's scrutiny, would sacrifice anything for acknowledgment.

We all knew that Mrs. Aster didn't like her daughter, because Caroline was what her mother liked to call "peculiar." Caroline later explained, after several months of friendship, a few drinks, and a vicious game of truth or dare that ended in Finch drinking a raw egg from a shot glass, that this meant that between the ages of six and eleven Caroline woke every night from a recurring and lucid night terror with ragged cuts across her biceps and thighs where her nails had scratched her back to a waking state, screaming all the while, claiming that there was a man crouching in the corner of her ceiling. The nightmares had only stopped after the intervention of an expensive counselor and a heavy dose of sleep medication that left Caroline too drowsy to stay awake in her fifth-grade classroom. The Asters promptly started pricey laser removal for the scars her nails left across her body and swapped her to an equally highbrow at-home tutor until high school, where Caroline excelled as an example of her family's beauty, intelligence, and drive. Her grandfather had been a Rotham legend—his name was on a placard beside a Sol LeWitt drawing in the library with profound grati- tude for his donation—and Caroline followed expectations by earning a legacy acceptance with a smile on her face. Her mother had been so proud—until a photo started circulating on Facebook of Caroline with another girl's face between her tits at a high school graduation party and a half-empty bottle of champagne held in one fist, foam spouting all over them both. Caroline made it her profile picture.

Under the threat of Kolesnik's assault, I wanted *that* Caroline—the one willing to wreak havoc if it meant putting someone else in their place, regardless of the consequences or the way it might sour her rep- utation. I wanted her to kill the pathetic part of me that still hoped Kolesnik might tell me I was capable of Soloing, to crush that desire underfoot even if it left a crucial part of me in pieces.

I looked at Caroline. Her eyes still held the same scolding quality they had over lunch, when she had begged me to let it go. If she would not allow us to go to the administration, what else could I do to defend her?

Saz leaned close to Caroline and rested her head on the other girl's shoulder. "What's up, Jo? Not hungry?"

I shook my head. Couldn't stop shaking it. Couldn't get a grasp on myself.

"You know what," I said, faltering. "You know what, fuck this, and fuck Kolesnik," I said. Every head swiveled. Even Pinhead stared back at me through the fuzzy TV screen. "Let's do the ritual."

"Yes, bitch!" Saz launched herself on me in glee, her arms squeezing around my middle as I laughed. Caroline straightened beside her. There was a triumphant joy etched in Saz's smile. "You mean it? No backing out now. If Jo's in, we're doing this. Come on."

The *come on* was directed at Amrita and Finch. Amrita shook her head, smiling, her ponytail bobbing with the movement. "Fine," she said, "I won't be the one to stop y'all. Let's do it."

Beside me, Finch shrugged indifferently but remained quiet. I could tell she was uncomfortable with the idea. And while her wariness left me uneasy, I was game for anything if it meant making them happy.

I needed Kolesnik to suffer—and if our thesis work happened to improve in the process, what harm could that be?

7

OFFERING TO THE OMNIPOTENT

Saz's Suburban was an industrial monster paid for with her parents' credit card. She typically rented a new one upon arriving back at Rotham, after she'd gone home for Christmas or summer break to stay at her family home just outside of London, and she consistently chose a sleek, ursine SUV. It was the only car between the five of us that could hold our collective comfortably. Saz always looked miniature behind its wheel, but she was far more confident directing it down dirt roads than I could have ever been.

The path she followed after Moody's class that day was pocked by years of tire tracks. Coming evening sucked the afternoon from the sky with a straw, and now all that remained were thin dregs of clouds and pockets of white-blue fading into a pinkened gray. Caroline sat in the passenger seat. Her phone was tethered to the stereo, one of our playlists depicted on the dash screen and reading: CINCINNATI BITCHES LOVE ME. It was a joke we made often about Saz—how the last four people she'd gone on a date with had all been from Ohio. The Suburban hit a pothole. The voice in the speakers gargled and writhed.

"You're really not going to tell us what we're doing out here in bumfuck nowhere?"

That was Finch, leaning forward and halfway across my lap, her fingers hooked around the seat next to Saz's right shoulder. Her jeans were stained with alizarin, the paint so vivid it suggested synthetic blood where it met a tear in the fabric across her thigh. My gaze kept dragging to the place where the threads pressed lines against her skin.

In the mirror, Saz's eyes were hidden behind chunky sunglasses. "I asked for patience and companionship. Chill out."

Amrita was quiet beside me, her head tipped back and her eyes shut. She let out a deep exhale, as if she could feel me watching but was too tired to acknowledge it. Her pupils moved behind the lids, back and forth and back and forth.

Finch's apprehension rubbed off on me. My palms were damp, pain prickling at my temples.

"How long do you think we'll be gone?" I called from the back row as we rattled over another dip in the road. I had to shout to be heard over the music. "Kolesnik asked to see an outline for my artist statement tomorrow, and I haven't started yet."

"All in good time, Jo," Saz sang.

There was something erratic about her, something godly and spellbinding about the fuzzing speakers and the inch of air Caroline's window let in, woodsmoke and dry earth and dying leaves. The thickets framing the road had that dusky look of the end of the world. I wasn't cold, but a shiver came over me anyway.

Saz pulled off where a cornfield began. Stalks stretched for what felt like miles, lush and higher than my head, and dense trees marked the distant boundaries of the farm. The SUV sat on a tilt where the dirt sloped down. We piled out after Saz, who slammed her door and circled to pop open the trunk.

"What's all this?" Amrita asked.

A large cardboard box took up most of the trunk, along with a few bags lined up beside it. It looked like the kind of stuff you'd drop off at a thrift store—old clothes, a pair of shoes, and something thick and downy that appeared to be a fur coat.

"You said you wanted to do the ritual," Saz declared, "so I prepared our sacrifice."

Finch sputtered. "Wait, you didn't tell us it was happening *now*."

"Spontaneity breeds success," Saz said brightly.

Caroline poked around in the box. Taper candles made a sound like a tongue popping against the roof of a mouth as they clacked together. She lifted a plastic baggie from the contents and held it between her index finger and thumb as if it were a used tissue—which made sense, considering it appeared to be stuffed with *several* used tissues, one crusty and brown with dried blood.

"Gag," she said. "Is this someone's snot? You were serious about all that 'bodily material' bullshit?"

Amrita leaned over the box, her eyes wide with horror. "Saz, you didn't. Please tell me you didn't."

We huddled closer to see what had caught Amrita's attention. Saz just grinned as Amrita lifted the fur coat. I could see, now that it was unobscured by the rest of the clothes in the box, that the hair was coarse as a mangy dog's. There was a hood attached to it, and atop the hood were two papier-mâché eyes. Below them sat a stuffed snout, thin where some of the fur had rubbed away to reveal painted-on nostrils. Protruding from the nose were two long tusks haphazardly glued to the fabric.

"The Boar King," Caroline whispered, struck with awe. "You stole Kolesnik's costume? You are so fucking cool. I could kiss you right now."

Saz sketched a bow. Her smile was radiant as she waved a set of keys in the air. "I had to borrow these to get it out of the case. Sorry, Jo."

She tossed the keys to me. I was so stunned that I almost didn't catch them. "How the hell did you get my keys? You're going to get me fired, Saz."

"Or me," Finch said, looking pale.

Saz just shrugged. I didn't recognize the look in her eyes when she pushed her sunglasses to the top of her head—unconstrained glee, smug satisfaction, an all-knowing lilt to the lips. "You said it yourself," she aimed at Finch. "Rotham security cameras are just props. What proof would they have?"

"I don't know," I started.

But she just hauled a bag out of the trunk and gestured toward the field. "Grab something and follow me. I'll explain when we reach the center."

"Wait. Wait a second, no way," Finch said, holding her hands up. "You guys can go all *Children of the Corn* on each other, but I'm not going in there. We need to take this shit back before they expel us. I don't care if they don't have you on camera. Jo and I will be so fucked if you don't—"

"Why don't you wait in the car, then?" Caroline snapped.

We stood in nervous silence. Finch wouldn't meet Caroline's eyes, her jaw clenched. Caroline hoisted the cardboard box and propped it on her hip. It was hilariously out of place against her delicate bracelets and pristine white sweater. She was taunting Finch. She wanted her to know that turning away now would make her weak. That it would separate her from the rest of us and leave her stranded.

"Fine," Finch said at last. "Let's get this over with."

A wooden pole rose above the maze of maize, barren and sun-bleached. Saz led us to it as if she had a compass behind her eyes, pushing stalks aside, flies buzzing between the ears. When we reached the center, she instructed us to drop the materials. She rifled around in the bags and the box and laid her findings out in the dirt—the Boar King's coat, a pair of men's pants and leather oxfords, the bag of tissues, three burlap sacks, paint markers, a pair of scissors, a soggy package of ground beef, and a needle in a pincushion threaded through with red embroidery floss.

"We're making a scarecrow," Saz announced, smoothing her hands down the front of her skirt. "Or, like, a poppet, I guess. Like I said before, the ritual requires a sacrifice. It's called sympathetic magic. We ask for spiritual awakening and the height of our creativity. And in return, we offer the downfall of another. So we're creating an effigy of Kolesnik, and we're hexing him."

"What's the meat for?" Amrita asked, looking ill.

"We needed something to represent his heart. You'd be surprised to learn how fuckin' hard it is to track down animal organs for sale in rural Indiana," Saz sighed. "Or maybe you wouldn't. I called a few butchers, and they acted like *I* was the weird one for asking. I mean, come on, don't be selfish. What else are you gonna do with it?"

I stared down at the Boar King's coat. Splayed in the dirt like that, it looked like something's shed skin. I could imagine it animated again with Kolesnik inside of it, the hood pulled over his skull and the tusks settling on either of his cheekbones. It was a sight I'd seen every year since I came to Rotham—a visual impossible to erase. In the Boar King's suit he was a feral creature, staked out high on his plinth at the Grotesque, the fur nearly obscuring everything but the grisly shadow of his beard. When I looked up again, Caroline had already begun to shuck leaves from the stalks of corn and drop them on the coat, stuffing them down the sleeves and into the scarecrow's torso until it was a plump animal in the dirt.

"Is this . . . morally right?" Amrita asked. "I know Kolesnik is awful, but aren't we just as bad if we curse him?"

"He deserves this and a whole lot more," I said, mostly to convince myself and quell the way my pulse pounded. "Especially after what he did to Caroline."

Caroline didn't respond, just continued filling out the pinstriped pants with grass and leaves. Her hair was a curtain, obscuring her expression.

The reminder kicked the rest of them into gear. I helped Amrita prop the shoes up at the ankles of the scarecrow's pants, stitching the pants to the shoes by shoving the needle through a few of the shoelace holes. Saz crafted a head out of a burlap sack. It was a ghoulish thing with marked indents where she placed two black stones for eyes. Beetles crawled over the face as she tore open the package of meat and dumped the contents into Kolesnik's new heart. Flies came like they'd been called. Saz peeled open the plastic baggie of tissues and shook them atop the wet, red matter.

Saz caught me staring at the napkins, stiff with snot and gore. "I had to dig through the trash," she admitted, making a face. "I told you, the ritual said we had to have bodily material."

"This is so fucked," Amrita muttered, but she tenderly fitted the burlap head into the hood and adjusted the tusks until they were just right.

Lying there in his completion, our Kolesnik scarecrow was a nightmare. His body was long—taller than any of us if we had stood him up on his ungainly legs. The Boar King's coat made him look like taxidermy, and the pinstriped pants gave him a kind of ridiculousness that had me smiling to myself, trying to contain the joke. His hooded head was unnerving. The tusks jutted skyward. The arms were splayed wide, black fur dusty with dirt.

Saz zipped up the coat around its new heart and straddled the bloated corpse. Kolesnik's husk-stuffed stomach swelled beneath her thighs, the boar's painted eyes staring up at the darkening sky. Her fingers disappeared into her bra cup and plucked a metal rectangle free from the lump it had made under the fabric—she kissed it in her fist, raised it before her, and flicked out a blade.

The box cutter sliced through the sack of the scarecrow's jaw with one smooth drag. Dry grass burst free beneath the tusks, right where the mouth would sit.

"Okay," Saz exhaled, gesturing to me with the knife a few times until I finally realized she was asking me to hold it. I did so gingerly. "Alright. Okay. Now, Caroline—hit me as hard as you can."

Caroline's eyes went wide. "Are you kidding me? I'm not going to do that."

"I will," Finch interrupted.

"I asked Caroline," Saz said, cutting her eyes at Finch. "Your rings would hurt too much."

"I'll take them off."

"Caroline," Saz pleaded, her smile slipping a bit. "Come on. We need to bleed on him, and I'm too squeamish to use the knife."

"This is ridiculous," Amrita said, but Caroline scooted forward until her knees were nearly framing the scarecrow's head. She touched her unblemished knuckles reverently.

"Come on, Saz, I don't wanna hit you."

Saz scoffed. "Of course you do. You called me a bitch yesterday."

"I was joking."

"Keep it up, funny guy, and hit me," Saz provoked, grinning.

Caroline grimaced. "Oh, shut the fuck up. You can't be mad, okay? You asked me to do this."

Saz's mouth fell open to answer, but Caroline's punch connected before she could speak. Her head cracked back. A wave of black hair bobbed with Saz's skull, and her hands flew up to her nose, cradling it, gasping in shock, her body rearing as if caught in the gravity of a crash. "Shit!" Caroline cried, immediately shaking out her hand. "I'm sorry! I'm so sorry!"

"Do it again!"

They didn't hesitate. Saz's hands fell away and gripped her knees, and Caroline swung, harder, knuckles landing with a resounding crunch. This time, the blood flow was immediate. It ran in fat rivers over Saz's lips as she careened forward, red spattering all over Kolesnik's fur and his burlap mouth.

"Jesus Christ," Finch whispered, heavy with horror.

Saz's cackle was high and delighted and red. "That's what I'm talking about. *That* is what I'm *talking* about!"

Beside me, Amrita was a clenched fist, half-risen to her knees to put an end to the whole mess. There was a dangerous nest inside of me where something horrible perched and festered, fed by their eagerness for violence and the lines they were willing to cross. I was afraid they would hit me next. I was afraid to be left out entirely unbeaten. Saz swiped a hand under her nose, smearing blood all over the lower half of her face.

"Gimme that," Caroline said to me, gesturing to the knife in my hands. I obeyed after a beat when she repeated herself. She thumbed out the blade again and slit it across her palm until a fast line formed and dribbled into the grass. She squeezed her fist over the effigy's mouth and let the drips land there.

Saz's teeth were rimmed with crimson along the gums when she grinned. Caroline dropped the knife and nursed her knuckles, cursing under her breath until the words dissolved into laughter, until she couldn't contain the sound any longer.

"This is so beyond fucked," Amrita said. "Next time I'm staying home." But to my shock she took the knife from its place beside Caroline's thigh and, after a sharp inhale, tore it across her palm. The skin split easily. She shuffled forward on her knees and bled onto the doll, and then the knife went to Finch. She hesitated, looking at the box cutter in her hands, and then turned to me as if asking for someone to remain on her side.

"I don't . . . ," she started, trailing off, her brow furrowing. "Come on, Jo. We are not doing this."

Pain was not a feeling I'd ever been able to wrangle. As a kid, my grandparents had banned me from going into the garage, where my granddad collected decades of parts and antiques in rows of metal shelving. But it was a maze made perfect for my wonder. On the day he left the garage door just slightly hinged open—only about a foot's width between the corrugated metal and the cement floor—I hunkered down and slipped inside, pacing past the precarious shelves with my body angled sideways to better shuffle between stacks. At the end of one row, he'd propped up a mirror—the sheet of unframed glass was splintered somewhere down the middle, and a large shard was missing from the bottom where it cut a jagged diagonal. In the dark mirror I was a ghoul, short hair curling with sweat around the temples, my teeth too big for my mouth, the collar of my tank top stained where my dirty hands had tugged it away to seek relief from the heat.

A creak had startled me coltish—I twisted to watch the garage door slide the rest of the way shut and hit the concrete with a bang, the room packed with close black, and in my stumble my bare foot darted back to catch me and slid down the sharpened edge of the mirror. The cut it left there was a perfect gory cleave all the way past my Achilles. I panted with pain and screamed until my grandma finally came to see what all the fuss was about. When she flicked the light on, there was a puddle already growing sticky beneath my heel.

Now I looked into Kolesnik's red mouth, where the grass soaked up their blood and melted it into one. All I could feel was that anticipation of a void—the valley the knife would make, the halves of my heart that wanted them to love me and wanted to remain untouched by their willingness.

I could say no. I could lean away from the intertwined thing they had become—Saz in the effigy's lap, Caroline at its helm, Amrita beside her with one hand pressed over the pulsing cut on the other, Finch hesitating at my side. If I asked to be left alone, they would clown me forever. But they would allow it. They would look at the space I had put between us, and they would not cross the moat of my heart.

But all I'd ever wanted was to be like them.

"Jo," Finch pleaded again. "Seriously."

Sweaty strands of hair stuck to her forehead. She pointed the knife away from her, as if afraid to look at it. Three sets of eyes flickered between the two of us. I knew what she wanted to say. I knew how she would scold me, the way disappointment would coat her tongue, how she always placed herself just beyond our boundaries.

But it was surprisingly easy to let her down. I took her hand and plied the knife from her grip. I gave it a swipe in the grass to clean the blade, and cut my heart line into two new lives. The feeling pounded all the way up to my teeth. I was immediately lightheaded as the blood welled. I tossed the knife back to Finch, and when it landed beside her knee again, she flinched. "Your turn," I said, and I splayed my shaking hand above the scarecrow's head, droplets spattering his mouth.

Finch's knuckles were white when she finally made the slice in her palm, hissing through her teeth. The accusing look she gave me cut deeper than the blade, which landed with a dead thump in the dirt beside her knee as she held her fist between the Boar King's tusks.

"*Yes*," Saz said, and I could hear how proud we'd made her even with my eyes shut.

When my eyes opened again, she was beaming down at Kolesnik, the bridge of her nose already swelling and reddened. She would have a black eye in a day or two. She would have to explain herself and what we had done.

But she wouldn't. She'd invent a story. We all would, and we would settle on the same page, and this moment would belong to us alone. The sun behind the trees leaving the world a crepuscular blue. The corn nodding in the breeze. The dirt beneath us so thirsty for rain. The pole jutting up from the corn as if waiting for us to erect Kolesnik's stuffed form atop it. The wound on my hand pulsing with its own heartbeat, cruor drying in the fine cracks. The blade tucked into Saz's bra again. Our mutual blood drying in his mouth, like a swear, like a pact, like a promise.

"What do we do now?" Caroline asked, her voice a little shaky, though it was hard to tell if it was from fear or barely concealed excitement.

Saz shrugged. "Maybe we should say something? The ritual had a whole section about incantations. You're supposed to make your intentions super clear."

Amrita waved her hand at the body in the dirt. "What, this isn't clear enough?"

"Nah, fuck it, I'm out of here," Finch said, getting to her feet and swiping her bloody hand just above the paint stains across her jeans. Amrita rose after her as Finch pushed through the corn, back in the direction of the car.

"Wait!" Saz called, then, "Finch! You're going to get lost!" She scrambled to her feet and disappeared between the stalks, calling for them to wait up. I started to rise, but Caroline stopped me with a hand on my forearm. Her wet palm slid down until it met mine, wound to wound.

"What would you say?" she asked.

"Me? Oh, I don't know." I blanked, flushing. "What do they say in that movie Saz loves?"

She paused to think, and then lifted my hand to her mouth.

"I drink of my sister," Caroline said.

I watched, horrified, as she licked across my weeping cut. Her cheeks hollowed. Then, with our hands still linked, she sloshed my blood around in her mouth and spat into the cavern of the effigy's chest. It landed frothy and pink amid the disgusting mass. She brought our hands to my mouth and fixed me with a stare.

There was so much coaxing in that look. I could feel my heart everywhere, pulse straining against my skin as if I'd been turned inside out, veins on display.

I said, "I drink of my sister."

I pulled her palm to my lips. Ran my tongue along the cut and felt my nostrils flare with the immediate salty tang of her blood in my mouth. I pushed saliva between my teeth, then followed suit, spitting where Caroline had a moment before.

"May you wither and rot and succumb. May you spoil and decay. May you fucking fester. So mote it be, or whatever," Caroline said in a low, terrible voice. Then she gave me an urgent nod.

"May you fester," I repeated, voice wavering. "So mote it be."

"Eat shit, you disgusting bastard," Caroline finished, zipping the fur coat the rest of the way up until the dead brush and our creation disappeared inside the Boar King's suit, then sat back on her heels. She offered the injured hand to me again. When I took it, she hauled us to our feet, shoulders bumping, and gave my fingers a squeeze.

"Thanks for not letting it slide," Caroline whispered, and the warmest hint of a smile bloomed before she wiped her mouth clean with the back of the hand she'd used to hit Saz. I couldn't help it. I beamed back at her and answered the squeeze with one of my own.

We left Kolesnik behind and found Amrita and Saz waiting outside of the Suburban. Finch was already in the back seat with the door hanging open, shadowed by the car's interior.

"There you are," Saz called as she leaned against the Suburban's passenger door. She licked her teeth clean and gave her car keys a playful shake. "I want Taco Bell. Who wants to drive?"

8

Brief Blessing of the Inevitable

Saz's black eye permitted the rest of the class to give our group a wider berth than usual. Even Moody seemed a little uneasy as we gathered for our first Friday critique with the five of us sitting front and center, all wearing matching bandages across the same palms, except for left-handed Caroline who had cut into her right. With the windows open and fans turning overhead, there was a permeating chill in the room. Fall staked its claim. I tugged lightly on the strings of my hoodie and shivered—the wound strained with pain, and I squeezed my hand into a fist to focus on the feeling.

An email had arrived in our inboxes that morning from the rest of Rotham's library staff, announcing that a few items had gone missing from the archive display case. The school requested that anyone who knew the whereabouts of "significant pieces of Rotham history" report to the library immediately. Just reading it had made me nauseous.

"Everyone have a good week?" Moody asked tentatively, perched on her stool with the heels of her tall boots hooked on the footrest.

We stared back in unified silence. Finch gave a delayed nod. Saz touched the skin around her nose gingerly.

"Mine was great," Phoebe spoke up. "I got tickets to see the new Helen Frankenthaler print exhibition this weekend. I know we've been talking about abstraction in my work, Professor Mooden, and I wanted to ask you what you think about—"

"That's wonderful, Phoebe, really great," Moody said, "and pardon my interruption, but I would like for us to get started with critique so we can see your piece and discuss what you might be able to take away from the show in relation to your work."

Phoebe deflated a little but nodded regardless.

Moody smiled. "Alright, it looks like we're going to get through four of you today, four next week, and the rest of you the week after that. If this structure works out, we'll repeat the same process every week, so you're receiving a critique every two weeks or so. First on the list, we have Caroline."

We watched her hang the canvases in silence. She mastered the drill and level like a carpenter, two screws protruding for two enormous pieces, each one as wide as her arm span. The pale blue of her dress made her a brilliant cutout against them until she stepped back and let us look.

The base layer of paint on both canvases was the thinnest sheen of near-black phthalo green. I hadn't thought that kind of color could be so full of light. On the left canvas, she'd stippled textural yellow ochre over it along the upper half of the painting, and then on top of the warmth, swans flocked in cold titanium white, their necks craning and tangling and snapping at one other. Clustered within the swans was a humanoid figure holding a red oval to its chest. The oval was lined with just the tiniest fingernail of the white, until it was intestinal and pulsing with heat.

The right canvas was swallowed up by more of that yellow ochre, a color so Caroline that it made me want to touch her and remind myself she was physical. This time the pigment seeped down into a tangled red pit at the bottom of the painting, interspersed with jagged lines that looked like roots unfurling in the dirt. Moody leaned close to it, one finger stopping just a hair away from the painting's surface as she traced the line of yellow.

"Visceral," Moody murmured. She straightened and turned back to us as Caroline took her seat. "Who wants to go first?"

Cameron waved a hand. "There's a real sense of light in both pieces. Normally I find that white can really dull a painting, but you managed to make them glow." He angled his head in Caroline's direction, but she remained stiffly composed with her arms crossed over her chest. She'd never been able to receive praise. I could see it in the clench of her jaw—she thought he was patronizing her.

Moody nodded. "Yes, there is a real illumination to those swans, and are those . . . entrails? At the bottom of the right piece?" Then to Caroline, she quickly added, "Not asking you to give us an answer yet, just thinking out loud."

"They are very gory," Yejun said, after clearing his throat. "They have a kind of butchered quality to them. Not in execution, but you know like, when you walk past a deli, and they have all the hunks of meat lined up in a row."

Saz coughed. I could hear the laugh she was trying to smother beneath it. Caroline straightened in her seat.

"Right, okay," Moody said, considering. "Anyone else?"

"This is some of the best work I've seen you make," Finch said, breathy and awed. We watched as she rose and went to the left painting, her unbandaged hand following the outline of the red shape the hunched figure clutched to its chest.

Caroline's knuckles were white where she squeezed her bicep.

"It's so possessive," Finch continued. "It's like the interior of the body splayed outward. It is gory, and it is intestinal, yeah, but there's something magical about it. The texture is so delicious, the layers so intentional, this—*organ*—so vivid and real. It feels like . . . a game of Operation. Like you cut into yourself and offered your insides for us to pluck, if we decide to try."

Moody smiled at Finch with the proud, pleased grin of a parent watching their child out in the world.

"You're right, Finchard. It is some of her best work," Moody said. "You're tapping into something here, Caroline. I'd like to see you push it further."

Caroline didn't smile. But her face softened when she nodded, relieved to some extent. She brushed her hair behind her ears and lifted her canvases off the wall, carting them back to her studio without another word.

"Alright," Moody declared, grinning, "who's next?"

At a certain point, our first critique crossed the line from real criticism into jubilance. Mars followed Caroline, and while their stitched-together fabric pieces were in the early stages of being stretched over large canvas frames without any paint on them yet, we still all oohed and aahed over the fine sewing and converging patterns turning the surfaces into kaleidoscoped shards of color. Cameron came next with a painting of his father in a field, the same forlorn and Andrew Wyeth–esque realist landscapes dotted with men on horseback he always preferred. This got some praise too, but also scrutiny. They were beautiful, finely done, easy to look at—but then Finch called them *digestible*, and Cameron's face shuttered with annoyance.

Then it was Amrita, with three new paintings on paper that were barely big enough to cover her torso. They were luminous, confectionery, packed with color and contemplation. Amrita was always thoughtful. It showed in her work. Each piece was laden with tiny details sketched first in pencil, then inked in graduating layers of gouache. They were rich illustrations—coiled dragons snaking through reeds, beheaded griffins with forked tongues lolling across the painting's border, fat clouds of smoke billowing around a girl perched on the back of a bull, hands hooked around the horns, trying not to be thrown.

"I call it my menagerie," Amrita said, eyes trained bashfully on Moody's shoes.

Moody's smile returned from wherever Cameron's critique had banished it. He slumped sullenly in his seat.

"She loved them," Saz exclaimed after class had ended and everyone else had gone home to reset. We gathered in Amrita's studio, marveling over the paintings and telling her how beautiful they were, Amrita blushing under all the praise.

"Moody is obsessed with you," Caroline said as she tipped one of the paintings back and forth, watching the overhead lights gleam off shimmery paint.

"I know," Amrita said, giddy. She dropped her voice to a whisper and gave us the kind of smile I would have started wars for. "I think whatever we did really worked. I was here all night working on these pieces, and I've never felt so *good* about what I'm making. It just . . . comes to me."

There was such a joyful gleam on her face. Finch seemed doubtful, but she was smiling wryly at the paintings too. "You just can't admit that you're a good painter. Caroline too," she added, though it was a useless olive branch that Caroline shrugged off.

"There's always room for improvement," Caroline said loftily. But she looked over her shoulder in the direction of her studio. And I could tell that she was excited—that she thought she was onto something too.

"I'm starving," Saz declared, plucking the painting out of Caroline's hands and laying it carefully atop Amrita's clean desk. "Fuck Bane. Let's go for a drive and eat something good."

There could be no denial of it. The ritual and its apparent success inspired a new hunger within us, a shared starvation for more, more, more.

In the days to follow that first critique, we went to the studio all the time—even more than we had before. Now that it felt as if the pieces might be falling into place, we wanted to claim them. We wanted control, and growth, and invention, and pride. I completed a new piece over the course of less than a week. This one felt more vulnerable than anything I'd ever made before. It was a close-up of Saz in the black corn, light all stolen away from the day, hands clutching her nose as blood ran through her fingers and over bared teeth. There was so much brilliance in her face. In the echoing triumph of her grin.

The hunger wicked something more literal to life within us too. We ate like animals—regardless of the hour, in great heaps, summoned by the body clock that dragged us from our beds like a bell in the middle of the night. Overhead light gleamed off the dining table, and the oven's clock blinked a red hour. We were insatiable and free of self-conscious doubt. I didn't think about my body and its limits with them. I just pulled up a chair. I let Saz craft me the perfect bite—chickpea and sweet potato and spinach on a fork, everything earthen and rich. The scent of Caroline's decaf filled the room and I accepted a mug of that, too, cinnamon dusted across the oat milk, heat curdling it into swirls. Amrita stacked salty chips with layers of garlic hummus and held it up in offering. I crunched it hard between my teeth, relishing the sodium and the affection of her hands building it for me. Finch wasn't there. But I imagined her fed.

In the span of quiet minutes filled only with the noise of our devouring, I'd start to consider all the sleep I was losing. But I couldn't have gone to bed—I was afraid that I'd never have them like this again, gathered around the table in too-big T-shirts and our underwear, someone's forgotten music spilling down from a floor overhead, the window opened to let night air combat the radiators. That kind of elation had its limits, and our days in the Manor were numbered. Besides, I kind of liked the wired, hallucinatory effects of my sleeplessness. It felt like accessing a deeper part of myself, something with the potential to be compelling enough to record on a canvas. Still, I knew, in the blackest corner of my heart, that it was a childish thought. I didn't need to suffer to be a painter.

I used to forget all my dreams. But I started to have nightmares that couldn't be shaken, my sleeping self always returning to the same white house in the woods where I'd grown up. Everything was as I'd left it: the stairs creaking under invisible feet, paint peeling off the siding, dogs barking in the trees. Familiarity wasn't comforting—I spent the majority of these lucidities witnessing horrors that would leave me clawing my way back to waking. I watched Caroline part the dark waves of Amrita's hair along the back of her head before she gently eased the halves of Amrita's mind apart and slid a hand inside. I pulled Saz from shallow water, her face swollen and blue until it dissolved into a million gnats. I cut Finch down from the rafters of Grainer with her own pocketknife and sat cross-legged on the slats of the porch staring at a television. Nothing played on the screen, yet I always woke with the knowledge that I'd been watching something. An end of some form. An apocalyptic rapture.

It was impossible to fall back asleep after waking. Some nights I turned on all the lights in my room and tried to sketch, determined to make something out of the images I couldn't banish from my mind. But the Manor had such an eerie quality in the dark, the only distinguishable sound a permeating buzz that never seemed to leave me alone. I googled the symptoms of tinnitus and assigned myself a diagnosis, thinking certainty might help. But all I could do was tune into that ringing hum.

A few nights after the ritual, with Monday on the horizon, I woke from a nightmare and went to refill my water glass. Glowing red Rotham-issued exit signs were the only source of light on the third and second floor, but as I descended the last staircase, I found the kitchen lamp already on and Amrita sitting at the table. She cupped a steaming mug and looked up at me.

"Can't sleep?"

I shook my head. I told her about that night's dream.

"Come on," she said, extending her hand. "Be sleepless with me."

I went to her. I leaned my head on her shoulder, sipped from her mug when she offered, and shut my eyes against the fabric of her T-shirt. This was different from our voraciousness. With Amrita I could fade into the background. There was no pressure to feed on what they gave me, to be funny or clever or lovable or coy. The dreams were just dreams. Conjurations my heart invented to hurt me and banished by Amrita's comfort. Anything impossible solved at once. Anything capable of killing simplified and slept.

But I had to go to bed at some point. I was terrified of possibility: how untethered and expansive it was, how there seemed to be no limit to our belief in the potential of magic. I was afraid that this was a precipice we could not walk back from.

The day before Halloween was a Wednesday. Normally Kolesnik sent out an email by Monday evening at the very latest detailing what he expected us to show up to class with, but my inbox remained empty. I tried to prepare myself anyway—the burgeoning anxiety that ruled most of my day-to-day tasks forced me to drum up something that he might find interesting. Only two out of the ten required pages of my thesis paper were written so far, and the five hundred or so words I had managed were limp and uninteresting. How could I put my thoughts on paper in a way that might make him understand? How could I describe the way I wanted to freeze us through the paint and immortalize us as we were? What could I say? The truth, maybe, even if it only made sense to me. That I was so greedy. I wanted nothing to change. I thought if it changed, any of it—if they went on to live lives that I couldn't be a part of—I'd turn to dust. And if I could capture it in the paintings, the world might keep moving on around me, but at least I'd have proof that it had existed in the first place.

Finch was already standing outside Kolesnik's classroom when we arrived. She had a hoodie on that I sometimes stole when I slept over, sleeves bunched up around her forearms. There were bags under her eyes.

"Canceled," she called. She inclined her head toward the room's shut door and the paper taped to it. "He left a note."

"Are you serious?" Amrita sighed, stepping up to touch the scrawled writing on the note. "He couldn't have sent an email last night so we could sleep in?"

"He wants us to suffer," Saz mumbled through a bite of a granola bar. Crumbs littered the pink silk of her top.

"He's probably just sick," I tried. I brushed a few bits of the granola off Saz. She gave me a full-mouthed smile.

"Maybe he canceled for Grotesque prep," Amrita suggested. "They still haven't figured out what · · · happened to the Boar King suit. I'm guessing they're going to make a new one?"

Caroline grinned. There was a cruel gleam in her eyes. "All they have to do is take a walk through the corn in a field off I-80."

"Shut the hell up," Amrita whispered, prodding Caroline's shoulder.

I had a vicious headache, likely a result of too many hours spent awake. At least a canceled class meant that I could go back to bed.

"Well, I'm not going to the studio yet if we don't have to. I'm going home to get some sleep," I said. "Wake me up if anything changes."

"Slacker," Caroline sang.

I flipped her off over my shoulder and started down the hall. Slatter Hall was a maze—everything the same dark hues of brown and green, from the high ceilings to the wood floors to the heavy doors. Most of the buildings across Rotham's campus connected somewhere along the way, either adjoining aboveground or under the promenade, and Slatter met the atrium down one of the east wing halls. It was a longer walk back to the Manor that way, but a prettier one, and I was so rarely alone on campus without a schedule that I wanted a moment to breathe.

I turned into the east wing and hesitated under its arched entryway. The overhead lights were off, usually triggered by movement in the afternoon when classes started to pick up. The only illumination came from the crosshatched windows, sunlight shaking on the floor as the wind outside blew through the leaves.

At the end of the hall stood a shadowed figure—stooped and somehow still massive, humanoid but bent in discomfort. The head drooped and hands went up to clutch the face. The black hall obscured most of its definition and turned it into an indistinct mass, until it finally staggered forward.

I rocked backward at the same time it stepped into the light. It convulsed again, hacking with a strained gag, but now the diamonds of sun lit up the face.

"Professor Kolesnik?" I whispered. "Are you okay?"

It *was* Kolesnik; I was sure now. In his white button-down and his black slacks, he looked like a penitent mourner. His shoulders made the same shape as when he would viciously blow the blood out of his nose—taut, drawn up by his ears as if in mid-flinch. Then he arched and made the rearing shape of an animal rising to its hind legs. One hand slid down to his chest, pressing against his rib cage as he stumbled closer.

My pulse pounded so hard in my ears I thought it might be the echo of footsteps behind us, but when I turned, we were still alone. The doors lining the hall remained shut. Kolesnik took another step forward, his body giving a shuddering, titanic heave as he gasped down a breath.

I tried to inventory my sanity. My voice, my hands, my heart—all shaking. "Do you need me to get someone? Do you need help?"

The questions were a reflex. I didn't know what the fuck to do. I just took a tentative step in his direction, like he might scare if I got too near.

He went down on one knee with a thud that rattled the hall. The floorboards wheezed as if all of Slatter was exhaling and cowering away from him. This close I could see blood coming out of his nose, collecting in the gray hairs of his beard. I thought about the stained tissues in the Boar King's heart. Kolesnik's gore sealed up inside of that chest forever and ever.

His eyes finally landed on me. But they were wild and dilated, his jaw working as he sank lower. A hoarse sound pushed out of his mouth. It was a broken moan, the whimper of a thing shot and intended for an end.

And then he began to scream.

He screamed and he screamed, fingers ripping into his chest, that dogged and awful howl carrying down the hall as I rushed forward and tried to yank him to his feet, my pleas for him to *stand up* and to *stop screaming* and *it'll be okay, you're okay, it's okay* all bowled over by the sound of his agony.

"HELP," he wailed, the sound only half a word, mostly the desperate caw a body releases when it can't find the breath to sustain itself. "HELP ME HELP ME HELP ME."

His eyes were bulging spheres of sclera with the iris all rolled away as he ripped at the collar around his neck, sweat beading at his temples. Blood running out of his nose made his lips a collage of color.

"What do I do? You need to tell me, I don't know how to help you, fuck, I don't know what's happening." The world blurred as tears rose to my eyes, and I tore helplessly at his blood-spattered tie, trying to clear his airway. "What the fuck do I do?"

The stone beneath my knees was so cold, his face a choked red. I watched something slacken in him—the onset of an absence of vitality.

"Jo, what the hell is going on?"

I didn't hear them come up behind me until Finch was pulling at my arms. Kolesnik keeled forward and hit the floor hard, the blood from his nose smearing a line across the stone.

"Oh god," Amrita whispered, her hand pressing over her mouth. The others gathered around her. Saz gasped a stream of horrified curses as Caroline rushed to Kolesnik to tip him onto his side and feel for a pulse.

"Someone call the dean, or fucking 911 or something!" Caroline snapped, but Amrita was already turning from us, her phone pressed to her ear.

Finch scrubbed at my arm with the hem of her hoodie, and that was when I saw the blood on my wrist from where Kolesnik had slumped against me. I drew in shallow breaths, my chest too tight, the hallway too hot, sun whiting out my sight.

"Hey hey hey," Finch whispered, squeezing my wrist. "Look at me, you're alright, everything's going to be fine."

I tried to look. My eyes kept snagging on her cheek and darting back to Kolesnik, panting against the ground, his eyes rolling back. The scream had died off. It was a rattling gargle of breath now. Caroline attempted to hold his head up, to keep it from lolling. She looked desperately to Amrita for help.

Finch turned my head back to her with a hand on my cheek. "What the hell happened, Jo?"

All I could think was—*we killed him, we killed him, we killed him, I killed him.*

9

The Masquerade Grotesque

The paramedics questioned us first, then administration. The process took several hours and mostly comprised prompts such as *Did you notice Professor Kolesnik struggling? Was he choking? Coughing? Wheezing? Did he speak to you? Are you okay? Do you need to sit down? Do you need a glass of water?*

Yes, to all the above. I was a hallucinatory kind of tired. My shirt was still speckled with blood, and there was a smear of it down my wrist.

Esther St. Roche, chair of the Fine Arts Department, was our main point of contact. She wouldn't let us out of her militant line of sight for the entirety of the afternoon. We had to sit in the stiff chairs outside of her office until the paramedics had long since loaded him in the back of an ambulance, until the only evidence that anything had ever happened were my stained clothes.

Amrita told them that I was the one who had found him, because I was mostly incapable of putting together words. St. Roche fixated on me after that—she wanted to know exactly what he had done, if I noticed him eating or drinking anything, if I believed he may have taken any medication, if Kolesnik had mentioned illness earlier than that day. I answered honestly: I didn't know. It was obvious that my responses weren't what St. Roche wanted to hear. She was a stocky woman, probably around my mother's age and height, but so broad and severe that she carried the aura of a dutiful knight. She crouched by my chair when she talked to me, so I could see all the ways her face changed with what I told her. A disappointed frown, a furrow of the eyebrows, teeth biting down on the inside of her cheek.

Administration let us go back to the Manor a little after dinner had officially ended, so my women ate like scavenger animals out of the fridge while I watched, my mouth all sandpaper and sourness, head pounding. Every loud noise was startling. I kept hearing that scream.

And though the image wouldn't leave my head—Kolesnik's cheek smashed against the stone, spit foamy and white at the corners of his mouth, eyes rolling, hands scrabbling at his chest—there was also a horrible, devouring part of me awestruck by the potential of what had occurred. I was afraid to open my mouth and let something unforgiveable seep out.

We gathered around the table in silence. Their hunger made a mountain of carrot sticks and hummus and microwaved pita and chopped apples. No one tried to force me to eat anything, though I knew they wanted to. But we didn't know how to broach what had happened.

Caroline's phone buzzed face down against the table, a bright edge glowing around it. A second later, so did the rest of ours. We looked in unison.

The first half of the email announced what we had expected. It was with the heaviest of hearts that the Rotham School announced the passing of the legendary professor Gabriel Kolesnik, in a sudden and unexpected tragedy. Grief counseling would be available as requested. Accommodations would be made for his thesis students along with updates for what to expect throughout the rest of the academic year.

Then, below that, came the unexpected part: despite the loss of the tradition's founder and the absence of his legendary Boar King costume, the school planned to go through with tomorrow's Masquerade Grotesque. *To postpone such an event would be like dismissing the influence of a brilliant mind like Kolesnik's on Rotham's legacy and culture,* St. Roche's email read, *and we plan to honor this celebration as a vigil for the professor.*

"Wow," Finch said finally. "They're still throwing the boogeyman convention."

"Good. If I wasted all that time on my costume when I could have been in the studio, I would have pitched a fit," Caroline sighed.

"Okay, priorities," Amrita said. "They've probably just already paid for caterers and don't want to deal with hosting another vigil later on."

We fell into silence. I read the email again and again, as if I might find a secret message between the lines intended just for me—St. Roche saying *you did this, you did this, you did this, it's your fault, his blood is on your hands.* The prickling pain in my temple worsened.

"Are we going to talk about it?" Saz the mind reader asked, twining a strand of her hair around one finger, the glitter from her eyeshadow dusted over the tops of her cheeks as if she'd cried out the shine.

Amrita drank deeply from her glass of water before saying, "About what?"

"Come on, you know what. Are we going to talk about our part in this? How we hexed him and basically wished his death on him?"

I could taste Caroline's blood everywhere, everywhere, everywhere.

"We have no part," Finch said, "because there is no *it.* Old people get sick, and they die."

"He was completely fine last week," Amrita said quietly. She was staring at her hands, pulling grapes off the vine and dropping them back into their plastic package.

"Fine? He blows a quart of blood out of his nose every class."

"Blew," Caroline corrected.

"Oh, fuck you," Finch snapped.

"Finchard." Saz frowned, tugging at the strand of hair in agitation now.

"*Sarah.*"

Saz rolled her eyes. "I'm asking a valid question! We cursed him, and he died a week later. You're telling me that's a coincidence?"

"We are not responsible for an old man having a heart attack. It was a wrong-place-wrong-time kind of thing, and it sucked, but we tried our best to help him." Some of the severity slipped from Finch's tone as she said, "I mean, we can all agree that bleeding on hamburger meat is not the same thing as murder, right?"

Caroline snorted a laugh but didn't say anything, just cut her eyes in my direction. I was afraid that my heart was beating loud enough for the rest of them to hear it.

"Okay," Saz started. "I'm not saying that it was our fault. I'm not. But if it was . . . didn't he deserve it?"

The pit in my stomach dropped another nine levels, to some perfidious circle of hell. Because he *did* deserve it, didn't he? If he had found it so easy to reach for Caroline, what else could he have done over the years? If our ritual and its subsequent hex caused his violent death, then what reason did we have to feel guilty about it?

I kept a fingertip pressed to my temple, trying to quell the dull roar, and flinched when Caroline's fingers caught my hand and gave it a squeeze.

"He was a self-absorbed dick who thought he could treat women like objects," Caroline said firmly. "He deserved it."

Silence enveloped us again. Amrita ate her neutered grapes one at a time. Caroline kept a grounding hand on me.

Amrita cleared her throat. "Does this mean we still have to write thesis papers?"

"What, so he can grade them in hell?" Caroline asked.

"Caroline, you dog," Saz gasped, a smile forming. She pressed her lips together to kill it. "You shouldn't speak ill of the dead."

Caroline grinned and bared her teeth. "We're not speaking ill. We're talking shit."

"Oh, Christ," Amrita said, sliding a hand over her eyes. But her mouth curled up at the corners just slightly.

Saz let the smile break through. "Okay, new hex idea. We saddle his soul with an eternity of burning somewhere subterranean."

"He's probably in the waiting room for hell as we speak. Sitting next to, fucking, I don't know, Beetlejuice."

"Nah, he's being tortured by Cenobites in the *Hellraiser* dimension. He's kicking it with that one who has big nasty teeth."

"Chatterer. Get it straight."

They were all talking over one another. Saz looked at me and grinned. "Look! You made Jo smile! She's smiling because Kolesnik's in hell!"

"Stop," I begged. I had to pin my hand over my mouth to hide my nervous cackle.

"We are such bad people," Finch said, but she couldn't stop laughing, and I loved when she laughed like that, the uncontrollable roll of it soaring high and happy, the way tears fell with her joy. "We are so fucking awful!"

"Awful!" Caroline echoed, slapping her hands against the table. "Horrific! Monstrous! Horrendous!"

"Awful, awful, awful!" The rest of us chanted, giggling now—we couldn't remember what had been funny about it. Saz tipped back in her chair, and when the leg wobbled and deposited her onto the kitchen floor, we laughed harder, hands on our stomachs, incapable of caging that joy.

I'd go back there, if I could. Just to that moment at the table, the lamplight hot and close, their laughter taking root in my heart, their delight disguising my guilt and leaving it somewhere deeper to fester. I'd go back to the way they banished the seed of fear in me. How they transformed it into power instead.

Even knowing what we had done. Even knowing the ways it would change us down the line. I'd go back, and I'd live in that moment forever.

◆ ◆ ◆

Classes were always canceled on the day of the Grotesque, but that Halloween was far more solemn than any of the three I'd experienced previously at Rotham.

Finch stayed the night, and we kept ourselves up for far too long, as if sleeping might cement the day's events in stone. I was afraid to be alone in my bed. Somehow, without vocalizing that fear, they understood—we dragged mattresses down the stairs and fit ourselves like sardines on the couch.

We woke to a desolate campus. In those first bleary moments, I nearly forgot what had unfolded the day before. But there was an email from Moody waiting on our phones that instructed us with what to expect for Friday's critique. She'd be taking over Kolesnik's role and operating as our sole advisor; no more Wednesday classes in Slatter, no more uncomfortable office hours, no more charismatic Kolesnik at the front of the lecture hall. Senior painters would be under the influence of Moody's opinion alone, an idea that intimidated us. But it was better than starting from scratch with a stranger.

We tried not to focus on what the rearrangement might mean for our ranks as potential Soloists. Instead, we spent the day working on our Grotesque costumes in the living room atop our makeshift beds, fine-tuning the last details as we pregamed with cheap liquor and cran-grape juice, dressing ourselves up and admiring the gruesome effects on each other's faces.

"If it wouldn't be so obvious, I'd drive out to the cornfield and don Kolesnik's boar suit myself," Saz said as she painted her eyes in her handheld mirror, the sweeping lines of black turning her corvine. "But now that we have proof the ritual worked, I'm never touching that thing. I don't want to risk screwing it up."

"*Proof* is a big word," I said, guilt rising in my chest. Amrita dabbed concealer on my jaw and tsked at me for moving.

"Hey, it's not like he can curse us back," Caroline said, the words shapeless as she held her mouth open to line her lips.

"I'm not worried about him. I'm more concerned about whatever higher power we currently have on our side," Saz answered.

"In Kolesnik's case, I think the higher power was a rogue blood clot." Finch's mask was pushed back to show her face and all the color Amrita had dusted across it—cool deathly greens and specks of orange around the eyes. The mask had the huge, membraned wings of an insect, thorax sloping down the bridge of her nose. There were eye holes cut in the delicate forewings. When she pulled it down over her face, you could see all the places she had painted replicas of her own eyes across the papier-mâché, until it was hard to distinguish which ones were real. Beside her, Saz's mask lay faceless on the ground, a barrage of black feathers interspersed with six different piercing beaks. It was heavy as fuck. I didn't know how she planned to keep it steady on her head all night.

Amrita was dressed in all white, her dark hair coiled at the nape of her neck. Her mask was a crescent moon with the cheeks and lips molded from clay. Jewels and stars hung from the jutting jaw of the moon—they twinkled when she moved, catching candlelight and tossing beams around the living room.

And Caroline looked magical—she'd sewn a swan with a long neck that coiled around her throat, the head resting at her collarbone when she wrapped and pinned it in place. She painted a red heart across the entirety of her face, rendering her harlequin and coy, her hair slicked back with little curls gelled against her forehead and around her ears.

The ram's head I created made me feel disgruntled against the rest of them. Fat horns curled at my temples in an imitation too like the Boar King's tusks for comfort. I had painted them to emphasize dimensionality—stripes of gray shaded with warm beige nestled in the rough faux fur I had painstakingly glued to the mask's frame. It covered my face down to the end of my nose and mostly obscured my eyes, upon which Amrita layered dark shadow. The pupils were cut out for me to see through, and my mouth was exposed beneath the furred edge of the mask.

Music lilted, a playlist of Saz's consisting of mostly the Cramps and the Cure. They talked over one another, fighting to hear each other above the music and the melding of voices. Half the time their yelling couldn't be deciphered as conversation or the lyrics to "Boys Don't Cry." Amrita and I sat together in comfortable silence as she dusted more powder around my eyes. The furrowed focus on her face was so endearing. I tried to lean into her distraction.

"You won't even be able to see any of this under the mask," I mumbled. She took my chin with sure hands and smeared a plummy black over my lips, the lipstick tacky and smelling of something artificially sweet.

"You'll be able to see *that*," she declared. "Sexy."

I couldn't help but laugh.

"Don't you dare. You look beautiful," Amrita said, clutching my face harder. "Say it."

"*You* look beautiful," I said petulantly. But I meant it—I couldn't take my eyes off the soft, exasperated way she smiled back at me. There was gold glitter all over her. Her eyes were a big affectionate brown, the kind of warm I could sleep in.

"You know what I mean," she scolded, and squeezed my cheeks between her fingers. "Say it back to me."

Her scrutiny made me hot all over. I swallowed and tried to imagine what she saw when looking at me. The pale and peaked corners of my face. The bloody mar on my bottom lip where I had chewed for too long. Dark circles that showed even past concealer. Brown hair brushing my shoulders, in desperate need of a cut or dye or anything to make it feel like less of an afterthought.

"I look beautiful," I whispered obediently.

"Better," she said, smile growing. "I almost believed you."

The Masquerade Grotesque was held in the atrium every year. The name made the room sound fancier than it really was—it had been a greenhouse constructed near the garden when the school first opened, and now the glass structure was mostly devoid of plants and used for benefit events when the administration raised money from devoted alumni. For the Grotesque, they decked it out with string lights and tables swathed in black tablecloths. Sculptures and busts were given masks of their own. As we walked from the Manor, appearing like five end-time omens, the typically spooky atmosphere inside the atrium now became sepulchral. Someone had decorated the walls with streamers of black and red cloth. Fake candles glittered on the table, and early aughts pop classics puttered out of a tower of speakers on either side of the hall.

The plinth in the center of the atrium bore a blown-up "In Memoriam" poster of Kolesnik's face, propped in his empty chair. It was clearly cropped from the faculty photo hanging in Banemast. The magnification gave his appearance a kind of Stanley Kubrick stare, grainy eyes piercing us as we stepped past the main doors.

"Jesus," Finch said, voice muffled behind her insectoid mask. "That's ghoulish."

In years past, Kolesnik would typically already be waiting in his designated seat with the Boar King's hood pulled over the thinning hair on his head. It was a place of honor—as the founder of the tradition, back in his first years as a Rotham professor, the school always revered him with that elevated throne. It made getting drunk and grinding on each other incredibly difficult when he sat in that panoptical position.

"We need to get trashed to deal with that looking at us all night." Caroline tapped her chest just below the swan's beak, fingernails clicking against a metal flask in her bra that she'd been swigging out of.

Up to this point, campus was barren and mournful. With all classes canceled, the only students out and about had been the ones heading to Banemast to eat. The lawn had remained empty, trees swaying in the breeze and dead leaves whipping cyclonic across the sidewalk. Now all of Rotham was concentrated in one charged spot. The crowded atrium hummed with rising voices—the masks made it nearly impossible to tell which of them were faculty and which were students. Our trained eyes, however, were a little better at picking up on the signs; the faculty masks were mostly reserved in their wildness, and some professors recycled their uniforms year after year. Professor Fujioka always wore the same porcelain sparrow mask with a long worm hanging from its beak, glazed a sickly pink. Same with Professor Bervoets, who framed her head with a birdcage every Grotesque, colorful parakeets resting on the bars within. And St. Roche had taught a course called Puppets and Performing Objects before she became our chair. Her costume consisted of a doll's face, with strings sewn into her clothes all the way down to her wrists where she could tug on the lines to make its jaw open and shut.

It was the kind of event that made my parents raise their eyebrows when I told them over dinner what unfolded in my time at school, how my classes went, what the faculty was known for. "The man dresses up as a *Boar King?*" my mother would ask in horror, twirling spaghetti around a fork. And then my dad's disbelieving echo: "You said she teaches *puppetry?*"

I was pleasantly half-drunk enough from the concoctions Saz plied me with to feel some of the dread of the past two days melt away. Amrita loaned me a dress, and I was stiff in it as we hovered near the doors—I couldn't remember the last time I'd put on something with a skirt. It left me feeling exposed, goose bumps prickling up my legs, the horns on my head heavy with the weight of plaster and fur. The mask smelled like acrylic paint and the dusty chalk of newspaper and glue, the eye holes barely big enough to see much more than what was directly in front of me. I had to turn my whole head to see anything outside of my peripherals that wasn't horn.

Someone tapped a microphone. The sound reared hot and shrill, and the music abruptly stopped. I twisted to get a glimpse of the dais where Kolesnik's image sat. St. Roche stood beside it, obscured by a ceramic smile, her doll's expression placid from the top of its finely molded hairline to the jut of its chin.

"This momentous occasion is dimmed by our institute's loss," St. Roche began, feedback half obscuring her words. "Professor Kolesnik dedicated his life to the Rotham School. As a student, he was the Soloist of the class of 1975 and went on to have an illustrious career that would have extended far into his life had he not experienced this abrupt and tragic end. We are grateful for what he gave our school, both as an incredible professor and a creator who formed enduring traditions such as tonight's thirtieth annual Masquerade Grotesque."

The atrium echoed with microphone static. Glasses clinked distantly. The lights gave a flicker, power struggling under the demand of hundreds of tiny bulbs.

"Is someone *crying*?" Caroline whispered beside my ear, holding my shoulder as she avoided the hook of a horn. Now that she'd said it, I could hear sniffling. I shrugged, feigning indifference. But the nerves in my stomach didn't mix well with the alcohol. It was eerie to look at St. Roche standing before us, the lips of her mask never moving as she spoke, its unblinking eyes boring through me no matter where I pointed my gaze.

"We mourn together," St. Roche's doll said. "We honor the life of a great man. And tonight, we continue his tradition in the hopes of inspiring many years of his legacy to come. It has broken our hearts to lose Professor Kolesnik, especially in the wake of his priceless Boar King costume disappearing. Again we ask that if you know anything of its whereabouts, that you share your knowledge with your advisors. Until then, we will honor his position with a moment of silence and our deepest condolences. As a reminder, counseling services will be available to all. Please enjoy your evening. This is a celebration of life and of the craft Gabriel Kolesnik so revered."

She fitted the microphone back into its stand. The photo of Kolesnik kept on smiling as a synthy '80s beat picked up. Everyone tittered, uncertain of how to start partying.

"Well, that was morbid. Who wants a drink?" Caroline asked, pointing around our group. The painted heart parted over her lips when she spoke. "Finch and I will get us something. Ginger ale? Spiked?"

"Sounds good to me!" Saz sang, hooking her hand in mine. "We'll be dancing, come find us!"

The room had filled out. Now Saz had to tug us through the crowd, her hand clutching my left and Amrita linked to my right. We wove past clownish wigs, an oversized Queen of Hearts playing card molded to fit a face, a plasticine horse head that looked like it came from Spirit Halloween. Saz procured us a spot close to a dry fountain in the center of the room, where Kolesnik's picture was mostly hidden by a cherub with its empty pitcher spilling no water into the basin. Pennies littered its dusty belly. The music was poppy and loud, and even with the echo of St. Roche's speech, the atrium was already growing hot with movement. Amrita spun me around, the chin of her moon bumping my shoulder every time we swayed. The stars glittered like a chime. Someone dressed as Joan of Arc jumped around behind her—I kept catching glimpses of a crown of thorns and three-dimensional tears spilling down the cheeks.

"Stop thinking so much and try to have some fun!" Amrita yelled over the speakers. I just nodded, letting her lead. I didn't feel capable of raising my voice to answer.

Caroline interrupted us with two cups in her hands, hips already swaying. She was ethereal under the fairy lights—the swan around her neck looked as if it could lift its head and nuzzle the heart of her face.

"Drink up," she encouraged. I let her lift the cup to my lips and took a sip before she turned to do the same for Amrita.

Finch filled the space Caroline left behind, her hand landing on my hip and pulling me into her as Saz sang along to Mariah Carey. There was something so funny about the clash of "Fantasy" and the resounding echo of Kolesnik's memorial speech. I started to giggle, chest bubbling with rising lightness, heartbeat echoing in my ears. I let myself meld into Finch's touch. We always danced on each other—all of us, without abandon—but it was never anything beyond the pleasure of movement. Still, Finch's hold on my waist and the way her thigh slid between mine as we moved had something coiling within me, a buzz of energy that started in my belly and prickled all the way up my spine. The ram's head kept me safe by obscuring my eyes, allowing me to watch her unabashedly. I liked the way her mask entangled with her hair, strands snagging on a wing. I liked the cool shadow it cast over her. I liked the exposed strength of her shoulders with the straps of her top digging into them, necklaces glinting along her collarbones with every sway. I liked the way the eyes on the mask's wings seemed thrilled by my gaze, coyly urging me on.

Every Grotesque unfurled like this—a jejune start building into a feral race to jump the highest, sing the loudest, get the drunkest. At a certain point the faculty would give us our floor or lean into it themselves. There was an unspoken permission to get as messy as we wanted, until someone threw up in the fountain or shattered a pane of the atrium's glass walls and St. Roche would send us all home.

I bounced between them, eyes shut, bass so loud I could feel it rattle in my jaw, hands over my head, mask bobbing back and forth, Amrita's skirt flouncing around my hips, goose bumps rising on my thighs. Fingers brushing the small of my back, the curve of my shoulder, the fat of my hip. The touch made me so hungry. My body kept angling toward it, seeking more. When my eyes slit open behind the ram's head, I caught phantasmagoric images: Phoebe and Veda dancing side by side, Phoebe shrouded in crinkling iridescent plastic and all of Veda's exposed skin painted with shadow puppet shapes. Each twist of her body revealed a new hand outline—a rabbit hopping, a bird taking flight, a fox biting down.

There was Caroline spinning Saz around with one hand, Saz laughing every time she collided with Amrita, crow wings shaking with the movement and seamlessly blending into her blunt dark hair where it wasn't streaked with pink. And Finch—I couldn't find Finch.

I slowed, seeking. I was unsteady on my feet. I shouldn't have taken that drink from Caroline. What was in it? She wouldn't give me something I couldn't handle, would she? Not without asking. Of course not. So why did I keep seeing flickers of shadow, blips in the glowing lights?

"You okay?" Caroline yelled from my right, the heart wrinkling when she frowned.

"Where's Finch?" I shouted back. My cup sloshed when someone jostled me. "What did you—what was in this drink?"

Her frown deepened. "I don't know, Finch fucked off somewhere. And the drink is just rum, Jo. Do you need to go home?"

I shook my head, though I wasn't sure I was telling the truth. "I'm just gonna get some air," I said, and I was pushing my way through the sea of coyotes and stars and spiders and cornucopias before any of them could stop me. Kolesnik's eyes followed me everywhere I went—I looked back once and found them on me, granular and heavy.

Outside smelled like the dead of fall. I prickled with cold. Leaves blew down the promenade between groups of people milling and laughing, masks abandoned for the contradiction of a cigarette and fresh air. Lampposts cast gold circles every few feet, and I followed the path down to the garden, past Lysander Gate, through the rows of naked bushes.

Most of the garden was empty, save for a few stragglers. But past the benches and the hedges a figure stood down by the pond.

"Hey," I called, voice wavering. I cleared my throat and tried again. "Hey, Finchard!"

The water rippled behind the person's outline. It was a dark, gibbous shape, head bent low, the arms held around itself. The moon was too thin to give it any real definition.

I pulled off my mask and held it against my chest. I waited for the figure to move. I wanted it to be Finch, waiting for me to find her. But the shape didn't answer or turn to acknowledge me. It gave a violent quiver as the breeze blew by. And slowly—quietly—I heard it begin to wail.

It was the same pained cry Kolesnik had released on the day of his death. That desperate croaking of a body unable to draw in breath. The silhouette rocked and howled, its edges indistinct, the shape of its back arching with each inhaled cry. It panted raggedly. The heaving sound was so loud that I thought I was closer to it than I was—when I took a step forward, I realized I was still standing among the sculptures, lamplight faint against my back, the moon an orange fragment.

"Kolesnik?" I called, like a terrified child staring at the cracked-open closet door and waiting for it to swing wide. The shape hunched low to the ground and tipped its misshapen head toward the clouds. Two jagged shapes protruded where a mouth might sit. A boar's tusks, waiting to gore.

Panic froze me where I stood. Part of me was afraid of the faint possibility that it really was an animal, rearing and snuffling against the ground, something raised in the woods and waiting to be fed. That was the reasonable terror. The rest of my dread belonged to the idea that what I was seeing wasn't real. That it existed for my eyes alone. Now I wanted a witness. Proof that this thing, whatever it was, had been called to life by our hands. Because it looked so *real*. I felt that I could reach out and touch it. That it was looking for me.

"What are you doing out here?" Finch called, and the sound of her voice called me back to myself and away from the sight of that creature. I turned and found her sitting on a stone bench. She'd taken her mask off, her makeup all smudged, the insect wings splayed faceless on the seat to her left. And to the right sat Thea, her hand perched horribly close to Finch's thigh, a rabbit mask pushed to the top of her head and long, floppy ears hanging down her back.

I turned back to the water. The mass was gone, and the water rippled beyond where the apparition had stood.

"Jo," Finch called again, "are you alright?"

The amused judgment on Thea's face seared me with embarrassment. I shook my head, fuzzy with drunkenness and delusion and a pounding fear that wouldn't let go of my heart no matter how many deep breaths I sucked in.

"I'm fine," I said, and I left them there with my ram mask hooked between my fingers, heading back to the Manor on my own. I didn't look to see who followed me. I didn't look to see if anything would follow me at all.

10

PITS AND STEMS AND FINELY STRETCHED SKIN

"You're being weird," Finch said.

To be fair, I *had* been staring at the computer screen in the equipment room for the last hour without clicking my mouse, while Finch ate cherries out of a Tupperware container and flicked concerned glances in my direction with the same hard ferocity as her spat-out pits. All I could do was let my eyes water as I hovered over a highlighted box waiting to be filled in with someone's camcorder return date. They were three days late.

I was sleeping only a few hours a night. The Manor's radiators finally kicked on with November's arrival, and they boiled the house to an inconceivable heat, one that left me kicking off my duvet every night and sweating beneath the top sheet. I'd drift off for a scant hour, my body in the dream space of half rest, and find myself in the same vicious nightmares. That white house forever. The same violent deaths of the people I loved most.

Even waking couldn't banish them—some nights, I'd stir in the dark to the sensation of something sitting on the end of my bed.

The first time was the night after the Grotesque ended. The others came home after they realized I was gone. Amrita knocked on my door asking if I was okay. I told her I was just too drunk and I wanted to go to sleep. Two hollow half-truths. Still, she let me sleep without pressing the issue, and I pushed my cheek deep into the pillow with makeup still smeared around my eyes. I always slept on my stomach with the lamp off, but someone had left the hall light on. I remembered drifting off with my eyes trained on the bar of light under my bedroom door. The dip of the mattress woke me—the distinct sensation of something else's weight.

My first assumption was that Amrita had come to check on me again. But I was pinned by the dregs of sleep paralysis. I couldn't flip my body around to see what perched behind me. The weight was an imposing pressure beside my feet. Sound wouldn't leave my mouth no matter how hard I tried, my mind still remembering how to call itself back from REM. Finally, I let out a little hum. Needles prickled all the way down my wrists as my limbs came back to life, and I pushed myself up on my elbows and twisted. Nothing. Just the black room. The distant hum of someone's fan, the creaking of the house, the clank of the radiator heating up.

I turned the lights back on and never went back to sleep. There was no way I could have eased the pounding of my heart. I went through the same process the next night, and the next. My head was impossible to clear. Everything held the slight tinge of unease and the potential outline of an apparition waiting in the dark.

In Moody's class I was dull-eyed and quiet. But I refused to waste any more time—instead, I spent long hours in the studio, both in class and out of it, determined to make something good out of all the ways my brain couldn't keep up with my body and unwilling to spend more time alone in my room. It was so embarrassing to lose control.

Personally, I thought I had been hiding it decently well. But I always assumed no one was looking at me and found myself shocked when they'd been watching the whole time.

Apparently, Finch had been alert. Tuned into a frequency I hadn't been aware I was putting off.

"You can talk to me, you know," Finch continued when I didn't answer her first prompt. She had her feet up on the work desk, her face creased with concern. "Sometimes you worry me. I think you spend so much time listening to the rest of them, and you keep important parts of yourself away. You're not honest about when you're going through something."

I hesitated, feeling overwhelmingly scrutinized and resentful that she was calling me out for it. I twisted the strings of my hoodie between my fingers and pulled. The hood scrunched closer around my face. "That's not true," I said, but it was a lie, and both of us heard the waver in it.

She looked at my fist. The bandage was finally gone, a wickedly pink half-formed scab now evident in my palm. Washing my hands in the studio had opened the wound on and off. I thought it might never heal.

"Okay," she said finally. "Well, I'm here, if you ever wanna vent."

Maybe I should have been pleased by the concern. But I was still smarting with the aftermath of finding Finch and Thea in the garden, disturbed by all the ways I could imagine them touching.

Besides—why would I complain to Finch when something innate was finally starting to click?

A week after the Grotesque, I signed up for critique. Finch started us off. Her canvases were cloudy with gradients of gray and blue and beige and taupe, like looking at the horizon with a magnifying glass and snaring the color you found there. Atop those surfaces she had sketched out portraits with half the face absent—they were just outlines of hair and shoulder blades, mouthless beings with the eyes filled in. Their gazes held wet, luscious detail, sparkling with unshed tears, peering past a gold wash of paint. Of course Moody loved them. They had that quality that Saz sometimes referred to as "Finchian," the one every professor ate up without fail, though Saz usually used the term as a replacement for calling something "fucking creepy." They were intangible, unsettling, all-knowing. They glowed from within.

But Moody also loved my new paintings. I had started to call them *Gatherings*; a collection depicting our group of five in mundane situations painted with the same chiaroscurist glow of a Renaissance piece, full of haunting light and umbral hues. I painted us eating at the table in Banemast with the fluorescent overheads replaced by candle glow, the walls black and deep, the table a cool green melting over our thighs. I painted Caroline with Saz in a headlock atop the sofa and the rest of us framing them, hands on thighs, fingertips digging into biceps, heads tossed back like we were worshipping the *Pietà*. Then another of us basking in the TV's blue glow, curled up in the dark in our massive bed of blankets across the living room floor, illuminated in a ghoulish writhe. I found that when prompted to make a record of them, I could draw every detail. I'd done it already, a hundred times, a thousand, and with these new paintings I kept finding ways to reinvent their image. Still—I found it hard to summon my own face without a mirror. I became my own Bloody Mary, apparent only when called.

Moody called them *eerie* and *nostalgic*. She dubbed them a *departure from my comfort zone*. She rhapsodized on their *magical quality*, their *poignant tension*, their *anticipatory beauty, as if awaiting the second that captured moment might end, like an archaeological excavation of a future that hadn't passed yet.* I lit up with all the praise. It made my enervated state a little more bearable. Of course, I was still terrified that there was something wrong with me after our ritual and Kolesnik's end, but I was also afraid that we had uncovered the answer—that maybe suffering really did make for a better artist. Clearly, it was working for me.

Moody's appreciation made me even more aware of the ways everyone promised that life after Rotham would change, all the warnings that my friends would go on to lead new lives. Insistences that I would think of them sometimes, not often, wistful for a time that was perfect only in its inevitable end. Premonitions that we'd marry and procreate and die.

But nothing about us adhered to tradition. At least, that was how it felt to me—I imagined that every relationship, platonic or romantic or some twist of the two, had the capability to leave you in reverence of it. You could only worship ordinary adoration for so long before it became sacred.

So I painted it. I tried to draw them closer to me, my hold on selfhood a loosening grip.

◆　◆　◆

The last few days before fall break were alight with frantic energy. We were all meant to head home for Thanksgiving, but I couldn't imagine a week away from the studio. Things were finally starting to fall into place, and taking a break felt like failure.

"When you return for the rest of the semester, you will have one week before Survey," Moody said to us on the Friday before break. "I understand that things have been strained without Kolesnik, but I believe that you all have the potential to move forward if you keep this momentum up. It's anyone's Solo."

Potential. That was the key.

Saz showed her work for critique, and Moody was overjoyed with the path she had taken. Saz's sketchy abstractions were gory with color. They were the kind of paintings my mother might declare childish, claiming she could do the same thing in an hour. But Saz's hand made them viscerally violent, moving beyond waxy scribbles into lines that suggested dripping lacerations. She painted on huge canvases with wide sweeps of the arm. Blaring fuchsias melted into pinks behind flat red animals, like something you might find carved into the belly of an amphora. They had the same ritual nature of the way Saz moved through the world—her abstracted icons and shapes and overlapping figures appearing like points along a constellation, like cards pulled in a tarot reading, like automatic drawings made with the eyes shut. Her energy exploded across the canvas, unrestrained.

Our paintings had such an unbridled newness to them. In the private chamber of my heart, I believed that the ritual had unlocked something important—something we couldn't have accessed without it.

Moody clearly thought so too. She was delighted by our progress and said so often. "I'm impressed by how many pieces you've been able to complete over the last few weeks," Moody told Saz as Amrita and I helped her take her work down. "From my perspective, it looks like you've found a rhythm that works for you, and the paintings are stronger for it. You've developed a signature style that feels inventive."

Saz's grin was full of giddy relief.

But we weren't the only ones reaping the benefits of hard work. The other painters kept their heads down and spent long nights in the studio. Grainer was never empty, the lights eternally on. We were all striving for perfection and trying not to get lost along the way—and Moody was an encouraging leader, enduringly honest. She chastised Phoebe for "laziness" when she didn't paint the edges of a canvas. She called Yejun's most recent painting "muddy" and instructed him to start it over without using any black. She read a section of Cameron's thesis paper out loud and asked the rest of us to point out what parts were confusing while he sat in front of us, head down and the tips of his ears red. She told Amrita that her palettes were overwhelming and instructed her to create three new pieces in monochromatic tones. She asked Caroline to push her textures further. To thin out her washes, build up the waxy drips, and give us more of an impact.

And she told me to keep it up, with a smile on her face.

I felt blessed by my apparent growth. Letting Moody down wasn't a possibility.

When everyone else started to clear out of the studio, I went into the hallway and made a call. The phone rang forever. I waited for an answer and watched Rotham darken past the windows. Campus was busy. Everyone leaving class and heading to dinner with hoods pulled over their heads. Leaves speckling the dying grass. The promenade wet with icy rain. The garden still lush with coniferous growth. The edge of the woods butting up against it, Lysander Gate blowing open and banging shut in the wind. I wondered what the Boar King looked like now. I imagined him soaked and tattered, that great head lolling in the dirt, stuffed arms limp at the sides. The fur all matted and sour. The stuffing melting into the meat and into the mud.

My mom's greeting finally came through the speaker. "Hey," I said, and then immediately followed with, "I'm not coming home."

"Oh," she said. Then, "Wait, what? Why not?"

"I have too much left to do. Survey is coming up, and if I went home, I'd fall behind. They're picking the top five students from our class to advance for Solo, and I need to get a spot in that group."

In an ideal scenario, those five spots would belong to us. I didn't know how to cope with any other outcome. The rest of what I wanted to say hung unsaid in the air—that there was no point if I didn't get the chance to Solo, I might as well drop out now, all this time and all this work just for nothing to come of it.

"Are you sure?" That was my dad. I felt betrayed by the speakerphone. Then his voice got closer, and I could hear movement, likely him taking the phone into the other room. "Do you want to fly in for just a night or two? It would make your mother happy, and it sounds like it would be good for you to spend some time clearing your head."

"It's not that I don't want to," I said, though I wasn't sure if that was true. A beetle crawled across the windowsill in front of me, and I crushed it with my thumb. A grassy scent clung to the air. "I just can't afford to leave right now."

It was, reluctantly, confirmed—I would stay at Rotham for break.

Saz never flew back to London for such a short period of time, and Finch would just drive home for the day, so I knew I wouldn't be alone on campus. But Caroline could never escape a holiday with her family, and Amrita loved heading south to see her parents and sisters in North Carolina. I didn't blame her—I'd visited once, and her mom had fed me so much that I had to buy two new pairs of pants just to have something to wear for the rest of the trip.

We threw our fourth annual Friendsgiving that night after critique, before Caroline and Amrita headed out. It was a tradition we had formed in our first year as friends after Saz asked for a "true American

Thanksgiving spread." We all helped with the cooking, though usually Amrita and I took over most of the work. None of us liked turkey much, so we stuffed a chicken with lemons and thyme and roasted it and seared a scored block of tofu for Amrita. The oven made the whole house so hot that we kept the back door open, wind blowing into the kitchen.

"You're really just going to stay on campus?" Amrita asked Saz and me. "Why don't you come home with one of us?"

I leaned against the kitchen counter and shrugged. Finch sipped a beer at the table, her knees splayed wide. Caroline sliced pats of butter into a bowl of mashed potatoes and tipped her head toward Finch, who poured some of the beer into her waiting mouth and laughed when it dribbled past Caroline's lips.

"Someone has to stick around to make sure that Jo doesn't make herself sick spending her whole vacation hard at work," Finch said lightly.

"Hey," I complained, flushing. "I'll be fine." I cranked open a can of cranberry sauce. Amrita had wanted the real stuff, made from scratch, but Finch insisted that it tasted best out of the can, and she had been the one to do the shopping. Something buzzed close to my head. I swatted next to my ear, annoyed.

"You can always come to dinner with my family," Caroline suggested. "The food sucks, and my mom will probably say you look dykey right after she finishes grace."

"Wow, that sounds awesome, you should totally do that, Jo," Finch said drily.

"I'll be fine, I want to be on campus for a reason. I need to have ten finished pieces by the end of the week, and two of them are still in progress. You guys are already leagues ahead of me, and I'll be lucky if I can catch up." The buzzing continued, the fat flutter of an insect's wings. I pressed a fingertip to my ear. "Is there a bug in here?"

"It's November," Saz said, like I was ridiculous for even suggesting it.

"Planet's melting, anything is possible." Caroline sucked mashed potatoes off the end of her finger. Saz coaxed Finch up to help her set the table. I tried to commit the sight of them to memory, imagining what it would look like in paint. Amrita tossing roasted carrots with spiced oil, Finch fiddling with the napkins beside each plate, Caroline with a bowl in each arm, Saz lifting the chicken out of the oven, Amrita rushing to clear a spot for her to put it down. Everyone pulling out a chair. Music playing from the speaker in the other room—the Cranberries. Saz lighting what felt like a hundred taper candles. Wax dripping down the sides and onto the tablecloth, which was really a piece of cobalt fabric that Finch had brought over from the studio. Brisk breeze creeping in past the open back door, a black cutout of night, lampposts glowing far down the promenade and lighting up the main door of Slatter Hall. The world a portrait of shadow. The memory of Kolesnik's shape standing by the pond.

"C'mon, sit," Amrita said, squeezing my wrist.

I sat. I watched them fill their plates. Saz heaped food onto mine and everything smelled heavenly, even though my stomach was tight with anxiety. I tried to lean into the simple pleasure of sitting with them, of enduring tradition, of all the ways we had claimed each other. I could have lived forever like that. Cooking a meal for them and watching them eat it.

There was no Boar King in this room. I sent him back to the corners of my self-doubt.

"This is so good," Saz moaned. "You guys should cook for us every day. Fuck Bane, I cannot eat another lukewarm penne Alfredo."

"It was mostly Jo," Amrita boasted, squeezing my knee under the table.

"Cheers to Jo, then." Finch raised her beer to me and fixed me with a knowing look. Caroline finished pouring the rest of us glasses of wine, and we raised them back, though I did it sheepishly, smiling and trying to hide it.

Finch was so pretty like that. There was an arrogant laziness to her stare that made her delicate and overwarm. She took another swig from her bottle and winked. She didn't even have to touch me—all it took was a look. I shivered and tried to play it off by fixing my napkin in my lap. I wanted to offer her something sweet and watch her chew in that open-mouthed way of hers, like the food was so good she couldn't remember to be polite about it.

My eyes kept drifting back to her mouth, too obviously. I didn't have it in me to rein the feeling in or remind myself that it was likely Thea she wanted, not me. Usually my brain would repeat the same frustrated mantra by now: *Don't fuck up your friendship don't fuck up your friendship don't fuck up your friendship don't fuck up your friendship don't fuck up your friendship.* The dull buzz picked up in my ear again.

"You have to try it," Saz was saying to Amrita, nudging the plate of cranberry jelly and watching it shake. Amrita made a face—her nose wrinkling, brows raised in disbelief.

"That thing is a travesty," she said.

"It's fuckin' good," Finch responded, hand over her chest in mock hurt.

"You might like it," I tried. "Just a bite?"

That did her in. Amrita rolled her eyes in my direction, but she dutifully slid the plate closer and forked a gelatinous piece into her mouth. Everyone went quiet as she chewed, her expression blank until it slowly started to crumple.

"Amrita hates it," Caroline said, gleeful. "You can see it all over her face."

"I do not! It tastes good!"

"She's practically gagging," Saz cried. "Look at her try to swallow it!"

"I hate you all," Amrita said after spitting into her napkin, but she was laughing hard enough to choke, and Caroline had to thump her heartily on the back. Finch slurped up her jelly and grinned, cranberry sauce viscous and red between her teeth.

"Gross!" Saz cackled, seizing my shoulders and trying to hide behind me.

I leaned into the laughter. If growth was an endless repetition of leaving them behind, I wanted stagnancy. We could stay like this no matter what time dropped in our laps. They weren't afraid of Survey, of the coming selection, of the possibility of some of us moving forward while the others did not. So what did I have to be scared of?

11

TINY MYTHS OF THE EMPTY HEART

It turned out I had plenty to fear. Without them all, the Manor was a fucking crypt. Even Saz's presence on the second floor wasn't enough to make the house less creepy—the empty attic with Caroline's door sitting ajar felt like an abandoned impression of her life. Still, those reminders and late nights spent with Saz were better than nothing. Spending my fall break entirely alone, while likely beneficial for my work ethic, would have driven me up the walls until I was sliding back down with plaster under my nails.

It was like someone had ordered winter in a catalog and paid for expedited shipping. Campus was sheathed in a carpet of leaf rot. Frost coated the windows in the mornings and nights. Saz swapped her summer clothes for her cold-weather wardrobe—chunky cable knit sweaters, bejeweled hair clips under bright beanies, thick tights under miniskirts, black boots pulled all the way over her knees. I wore what I always did: my brother's hand-me-downs, with a heavier jacket thrown on top. I started to find little holes in my shirts. Places where I had nicked the fabric carelessly with a palette knife, or where something had burrowed into the cloth. Thoughtlessly, I often found myself pressing a finger through the holes, straining the edges of the fabric.

The studio was mostly empty, but there were a few cubicles occupied by familiar faces. I waved to Mars and passed Yejun hunched over
something on his desk. It surprised me to see that Finch, Saz, and I
weren't the only ones who skipped out on heading home for the holiday.

I hovered in the doorway of Saz's studio as she shrugged off her
puffy jacket and let it join the heap of papers scattered across the floor.
Some of them were beautiful sketches—messy scribblings of gouache,
pale washes of color over illustrations outlined in her favored red. Some
of those nice ones had boot prints on them. One had torn down the
middle where the leg of her stool caught it and ripped. They were a tes-
tament to how little regard Saz gave to the pieces the rest of us thought
were her best. She was never satisfied, forever wiping a canvas clean
and building it back up from the start. Still, she somehow had more
technically "finished" pieces than I had at thirteen to my eight.

"Quit lurking over there, I need to get something done without you
breathing down my neck," Saz called. I held my hands up in surrender
and did as I was told, heading back to my own studio beside Finch.

Wind pushed past the crack in my window. The Chapel was a dark
outline against the purpled sky. That dull light filled my cubicle, illu-
minating the sketchbooks on my desk and the drying slabs of paint on
my palette. I perched on my stool and wondered what my women were
doing. If Caroline was playing backgammon with her grandmother
in the same sunroom she always sent us pictures of, if Amrita's sister
brought her newborn baby to the house for Amrita to coo over. I could
have checked our group chat—it had been buzzing with the explosion
of a hundred different texts since the moment they left. But I had a
hard time looking at it more than a few times a day. The steady funnel
of screenshotted memes and complaints posed a distant normalcy that
made me uncomfortable with longing.

The canvas pinned to my wall was smeared with orange, the color
of headlights and sun coming through fingers. I dragged a blue-coated
brush over it, lightening my touch where I wanted the warmth to come

through the layers. Illumination was the goal. The kind of brilliant glow that couldn't be ignored.

Could the hand move separately from the mind? Could my body translate something buried insensate, speak it through strokes and image? Wrist twisting innately, color spreading in broad washes, figures forming out of the cold blue?

If there was a threshold between myself and creation, I felt that the ritual had carried me over it. Because that had to be the reason, didn't it? There was a veil between the work I made now and all the ways it had shifted from the past. It was the sensation of surety in the marks I made. I leaned close to the canvas and worked until the studio lights came on, until Saz left to find something to eat and Yejun's music shut off. Until all I could smell was turpentine and the spice of oil paint, that combustible cling, that mineral grit.

"Wow, that's fucked up," someone called from the doorway. I looked up immediately, surprised I could hear them at all. I hadn't even thought to put my headphones on.

It was Thea with Finch close behind her. Schooling the disappointment in my face at seeing them together was next to impossible.

"Can I take a closer look?" Thea asked, already stepping into the studio. I angled, hesitant, not wanting her to fully see what I had made. Finch gave me an apologetic smile from the doorway. What did she have to be sorry for? If she could tell Thea was irritating me, why didn't she ask her to fucking leave?

That hot build of aggression startled me. I pushed my stool away from the canvas to let them look.

"This is wild, Joanna," Thea murmured. The paint had a satin sheen under the bright overheads. The shapes had been sketched by my hand, but they felt detached, like someone else's creation. I felt I could see the piece for the first time through Thea's eyes.

It was the five of us, kneeling, just shadowed shapes without any features. The blue-black night around us. Mustardy earth meeting our crouched forms, a thin line of orange delineating the boundary of the sky and the ground. Small glowing spots marking the wicks of candles. Stalks of corn framing our bent heads. Our little conglomeration holding an indistinct black mass in the center, a limp body without the necessary bones to bring it to life. Somehow, without knowing, I painted the ritual.

"What is it supposed to represent?" Thea asked. She looked at me out of the corner of her eyes, and I wrung my hands behind my back.

"Sacrifice," I said, like a fool.

Finch let out a choked sound. It was hard to tell if it was a suppressed laugh or a disbelieving scoff.

"Well, Moody will think it's good." Thea looked at Finch in question. I wanted to know what she was communicating there, what they were saying without me.

"I'm gonna get dinner with Jo," Finch said finally, "go ahead."

Thea gave the two of us a long glance and then shrugged and turned to go. When I heard her sneakers squeak past the main doors, I said, "Got tired of hanging out with your girlfriend?"

"Don't be a dick," she answered lightly. "You know, Saz was right, it wouldn't kill you to have friends outside of them." She gestured at the painting.

"I hate when you say *them*, as if you're not one of us."

"I can be your friend and still have a sense of individuality."

"Riiight, I forgot," I said, rolling my eyes as I wiped my hands clean on the paint-stiff rag tucked in my front pocket.

Finch gave me a flat stare. "Why are you in such a bad mood?"

"I'm not." I scowled. Then, childishly, I said, "Why do you insist on bringing Thea in here when you know I don't like her?"

"I didn't think it was that deep. What reason do you even have to hate her? Thea's chill, and she makes cool work." Finch crossed her arms over her chest. Her jacket looked too thin for the weather. My irritation faded, just slightly—I wanted to put my own coat around her shoulders and warm her up.

"I don't know," I said. "Sorry. Forget it."

We were silent. Neither of us could forget it. There was so much hanging between us, so much I couldn't say. I tried to straighten up my desk a little, unwilling to look in her direction.

"It's fine. We're all on edge right now. But seriously, try to take a break and sleep in or something. You look fucking exhausted."

If I answered that, I would burst into tears. The feeling constricted in my throat. I just shrugged and turned to the canvas. The painting stared back at me, our five forms intertwined among the illumination of the candles and the ears of corn. There was something jarring about the way I had arranged us—together, we looked like a poor imitation of Francisco Goya's *Witches' Sabbath*. I expected the creature between us to stand and rise a foot above the ground.

"A little on the nose, don't you think?" Finch said at last, her voice strained as she pointed at the painting. "Do you think that's smart, considering how it could implicate us if they ever find the suit?"

All I could do was shrug.

When I finished cleaning up, Finch followed me home, the two of us searching for Saz and something sustaining to put in our stomachs. We found her in the living room eating pretzels on the sofa, a sitcom on the TV.

"Finally," she said when she saw us, crumbs littering her too-big T-shirt. "This place is terrifying without anyone else here."

We curled up on the couch together. I was a bone-deep kind of exhausted, and I desperately needed to shower, but it was rare that we gathered like this. Finch and I spent time together alone at work, but I liked witnessing Saz and Finch interact—I could unlock all the ways they fit together individually, what pieces of us made the most sense to one another. And even though it was different without Caroline and Amrita there, it still worked. Saz rested her feet in my lap, and Finch tipped her head onto my shoulder, the room dark save for the TV screen glowing back at us.

It was past two by the time Finch rose to find her shoes, and we were all half-asleep as she went back to her apartment. She always left us like that, even when it was too late in the night and we tried to convince her to stay and take one of the other's beds. But tomorrow was Thanksgiving. I had kind of hoped she would stay. That we could wake up together and do something that felt a little festive, even though I knew she would head home to eat at her parents' table, hating it all the while.

"You going to bed too?" Saz asked when the door shut behind Finch.

I hesitated and then shook my head. "Not yet. Haven't been sleeping well, I don't really want to be in my room."

Her eyes softened. I loved that about Saz—how open her face was, how readily she showed her affection. Everything she felt made itself evident in her mouth. She nudged me until I lay down on the couch and then snuggled up with her head on my shoulder and an arm thrown around my waist.

"Let's stay here like this," she mumbled into my shirt. "Let's have a sleepover and share secrets."

I dragged my fingers over her back and shut my eyes. "You go first," I whispered.

"I'm afraid of ghosts," Saz said immediately, "even though I really want to see one, one day."

"Not a secret. That's obvious."

"Okay, whatever. Your turn."

The quiet buzz of the room, the dim hiss of the radiator, the rise and fall of her chest against me. I felt I could say anything and let it die in the air between us.

"It's a big secret," I said finally. "You can't tell anyone."

Saz wriggled a little. "I won't."

"For real."

"For real! I'm honored you'd even want to tell me anything. I thought you reserved that kind of thing for Amrita or Finch."

There was something about the dead quiet of the house and the reassuring nearness of Saz's heartbeat that made me want to confess.

What I wanted to say was *I think something's wrong with me. I'm afraid that I gave a vital piece of my mind to that ritual.*

But that felt too enormous to release. I wanted her to know what I needed to say without my having to speak it aloud. The core of me begged to ask, *Do you see something in that corner? Is it looking at us? Do you feel it at the end of your bed? Do you remember bleeding into that effigy and wishing upon something bigger? Did you feel it come home with us? Did we fuck it all up?*

Something brushed against my neck—a strand of hair or the tickle of an insect. I tried not to flinch so I wouldn't scare her. Above all else, I didn't want to scare her.

"Well," I started, and then I just kept going, the words spilling out in an adolescent rush. "I can't because—it's actually—I think I have a crush on someone. And I can't tell them."

Useless mouth, hopeless heart. Saz tipped her head back and fixed me with a look; gentle, probing, a little pitying. "Why can't you tell them?" She said *them* like she meant to say *her.* I hated how well she could see me.

"I don't think I'm made for a relationship," I said, the admission muffled by her forehead bumping my cheek. "I don't think I'm like . . . romantic. I don't know how to make it last."

"What do you call all this, then?"

I shrugged in her hold. "What do you mean?"

"Us," she clarified, tapping once on my chest. "All of us. Haven't we dedicated ourselves to each other, for the long haul?"

I went quiet, dumbfounded. She smiled at me as if I were a particularly naive child.

"Besides, isn't this all temporary? I mean, not us. We'll be friends forever. But we'll grow and change, and we'll do really fucking cool things. Solo isn't life. There's more beyond the studio being your life. Of course, it doesn't feel that way now, when we're like, in the thick of it. But we have so much time to figure it out. Graduation is only a few months away, and then we can let go of Rotham forever and you can kiss as many girls as you want."

I closed my eyes.

"Aren't you excited?" Saz asked. I could hear the smile in her voice. "Aren't you ready for our lives to finally begin?"

Begin? I was in the middle. Hell, I was close to the end. I wondered where the fundamental shift between Saz and I lived, what delineated my devastation as her invention of the world. I tried to hold it all in my hands and failed despicably.

"I don't know if we're on the same path," I admitted. "I think I'm doing a bad job."

"Come on, we're not so bad," Saz said, her hand fisting in the fabric of my shirt. "We've done enough suffering. I think we can take a break for love."

I swallowed. "Whatever you say."

The room felt too dark. I kind of had to pee, but I was too afraid to leave the safety of the living room, to slip out of Saz's hold. Her voice was so near that it vibrated against my chest every time she spoke.

"You worry us. Our tortured Jo."

I couldn't speak. That flutter again, up against my ear. This time I did flinch. I couldn't help it.

"If you need my help, you can ask me. You know that, right?" Saz murmured, shifting against me. "Just ask me."

It was a lifetime before I could coax my voice back into my mouth. Finally, I said, "I don't know how to do that."

But she didn't answer. I could feel the breath of her sleep rise and fall, rise and fall, rise and fall with the desperate swell of my chest.

12

RITES AS SUTURE

It rained the rest of the week. Dead storms, soundless and gray, the clouds a thin threat overhead.

Saz and I got up early each day and went to bed late. I don't think she actually wanted to spend as much time in the studio as I did, but there was mutual pressure between us—if Finch and I went, Saz would too, and she'd last throughout the day as long as her interest would hold. But she was a faster painter, and surer of herself. Now Saz had fourteen pieces to show at Survey. And they were *good* pieces, though I was biased. But these recent paintings were special; iconographic canvases with fragments of Saz's life worked into the smaller, sketchy details, like a road sign from her grandparents' street in South Korea, the phone booth she could see from her childhood bedroom in London, the outline of the window in the Manor's living room. Each one felt like getting to know her all over again.

Finch, Saz, and I left the studio by dinnertime on Sunday. Campus was filling up again. Suitcases rolled over brick. The air smelled like the possibility of snow. I burrowed my fists deep in my pockets, trying to stay warm. The chill cut down to the bone anyway.

But the Manor was aglow. It stood like a queen on a throne at the end of the promenade. All peaks and eaves and gingerbread, those imposing stairs, those crosshatched windows, elegant columns that had stood the test of time. Lights on in every window. Figures moving behind the curtains and glass. I could see the shadow of Caroline there, at the top, and someone in the hallway on the second floor, head bobbing near the little circular window. They'd turned the porch light on, knowing we'd come back eventually and need it.

"Looks like everyone's home," Saz said with affection.

We kicked our shoes off at the back door. I could smell someone's lingering coffee made too late in the day. Amrita's red scarf hung over a dining chair, and weed smoke clung in the air. The clock read 7:36, and my heart swelled with anticipation of hearing their delight come pouring down the stairs when the minute changed. I closed my eyes and stood there beside the stove, listening.

"Seven thirty-seven!" Saz called, and the distant chorus answered her. Coming home to them would never get old.

We piled around the dining table that night. Caroline had been the one smoking, and she brought her ashtray downstairs to pass around the joint. She sat shirtless in a lacy bralette as the radiator cooked the room. Someone had trimmed her hair while she was away. Now it sat just past her shoulders. She frowned around the joint as a long pull flared the end red, and then said, "I hate being back at that house."

Saz put an arm around her. Low music played from a speaker. Every so often the Manor's poor wiring would falter, and the lights would give a halfhearted flicker.

"Well, you're home now," Amrita said gently. "You don't have to think about it anymore."

Saz smiled. "Yeah, next time we'll just go back with you. Then you won't have to deal with it alone."

Caroline looked like she wanted to say something self-pitying, so I cleared my throat and interrupted. "Can you imagine how fun it would have been if we grew up together? What it would have been like to be teenagers at the same time?"

Finch said, "Caroline would have bullied us. She's too hot."

Caroline shoved Finch's shoulder, but the look that passed over her softened. She cracked a grin.

"Sometimes I can't believe I didn't grow up with you all." Saz smiled. "You're too important."

Amrita's laugh was bashful. "Please don't be earnest, I've been up since six."

Finch was grinning. "Seriously. We would have worn those necklaces that are two halves of a heart and played with Ouija boards, or pierced our ears with sewing needles and apples."

"We would have started a band."

"We should still start a band."

"We would have been so fucking insufferable. Like seriously annoying."

"Our parents would have disowned us."

"We would have gotten expelled from whatever school was unlucky enough to enroll us."

"I was already halfway to expulsion," Finch cut in again through the overlapping voices. "My mom always said I was a horrible kid."

I could imagine them younger. I'd seen their baby pictures, their downy adolescence, and I'd shown them mine. Sure, I guess we were still kids. At least, we were hardly adults—we played at maturity as if claiming it might make it true, like our dedication was enough to prove that we deserved to say we knew what we were doing.

"I wish I'd been worse," Amrita admitted. She rested her chin on a fist and touched the candle Saz had lit in the center, toying with the wax. "I think that's the only thing I would change, if I could."

"What, you wish you had our bad influence?" Finch asked, giving a piece of Amrita's hair a gentle tug.

Amrita tipped her head at Finch and smiled. "Honestly, yeah."

There was a lull, the five of us steeping in the quiet.

"We could do something to prove our friendship," Finch said.

"Didn't we already sacrifice the life of our worst enemy in girlish solidarity?" Caroline asked as she raised the joint to her mouth again.

"I mean like, a friendship bracelet. But forever."

Amrita's fingers danced up the candle, dangerously close to the wick. "Like what? Want me to brand you with my initials?"

Finch shook her head, smiling. "Nah, I have a better idea."

She slid away from the table and up the stairs, sock feet thumping the whole way up. Saz raised her eyebrows in a silent question. We shrugged in unison. Finch reemerged with something in her hands that appeared to be a shoebox.

"Oh my god," Saz said, sitting up straighter.

"What is that?" Amrita asked, nervous now.

"My stick-and-poke kit," Finch said. "I let Saz borrow it."

"You were going to tattoo yourself?" I asked Saz, incredulous.

She shrugged. "Finch said it was easy."

"It is easy."

"No way. You are not sticking a needle into me," Caroline said immediately.

Finch gave Caroline a real, true-to-life pout.

"No fucking way," Caroline repeated.

Amrita surveyed the box suspiciously. "Is it . . . sanitary?"

Finch scoffed. "You know I'd never hurt you."

We answered her with hesitant silence again. Finch looked exasperated. "Seriously! Come on, I'll do it to myself first."

"You're high," I said, looking for an out.

"Only a little. It'll hurt less like this."

"I don't know if that's how it works," Saz said doubtfully.

The kitchen chair made a ragged sound when Finch pulled it out again. We watched her set up all the materials—a vial of India ink, a packet of long needles, latex gloves, alcohol wipes, a bottle of witch hazel. The lights wavered overhead, and the music fluctuated with them.

"This is probably a bad idea," I said.

"Jo, do you love me?"

Finch gave me a beseeching look. Her brows arched up as if daring me to challenge her, prepared to challenge me back.

"Of course," I said.

Her answering smile beamed at me. "See, Jo gets it. You've all said that you wanted a tattoo at some point, and now that I'm giving you the opportunity, you want to shoot me down?"

"I meant from a professional," Caroline answered. "Like, with a license and the right equipment."

Amrita picked up the India ink and examined it, her expression thoughtful. I thought if anyone would cling to sensibility, it would be Amrita. The rest of us had less backbone. She'd always been a stable pillar.

"Okay," Amrita relented. "I did say I wanted one."

Saz laughed, giddy with permission. "Hey, if Amrita does it, I will."

"My mom would fucking crucify me," Caroline said.

"Isn't that half the fun of it?" Finch asked.

Caroline hesitated, but a smile forced its way through. "You know what? You're right. Fuck it."

Fuck it was right. Finch began to set up a little cup filled with ink, leaning down to eyeball the liquid's level. When she deemed it acceptable, she rose and undid her belt, then slid her jeans down around her thighs. We whooped accordingly. I cupped my hands around my mouth as we cheered, mostly to disguise the immediate heat that rose to my cheeks.

We crowded to watch Finch ready herself as she cleaned her thigh and prepped the needles. She met my eyes when she asked, "What should we tattoo? We all have to match."

"The Rotham insignia."

"Gag, that's ridiculous."

"Moody's name."

"The Manor."

"Do I look like I'm capable of that kinda detail?"

"Oh, my bad, I thought you were an *artist*."

"Give me something easier. Like, a leaf, or something small I can't fuck up."

"That gives me a lot of faith in your abilities."

"I'm just being straight up."

"You've never been straight. Not even for that spring semester in sophomore year when you pretended so a guy would give you free tickets to see The Internet."

"You *promised* that you would never bring that up again."

"Can you do a flower?" I interrupted. "Something with meaning?"

Saz sighed. "Jo, that's corny."

"No, it's cute." Finch's eyes gleamed. "What are you thinking?"

They were all looking at me. I thought about the allegorical vanitas paintings we loved, and all the gravity in a memento mori. I cleared my throat and said, "In Greek mythology, hyacinths are supposed to represent devotion beyond death."

Finch gave me a lingering look. Finally, she said, "Okay, that's kind of metal. Someone pull up a pic and let's get to work."

Amrita obeyed, propping her phone against someone's beer bottle. Finch swiped her leg clean again and got to work. It was a meditative process, with the in and out of the needle and her brow furrowed in focus. The lines were more even than she had promised they would be—she was actually good at it.

"Look at that," Saz said, marveling.

It really was beautiful, after she wiped away dots of blood with an alcohol pad. The design was small and delicate. Outlined petals burst from the stem, lupine leaves soft as a rabbit's ear, Finch's careful hand etching the shape along the top of her thigh. Caroline volunteered to go next. She wanted the flower along her ribs where she might be able to hide it from her mother for a little while. If it hurt, she didn't show it—her expression remained pleased. Saz followed after Caroline's was cleaned up, with Saz's inked on the inside of her left bicep where it could press close to her heart, and then I gave a little wave.

"I'll go," I said.

It was just after midnight. Something bumped against the kitchen window with a dithering hum—a moth beating its wings against the glass. Finch motioned for me to take my sweatshirt off, and I obeyed, sitting there in my sports bra with my bicep clutched in her hands. She wiped down the skin and gave me a look of confirmation. "You can start," I reassured.

"Just tell me if you want me to stop," Finch said with a reassuring brush of her thumb. My skin prickled beneath her touch.

"And leave me with a half-finished tattoo? Yeah fucking right."

My stomach tittered with the same fluttering motion of the moth. I sucked in a hard breath, and Finch gave my bicep one more little squeeze. "Alright, Jo. One, two, three . . ."

The first poke was just a light prick. Finch was quick and sure of herself, acutely aware of my skin and how to maneuver it. Her thumbs stretched my bicep taut. I leaned into the touch, my head fuzzy, the room too close, something creaking upstairs. But we were all down here, weren't we? Who could be standing above us?

There was a damp titter beside my ear, like something with wings taking flight. I flinched.

"Quit moving," Finch said softly, her exhale fanning across my cheek. I closed my eyes—

And opened them again in a daze. My back was against the floor. I had slouched out of the chair at some point, limp with forgetting. Caroline peered down at me, framed by the comet of the overhead light behind her head.

"Look at me," Caroline said, her hands cold against my cheeks. "You're okay, just take a deep breath and relax."

"What happened?" I asked. Fingers combed through my hair, a little rougher than needed but kind all the same.

"You fainted, baby," Saz's voice answered. "For no reason, really. It's just a little needle. Come on, sit up. Amrita, get her some water please. No, don't splash her with it, let her drink."

I felt for my head, which was already pounding with the promise of a lump. My fingers prodded a tender spot, and I winced. It was like cracking open the back of a beetle, hearing the crisp exoskeleton crunch. Amrita was there in a blurred-out shape, and I felt her press the glass to my lips, heard her encourage me to swallow. When I finally focused my gaze, it landed on Caroline again, scrubbing my skin with a spit-dampened thumb. Her eyes were blown wild and wide, blue pupils pale as chemtrails. She gave me a grin and turned her teeth into a barrier.

"Good morning," she said.

My arm throbbed. The skin above my elbow was tender as a fresh burn. I reached for it, instinctively, and then Finch was there to push my hand away.

"Don't touch it," she said under her breath, hand just grazing around the place that stung. "You'll get something infected."

My eyes fell on the flower blooming half-finished in Finch's line-work. The tattoo wept fresh red tears.

"We match now," Saz said with a grin. She held her arm up, a diagonal blur of skin. I struggled to trace the hyacinth petals inked into place there.

Finch pushed a strand of hair away from my eyes. "I didn't get to finish yours. Do you feel well enough to sit up?"

The whole weight of my body pressed down on my elbows against the kitchen floor. That room felt like a staged scene, a sculpture about to tip. Like one of my paintings carved out of the canvas. Each of them sat around me in a circle, angling into my space as if they thought I might speak a prophecy out loud, some lasting and strange insistence.

"Jo?" Amrita asked, her fingers pressing into her lips as she studied me. "Are you alright? Should we call the clinic?"

"Are you kidding? We'll get kicked out for the tattoo alone," Caroline cut in.

"I'm fine," I insisted thickly, my tongue heavy in my mouth. "Sorry, that's so embarrassing. I can't believe I fainted."

"Yeah, me neither," Saz laughed. She helped me sit up all the way, and they got me back into the chair as Finch ran her fingers over my skin, right where the tattoo ended.

"Finish it up," I said. "I'll just look away."

Finch sighed. But her hand slid down my arm and intertwined with my own, fingers locking with fingers, palm to palm. She gave it a squeeze, and I set my spine straighter. Then she released my hand and tugged my arm into her lap. The needle in her hand steadied again. She dipped it into her pot of ink. I kept my eyes trained on Caroline, who sat with her arms wrapped around her knees, her own tattoo bandaged in plastic wrap.

She smiled when she caught me watching and gave me a thumbs-up. I let that gesture and the feeling of Finch's hand in my own carry me.

"Almost done," Finch said softly. When I shut my eyes this time, I remained upright. I went somewhere else in my head, sank deeper into the moment and their touch and their collective joy in watching me join them. It felt like an answer to our sacrifice. Like we actually held all the power we had taken from Kolesnik with our Boar King effigy. Like we were witches, conjurers, necromancers, animating the life out of his body, drinking it into our own.

Or maybe we were just girls obsessed with the occult, and each other, and all the different ways we could mutilate ourselves. Playing at liturgy until we could call it our own.

But couldn't this be ritual enough? Couldn't it be religion, the way I felt beside them? Did anyone else feel like this? Had I found the hidden panel in the wall, the sliding bookcase, the peeling crack in the plaster?

Finch dragged a soothing thumb along the skin that framed the tattoo. I slitted my eyes open and met her searching ones. "Done," she murmured, and she gave me one final squeeze.

My arm stung desperately. I reached for it, longing to scratch, to dig my nails into the wound and rip it farther open. But I just pushed my fingertips into the soft fat padding my bicep instead. I pressed down and down and down until the hurt was the only feeling that remained.

13

BUILD THE RIVER AND THE RAFT

The itching wound woke me early the next morning far before I was meant to be up for studio, the sun not yet awake, the sky still that pinkened breath of predawn. My nails ripped into it again before my mind blinked back to life, and I pulled my hands away wet with blood. Some was already half-clotted beneath my nails. Caroline was sitting on my bed.

"Jesus Christ," I said. "When did you get here? I thought I locked the door?"

She was in a little lavender satin nightgown with her hair hanging down around her face, dewy with sweat. Her tattoo was red beneath the plastic wrap and tape—I could see the faintest edge of it peek just past the armpit of the satin beneath her bicep. "Check your email," she said.

I pushed my hair out of my eyes and stared back at her. Past the gauze of curtain, I could see pinprick lights glowing in Grainer. I was half-afraid I might look at her and see that light poke through the thin planes of her face. That she was an apparition I had summoned from my head. Some new form the ghoulish Boar King had taken—a shape I was more likely to trust and less inclined to run from. If that was true, it wasn't doing a very good job. I still wanted to run.

"What time is it?" I asked, but she just shrugged, the look on her face intensely pensive. There was an eeriness to the rigid angle she held herself at. As if the news she had to give me were something life-ending.

I reached for my phone, still sorting through questions in my head: When had I fallen asleep? How long had I been dead to the world? Why hadn't I heard her come in?

There was a notification highlighted at the top of my phone with St. Roche's name on it. Fear curdled in my belly with the memory of Kolesnik's death announcement.

"What is this?" I asked, but Caroline just wrapped her fingers around my ankle through my blanket, sweat beading along her upper lip. My eyes kept flicking around the room and back to my phone screen, finding nothing safe to land on. It was a campus-wide email with the official Rotham crest in the signature. I read it once, twice, three times, four. "What the fuck? Did you tell the others yet?"

"Just you," Caroline said.

St. Roche's scathing words were a slew of emotions like *disappointed, confused, appalled, crestfallen, stricken*, all used to describe what she stated "a local farmer had discovered in a field": Kolesnik's Boar King suit, defiled in a dirty patch of cornfield. Our ritual.

The end of the email stated that Rotham advisors were expected to speak to their students about what had happened to the suit. If faculty had reason to believe that one of their students removed the suit from its case, punishment would be meted out appropriately.

"We're done for," I said. "It's fucking Survey on Friday. We'll be expelled."

"That's not what I'm worried about," Caroline said.

"What the hell are you worried about, then?"

Fury rose until my first instinct was to say something hateful, something like *of course that's not what you're worried about*. Because Caroline would always be okay. Her parents were far more entrenched in Rotham's history and culture than any of the rest of us were, with deep pockets to prove it. Caroline could burn down Grainer, and St. Roche would let her Solo with the tiniest disapproving pat on the hand.

The longer I looked at her, the more I wanted to snap. Panic constricted me tighter and tighter, every opportunity for our inevitable end cycling through my head. Now that they had the costume and could see what we had done with it, they would be questioning everyone on campus. Who knew how long we'd be able to stave them off? Saz was such a bad fucking liar.

Caroline leaned closer. Strands of hair stuck to her forehead, one caught in her mouth. Her eyes were a pallid blue. "Can't you feel it?" she whispered. "Can't you see it around us? They disrupted what we created. They cut our ties to a higher power."

Frost coated the window. Another light blinked on in Grainer, then another, as the lampposts down the promenade slowly blipped out.

That was the first time, with Caroline on my bed and that wild gleam in her eyes. That was the moment I knew I wasn't alone with my horrors—that even unsaid, we could all feel the shift. Whatever we had invited in had staked its claim deep within us. I could still smell her blood, feel her rough tongue against my palm.

I asked Caroline to go. I got dressed. Wordlessly, we gathered. We pretended that none of it had ever happened, and we went to class.

Moody avoided the subject of anything Kolesnik-related, though clearly St. Roche's email had bothered her. It had everyone in a frenzy. Yejun pulled the email up on his phone, and we abandoned the half-moon of chairs to read over his shoulder.

"This is so fucked," Phoebe said from my right. Her voice was laden with excitement. "Like, who thinks of this shit? And to do it after Kolesnik dies? Spit on his grave, why don't you. I wish we could see what it looked like."

Thea plucked Yejun's phone out of his hands and read over the email again. I avoided her eyes at all costs, pulse thudding loud as footsteps in my ears. All I could think about was Thea in my studio. How she'd leaned in to peer at the painting of the five of us in the cornfield. I wiped my sticky palms against my jeans.

But she just scoffed and tossed the phone back into Yejun's lap. "Who said it was made after he died? Maybe he did it himself. Maybe it was his final sculpture before he keeled over."

"He wasn't that creative," Cameron said, shaking his head.

Phoebe rolled her eyes. "Who do you think made it, Jo?"

My head snapped up. "What?"

"Do you think it was one of us? It seems the most likely, right?"

I floundered. "I mean . . . ," I started, before turning to find the others behind me—Amrita claiming the seat to my left, Finch hovering at the back with Saz to her right, Caroline relentlessly biting at the raw skin around her thumbnail. It was the only habit of hers that I'd ever been able to clock as distasteful. Blood collected in the torn skin like she'd been eating cherries.

"Why would any of us risk our Solo position like that?" Amrita answered Phoebe for me, her expression neutral and pleasant. "It was probably one of the juniors Kirsten hires to make the library displays. Sculpture majors always think they're so funny, it's ridiculous."

"They're wild," I agreed.

"Twisted," Saz said lightly. Finch nodded.

"Totally fucked," Caroline finished.

"I think we have far more important subjects to focus on this week, don't you all think?" Moody interrupted. She stood beside her stool, apparently too on edge to sit. Finch mirrored her when I glanced back and caught her eye, with her arms crossed over her chest and bottom lip caught in her teeth.

"Right on," Cameron said. "Let's get to work."

Moody's smile was weak. "This is your last week to collect your materials for Friday, when you will present the introduction to your thesis with the intention of expanding it throughout the winter and early spring for exhibition, whether that be in the Grainer Gallery or as a Soloist. I'll remind you that what you show will be a determining factor in our selection of the five candidates for Solo. Please present your best selves."

"Aye, aye, Captain," Saz said.

Moody smiled again, a little looser this time. She waved her hands at us. "Alright, go on. I'll come and find you."

We split up, conversations still lingering about the Boar King. I could hear flashes of awe and disgust—*Can you imagine finding it? I would have thought I was stumbling across a murder*—but I kept silent.

In the studio I fretted over what I had to show to Moody: a collection of twelve *Gatherings*. The scene at the dining table. Saz's nose spouting blood like a cracked faucet. All of us piled into the living room or sitting in rows in Saz's SUV. Our collective on the beach in Michigan, painted from the last photo I had taken before senior year began. Amrita standing at the top of the Manor stairs. Caroline crouched at the bottom, invented candles sitting on each step. Caroline's head peeking around the shower curtain, Saz applying false lashes in the mirror, Finch perched crisscross on the toilet lid, Amrita leaning into the doorway mid-shout. A series of us coming together over, and over, and over. A life crafted from the spaces in between us. All the shapes we made out of shadows and all the light we ferried with us. Our sabbath around the Boar King in the field, each of us with a hand on its body, spines arched and limbs entangled.

Right. Fuck.

I tore the canvas from the wall, pins clattering around my cubicle. The paint was just dry enough that it wouldn't smear, still a little tacky to the touch. I rolled it frantically into a limp tube and stuffed it in the corner of my cubicle just as Moody rapped her knuckles on the wall beside the doorway. "Jo, ready for a chat?"

I nodded and tried to look anywhere but at the canvas. She leaned against my desk, her pants pressing into the edge of raw wood. I was afraid of being a mess. My worst fear was that she would stand up again and I'd find evidence of all my chaos on her in a mark of paint across the back of her thighs.

"You've been working hard," she said. She traced a finger over a pile of discarded sketches, then drifted to my stack of loose canvases. She gestured to the one on top—the painting of the five of us on the beach. "That one's new. Did you have a good break?"

I searched for an answer that wasn't pitiful and ended up with "I never left."

She hummed. "Hard worker. How do you feel about Survey?"

Wasn't that the question? Knowing my own feelings felt like wisdom out of my reach. I needed someone else to fill me in after reading it on my face.

"I want to ask you how I should feel," I admitted, "but I know that's a terrible question."

Moody laughed. "I can tell you what *I* feel. I think you've created some special pieces. The past few months have pushed you to explore something that really matters to you, and that value comes across in the work."

I followed her eyes as they scanned the beach painting. On the canvas, we were eons from winter. White sun overhead, dark water sloshing against the rocky shore, dunes sloping like a mountain range. Five women standing in the water. Light refracting across the world.

That summer trip, Finch drove us everywhere. We liked to be in the car more than anything, Caroline queuing songs we'd all loved as teenagers—"Diplomat's Son," "Silver Soul," "Congratulations." Amrita sat up front with Finch, fiddling with the aux cord when its loose wiring would give out. We hung our arms out the windows. We listened to "Super Rich Kids" four times in a row because Saz kept saying, "*Again! Again!*" like she was a little kid on a roller coaster, hands flung up in the air, waiting for the drop.

It was music all the time. On the beach, in the kitchen, sound warbling out of my waterlogged speaker on Caroline's back porch. It was enough tequila to fend off an inevitable hangover, hair of the dog, except the dog never strayed anywhere we couldn't easily call it back from. Finch was our bartender. Squeezing limes all night. She liked to make things personal, liked to watch you take the first sip. By the end of the night, we all just wanted a heavy pour in a cup of something carbonated or sweet, but Finch still insisted. Wanted to be the one the rest of us could depend on.

In the mornings, Amrita made us breakfast. We relied on the raspberries we plucked from the tree line, endless baskets of red with each haul sweeter than the last. Caroline would sit at her grandmother's piano and bang out tunes while we ate. Saz liked to lay herself halfway across its sleek body, crooning like a jazz singer to the repetition of "Hot Cross Buns." She wanted to make us laugh. She was so good at it.

We mostly wore Caroline's clothes, each of us somehow finding something that fit—oversized sweatshirts, loose summer dresses—and we kept laughing and saying, *sisterhood, sisterhood, sisterhood.* By the end of the week, everything smelled like woodsmoke and old sun. Grass stains on the elbows. Sunscreen clinging to the collars.

At night by the fire, Saz talked about stars and birth charts and told us all the ways the universe predicted our lives in signs and nodes. The water was a deeper black than evening. I couldn't believe how old I was and how fucking young I felt. It was like playing at adulthood, ignoring all the ways we ought to grow up.

I imagined that this was what it was like to be in love: how people said it rose unbidden and unnamable.

Sometimes I forgot that we'd been a complete unit for only two years, that there were things they didn't know about me and they had secrets I wasn't privy to. That week on the beach came with a shift— some innate understanding that we were safe with one another. We had time to unfurl. Maybe they didn't know me entirely yet, but they liked me so far. If I spoke up, they'd look at me and listen.

"I'd live like this forever," Caroline had said, sprawled out on her back under the stars, fire painting her in shades of hell. "We could get a house, just us, and spend the rest of our days exactly like this."

"You want kids, though," I said, because I wanted her to know I remembered.

She cocked her head thoughtfully. "Yeah, I guess I do. But you guys could be their aunts. It'd be a cool way to grow up."

Amrita hummed like she was sloshing the idea around in her mouth. "I think we'd make great aunts. I'll have some practice when my sister's baby arrives."

"Will she let me test my aunt skills on that baby too?" Saz asked, laughing and ducking when Amrita flicked sand in her direction.

"Your kid would grow up to be such a dick with us in the picture," Finch said. Her smile pressed into her bare knee as her arms wrapped around her legs.

Caroline laughed. "Perfect, that's what I'm hoping for."

"Imagine if they were straight," Saz said, horrified. "What the hell would we do?"

Caroline's laugh became a cackle. That set the rest of us off. I couldn't tell if it was the fire making me feel so warm or if it was the thought that life could continue like this with them by my side.

It was the first time that anyone had suggested such an idea. The first time I learned it was the only thing I'd ever wanted enough to make myself sick.

That moment on the beach seemed so far from me now as Moody hovered a few inches away from the painting. When she straightened again, her eyes caught on the rolled-up canvas in the corner. I held my breath until Moody gave me her full attention again.

"You're still keeping something out of the viewer's reach. You give us these scenes of intimacy, and you make us feel excluded from them. I don't think that's entirely a problem, because maybe that's the point. Maybe we're supposed to be aware that we don't fit into this group and we never will, no matter how many private moments we're permitted to witness. But if you won't let us love them, we need to understand why you do. And to me, it still feels like you've built a barrier between your audience and your subject. One that you probably keep between yourself and your subject as well. If you can't cross it, how do you expect the rest of us to try?"

I followed her gaze to where Caroline's head was outlined in the faintest trace of yellow, hair whipping in the wind. Finch with her arms looped through mine and Caroline's. Saz half-turned, knee-deep in the water. Amrita leading us farther into the depths.

"Kolesnik said the same thing once," I said quietly.

"Kolesnik was an asshole," Moody said. "I'll be the first to admit that. He was sexist, and self-absorbed, and he held little regard for anyone's feelings other than his own. He was my professor, too, you know, in his first years at Rotham during my undergrad. I'm no stranger to the way he carries himself—or, carried. Sorry."

Truthfully, I hadn't known that. Moody ran her thumb along the frayed edge of my canvas. "I have to ask everyone about what St. Roche found. I've always been honest with you, Jo. I hope you all will be honest with me."

Looking at her would have given me away. I made a fist around the brushes in my hand, thin wood crackled from sitting in cups of solvent for too long.

"Of course," I finally answered, knowing I was a liar, knowing that I would be forever if it meant keeping that ritual to us alone. Maybe that was part of what Moody was talking about: my inability to take down the walls that encased my deepest desires could end in my own destruction.

I considered it and decided that I didn't really care. It was such an easy pleasure to keep them all to myself, to let everyone else know they'd never see inside.

"You didn't have anything to do with it, did you? You wouldn't have disrespected Rotham property like that."

She ended with a statement rather than a question. She gave me so much room to slip out of her reach.

"Never," I said.

"Good." She gave my painting one more glance and waved her hand in its direction. "You know · · · what if you brought the viewer into the painting? You have these defined figures that almost become characters in your narrative. What if you painted some kind of representation, like a blank figure, or a symbol, that lived in each painting like a stand-in for the audience?"

I nodded and considered. "I like that," I said.

Moody grinned. "Good. Give it a try. Now I won't take up any more of your time, I'm sure you have plenty of preparation to do."

"I'll keep working," I said. "I'll be ready for Friday."

Winter

INFESTATION

14

FAILURE TO CONJURE

Saz threw up the morning of Survey. Amrita sat on the edge of the bathtub and held her hair back as Saz clutched the toilet with a white-knuckled grip.

"I'm so fucked," Saz wailed into the bowl. "I'm so, so fucked."

"Saz, everything is going to be fine," I said from the doorway. I watched them in the mirror, Amrita's hands twined in Saz's black hair, Saz's shoulders heaving again. My stomach churned. I had to close my eyes.

"I told you that Moody said she didn't think I was ready," Saz wept. "It's that farmer's fault, he screwed everything up by finding the Boar King. The book said never to move the effigy unless you were prepared for the spell to unravel. Now Moody thinks everything I make isn't good enough, and I'm supposed to show up with a smile on my face? Not happening."

Amrita shifted her grasp on Saz's hair. "I thought you said you found the ritual on Reddit?"

"Whatever, that's what I meant," Saz answered as she pressed her forehead to the porcelain.

"Moody just said that she could tell you didn't feel confident about the pieces you're showing," I tried. "And I mean, she was kind of right. Your face is in the toilet."

"Jo, if I could stand right now, I'd throttle you," Saz said weakly.

"No throttling, we're going to be late."

That was Caroline's voice from behind me. I turned to find her inches away from me, her cool eyes fixed on Saz.

There was something so eerie about Caroline over the past week, a chilling distance to the way she moved throughout the house. It was like a switch had flipped since she returned from break. She was on edge, increasingly erratic. The behavior sparked a new fear in me; it felt like further evidence that our ritual had changed something. The Caroline who awakened me before dawn in my bed did not feel like my friend.

"Moody ragged on the rest of us all week too," Amrita said softly to Saz, giving Caroline a look out of the corner of her eye that said, *please, not now.* "Everyone is stressed over Survey. It's not the 'failing ritual' or a symptom of your work. You're a good painter, and the fact that you got to this point is enough to prove that." She paused, waiting for Saz's acknowledgment. "Okay?"

"Okay," Saz whimpered.

Amrita smoothed Saz's hair back and tied it with an elastic. "Alright, come on. Let's get you cleaned up and feed you a piece of bread. No coffee until you have something in your stomach."

I stepped back to give them room and found that Caroline was already gone, the doorway empty and the house quiet.

Survey was held in the gallery on the ground floor of Grainer, where the walls were freshly painted and lights made bright circles against the plaster. It was the same space where everyone who didn't end up Soloing would show our collective group work. Tall windows welcomed in morning light. The hall that led from Grainer's entrance to the gallery door was lined with stacks of paintings, with Phoebe at the front preparing to go first, then Veda and Cameron behind her with two spots left in front of them for Caroline and Amrita. We filed in accordingly to prop up our work against the wall. Inside the gallery, the floor was coated with layer after layer of gray paint to make the space neutral enough to complement any work that was hung. Rows of wooden folding chairs filled the room, enough for our critiquing panel as well as students from different majors who wanted to tune in for the show. The first row was seated: Moody predictably at the center with St. Roche to her right, and our surprise guests on either side of them. I didn't recognize a few of the faces—they were likely local artists or critics with some debt to Rotham, or alumni that wanted to see the work our class was making. Interspersed throughout those strangers were some familiar professors: Lizbeth Enriquez, Jessica Fujioka, Pat Williams, and an empty chair with a photo of Kolesnik on it. Another memorial to a poltergeist.

"We have to look at *him* the whole time?" Amrita muttered beside me as we hunted for seats.

"It's sabotage," Saz whispered, still looking green. "They want to watch me spiral."

Caroline sighed. "Not everything is about you, Saz."

Caroline sat at the end of our row—she was first out of our group to go, alphabetically right after Phoebe, so she wanted to be able to slip out easily. Saz flipped Caroline off as Phoebe pinned up her collages. My leg bounced ceaselessly. Saz's anxiety had rubbed off on me, clung like taffy to my teeth. It had been another sleepless week of struggling to fine-tune what work we were going to present. At this point, I was pretty sure my body was 85 percent caffeine. My sweat would perspire the color of weak coffee.

Moody stood at the head of the room. Phoebe teetered behind her atop a ladder, hammering pins through her painting into the wall. Moody had to raise her voice to be heard over the hammer.

"I'm sure many of you are familiar with the process of Survey. But we'll run through it again for our distinguished guests." She gave said guests a gratifying smile. Her hair was swept out of her face—the one earring glittered under the gallery lights.

"There are eleven of you showing your work this year. Each of you will have ten minutes to set up and take down your work, and thirty minutes of actual critique. We'll open the last few minutes up for any students who might like to comment on their peers' work. I encourage you all to take notes, ask questions, and absorb the feedback our guests provide. On Monday morning we will post our list of the five students who have a chance to advance to Solo. Out of those five students, we will evaluate the growth you apply to your work throughout the spring semester and select from your ranks our Solo candidate."

She clasped her hands in front of her and smiled. "Good luck to you all."

Phoebe descended the ladder. "Ready to go, Captain."

"The floor is yours, Ms. Arnett," Moody said as she returned to her seat in the front row.

It was a bit of a curse to show your work first. Phoebe likely resented her last name for designating her placement. We'd all been coming to public Surveys for the painting students ever since our freshman year—they were tense back-and-forths, exemplary presentations, scourings of vulnerability. We knew what to expect.

Phoebe cleared her throat once, twice, and said, "Hey, guys!"

"I'm already tired," Amrita whispered, fingertip pressed to her temple.

Phoebe's collages were not my favorite, but objectively intriguing. We took them in for a few silent moments—layered pieces of fabric and canvas in electric shades of pink clashing with yellow floral and blue denim. A shadow passed by the windows in front of the gallery and blotted darkness across the paintings. Beneath it I could just make out Phoebe's details. Small stitches of red and black, like ants on a picnic blanket. Real shoelaces woven through cuts she had made with a blade. Paint scrubbed here and there, as if she had needed to reach a requirement: a suggested horse, seashells outlined with white, the faint trace of a woman's profile.

"Your attention to detail is lovely, but it's difficult to discern where you intended the eye to follow," one of the guest speakers began. Phoebe's face rose and fell. "There's just so much happening at once. If you hoped to overwhelm the viewer, you've succeeded."

That fed the rest of them. The critiques began to flow. Phoebe was a stoic force with a smile still clinging to her face, and I had to hand it to her. Somehow she remained professional throughout their dissection.

"I need a smoke," Finch muttered, slipping out of her seat before I could catch her sleeve and stop her.

"We *just* sat down," I whispered, loud enough to have a few heads swiveling in our direction. But they quickly lost interest in us and followed Finch out of the room with their eyes until their heads were all the way back on Phoebe, whose expression had soured.

Thirty minutes felt like thirty seconds. I'd bitten my bottom lip bloody by the time Moody announced that Caroline would be next. Finch reclaimed her seat, smelling of smoke.

Veda and Mars helped Phoebe deinstall her pieces, and Mars kept a comforting hand on her shoulder. They were too far away for us to hear what they were saying, but I figured it was something encouraging to bandage the way the panel had just torn her work apart.

Moody gestured toward our row, and I followed Caroline into the hall to help her hang everything. The canvases were massive. We had to carry them one at a time with each frame held in our wingspan. "Careful with that one," Caroline said as I lifted one of the newer paintings. "It's still wet."

I obeyed, holding the canvas as far from my body as possible. Caroline took her place at the front of the room. There were five paintings in total—she had more, much more—but space only allowed for so many pieces, and these ones dwarfed everyone in the room. Caroline paused before the painting in the center as I hauled the ladder over and started drilling into the studs to hang the rest. The room was alight with low chatter. The closer I got to the overhead lights, the hotter they were against my hair.

"What the fuck?" she muttered, a hand grazing across her painting. She stopped at a gap in the canvas—a hole with the edges eaten away. Caroline spun and faced the rows of chairs. Everyone hushed, watching her, waiting. From above I could see her lip curling back, strands of hair sticking to her temples.

"Caroline?" I whispered. "You alright?"

She didn't answer me. Her eyes focused on a face in the crowd—Finch stared back with an eyebrow cocked in confusion.

"I'll kill her," Caroline whispered.

"Ms. Aster?" Moody prompted. "Your critique begins in two minutes."

Caroline pivoted back to the paintings without another word. There was seething rage in her face, the kind of anger I hadn't seen since the time her dad called junior year and threatened to pull her out of Rotham entirely if he didn't see her on the dean's list. I climbed back down the ladder and rushed to get it out of her way. Caroline thrust the last painting onto the screws and took her seat, all the fury schooled, the smile on her face a picture of excellence.

"Our guests will take time to consider your work," Moody said, "and then we will open the floor to you to hear your thesis."

Caroline nodded, but the flat heat in her eyes concealed something terrifying. I thumped into my seat in the back row again beside Finch, then stabilized myself with a prodding finger on her thigh. "What happened?" I whispered in a rush. "What did you do?"

Finch reared back. "What did *I* do? What are you talking about?"

Two of the guest critics stood to give Caroline's work a closer look. The paintings were expansive, primarily consumed by dark hues and texture. Deep cobalts, burnt maroons, lush emeralds. There was that swan painting from her first critique and an image of a woman clutching the belly of a tree, bark crawling over her skin where her thigh pressed against it. Another painting where the sky glowed a dirty, apocalyptic orange and birds were carved out of the paint rather than etched on top of it. Caroline's careful hand had marked out lavish details among broad strokes. Each one felt like the kind of landscape you'd find in a nightmare, some disquieting purgatory. They were all-consuming, precarious, devastating. The one in the middle was spotlighted by one of the bulbs overhead—it shone on the hole where something had eaten away at the canvas's fabric, the size of a child's fist.

"The scope of the work is fantastic," an elderly woman in the front row said. She had her hands clasped in a knot, fingers gnarled with age. "They're quite dystopic, are they not?"

"Absolutely," agreed Moody, "that's just the word I would have used."

"Like a scene from Dante's Inferno. Have you ever seen the Paris catacombs in person?" That was a pale bald man with frameless glasses in a tailored suit.

"Of course," Caroline said easily. Sometimes I forgot who she was—that when she said *of course,* she meant it, because it was true.

"You're a fan of Anselm Kiefer, I presume. Your work appears like his more colorful sister." The jovial voice belonged to a younger man, the long-haired, tortoiseshell-glasses type. Caroline nodded and laughed politely. He pointed to the hole in Caroline's central painting. "Can you tell me a little more about this?"

Caroline's smile calcified. "I prefer to let the physical details speak for themselves."

Moody waved a hand. "That's alright, you can go ahead and give us a little background about the work."

Caroline looked like she wanted to choke Moody silent. "That wasn't intentional," she said finally.

I nudged Finch. "I saw it up there, it looks like a burn. She's pissed."

Finch cut her eyes at me. "Okay? What're you trying to say, Jo? You think it's my fault that she screwed her work up?"

"Can you two please be quiet?" Amrita whispered.

I slouched in my seat, scolded. The way Caroline fixed her gaze on Finch as she said *I'll kill her* had me convinced that she believed Finch was to blame. I anticipated fallout—the arrival of that shadowed self

Caroline kept tucking out of view. But Finch just scoffed and turned back to face the display.

The young man stood before Caroline. "If it's damage, it's nicely done. I'd like to see what one of these would look like with a larger section burned out of them, maybe even sutured back together afterward. Not that I don't enjoy what you've added already, but I think you might as well embrace how destructive they are."

Destructive. I saw the word take root in Caroline. Her smile wavered, just a fraction.

Tortoiseshell man nodded. "There's a sense of loneliness in these huge expanses with such small figures, little vegetation, wounded animals. It's a scary place to be. I assume that's what you want us to feel— ultimate fear?"

Caroline hesitated. The gallery lights made spidery shadows out of her eye sockets. Her spine was rigid, her mouth cruel, eyes glassy.

"I think of them as the moments in between," she said. "It's a place to cross in search of somewhere better. You know that feeling when you're on a road trip driving somewhere remote and the land you're passing through feels like a simulacrum of the world? Something your mind fills in to make sense of all that space you're leaving behind? It's never felt real to me. I'm trying to capture that feeling—a test of mettle, to see if you can find your way out of that ersatz space."

"Nobody knows what the hell *ersatz* means," Saz mumbled, but the professors in the front row were nodding sagely and looking at Caroline with revered awe.

"Any comments from the crowd?" Moody asked. When no one responded, she checked her watch and announced, "Well, that's time anyway. Amrita Balakrishnan, you're up next."

15

Compel Fictions, Devour Visions

Saz went to help Caroline take her paintings down and cart them back upstairs to the studio while Amrita and I hung her work up. The process was simpler than hanging Caroline's had been—Amrita's paintings were all pieces of paper attached to thin board. All we had to do was stick museum putty in the corners and eye each piece with a level.

"Whimsical," the elderly woman said as Amrita took her seat, pen poised for notes.

"Such a wonderful sensibility for color," Fujioka said.

The comments for Amrita were kind but hesitant, as if they didn't quite know what to say. Her row of ten paintings all sat at the same size, about the height and width of her torso. They were rich with warm hues of yellow and lavender and sky blue painted with the attention of a light, illustrative hand.

"My mother liked to tell stories about our family," Amrita said. "As a kid, I always blew those stories out of proportion until they became myths. My grandmother riding a horse across town became a legendary outlaw preparing to lasso the love of her life. My mother stepping in an anthill became a specter standing in a field, body made entirely of insects. I wanted to make those daydreams physical and let the invented stories live on, larger."

Moody called her time, and I wanted to get the whole crowd on their feet to clap. Instead, the room rustled quietly, and Amrita plucked each painting carefully off the wall and stacked them together.

Then it was Veda, whose surrealist abstractions the panel compared to "putting Salvador Dalí in a blender and hoping the mixture didn't come out gray." Cameron followed, and they ate up everything he presented, much to Veda's (and the rest of ours) dismay. Finch had another cigarette during Cameron's critique—when she sat back down, I saw her hands shaking against her thighs.

"Alright, Jodie Finchard, come on up," Moody called.

Caroline resumed her seat at the end of the row. She had the distant look of someone deep in thought as Finch and Saz hung up the twelve pieces Finch had selected. The lights seemed to dim as I stared into those portraits—each one was a haunting removal of anything bodily, with the faintest outline of hair and shoulders against a rich panel of color. Only the eyes remained illustrated with care.

"There is so much light in these," Moody said proudly. "You've really mastered letting them glow beyond all the dark hues. And the contrast of your rendering of the eyes against the loose, painterly landscape is just delicious."

Someone in the crowd scoffed. Finch remained unbothered, shoulders slumped casually, elbows resting on her knees as she splayed them wide.

"*Delicious* is a great word. They're saturated with feeling." Tortoiseshell gave Finch an approving nod.

Something thumped behind me. The hair on my arms stood on end. I turned and caught a glimpse of the windows out of the corner of my eye—a fat insect bumped its body against the glass, trying to get inside. It was moving so quickly that its wings were a blur. It hit again. Then again, harder, so hard I almost expected to find a fine crack beneath its wings. There was a moment where I thought I could hear it flutter against my ear, and my fingers flew up to feel for it with a full-body flinch.

But the glass just kept thudding as the panel's voices fell into a dull drone. My mouth was dry. I dragged my tongue over my lips and swallowed nothing.

"You good?" Amrita whispered, and I just shrugged as Finch's voice called me back.

"They're meant to represent partial memories, the ones just out of grasp. Like spending time away from home and then trying to remember all the specifics of your father's face, and only being able to recall some of the most prominent details."

The panel hummed appreciatively. Caroline was rigid. The bug's body went *pat, pat, pat.* It looked like a moth—thick and gray with heavy wings. The sound made the hair at the nape of my neck prickle. I pressed down on my ear and muffled it.

"Any comments from the student body?" Moody posed, turning to face us.

"Yeah, I have one," Caroline said, with her hand lifted in the air. Every head swiveled to look at her. "Can you talk about your process? Where exactly do you find inspiration for your work?"

Finch had a slow, suspicious smile on her face. She spoke languidly, as if placating Caroline for asking something she already knew the answer to. "I don't really like to use any references. I try to sketch the same image ten or more times until the composition feels right, usually in pastels."

Caroline smiled back. "Let me rephrase my question. You mentioned your father and how you can't seem to remember his exact facial structure. When was it that you realized you couldn't bring the image to mind? Was it after he called you a miserable dyke?"

The room drew in a collective gasp. Amrita said Caroline's name like it was a curse. I was frozen. All I could think about was lying on the porch that last summer, spent from the sun, the five of us in a lapdog puddle. The house empty and dark. All of us a little high as Finch told us about the time she'd run away for a week when she was sixteen and exactly what her father had said to make her go. The way Caroline had leaned on Finch's shoulder, eyes squeezed shut and a hand on her knee and said—*I'm sorry, Finchard. Fuck that guy.*

"That must've been it," Finch responded lightly, "or it might have been the time yours told you your life wasn't worth the change he dropped between couch cushions."

A beat of profound silence. All I could hear was the gritting of Caroline's teeth and that moth's incessant thump. My fingernails dug into the skin of my earlobe until it stung.

"That's enough." The light drained from Moody's face. "If you have constructive criticism to share, I invite you to do so. But I'll remind you to be cordial to your peers while they're presenting. Let's take a break. Caroline, may I speak with you?"

Caroline followed Moody without a word. The room filled with rushed whispers. Thea spun around in her seat to face the remains of our group—Saz, Amrita, and me—and said, "Trouble in paradise?"

"I need a coffee," I muttered.

Caroline and Moody stood in the hallway as I left the gallery. I caught them on the fringe of whatever Caroline was saying—it sounded like *infantile behavior, no regard for anyone else's work*—and they clammed up when I passed.

I kept my head down the whole walk to Banemast, where the cafeteria was mostly empty. When I returned, paper coffee cup searing my scarred palm, everyone was seated again for Mars's critique. I could barely hear anything the panel said. Couldn't hold Mars's work in my head, all its patterning and vivid colors blurring before my eyes until it was nothing more than a hallucinatory glow. I didn't even have it in me to feel anxious about my critique coming next as Yejun followed Mars. All I could think about was the heat in my ears and the hum of the overhead lights and the thumping, the thumping, the thumping, the thumping.

Moody called my name. Everything tasted like static. Amrita's grasp on my fingers was the only thing that let me know I'd been shaking. She said something about helping me hang my work that I only half registered, and I moved like I'd been programmed, hauling my paintings into the gallery with Amrita on my heels and leaning them up against the wall where they were meant to hang. Caroline was still gone—only Saz and Finch sat in our row, watching me like I was an animal limping away from the scene of a hit-and-run.

As a collective the paintings were an exposed vein, pressed on and spurting. I could hardly bear to look at them and preferred to watch the panel's faces as they took them in. I'd spent so long planning how they might appear on the gallery wall that I could describe it without a glance. The *Gatherings* included the painting of the four of them around the table, several portraits of late dinners and our group surrounding the glow of the blue TV, a depiction of the Manor at night with them all peering out at me from their bedroom windows and backed by gold light, and finally, the five of us standing in Lake Michigan. More than anything, I'd wanted to hang the painting of our cornfield ritual. It was the piece I was proudest of out of anything I'd made yet—but it was too damning. I had, however, taken Moody's suggestion and worked a shadow figure into each of the paintings. Sometimes it was an active participant in our world. Sometimes it was just a distant blip on the horizon.

"You've managed to build an impressive collection," Moody said.

The ceramics professor chimed in right after her. "It's rare for a student to present a body of work that feels this cohesive. You seem to have a firm grasp on theme, and your depictions have a lovely sense of chiaroscuro."

"I agree, they're very cinematic and eerie. Like stills from a horror film," Tortoiseshell said. "Did you intend for your figures to feel so impenetrable?"

It probably wasn't his intention, but I took it like a compliment. I gave a weak smile and tried to direct my gaze somewhere other than his stare as I answered. But my eyes fell on the memorialized chair with Kolesnik's photo.

The photo was gone. The seat was now occupied by an increasingly familiar horned shape. It was less an animal and closer to human, like a body in an ill-fitting costume, the limbs too long, the edges of it frayed with the impression of fur. Its tusks curled up and over the mouth and nose. Lidless amber eyes peered back at me. The dry corner of my lips cracked, and copper flooded my mouth with the sting.

Moody's face crinkled with concern as she turned to look at the spot I couldn't tear my gaze away from. The creature stared at me, unbothered. Its eyes were so alive. They seemed to beg me to speak.

"It hurts," it said with Kolesnik's voice.

Said was the wrong word. It was more like the echo of a scream, as if Kolesnik's voice started down in hell and crawled along a thread, tin cans held to the ears, a makeshift séance between worlds.

"Jo? Is everything alright?"

"I'm . . ." The words wouldn't come. I blinked a hundred times and opened my eyes each time to find that boar man. It was so massive, so impossibly opaque. The room filled with the snuffling sound of its breath. A low whine slipped from its spent throat. Saz stood up, her face appearing over its shoulder with worry written all over it.

The creature keened a desperate sound. The head rolled back and forth. "It hurts," it wailed again. "It hurts it hurts it hurts it hurts."

The gallery's door slammed shut. I looked away from the creature to find Caroline hovering in the doorway. Her gaze flitted over the panel and finally fixed me with a burning stare.

"I'm so sorry," my body said. "I think I need some air."

"Must be the nerves," I heard someone say behind me, but I was already brushing past Caroline and hurrying down the hall. "No need for them, really, her work is quite moving."

I didn't know where to go. I let my feet take me down the promenade to Lysander Gate, where the garden slept dormant. Topiaries and sculptures watched me hurry forward. I nearly made it to the water before I had to crouch and dry heave in the grass. When I finally stopped retching, I wiped the back of my hand across my mouth and slid my fingers over my eyes, shaking, unraveling.

Tears had fallen without my noticing. They dried in frozen tracks, toes numb in my boots. The grass crunched when I sat. It was barely afternoon, and the world already felt close to dark. Evening kept coming quicker and quicker.

I didn't know how long I'd been gone, but the cold drove down to my core. As the sun fell, I was immediately aware of the consequences of being in the garden alone—the trees were too close, the woods too dark, water sloshing roughly at the pond's edge. I got to my feet. I'd missed Saz's critique by now. How long had everyone waited before they realized I wasn't coming back? Who had taken down my work?

By the time I got back to Grainer, the gallery was dark. The room had been cleaned and the chairs neatly put away. I carried myself up, and up, and up the old staircase, winding my way to the top. The studio was alive with rustling and stools screeching and someone hammering a nail into place. I followed the noise and found Finch in her studio. She whipped her head up when I knocked on the doorframe.

"Fuck, there you are. Where the hell did you go?"

"I—" I started, then faltered again. "I needed some air. Didn't feel well, but I'm okay now. Are you and Caroline . . . fine? How did Saz do?"

Finch grimaced. "The whole day was a shitshow, but they did okay. They called Saz's work 'dense' but 'intriguing,' which felt like code for 'we don't know what the hell we're talking about.' I guess shit hit the fan for all of us in some way. Are you sure you're alright? You look like you're about to throw up."

"I think they liked you," I said softly, letting the rest of her words fall away.

A new voice interrupted us. "Of course they liked her. All she does is throw the rest of us under the bus and kiss their asses in the meantime."

I turned to find Caroline in the doorway. Saz and Amrita followed close behind, likely anticipating the mess that was about to unfold with Caroline's raised voice.

Finch froze. "What exactly do you mean by that?"

"You know what I mean," Caroline said, smiling.

"No, I don't think I do. If you're going to accuse me, then accuse me. Have a fucking conversation with me instead of trying to make insulting quips during my Survey."

"I just think it's funny that you take a smoke break right before my critique, and then I find a massive burn in my painting."

Said painting was propped against the wall outside of Caroline's studio now. The burn almost appeared bigger, blackened around the edges as if it had spread in the short time between Survey and now.

Finch gave a disbelieving laugh. "You're ridiculous. You know I wouldn't do that."

"Do I?" Caroline's stare was a challenge. Her pale dress made her appear taller, as if she were growing toward the ceiling where the fans spun, flickering light and shadow, light and shadow, light and shadow. "I think you'd do anything to be chosen for Solo."

"Are you serious? *I'm* the one who would do anything? I don't give a fuck what happens, Caroline! You're the one whose parents pin her whole worth on whether she shows twenty paintings to a bunch of washed-up, wine-drunk professors."

"Finch, stop," Saz pleaded. "Both of you, come on."

Caroline ignored Saz and stepped closer to Finch, index finger pointing hard. "I'm sick of you acting like you're better than the rest of us."

Finch rolled her eyes. "Jesus, this again. When have I ever said that?"

"You don't have to say it. I can—" Caroline cut herself off, her chest heaving.

"Go ahead, speak your fucking mind," Finch snapped.

"You want to win without having to accept accountability," Caroline said immediately, her lip pulling back in disgust. "If the rest of us fail, it makes it easy for you to reap the benefits and go on being Moody's favorite pet. You don't care what that means for us. What we'll lose in the process."

"As if *you* could ever lose anything," Finch said, her smile cold and mocking. She shrugged and said, "You'll be fine, Caroline. You're just mad they liked my work better."

Amrita stepped between them. "Enough. Get out. Go."

Finch looked at her, appalled. "Why do I have to leave? She interrupted *my* Survey!"

Saz had an arm around Caroline, steering her away, murmuring something under her breath.

Amrita's voice was strained. "I cannot have you both in this room right now. You're friends, remember? You're supposed to care about each other and not ruin what was supposed to be a good day."

"God," Finch sighed, fingertips pressed over her eyes. "Whatever, fuck this. I need to get my bag from the Manor. Jo, can you let me in?"

I blinked back, surprised. "Sure, yeah, of course."

I gave Caroline one more glance over my shoulder as we left Grainer. She stood rigidly outside of her studio, staring at the burned painting. Saz put a gentle hand on Caroline's arm as if hoping to comfort. But I knew she couldn't. Caroline was too close to immolating.

Finch called my name one more time, and I followed. We walked the promenade in silence.

"I know what you're thinking," Finch snapped, "and I didn't do it."

I stayed quiet. I was thinking about the burn. But I was also thinking about Caroline and how worried I was that something crucial had snapped within her. Caroline needed Solo like it would keep her alive, but so did the rest of us. There was no way to win.

"I don't understand why you always take her side," Finch said when I still hadn't answered. "You let her get away with anything just because she's Caroline. She could kill someone, and you'd go about your day as if nothing had happened, saying the person had probably deserved it."

I flared with a combination of guilt and irritation. "*We* killed someone and he *did* deserve it."

Finch balked. "You don't actually believe that, do you? He was old as dirt, Jo, and blew half his brains out with a tissue box every week. We are not responsible for the natural order of life, no matter how many internet rituals we act out."

We paused at the Manor's front door. I fumbled with my keys. "Listen, I'm not taking her side. I'm not taking anyone's side. I just want us all to make it through this year without losing our minds."

Finch stopped my fidgeting with her hand on my wrist. Her fingers were so cold. I wished I had gloves to give her, that I could tuck her fingers inside of them and clutch them between my own.

"I didn't do it," Finch whispered. "I need you to believe me. You especially, out of all of them, or else I have nothing to stand for."

Everything about her face pleaded with me—the wisps of her hair curling out from beneath her hat, the pink of her cheeks, the intensity of her gaze.

"I know you didn't," I said, and as the words rushed out, I realized that they were true. Finch was evasive, clever, too blunt—but she could never be cruel. That was what made her and Caroline so similar, what made them grate against each other so viciously. They could pick and prod at one another, but the tension always melted away to reveal barely concealed admiration.

And while I knew that, there was a terrified part of me that wondered what had burned the painting, if not Finch. I thought about the shadow of the Boar King by the water, perched on the end of my bed, seated at the gallery, living in the blackest corners of my mind. I wondered how physical something had to become before it could cause harm.

When she didn't answer, I said, "I'm sorry, of course you didn't. I know you wouldn't do something like that."

We stepped inside, and she grabbed her bag off the sofa before hesitating. Hypocritically, she said, "You look exhausted. Promise me you'll try to get some sleep."

I promised her. Finch pulled me into a hug, her breath warm against my cheek, hands firm at the small of my back. I shut my eyes and inhaled the scent I'd always associated with her—smoke, apple, something warm and nutty.

"I don't like any of this," she whispered. "It scares me."

With my eyes closed, I could feel her pulse where my forehead met the thin, cool skin of her temple. My brain sabotaged me with images against my eyelids—the eyes of the boar and its hulking humanoid shape.

"We'll be alright," I murmured.

Voices rose in the distance, coming closer—Amrita arguing with Saz, the words impossible to make out but the tone unforgettable. Finch stepped back and said she had to go. I let her walk away, let her leave us behind, let the rip down our center stretch wider. I closed the door behind her.

In my room I tried to wipe the day from my mind. Clearly there was something wrong with me, if no one else could see the monster we had created. If I could fix it—if I could make up for my faults, for all the ways we had fucked up—maybe Kolesnik would leave me alone.

Amrita knocked on my door and asked if I wanted to talk. I pretended to be asleep until she went away, and when the house at last grew quiet, I went around my room and took all the mirrors down.

Out of sight, out of mind. The night passed with only a blink of sleep. Was I out of my mind?

16

THE PASTORAL STAIN

Mid-December brought the season's first snow. Winter in Indiana had a parasitic cold that burrowed deep in my teeth, smarted in my throat until it left a twinge of pain with every swallow. We were instructed not to fuck with the Manor's old fireplace, but Saz made it her mission to coax the hearth to life. This involved several trips to the woods past the garden and lots of crumpled newsprint subjected to Saz's lighter. The radiators already kept the house too hot, and the thought of a fire was awful enough to make me want to sleep in Grainer. But the idea of more time in Grainer was its own hell.

We spent the weekend after Survey on edge, Finch flighty and Caroline shut up in her room. If she ate or used the bathroom, I never saw it happen. Snacks and cold mugs of tea collected outside her door. I could hear her talking through the wall we shared. It was an endless, furious muttering, the kind of relentless monologue that left me unsure if she was taking several phone calls or talking heatedly to herself in the mirror.

Amrita and I went on a walk to get away from the Manor, she enthusiastically and I reluctantly, wind biting down to bone and leaving me shivering by the time we circled the promenade. Finch's hyacinth had crusted over on my arm and kept opening again every time

I showered. I could feel its raw edges rub up against the material of my sweatshirt beneath my coat.

Amrita looped her arm in mine and slid her hand into my coat pocket. Our fingers laced together, and her palm kissed heat against my own.

"You know you can talk to me about anything," Amrita urged after a while, the only sound the soft huffs of our exhales. "You haven't been acting like yourself ever since all that stuff went down with Kolesnik, and I still don't understand what happened at Survey."

Amrita and I had known each other longer than anyone else. She held my hair the first time I got sick from drinking, made me soup on the common-room stove, rubbed my back after nightmares that woke us both. When she broke her ankle freshman year after we tried to sled down a hill in the garden, I slept beside her hospital bed, slumped in a chair with my head pillowed on her thigh. I don't know why it always surprised me when she knew me—when she could see past the weak barriers I tried to build.

"I know. I'm sorry," I said, the words rough with shame. "I still feel horrible for missing Saz's critique."

"That's not what I'm talking about, and you know it. You ran out like something was after you, Jo. I've never seen you so scared."

I risked a glance in her direction. She focused ahead, her profile the only thing in sight—the long slope of her nose, black lashes, full lips pressed into a concerned line, color deepening in her cheeks with the chill, thick hair bunching up around a scarf that used to be Caroline's.

"Everything was overwhelming," I said finally. "You know, Finch and Caroline were at each other's throats, and I guess I panicked after they started to fight. I just wanted everything to go smoothly. And I haven't been sleeping much. I don't know, I think it's all catching up with me."

Another squeeze. Amrita's brow furrowed, but she didn't push me any further.

I didn't tell any of them what I'd seen. I was terrified of being the one that couldn't take the heat, of fracturing us further and outlining all the thin places we could shatter. They were already so aware of my mannerisms that I had made it easy for them to know I was suffering. There would be no concealment of emotion—but I made a pact with myself. My demons would remain my own.

With Monday came the threat of Moody's list.

Our first class after Survey felt like a funeral. Caroline stood as far away from Finch as she could get. The room tittered with awareness, everyone recalling the way Finch and Caroline had publicly negged each other and my untimely exit. Saz crossed and uncrossed her legs again and again as Moody settled onto her stool. I had another goddamn headache. It was hard to remember the last time I'd felt healthy. Something in the studio smelled metallic, like a coming nosebleed.

"To say I'm disappointed would be an understatement," Moody started. "Rotham expects a certain respect for your peers, your predecessors, and yourself. Several of you"—she paused to give us a hard look—"disregarded these values."

I slumped lower in my seat and hoped to dissolve into dust.

"However, the events of your Senior Survey have made it clear to me that the loss of Kolesnik had a greater toll on you than I had previously realized. I explained the recent tragedy to our panel of critics, and, luckily, they were very understanding. They were impressed by the caliber of your artwork, despite all interruptions."

The paper in her hands was creased with months of reading. It was the same roster she'd greeted us with on day one.

Amrita touched my shoulder from her perch on the stool behind me. It was likely supposed to be a show of comfort, but I seized up beneath her hand, heartbeat roaring in my ears.

"We've narrowed down our Solo selection to the five students we believe to be most capable of presenting a unified body of work at the end of the semester. You've all worked incredibly hard and deserve to be recognized for it. But Rotham is a rigorous institute, and our Soloist's revered position exemplifies dedication. The following five students have the chance to show *en Solo*."

I folded my arms across my chest and pinned my hands beneath my armpits to stop their shaking. I inhaled until my chest began to ache.

"Caroline Aster," Moody began. "Amrita Balakrishnan, Jodie Finchard, Mars Jackson, and Joanna Kozak."

Silence settled over the room as Amrita's hand on my shoulder squeezed hard enough to clutch bone. I heard her whisper something that sounded like *shit, Jo.* My ears rang, the skin there so hot I thought it might be wet.

The others made sense—but *me*? I could hardly remember if the panel had even said anything good about my work. It was over the moment I locked eyes with the specter in Kolesnik's seat.

And she didn't say Saz's name.

Cameron said, "Are you fucking serious?"

"Excuse me?" Moody asked, flushing pink.

"Aster and Finchard treat Solo like a dick-measuring contest, and Jo didn't even hear her critique for more than five minutes before she had to leave. The only people on that list who deserve a Solo spot are Mars and Amrita."

"Good thing they're on the list and vying for a spot then, right, Mr. De Luca?" Moody said sharply. "As I said, our decisions were made based on merit and the quality of a painter's work. Of course, critique is an important factor. But in a gallery setting, the work will speak for itself. We brought the same considerations into our evaluation."

Cameron simmered with anger. The rest of the class sat in stunned silence.

If Moody were honest, she would admit that Rotham wanted a bloody showdown, wanted to pit us against each other and watch how we'd descend into madness. Because that had to be the answer. If merit was meant to carry me, I should have been dropped somewhere along the line. Every painter at Rotham knew that the best Solos were always the ones born out of chaos and competition. You got vicious, laudable work when you thought it was the only chance you'd ever get. And this *was* our only chance—one that had to be seized, wriggling and desperate.

We were supposed to put on a show. I would play the part of unsound augur facilitating my own end, and Caroline and Finch would tear each other apart. Mars was entirely capable and deserving of the spot, but I closed my eyes and prayed it would be Amrita. No one could ever stay mad at her, and her work was incredible. Besides, if Caroline and Finch had nothing left to hold over one another, what reason would they have to hate each other?

Moody tapped her pen against her palm. "On Thursday, we'll take the train into Chicago to view the Art Institute's Henry Fuseli exhibition. I want you to use this visit to consider the works that inspire you and to take notes on how you experience them in person. Regardless of the post-Survey decision, you are all expected to complete your thesis papers for submission at the end of spring semester."

Cameron got up, his stool sliding with a hard grate as he headed for his studio. Moody released a long exhale through her nose. "Any questions? No? Good. I'll be going around to have a chat with each of you. Meet me at the train station to take the eight o'clock to Chicago, bright and early."

Caroline was gone by the time I turned toward the studios—I expected she had followed Cameron's example and headed to her cubicle.

"I don't understand what her problem is," Finch sighed when I fell in step beside her. Amrita and Saz were already paces ahead of us, Amrita with a hand on Saz's back, rubbing slow circles.

"Who?" I asked, distracted. I wanted them to wait up. I wanted to tell Saz I was sorry.

"Caroline," Finch continued. "She got exactly what she wanted, and she's still throwing a fit."

"Well, she's mad about the burn. You'd be upset if you were in her place."

"Yeah, at one of *them*," Finch emphasized, gesturing loosely around the studios. "Never any of you. We wouldn't do that to each other."

The words warmed me. I was always so afraid that she didn't feel the way about us that we felt about her. Or, at least, how *I* felt about her.

Saz stopped in the doorway of her studio ahead of us. Finch faltered when she noticed me slow down. "What's up?"

"We should talk to Saz."

Finch's face fell, just a fraction. "She might want some space."

I ignored that and said, "Go ahead. I'll catch up."

I could feel her eyes on me but waved her on again without meeting them. I didn't want to have to address whatever I might find there. When she finally went on without me, I retraced my steps to Saz's studio doorway.

She crouched in her studio, the contents of a tote bag emptied on the floor as she rummaged for something. Her skirt made a splayed circle across a pile of abandoned drawings.

"You should be on that list," I said to her back, "not me."

Saz paused with her hand around a lighter. She flicked it once, twice, and then thrust it back into her bag without looking at me. "None of that," she said at last. "If anyone was going to be nominated, I'm glad it was you. You're amazing, Jo, and you deserve your spot."

"You know you're equally incredible," I answered, because I knew putting myself down would only make her angry.

"Well, you didn't see my critique, did you?" Saz smiled. Her lashes were wet. She kept herself mostly angled away from me, but those tears in her eyes broke me up inside.

"I'm sorry, Saz," I mumbled, another useless apology. Guilt was a mechanism built into my heart. I ran on shame.

"Shut up, no apologies. I'm happy for you, Jo, I'm just sad for me, too."

She held her hand out. I took it, made a bridge out of us in that little room.

"I can talk to Moody," I tried again. "I think she's made a mistake. I can offer my spot, or maybe we can—maybe she'll reevaluate, maybe—"

I saw the frustration rise in her face. "Seriously, drop it. I can't—I can't do all this right now. Thanks, but it's too much." Saz's eyes were flat when her fingers squeezed mine and then slipped away. "Go. Moody will be making her rounds soon."

I didn't even try to find Caroline, too afraid of the barbs I might uncover. Obediently, I went to my studio. One of them had collected my paintings after Survey and stacked them in a pile on my desk. They waited there with the cornfield canvas still rolled up in the corner. The sight made my throat sting with emotion.

I'd spent so much time comparing myself to the rest of them. I didn't know how to be proactive about my hope the way they always had, intentional about their desires and distinct in their dreams. Saz wanted a piece in the Tate Modern. What did I have to show for myself other than the prayer that my parents wouldn't disown me for choosing a school whose scholarship barely covered my housing? I knew that we were alike in a million ways, but it was the ways we were different that made us quiet.

And painting was a necessity by now, same as drinking water or sleeping more than a few hours or choking down something sustaining. Still, those necessities had failed me plenty of times. Sleep eluded me, and I had a hard time keeping anything down unless it was bland and tasteless. Dark shapes blotted the corners of my vision. I couldn't trust my own mind.

"You okay, Jo?"

Moody's simple question was enough to summon grief in me. I had to shut my eyes against the constriction of my throat. When I blinked them open again, I found her waiting next to my easel, unwilling to sit. Her discomfort was apparent—I made her uneasy. I wondered if we shared the same sleeplessness. There were bags under her eyes, tension written in the lines of her face.

"I thought you'd be more excited," Moody continued. "About the results of Survey."

"Why me?"

Banal question. Thoughtless tongue, roguish mouth. I knew it sounded like I was ungrateful, but I meant what I asked. Why would they choose me after the way I collapsed? If I couldn't trust myself to make it through Survey, how could I be expected to Solo?

Moody frowned. "Didn't you come to Rotham to create artwork that could stand on its own? Did you expect to be beside it every time an audience experienced it, explaining your meaning and ensuring that no one would ever misunderstand what you're trying to portray? That's the nature of art, Jo. You make it, and then you lose control. Interpretation is beyond your boundaries. In some ways, it's an awful idea to come to terms with, and in others, it's remarkably freeing. You can keel over in the middle of a critique, and if the panel's still enraptured when you're gone, you've done something right. You did it right. You made them want more."

I had to lean against my desk for stability. The edge of the table dug into the backs of my thighs. "More?" I murmured, wrapping my arms around my middle.

"Solo is important for a reason. Rotham creates an environment that pushes you beyond your limits. It's meant to force you as far as you can go, to test your relationships with your peers and your work and your drive. The student that Solos shows us that they can sustain a life like the one Rotham has given you."

"I don't know if I'm that kind of student," I said.

"Should I offer your spot to someone else?"

"No!" I rushed, shame slick in my mouth. No, of course not, but simultaneously yes—*give it to Saz, give it to anyone but me, don't let me be the one to bear it.*

"You earned it," Moody said, as if it didn't shatter me, as if I could take it. "It's an honor, Joanna, not a death sentence. The others will understand. It breaks them, for a bit. But down the line, those who don't Solo make do without it. You're all talented. But success takes a certain degree of risk that not everyone can accept."

And I can? I wanted to ask, but the words that tumbled out of my mouth surprised us both. "How do you cope with it? How can you bear getting what you want when it could mean leaving the rest of them behind?"

"I wish this wasn't the truth," Moody started, faltering. "But this life is temporary, Joanna. Friends move on. Peers lose touch. Community is important, but competition is hard. There were Jean-Michel Basquiat and Andy Warhol, Sally Mann and Cy Twombly, Paul Gauguin and Vincent Van Gogh, Helen Frankenthaler and Grace Hartigan, Edgar Degas and Édouard Manet. Friends, yes, but tragedies too. They were close but painfully critical, and many of them grew apart. Some people can't take that kind of scrutiny."

"We aren't like that," I said immediately. *Make me better than I am,* my heart begged simultaneously, *reinvent me.*

Moody's face fell, full of pity. "You chose this practice, and you get the consequences that come along with it," she responded softly. It wasn't really an answer at all, but it was clear that it was all I was going to get as she turned to go. "We'll discuss your thesis over the next few weeks as you prepare your Solo propositions. If you have any questions, you know where to find me."

She was right, in most ways—I'd chosen Rotham for the ways it would force me to grow, not for companionship. But now that I'd found my women, I couldn't imagine giving them up for anything else. Who was I as a Soloist, up there alone? They'd become the reason I wanted to paint anything at all.

I wanted someone wiser to tell me the answer. I thought that was why I came to Rotham in the first place—to be instructed and made anew. The only part of myself that I was certain about was my capability in loving them. The rest seemed inconsequential. Some part of me would always crawl toward the idea of "better." I wanted to fucking rest.

And really, if I was honest with myself, the worst part was the comparison. I wanted to be the kind of girl who didn't need sleep, who could survive on a coffee and a cigarette, who could paint until the automatic lights went off and fall asleep on the studio floor. But I was so tired. The corners of my life were crowded with phantoms.

What had we done the ritual for if the goal wasn't mutual ascension? To be closer to greatness and to one another? To make the most of this fear and to transform it into something beautiful?

17

GREEN CLING OF THE TRAMPLED

On Thursday, we took the train into Chicago. It was the kind of cold outside that made it hurt to breathe, cold the color of frostbite, cold like the dizzying scent of woodsmoke. The landscape beyond the train's windows was a sheen of gray and white, snow over everything, trees bending with the weight. It was the first time I'd been off campus in weeks. I didn't realize I was bouncing my knee nervously until Finch turned around in the seat in front of me to tell me to stop.

I sat with Saz, who slept on my shoulder the whole three-hour ride, bundled up in a puffy pink coat that nearly swallowed her whole. Her head poked out of the collar, a dark lump of hair brushing my chin whenever I shifted. The peachy warmth of her shampoo and her floral perfume rose around me in a cloud. She'd been quiet after the Survey decision, some of her light snuffed out, listless in her desires and her willingness to show up nearly on time for class. It was hard to get her out of bed before. Now she rarely set an alarm.

The city was adorned for the holidays with the same grace of a department store window, wreaths around the lampposts and the necks of statues, slush in the streets, gold lights glittering from awnings. We got off the Amtrak and took the L straight to the Art Institute of Chicago, where we'd spend the day considering influences for our thesis papers and examining the latest exhibitions. It was supposed to be a treat, Moody told us. A chance to think about something other than Solo and its inevitability—or, for the other six painters, its impossibility. She was our steadfast leader in fitted brown trousers, a thick beige turtleneck, and a pair of frameless glasses. Out of all the cliques that had formed within our class—Veda and Phoebe and Yejun clustered at the front vying for Moody's attention, Cameron with his arm around Mars, Thea behind them throwing looks over her shoulder at Finch—our five remained surprisingly quiet. Saz kept her arm looped in mine but her eyes on her phone. Finch checked her watch with a frown. Amrita sipped from a cup of train coffee that smelled amazing, but after she offered me a taste it settled on my tongue like tar. Caroline was dressed like she had come for a funeral: black dress to her knees, tall boots that rose to meet its hem, hair whipping in the wind. The only color was in the faint dusting of blue over her eyelids and the bloody bitten line of her mouth.

Painting students at Rotham made this trip annually. Past visits to the Art Institute had been some of my favorite extracurricular experiences—campus was so isolated from the rest of the world that it was hard to spend time with work that wasn't a part of Rotham's collection. Knowing that our thesis papers would play a part in who would Solo amped up the stress as the deadline loomed closer. I had a sketchbook in my bag with a pen hooked over its cover ready for the occasion. In its current state, my paper consisted of nothing more than fragments and the beginning of a thought from my notes app where I had started to type out a thought and fell asleep halfway through, the text devolving into a long line of hhhhhhhhhhhhhhhhh-hhhhhhh where my thumb had pressed down in my sleep.

We split up inside the museum, and I took my time meandering. Yearly visits had given me time to curate out my favored niches. I liked to start in the Arts of the Americas exhibition; there was always a crowd around Edward Hopper's *Nighthawks*, but I circumvented them in favor of trompe l'oeil still lifes of fruit and skinned birds, an avant-garde

Florine Stettheimer portrait that reminded me of Saz, lush Georgia O'Keeffe watercolors, a sweet Mary Cassatt depicting a woman bathing a child's feet. I took the long way around past the blue glow of Marc Chagall's stained-glass windows, through the Photography and Media gallery with Sally Mann's *Immediate Family* gelatin silver prints. Upstairs, I didn't slow until I reached the gallery I loved the most—Painting and Sculpture of Europe.

My affection had nothing to do with Europe itself. It was in the expansive nature of the collection—the massive Impressionistic pieces and sweeping old master paintings, that haunting intersection of religious iconography, fleeting glances of eighteenth-century life, Romantic disasters at sea. Again, I bypassed the spectators admiring Georges Seurat's *A Sunday on La Grande Jatte* and sought out a few of my favorites: *Resting* by Antonio Mancini, in which a nude woman reclined among downy pillows, her expression distraught, the paint built up with such a thick impasto effect that it seemed like she had been carved out of clay. Jules Adolphe Breton's portrait *The Song of the Lark*, depicting a lone barefoot woman in a field as she stood under a setting sun with a sickle in hand and her mouth hanging open as if in mid-plea. Then Juan Sánchez Cotán's still lifes of hanging fowl and peeled melon waiting to be devoured, hunger coiling in my stomach.

Finally, Francisco Goya's *Boy on a Ram*. It was a painting I returned to without fail. A young boy sat on a ram's back in decadent clothing. His hammy fist raised a switch high in the air. The ram beneath him had its head twisted away from the switch and the leaning boy, one serpentine eye gleaming red and wide. Behind them was a pastoral landscape, barely sketched out in pastel greens and blues. The boy's face was doll-like and blank. I'd sketched the composition a hundred times. I'd used the ram itself as inspiration for my Grotesque mask. There was something fascinating about the eerie distance of the boy's expression, the ram's wild eye, the startling juxtaposition of the boy's prepared violence and the idyllic landscape.

I leaned as close to the painting as I could manage without tripping any alarms. The overheads illuminated the boy's bulbous eyes and cherubic cheeks. Beneath one of the eyes I found a slit—the finest cut in canvas, a weeping wound.

Blinking wouldn't banish the sight. It only revealed new slices to me unfurling all over the boy's body, his fine clothes, the ram's toiling head. It looked like someone had taken an X-Acto knife to the whole portrait. Beneath each fine laceration was a black gap, an oily promise, like tearing open the fabric of a night sky and letting stardust pour out. A high-pitched whine kicked off in my ears, a close and bleating scream, the kind that nearly sent me to my knees.

"Miss! Step back!"

It took me far too long to register that the voice was aimed at me. My vision stuttered, and I yanked my hand back. One finger had been pressed to the surface of the painting, a nail digging against the ram's eye, threatening to puncture right through the canvas. I rocked away from the painting and held my hands up in defense. The shrill noise finally stopped ringing in my ears—it had been the sound of the alarm going off when a body got too close to the art.

The glaring security guard who had reprimanded me had one hand on his radio. "No touching the paintings. I have to ask you to move on before we need to escort you from the building."

"Right, sorry, I'm so sorry." My heart was pounding. "I didn't mean to. I'm sorry."

Every head in the room pointed in my direction. A quick and grateful glance told me that none of my women had witnessed my fuckup. The only familiar face I landed on was Thea, standing in the doorway to the gallery with her eyes narrowed directly on me. Cameron followed close behind her, laughing at something Mars said as they trailed in. I sped past them with the boy on his ram at my back, canvas unblemished despite the threat my thumb had posed. Like wiggling a finger into a wound and working it open, exposing the meat underneath.

The image was difficult to shake. I was scaring myself.

Unsettled, I wandered Contemporary Art in search of an escape, plucked a piece from Felix Gonzalez-Torres's carefully weighed mountain of plastic-wrapped candies and sucked it around my tongue for a sugar distraction, lingered by Kerry James Marshall's massive *Many Mansions*, let myself get lost in one of Agnes Martin's untitled grids. The abstract pieces in this gallery reminded me of Saz: Eva Hesse, Lee Krasner, Joan Mitchell, explosions of color and expressive brushstrokes. Finally, I found the back of a familiar head in the center of the room, seated before a Cy Twombly painting.

I slid onto the bench next to Finch and sat on my hands to hide the way they were shaking. "Knew I'd find you here," I said.

She was quiet, focused on Twombly's *Untitled (to Sappho)*. I watched her for a moment—her sharp profile, straight nose, fluttering lashes. Most of her hair was pulled away from her face with a clip, but choppy strands hung across her brow. Beneath them, her eyes flickered back and forth, back and forth.

I followed her gaze to the painting. It was a framed sheet of paper about the width and height of my arms if I held them out at my sides, mostly blank space, the creamy color of milk gone slightly beige with age and time. There were smudges and flecks of paint marked in spots. Accident, or the smallest hint of detail. On the left side was an oily purple mass, like a scribble marked out in crayon, the kind of shape you might imagine hanging over a cartoon character's head after an argument. A cloud of lavender and graphite, layer upon layer of wax and pencil. And to the bottom right were Sappho's words in Twombly's frenetic handwriting:

Voice like a hyacinth in
the mountains, trampled
by shepherds until
only a purple stain
remains on the ground

"He loved ancient Greece," Finch said. She was crying a little. She did that sometimes when she really loved a painting. The corners of her eyes glimmered with the feeling, and I pretended not to notice out of fear that my concern might make her stop speaking. "He's from Virginia, though I'm sure you know that. But he had a studio in Rome. People always look at his work and say shit like 'I could do that' or 'It looks like a child painted it,' but they don't see how devotional it is, how he linked this modern practice to such an enduring mythology, how he gave us these stories of divinity and queerness and devotion."

Finch shook her head and sucked her bottom lip between her teeth, then the top. "It's a sad fucking poem about the way marriage changes a woman. The girl's the hyacinth. We don't know how the marriage unfolds. We just know she's lost her freedom along the way. The original poem doesn't include the word *voice*, but I like to think that by adding it, he's telling us someone is speaking the words aloud and giving the painting a voice of its own. I don't know, I probably sound ridiculous. It's tough to even decipher his handwriting. But that's how the words make me feel. Like by reading the poem aloud with him, I'm following instructions and becoming that voice."

I didn't try to interrupt. Just let her ramble on about the emotion in the downward slope of his handwriting, as if Twombly's thoughts trailed off into nothing at the end. My gaze lingered on her thigh where I knew her own hyacinth was inked forever.

"I always think of you when I see this painting," I admitted after we'd been staring in silence for a while. Her face crumpled. I slid a hand free and circled my fingers around her wrist. Held tight.

"Sometimes I worry that it's a bad thing we know each other so well," she said finally. "I think it's hurting us."

You don't know everything about me, I wanted to say, but I was afraid it would be a lie. Instead, I shrugged and tried to keep my voice steady when I said, "I want to know you better than anyone. I don't care if it hurts."

Finch looked at me. Her smile was wry, her damp eyes halfway to rolling. "Fuck off," she murmured, that smile growing. Her pulse pounded in the thin skin beneath my thumb.

I was afraid that by loving her, I'd leashed her. There was nowhere she could go where I hadn't already touched. We were already so scuffed by each other and the downward spiral of this year. But the way she watched me was so open, so trusting, so calm—I wanted to tell her everything. The ripped-up ram. The Boar King in his front-row Survey seat. The figure at the edge of the pond, at the end of the bed, in the dark corners of my brain. The uneasiness Caroline's presence produced and Saz's desperate hope for magic.

But she had enough on her plate—we both did—with Solo's impending threat and Caroline's insistence on arguing. Despite her hardened exterior, Finch could be sensitive and overwarm, too willing to trust, too easy to wound. I wouldn't be another perpetrator of that hurt. Couldn't give her something else to worry about.

"There you are," a hard voice said to my right. I looked up and met Caroline's irritated expression. "You're late. We were all supposed to meet Moody on the Grand Staircase for lunch."

Her eyes flickered down to where I still held Finch's wrist. Disdain warred with something heavier in her face. I pulled my hand away and let it fall in my lap.

"Sorry. Thanks for finding us."

Finch tucked her hands back in her jacket pockets. She wouldn't look at me. I felt as if I'd done something wrong—crossed a line I shouldn't have, deepened an unseen rift. "Lead the way, Caroline," she said.

Caroline paused, gaze floating over our heads and landing on Twombly's Sapphic devotion.

"I hate that painting," she muttered, and then she turned from the room with us trailing after her like scolded children.

18

PRACTICE, PRACTICE, CRAFTED PRACTICE

Now that a Survey decision had been made, I set my alarm to go off before sunrise. Finch hardly stopped by the Manor anymore—she mostly circulated between Grainer, the library, and her apartment in Tuck House. Amrita kept her headphones on most of the time. She filled sketchbook after sketchbook with cramped drawings. Saz avoided the topic of Solo altogether and spent long nights in the studio working on a piece that took up an entire wall. She refused to let the rest of us see it. She claimed we could look when it was ready, but I was afraid that she was embarrassed to be left out, and hesitant to be perceived again.

And against Moody's clear instruction, Caroline occasionally slept on a cot in her white cubicle, though there wasn't much remaining white space to speak of. Anywhere that didn't hold a painting had been covered with magazine clippings from *Artforum* or *Hyperallergic*, collages and sketches, color palettes and reference photos. Her scribblings butted up against reproductions of paintings torn from the expensive coffee-table books Caroline ordered in droves—abstractions by Helen Frankenthaler, Renaissance depictions of the *Pietà*, and Jean Broc's dramatic and intimate *The Death of Hyacinthos*, in which a mournful Apollo cradled the slack dead body of his lover.

Sometimes we gathered in Banemast for dinner, though Caroline rarely stayed for longer than twenty minutes. She sat as far away from Finch as she could get and picked at her fingernails the whole time. Amrita's brow took on a permanent furrow of concern. Saz poked at her food while her phone buzzed with notifications—Instagram comments, package delivery notifications, dating app matches.

Our five had always established that Solo would not affect our friendships. Now I felt we'd been fractured—Finch, Caroline, Amrita, and I on one side, and Saz on the other without a direction to walk in.

I wanted to go back to our summer, back to a time before Solo had to be addressed. I was so afraid to be the last one missing them—terrified that I might be the only one who remembered who we had been and the pacts we made. If they forgot me, how could I show my face? How could I deal with the idea that maybe I loved them more than they loved me, that this mattered most to me, that they were okay with letting it dissolve?

I wanted to be free of all that fear. I followed routine and I went to the studio. I put the feeling in a painting, so something else could carry it for a while.

Moody had just left my studio for the last chat of the day when Saz appeared in the doorway. There was blue paint all over her dress, as if she'd been drenched in water. She gestured to my headphones. I slid them off. "Do you always have to wear those things? Don't you ever just sit alone with your thoughts?"

"I don't hate myself enough to do that," I answered, hooking the headphones around my neck. Tinny music played below my ears. "What's up?"

"We should have a movie night."

I blinked back at her. "Tonight? All of us?"

"No, Jo, next year."

I didn't dignify that one with a direct answer. "It's Thursday. We have critique tomorrow."

"So what? It's not like we haven't done it before."

The reminder felt pointed—a callback to who we'd always been. The smile on her face was hesitant, as if afraid I might actually turn her down.

I shifted on my stool. The painting before me was still wet. It was a landscape depicting the line of trees beyond Rotham, with the five of us sketched out between the trunks like iterations of Mother Crone and a shadow figure haunting us in the back. Moody had called it "phantasmal and unsettling," though she had appeared uneasy to say so. I couldn't get any of their faces right. I'd painted over each one what felt like a hundred times. The only thing that did feel right was the shadow figure—a perfect blur of deep green radiating out into gold.

"Have you asked everyone else?" I prompted, testing the waters.

"'Course. Even Finch said yes."

My heart loosened. "Whatever, I get it, ask me last."

Saz's smile melted into a grin. I was so happy to have put that look on her face, so delighted to watch her light up with feeling for the first time in what felt like forever.

We all met in the Manor after dinner and showers, wet hair plastered to the nape of my neck where it nearly froze in thick tendrils. The radiators were acting up and left the house colder than normal, so we made a nest of blankets on the living room floor. Saz coaxed a fire to life in the hearth. Finch settled onto the sofa beside Amrita, looking deliciously soft in her hoodie and sweatpants, haphazardly rinsed off eye makeup clinging to her waterline. Caroline sprawled out on her stomach to watch Sigourney Weaver grace the screen as *Alien* began. Saz sat beside me, our backs against the couch, my torso framed by Amrita's legs. Finch's knee brushed my left shoulder. I could have turned my head and kissed it.

It almost felt normal, all of us in that room, bundled close to each other with the lights off and another movie starred on the list beside the TV. Popcorn in a bowl. Beer bottles and hot toddies warring for space on our limited table surfaces. A candle burning somewhere, Saz's doing—cinnamon and vetiver and clove. Amrita made a comment about Sigourney's hair on the screen and how she thought mine might hold a curl like it, then scrunched her fingers through the wet ends. Finch stretched a foot out as her arms rose above her head, catlike and elongated, and the end of her socked foot bumped into Caroline's thigh.

Caroline jerked away as if burned. They gave each other sharp looks, Caroline's halfway to a sneer. Saz paused the movie and the room erupted in complaints.

"This has gone on for way too long," Saz declared. "You two are pissing me off. Squash whatever beef you have, now."

Caroline rolled over and sat up. "She burned my fucking painting," she said immediately.

"You cannot possibly still be hung up on that. Why would I burn it? What proof do you have?" Finch leaned closer to Caroline. Their eyes bored into each other. "Go ahead, tell me. I'd love to know."

"You went out to smoke just before my critique."

Finch scoffed. "Okay, and? So did Cameron, and Thea, and Yejun. We were back and forth all day. It's Survey, it's hectic."

"You're the only one who has a reason to sabotage me like that," Caroline snapped.

Finch's face was full of barely restrained grief. "Are you serious? You could say the same thing about Saz. Everyone in our class wanted a spot in the top five."

"I would never!" Saz said, horrified.

Finch gestured in Saz's direction, as if to say *see?* "Caroline, I'm sorry someone burned your painting. I really am. But if you think that I'm the kind of person who's capable of that, then I don't know what you've possibly seen in me as your friend. Obviously, I want to Solo. All of us did at one point or another, and still do. But we'd never do something like that. Not to each other." She pointed a finger at Caroline. "I love you, you bitch. Don't make me out to be someone I'm not."

Caroline hesitated. The TV's glow painted her like a ghost. Amrita said, "Are you good now? Is it squashed?"

"Fine," Caroline answered. She wouldn't quite meet Finch's eyes. "But that doesn't help me know who burned my painting."

"It was probably Cameron," I supplied, trying to mediate. "He hates our guts. I wouldn't put it past him, especially on the day of Survey."

Caroline nodded, but her apprehension lingered. Finch waved at the screen. "Can I put the movie back on? I need to see my xenomorph girl."

Saz shivered beside me as the movie started playing again. I squeezed her arm. "Cold?" I asked, and she nodded, resting her temple against my shoulder. Her half-shut eyes made me emotional. I felt halfway responsible for that subdued look on her face, the absence of her usual fire—I felt I always would, with the knowledge that I had claimed a Solo spot that potentially could have been hers. So I said, "I can grab you a sweatshirt."

"Pipe down, front row," Finch demanded as Saz started to protest, but I was already getting to my feet. "Jo, come on, we are not pausing again!"

"I'll be right back!" I called as I jogged up the stairs to the second floor. Saz's door sat ajar. Her duvet was bunched up in a ball, sheets ruffled beneath it. A hoodie hung from the back of her desk chair. I grabbed it and turned to go but paused when I saw the familiar edge of a book poking out of the mess of papers on her desk.

Tugging it free revealed the cover of *ANTHROPOMANCY*. The pages were marked with tabs and slips of paper in different pastel shades. I flipped through. I landed on an early page with a tasseled bookmark. The image spanning it was the sprawled figure of a body, splayed like Leonardo da Vinci's *Vitruvian Man* with his arms and legs at perfect angles. I skimmed the text beside it, lines highlighted and annotated in Saz's delicate hand throughout: *Modern divination practices redefine the sacrifice by substituting bodily material of any kind in the representation of a human being and reading from the interior, finding the heavens reflected in the meat of the body.*

I read the passages once, twice, three times. I thought about Saz on her knees in front of the toilet, Amrita holding her hair back and saying, "I thought you said you found the ritual on Reddit?" and Saz skirting her question. But why? What was so wrong with the ritual originating from *ANTHROPOMANCY*? If the spell had come from some new age forum, then maybe its seriousness could be played off. But the sight of those words in print—*divination* and *sacrifice*—made our actions feel less capable of dismissal.

I turned from Saz's room with the book tucked against my chest and her hoodie flung over my arm. I brought the sweater to her as intended—but first, I hid that leather-bound tome beneath my mattress, where I could learn exactly what we had done.

Work was a slog, but I couldn't afford not to go—the job at the library supplemented my paints and canvas, and I still hoped to finish a few more pieces before Solo came around. Finch left our shift early with a headache, so I spent most of the evening on my own in the equipment room. The overhead lights buzzed all night. The archive desk closed around dinnertime and left me as the only one in the basement, just a few feet from the empty glass case where the Boar King's suit had once hung. I was simultaneously nervous to be left there alone and relieved that Kirsten was finally gone—I knew she'd been interviewing the sculpture majors who curated the display case in search of the one who'd removed Kolesnik's costume without results, and I was afraid that she'd remember Finch and I had keys of our own. She asked me once if I'd noticed anything strange before the costume disappeared. I, truthfully, answered no, and then tried to keep myself scarce to avoid catching her attention again.

With the realization that our ritual could have come from *ANTHROPOMANCY*, I'd been racking my brain all day about the box where Finch had found it. Who donated it? Was there anything truly powerful about it, or was I too willing to prefer the pagan above all else if it meant retaining some fraction of my mind?

Closing was the worst part. Half the lights shut off automatically in the library's basement, and most of the time the librarians who worked upstairs at the front desk forgot I was down there if I didn't get up and wave my arms around. Sometimes they'd shut down too early and jump a foot in the air when I had to call down the hall, reminding them I was still at work for another hour.

That night I locked everything just after nine. The hallways glistened red as the exit signs beamed on. The only sounds were the clink of my keys clipped to my hip and the swishing of my jeans when I walked. I turned from the equipment room and faced the hall, that display case forever illuminated by the hot gold of the puck lights.

Someone stood behind the glass.

Maybe they'd replaced the Boar King's suit while I was working, hoping to display new work and disguise the empty space. I hesitated by the equipment room's door. I'd have to walk past the case to leave. The library basement smelled wet and alive, like digging up dirt with your hands, earth clinging beneath your fingernails.

"I'm still here," I called out foolishly, as if that might summon something to save me. But my voice was so small in that hallway. The red light flickered. The figure in the case was still enough to convince me of its inanimateness, of my safety. I took a few hurried steps forward until I was only feet away from it. And then it groaned.

The sound was muffled behind the case. The creature keeled forward, nose pressed up against the glass, steam billowing out from where the snout left a wet print. Closer now, I could see it was the same nightmare that had claimed Kolesnik's seat in Survey. Animal eyes peered back at me, slit pupils rolling, each breath casting a new damp circle around the nose.

Its strangled plea disintegrated behind the barrier between us. The hands—*hands* was a generous word, my mind trying to make up for what I was looking at—scrabbled against the case, the figure slumping as if shot and trying to keep itself upright. There was an undulating desperation in its eyes. I got the sense that it was asking me for something. Like I might be capable of putting it out of its misery.

"I'm sorry," I whispered. "I don't know what you want me to do."

It reared its head back. The horns jutting from its snout curled up and over the nostrils. The eyes gave another terrifying roll, and it crashed its head into the glass.

I flinched, hands coming up to block my face. But the case just released a low creak as the head ricocheted off the barrier with a slick thud. The creature's chest heaved, panting like a bull preparing to gore its way to the end.

The words coming out of my mouth were closer to desperate begging, "*Please stop*" spiraling past my lips in a repetitive mess as I slowly backed away. It slammed its head against the case again, and then again, and then again, until a splinter jutted away from the point of impact. The crack woke something in me. I stumbled backward and took off at a run toward the stairs.

Another slam. Another. Another. Another. Another. Then the resounding shatter of the glass case filled the room, shards twinkling to the floor behind me as the creature released a wail that followed me all the way up the stairs.

I didn't look back, not even when one of the janitors on the library's main floor called out and asked if I was alright. I just ran as fast as I could, slamming a shoulder against one of the main doors and exploding out into the night. Outside was so bitterly cold that it hurt to inhale. I focused on that stinging pain, the way it tore me up each time my lungs expanded. There were two possibilities behind me—either what I witnessed was real and there was now a creature loose in the library archives, or I had just hallucinated the Boar King's skin becoming animate and would return to find the display case the same as it had always been. Neither idea was comforting.

I stayed like that, hunched over with my hands on my knees, the path a steadying force beneath me. My feet begged to run again. To go wherever they would carry me. When I finally lifted my head and straightened, a ghost breezed down the promenade to the enormous doors of Slatter Hall.

No, not a ghost. Caroline, the pale sheen of her hair like a gibbous moon in the dark. I watched her heave the door open and slip inside of Slatter as it closed behind her without a sound.

How was I supposed to know what was real when no one witnessed what I had? How, when it seemed no one ever would? Maybe Caroline's apparition was just another specter, trying to lure me somewhere where it could finish me off. Whatever I had wronged with Kolesnik's sacrifice seemed intent on ruining me. I was losing to the invisible.

Still—if that was really Caroline, then I couldn't go home without knowing she was okay. I jogged down the promenade, sneakers crunching over dead leaves and ice. There was no moon overhead. Campus was desolate, everyone already in bed or hiding from the cold.

Slatter was silent. I hadn't been inside the building since Kolesnik's death. I started up the stairs, then glanced over my shoulder as if expecting the creature to have followed me. The idea didn't seem so nonsensical anymore—every shadow had the potential to stand up.

She wasn't in the main entryway where the walls were lined with the ornate benches we'd waited on before Kolesnik's class—now they were mournfully empty, like pews in an abandoned church. The lights were mostly off save for a few of the classrooms and the motion-activated overheads in each hall. Pipes clanked distantly. A door creaked open.

I went toward the sound, trying to keep to the shadows. It felt pathetic to sneak after her like that. But Caroline had been so secretive. I could see it in the way she moved, in the little time she spent at home, in the haunting paintings she created and then scrapped again and again. There had been a shift. Whatever trust she once held in us had stretched thin.

Somehow, I'd known where she would go. The door to Kolesnik's old classroom hung ajar, and the desk lamp glowed past it. I peered into the sliver of space between the door and the jamb, feeling like a ridiculous recreation of that day when I'd first seen him put his hands on Caroline.

She stood before his desk and stared at the empty chair, one finger dragging over the oiled wood. She pulled her hand away and looked at it, rubbed dust between her index and thumb. Caroline's eyes were mostly sclera, the irises pale, head tilted down and lashes painted against her brow. Her jacket hung around her like a shroud. The light made her an indistinct ghoul. Her lips parted—I almost expected her to talk to herself, the feverish rambling I'd listened to on the other side of our shared bedroom wall for weeks—but she just dusted her hands off on her pants.

The light dulled as Caroline circled the desk. She stopped in front of it and started ripping open drawers. Each one gave a vicious rattle. Slatter was likely empty, but she wasn't moving like she cared. Drawers flung open and slammed shut again and again as she hunted. When she came up empty, she let out a frustrated huff.

"You might as well come in," Caroline snapped. She didn't turn to the door when she said it, just kept rifling through a drawer, pens and paperclips rustling under her touch. I straightened and pushed the door the rest of the way open, blushing. "What do you want, Jo?"

To apologize, to ask her what she was doing, to tell her to come home with me and leave whatever this was behind. To tell her what I had seen. For her to tell me everything was going to be okay, that I was salvageable and hers.

"Are you okay?" I asked.

"Oh, just fine." She tore a drawer out of the desk and upended it onto the floor. Pens went spinning across the floorboards, pins and rubber bands and paperclips raining after them, half-used notepads fluttering like clipped birds. I watched them fall, something seizing in my chest—once, Saz made a sculpture with rubber bands and spent a semester hunting for them everywhere. They became a priceless commodity to me; I hadn't yet been able to turn that magpie sense off.

"You don't seem fine," I said, mouth dry.

"What would you know about *fine* and *not fine?*" Now she looked at me, really looked. "You're hanging on by a thread. Don't shake your head at me. I know you. You're hiding something, I can see it."

"I don't know what you're talking about," I mumbled.

Caroline scoffed and kicked a pen away. It rolled to the other side of the room as she dropped into a crouch behind the desk and began digging in Kolesnik's trash can. It must have been empty—she let out a furious growl.

"You just going to stand there, or are you going to help me?" she asked, her voice muffled beneath the desk.

I stepped farther into the classroom. Inside, it had the stale, sleepy smell of a space that hadn't seen life in a while. The chairs and desks were the same as they'd been on that last day of class, half-empty tissue box sitting on the edge of his table, chair rolled away to let Caroline under it.

"I can't help if I don't know what you're doing," I said.

"I'm fixing it," she said. "I'm repairing the ritual." Her head popped up from behind the desk again—just her exposed brow, the faint divot in her forehead where a scar remained from a childhood accident.

"Caroline," I started.

She rose to her knees. "Everything was going great until that farmer fucked with our Boar King scarecrow. Now my painting is ruined, and Moody won't stop chewing me out in our one-on-ones, and I swear that I can hear—I mean, I keep seeing—" Caroline hesitated. "I'm just not sleeping well," she said finally, "and I know you aren't either. I can hear you watching movies on your laptop through the wall all night."

"So what?" I asked. "You're here to curse Kolesnik again? He's already dead. What more can we do?"

"Exactly. He's dead. We killed him and earned that power. The ritual is just . . . out of alignment. I'm going to find something new to put inside a recreated Boar King suit, and I'm going to fix it up and make it right."

I didn't know what to say. The Caroline in front of me warred with everything I thought to be true about the one I knew—a pragmatic girl, skeptical and smart, sensible to a fault unless she believed it might piss her mother off. Sure, she'd been game for the ritual, but so had the rest of us, albeit reluctantly. I wanted to ask her why she believed it was real, if something had been following her too, if she was afraid to turn out the lights at night, if she could hear it breathing in the room with her. But they were dangerous questions to pose; acknowledgment felt like giving those horrors solidity.

"Say whatever you want," Caroline urged when I'd been quiet for too long, her head thrown back to face me and the shadow of the desk bisecting her expression into snarling halves. "Call me hysterical."

I swallowed around the sting in my throat. "I wouldn't."

That made her smile. A real smile, one I hadn't seen in a long time, small but bright. "I'm sorry, Jo," she said. "I know you wouldn't."

She rose and gave the mess she'd made a cursory glance. "It doesn't matter anyway. Custodians must have already given this place a once-over. I was hoping to find another tissue or his hair or something, considering how intent St. Roche is on making everything he touched a fucking memorial." Her voice dropped an octave, into a private, nervous lull. "I just want everything to work out."

That made two of us. I wanted to retrace my steps to a different time, a different body, the world before we'd let it wreck us.

"You're on the list for a potential Solo," I reassured. "You've put in the hours, and they loved your Survey. You're going to blow them out of the water."

Caroline pulled her coat tighter around her. She looked peaky and too thin, the circles beneath her eyes deepening in that lamplight as she shrugged.

"It doesn't matter," she murmured again. "Let's go home before the rest of them send out a search party to find us."

I didn't push it. I just let her lead the way.

19

THE CYCLE OF VIOLENCE

Finch, Caroline, and I were the last of us left on campus at the end of the semester. The camaraderie of fall break was nowhere to be found—while Finch and Caroline had inched away from wanting to kill each other, they were still tense anytime they found themselves in the same room. The Manor was mostly empty. Finch gave Amrita a ride to the airport; she'd spend the next week in North Carolina collecting photos of her new niece to share. Saz would be gone for two—her flight to London had left before any of us had even started to pack. In two days, I'd fly back to Virginia.

Rotham took on a deathly quiet—the woods spindly and eviscerated, the promenade blanketed in snow and salt. It was the three of us, the remaining Banemast staff, and a few international students. I wanted everyone back the moment they left, but it was also nice to share the Manor with only Caroline. After our mutual distress in Kolesnik's classroom, I liked being able to keep an eye on her.

Still—there was something clawing at Caroline that she clearly hadn't fully admitted to me. I never saw her return to Slatter, but she continued to talk to herself through our wall. The timbre was too low to ever make out the words, just a constant hum. We spent a day in Grainer together, though when I left to find something for dinner, she just promised me she'd meet me later. I left her sitting on the floor of her studio and staring at the painting nailed to her wall—her back to me, knees pulled to her chest, T-shirt strained over the prominent knobs of her spine.

And over those last isolated days, I found that Caroline was saving her hair. I stepped into the shower early in the morning when the sun was only fingers of light beyond the bathroom window, and discovered swirls of shed hair plastered to the tiles where she'd gathered and left them to dry. Against the gleaming white, they looked like runes. Symbols of a darker intention. Or she was just a forgetful slob and she'd left them for eventual cleanup.

I wanted to believe in the latter. But the festering fear inside of me wouldn't be banished. I kept seeing things out of the corners of my eyes everywhere in the Manor. It took me hours to fall asleep—there was an insect in my room that just wouldn't die and the pervasive smell of something chemical that made me lightheaded. Everything I touched in the studio seemed to turn to waste beneath my hands. I'd finished several paintings in a row, only to wet a rag with turpentine and wipe them clean again, solvent burning my nose with every inhale.

On the last day before break, I met Finch in the library for our final shift of the semester.

She arrived at work before me to make up for the shift she'd missed the other night. I awaited a text—something full of horror telling me that *they smashed the display case where the Boar King's suit used to live, there's glass everywhere, you were the last person seen downstairs.* But nothing ever came. And when I arrived at the archives again, the case was perfectly normal, the Boar King's stand still an empty white pillar.

Finch never went home if she could help it. Her parents lived forty minutes from Rotham—she told me she'd make the drive on Christmas Eve and come right back the next day. She didn't want to spend any time away from the studio.

"You should stay too," she coaxed as she leaned over the desk. It was still piled high with materials that the two of us were meant to catalog—there had been a rush of last-minute returns that morning, Rotham's least reliable students rushing to avoid the late fee that would come with film equipment sitting in their dorm rooms. "You can come home with me if you want Christmas dinner and everything, though I can't promise the food won't be shitty."

I clicked around a spreadsheet and pretended to be intently focused. The library basement emitted a bone-deep cold, and the hand I kept on the mouse trembled. Finch raised her eyebrows when I shivered. "Okay, it won't be *that* shitty," she said, but I just laughed and rubbed my hands up and down the sleeves of my hoodie.

"My parents would kill me," I answered, though I wasn't sure if that was even true. They hadn't thrown that big of a fit over fall break, despite our subsequent calls being a little tense and even less frequent. They would likely be disappointed if I stayed again. But they were disappointed even when I did return home. I was never there long or often enough. Something about going back reduced me to a child again, unequipped for the expected role.

Finch didn't answer. I could tell she was disappointed, too, though that lit a different sort of fire in me. I was buoyed by her apparent desire for my company. I imagined a Christmas with her. The two of us curled in her twin bed, acutely aware of all the places we didn't touch. I'd been to her parents' place once, back when we were sophomores and we decided to thrift some frames to make collages with. Finch claimed there were a ton of spots by her childhood home where we could find cheap options, so we piled into her car and let her lead the way. The whole time, all I could do was imagine her growing up alone—her brother and sister more than a decade older and already building their own families by the time she was a teenager, her mother overly polite and reserved and her father a distant force. It made me too sad, even then, when we were still new to each other. The house had no life, save for the relic of her room. There were still magazine clippings stuck to the walls with clear tape. *Alternative Press* and *Paramore*, Manic Panic jars scrubbed clean and stuffed with colored pencils, early self-portraits where she was scrappy and frowning, fragments of poems she loved, like the Emily Dickinson one that I'd also memorized as a kid. I pictured her reading it—her rough voice softened by youth, hair chin-length and mousy, mouth unbraced. I imagined how her recitation might ignite something in my heart. How I might come to believe that hope really was the thing with feathers.

Spending Christmas there would be like witnessing a version of Finch that neither of us wanted to unearth. I knew she'd only invited me to be nice. Still. In the darkest recesses of my hope, I wanted to fall asleep on her shoulder in a childhood bed, sharing her dreams.

But beyond that, I wanted to know that by staying at Rotham, I was one of the few willing to make a sacrifice. That, like Finch, I would give up my holiday again, and my family, all in favor of toiling away in the studio until the overhead lights shut off for good. As alluring as the idea was, the logical part of my brain hoped that leaving campus might be the reset I needed.

"I'll try to come back early," I said instead when she didn't answer my first deflection. Finch fell back into her seat with a shrug and started to tap away at her laptop. Somehow her iced coffee had melted—I couldn't imagine how, or why she'd picked iced in the first place in this frigid room—but she sipped it as if it were fresh and went back to her work.

When I returned to the Manor that evening, raised voices cascaded down the stairs. I hesitated in the kitchen, listening. Caroline's was sharpened to a point—it sparred with her mother's piercing tone and had me immediately turning to face the back door, considering if I should try to slip out unnoticed. I always tried to hide in my room when the Asters arrived, and I had missed my opportunity to disappear. They were already coming down the stairs and still arguing the whole way.

"You look malnourished," Mrs. Aster said, her heels clicking like a tongue against teeth. "Normally I like it when you thin out, but you look drug addled."

"You know how to give a compliment."

Caroline led the way down the stairs and spotted me hovering in the doorway. Her face softened, an apology. "Mom, you remember Jo," she said as they descended.

Mrs. Aster gave me a polite smile. Her eyes landed somewhere other than my face, distant and removed. "Right, hi. Caroline, I'll meet you in the car. Please don't take longer than five minutes."

I stepped out of her way. The door closed with a polite click, and Caroline reached for me. The hug she pulled me into was too tight, a staked claim and a desperate plea, her fingers a vise where my T-shirt collar met my neck. "Don't make me go with her," she mumbled against my hair. "She asked me if you and I were fucking after she saw your sweatshirt on my desk. And when I said no, she asked if you were the one giving me drugs."

The idea made me flush red. "Did you tell her that you're the one always corrupting me?" I offered, hoping to hear her laugh. She rewarded me with one.

"Bitch. Maybe I won't share my drugs with you anymore, how about that?"

It probably would have been a smarter promise. Temptation consumed me, the longing to filch every substance from her room and flush it away, leave us unaffected and alive.

Instead, I said, "You love me too much to follow through with that," and she just squeezed tighter, exhaling one long breath as Mrs. Aster laid on the horn where she'd parked her sleek black car in front of the Manor. Caroline's stiffening traveled across her body, echoed through me where we were connected.

"Yeah," she murmured, "I do."

◆ ◆ ◆

The flight home left me delirious, some other girl's body shuffled through South Bend's airport. My dad picked me up when I landed and drove the hour and a half it took to get us back home. I rode the whole way with the window rolled halfway down, and he only chided me about it once, giving up with a smile he tried to hide when I admitted I just wanted to smell the air. There was snow on the mountains. The world held that frosty scent of wet earth. It was warmer than Indiana but freezing for Virginia, and the cold was different, smokier and heavier as we twisted down I-81. The interstate gave way to two-lane highways, everything endlessly perse, the houses tucked away in the hills decked out in mismatched Christmas lights—mostly the kind my mom hated, multicolored bulbs clashing against gold clashing against Technicolor blue.

I was the last to arrive. The rest of the house was already asleep. Tomorrow was Christmas Eve, and Caleb had driven in from his school the day before. My room was given to my grandmother, which left me with the couch. The living room smelled of laundry. The decorated tree cast the only light. A blanket draped over the back of the couch boasted the insignia of Caleb's university, all maroons and golds. There was nothing in the house signaling Rotham's existence, save for a photo of me and my parents on the mantel posing in front of Lysander Gate from my first move-in. The sight of it was unbearable. I wanted to turn right back around. I wondered if my women felt the same way—wanted to know where they were now, if Caroline and her mother had fought more, if Finch was alone in her apartment feeling as lost as I did.

"Let me know if you need anything," Dad said, giving my shoulder a squeeze before he ascended the stairs to their bedroom.

My first year at Rotham, I used to call my mom at all hours of the night, stomach tossing with anxiety. I had dreams of fire erupting in the kitchen, alarms melted down to pools of battery. Where had that girl gone? When did I stop wanting to go home?

I changed in the bathroom, my pajamas just a Rotham shirt and a pair of boxers, and pulled the couch blanket over me. Past the windows the night was a black curtain. The Christmas tree still twinkled—I didn't want to turn it off, afraid that I'd find the Boar King had followed me home, waiting to show his face in the dark. I closed my eyes against the idea. For the first time in what felt like months, I slept.

Christmas Eve passed in a mad flurry of last-minute shopping, wrapping, and cooking. We always had an ornate dinner before Grandma left the next day. That meant Caleb spent the afternoon on the phone with his girlfriend, conveniently unable to be conned into any help, while I was trapped in the kitchen with Mom and Grandma.

"At least you're here this time," Mom said, cutting her eyes at me. "I still can't believe you didn't come home for Thanksgiving. Sometimes I think the only thing that school teaches you is how to avoid real life."

"Oh, lay off her," Grandma said, touching my back as she passed behind me to rinse peeled potatoes under the sink faucet. "Jo is the only chance this family has of making a memorable impact on the world. Isn't that right, honey?"

Memorable was close to correct, though I doubted its truth would be for any of the right reasons. It was difficult to delineate exactly when I had become so out of place in that house, but it likely fell somewhere along the timeline of my queerness. I came out to my family two years ago in a restaurant, a few months after I cut my hair scalp-short for the first time and got tired of answering "of course not" every time my mother asked if I was a lesbian. It went about as well as I had expected it to—my parents stated that they loved me no matter what, and each gave me a cursory hug. Caleb made a joke, asking if I was a boob or butt guy.

Now my mom looked at my clothes like she could burn them with her gaze alone, cook Saz's old shirt off my body, sear away the paint-stained jeans I wore in place of the flared ones with the heart-shaped back pockets she'd bought me last summer. Examined my sloppy hair-cut kept haphazard by Finch's scissors with the kind of intense stare that willed it longer.

What they didn't understand was this—it was never about being out and proud or feeling understood by them. I never expected my family to kick me out or disown me. I was lucky in that way, unlike Caroline or Amrita whose parents might never forgive them for being queer, both safer keeping their interior life just that—interior. But I'd known the direction my life would turn once my parents knew I was a lesbian. That I'd never be free to act like myself without that knowledge souring the idea of me in their minds no matter how much they loved me.

And while I knew the reality of the situation—that I'd always been a lesbian, even if it took time for me to come to that understanding and even longer to share it—my parents associated my coming out with my Rotham education, further resenting the hold it had on me.

We sat down for dinner at a table laden with our usual favorites: sugar-glazed ham, frothy potatoes mashed with garlic, carrots roasted and curled, butter beans spiced in their bowl, parsley dusting everything like green confetti. Rolls swollen and yeasty, olives in the good crystal, gravy in the good china, yams in the good stoneware.

Grandma said grace with her head bowed. I clasped my hands in front of my nose and closed my eyes, thinking *please let him be gone forever, please leave me be, please let me wake without needing to scream.*

We ate. I wanted to scratch at the tattoo under my sweater but was afraid to draw attention to the scabby wound of the hyacinth. I didn't want to listen to them curse me for doing something as foolish as getting a stick-and-poke dorm tattoo. But I was more concerned that I was incapable of healing. What was wrong with me? What made it so impossible to move forward?

"You know, Joanna was selected for her art show," Dad said proudly between bites.

"Oh, that's wonderful! That's what you wanted, right? That means you get to show all your work?" Grandma's enthusiasm was a kind balm, but it couldn't prevent the words from cutting. I swallowed a stone of half-chewed meat.

"They're just narrowing down which students have an opportunity to show their work in a Solo presentation," I clarified. "I've been chosen with four other students to reach the next level of selections, but the Soloist hasn't been decided yet."

Caleb snorted. There was a beer beside his plate, something that pissed me off to see. Our parents would have killed me if they saw me have even a sip of alcohol while underage. "Seems like a waste of time if you're not the one chosen," he said, simmering the heat in me further.

Mom laughed. "We spend so much money on your education, and you come back with ghost stories and—crafts."

The hitch in her words made me think she intended to say something different and decided to soften the blow at the last minute.

"Ghost stories? I'd like to hear some of those," Grandma prompted.

"Joanna says her dorm is haunted," Mom sneered, wineglass in her hand.

It had been a throwaway comment over the phone intended to make light of reality, a weak grasp at connecting with her. But now I regretted opening my mouth at all. Dad cleared his throat and asked for more potatoes. I pushed mine around on my plate.

"You've barely eaten your dinner," he tried, and I just shrugged, said that I wasn't feeling well. It was the truth. Anything I swallowed felt like it had the potential to come back up. There was an acidic curdle in my stomach.

I imagined telling them the truth. Kolesnik's death and the smear of his blood across my shirt, Saz's nose dripping over the scarecrow's body, the hallucinated slits in Goya's painting, the creature shattering its way through the display glass. It was all too much, entirely unbelievable. They'd pull me out of school. I'd leave Rotham with Solo just out of my reach and an empty room in the Manor. I let the silence fester and scraped my full plate into the garbage.

Grandma sat on the porch after dinner, long after everyone had gone to bed. The forecast said more snow—my phone kept lighting up with the alert, a little red exclamation point promising the first white Christmas in years.

I went to find her with a blanket hooked over one arm in case her coat wasn't enough. There was a cigarette stubbed out in the ashtray beside her hand and another lit between the fingers. The familiar smell seized my heart—she had always preferred a box of Benson & Hedges. Smoke rose to the slats of the ceiling and coiled there.

"I won't tell," I said when she startled and turned to find me in the doorway. The smile that crossed her face was an instant comfort. She patted the swing beside her with a wrinkled hand, and I went to sit, leaning my head on her shoulder. The blanket made our laps two hilly expanses.

"Aren't you cold?" I asked. She shook her head against me.

"I've always loved winter." She coughed once and cleared her throat. "I like how clean the air feels."

We were safe under the awning as the first flakes started to fall. The sky was starless with storm. I was cold down to the bone, my jacket not thick enough and my hands fisted in the blanket, but I didn't want to leave that moment behind.

"You know," she said finally, after I gave a hard shiver against her side. "I see your uncle at the foot of my bed all the time. He's this hazy, black outline, and yet somehow I know it's him as soon as I open my eyes. He talks to me just like he did when he was alive. He calls me Mama, and he tells me he's okay, and not to worry too much, and to go back to sleep."

We rocked slowly, the swing's chains creaking and stiff. Her hand patted my knee. My eyes traced all the lines around her knuckles, the evidence of her years. "I've never told anyone that. I didn't want them to think I was already losing my mind and put me in some home to die. But I thought you might be the only one who would believe me."

Snow piled upon the dead grass. I inhaled cold and cutting air. She was right about the cleanliness—I felt its sharpness revive me, slicing down my throat and all over my lungs, leaving holes for the hurt to seep in.

"I believe you," I said, and I meant it.

20

RAIL AND RAVE AND RAVAGE

The Wrangler had seen better days. Caleb's time with it nearly ran it into the ground, and he was still resentful about me reclaiming it to drive back to Rotham two days after Christmas. Dad checked the oil three times before he gave me the keys, suspiciously eyeing the engine as we stood in the driveway like the hood might pop open and snap at him. It was a reptilian shape—the front end was spiked with metal accents, its deep green body like something lurking just beneath the surface of a mossy pond. But it was such a relief to see it. I couldn't get on another plane. I wanted to be in control of my own pace, needed the option to pull over and breathe.

"It's icy," Mom said for the tenth time, dropping my backpack into the passenger seat and slamming the door shut. She had her bathrobe on over her Christmas pajamas. The combination made her look so small. I wished there wasn't so much resentment in my heart. That I could banish the sound of her saying *we spend so much money on your education, and you come back with ghost stories* playing on a loop in my head.

"It's always icy this time of year," I answered. "I'll be fine, I promise."

"It's a nine-hour drive, Joanna. You really shouldn't be going alone."

Honestly, it didn't sound so bad. I couldn't remember the last time I'd been alone for more than a few hours, and Rotham lured me in— Finch was already back on campus, and Amrita would arrive the day after I did. Caroline was supposed to follow close behind her, with Saz the last one to come home. I wanted to get back to them, even if I was afraid of the fallout that might come along with our reunion.

"I just don't get why you have to go so early," Mom said, frowning. "You said you were going to stay for two weeks."

"That was before Survey. Now that I have a chance of showing my work, I'd fuck myself over if I wasted that time when I could use it to get ahead."

"Language," Dad said.

But that was what they wanted after all, wasn't it? Proof that I was taking advantage of every opportunity. Mom just shook her head, mouth wrung up like a rag, her hands pushed so deep in the pockets of her robe that I thought they might tear through the cloth.

They let me go with only brief goodbyes. It was brutally cold, morning-on-the-mountain kind of cold. Weak heat puttered out of the car's vents. I alternated between holding the wheel and waving my hands in front of the tepid air.

The first few hours of the drive were easy once the car finally warmed up. I kept myself entertained with podcasts and a playlist of Finch's playing over the speakers. The only stops I allowed were coffee and pee breaks, though I tried to limit them to as few as I thought my body could handle without my kidneys melting.

It was the setting sun that got to me. There was only an hour left in the drive when darkness blanketed the road—I'd left early, but winter's stolen daylight didn't care. The roads closer to Rotham were in desperate need of repaving. Dormant trees bent close. There was hardly anyone else around, everyone still at home for the holidays.

The Wrangler ate up yellow lines. I looked at the road. I looked at the trees. I looked at the rearview mirror and then back at the road. Was there ever a point when the brain got bored enough to conjure a new vision, to replace the one it was seeing? Fuzzy warmth from the vents made me sleepy and spent. A woman waved at me from the woods. A woman waved at me from the woods?

My head snapped up from where it'd nearly drooped to my chest, and the car's tires roared against the rumble strip. Thudding heartbeats nearly drowned out the stereo I'd cranked up to stay awake. A frantic glance over my shoulder told me there was no one in the woods, that I hadn't seen anyone, that I needed to pull over and go the fuck to sleep. But I was so close. Just twenty more minutes. I could go twenty more minutes.

I ripped my eyes away from the woods in my rearview mirror, and they landed on a black animal darting across the road.

This time I swerved hard. Screaming was an instinct—all sound, no words, just a desperate body-deep wail. The car's grille connected with something hard as I barreled into the grass, barely wrenching to a stop before it could crash headlong into the trees. Headlights lit up the trunks. Finch's playlist blared '80s pop at me. I shut it up with a violent twist of the dial.

When I flung the door open, everything smelled of cooked rubber and churned mud. Beneath that earthiness was the musk of animal pelt, a sleeping scent, unwashed. Something on the dashboard beeped incessantly as I slid out of the driver's seat. I was shaking too hard to let go of the door handle. Everything else remained impossibly quiet—no rolling tires, no wind in the trees.

Then Kolesnik screamed.

The dragged-out cry bleated from the mouth of the animal slumped on the asphalt. I staggered toward it. Swallowed the lump in my throat that made me think I might vomit. Frost crunched under my boots, dead grass flattening. "Not real," I whispered, "not real not real not real."

Because it was a wild boar lying on its side, hind legs a twisted mess, the snout huffing clouds against the pavement and front legs pedaling wildly. The hips wouldn't obey. I'd injured it. The mouth parted, tusks jutting out of the jaw as it released another echoing scream, that endless *HELP ME HELP ME HELP ME.*

"Not real," I whispered again as I crouched as close as I could while staying out of the creature's line of sight. The shattered glass hadn't been real. So there was no way this could be either. I was sleep deprived and buzzing from too many cups of gas station coffee. But I'd felt the impact in the steering wheel.

It was so much smaller than I might have once expected a boar to be after seeing Kolesnik's hulking apparition. It was round and wiry with the same seeking eyes but lacked all the humanoid mass—save for its voice, Kolesnik's stolen and recreated. I wanted to touch it and prove that it wasn't real. But I was so scared to feel the heat of its fading life. I reached for it, shaking.

My phone rang from the car. Headlights blinded me when I twisted to get to my feet, scrambling to answer. The screen flashed *MOM* in big white letters, and I swiped to answer. "Hey," I said shakily. "Sorry I didn't call yet, I'm almost back."

"HELP ME," the voice on the other end of the line wept, and for one seizing moment it was her. Then the shift came over my mother's familiar tone—wiped it away and replaced it again with Kolesnik's last plea—"PLEASE HELP ME."

The boar began to echo the cry until the words seemed to come from every direction, booming between the trees: *HELPMEHELPMEHELPMEHELPMEHELPME.*

I threw the phone, and it clattered across the pavement. It came to a stop beside the boar's body just as it let out a squeal. Its body stilled. Immediately the screen lit up again, the same jolly ringtone chirping into the dark.

"Stop it!" I screamed. "Leave me the fuck alone!"

The phone went black. I stared at the boar and the knot of its hind legs. Then the ringtone began again. I snatched it up to answer, shards of the shattered screen cutting into my thumb. *"What the hell do you want?"*

"Jo?"

It was Finch. My Finch, warmth and worry in her voice. "Oh, fuck," I panted with my head in my hands, phone pressed harder against my cheek to ground myself with the pain. "Fuck, I'm sorry. I thought—I didn't realize it was you."

"Are you alright? You were supposed to be home by now. I went by the Manor and it was empty."

The cold made it hard to hold the phone. I nearly dropped it and shattered it further, stranding me without her voice. "I'm okay," I said, shakily. "I didn't mean to worry you. I'm close to campus. I just—I hit something with my car."

"What? Are you okay? Do you need me to come and get you?" The panic in her voice shocked me back into my body. I shook my head, shut my eyes against the headlights. "I'm getting my keys. Just give me five minutes and I'll be in the car. Can you send me your location?"

"No." The boar's eyes stared into the street. I could hear tires for the first time in what felt like hours—a car coming down the road. I needed to get out of the way. "I'm okay, the car's okay, everything is fine. I just had to catch my breath. I'll be back soon."

Her exhalation was long and loud. I could imagine her, fingers pressed to her forehead, rearing to scold. A car came around the bend about fifty feet back and slowed to a crawl when it saw me and the boar. I kept Finch against my ear as an older woman pulled up, rolling down her window. "You alright, sweetie? What happened here? Did you hit that thing?"

Finch was saying something I couldn't hear as I waved the woman on, even as my stomach sank. The woman's horrified eyes on the boar were confirmation. She could see it. It was real.

"I'm fine, car's fine," I said again. "I'm just going to move it out of the road. Thank you for stopping."

"Never seen one of those around here before," she said with wonder, unable to peel her eyes away from it.

I hadn't either. No one really had, except for Kolesnik—it had been the inspiration for his very first Masquerade Grotesque costume, the reason it came into existence at all. He'd seen a feral pig outside of his cottage on campus, rooting in the garden, tearing up all the green until he chased it off with a gun on his shoulder. He used to tell everyone who would listen that they were violent things.

"Jo," Finch said. "Jo!"

"You can go ahead," I said to the woman. She just gave me a concerned nod and slowly picked up speed again, tires crunching over the rumble strip until she grew smaller and smaller in the distance.

I pressed my fingers to my temple, tried to inhale without feeling as if I might split in two. "Sorry. What did you say?"

"Can you drive?"

"Yeah, of course," I whispered, eyes shut.

"Come over," Finch said, her voice stern over the phone's frayed line. "We don't have to be at the airport until eleven tomorrow, and I don't think you should be alone right now."

I nodded, forgetting she couldn't see me. The knees of my jeans were wet with something—mud, or the boar's blood, everything too dark to decipher.

"I'll be there soon," I said, and ended the call. The boar lay on its side. Trembling, I took it by one massive tusk, the head dragging limply with my straining pull. It was so impossibly heavy. I thought that nothing this heavy could be dead—that whatever abandoned a body must leave it lighter than before. It took all my strength to move it into the grass where it would lie until someone else came to find it, police or animal control or someone more capable than me.

A smothered cry ripped up my throat and out of my mouth: the sound of pent-up horror and the sense that a steadfast piece of myself had snapped off. Then I sucked the breath back in. Left the boar behind. Got behind the wheel of the car and turned the key and drove the last twenty minutes back to Rotham to the sound of nothing but the engine and my pounding heart.

21

WAIT AND DROWN IN DUST

Finch's apartment in Tuck House was so different from the Manor. It had her all over it—towers of books both read and unread, stumps of candles on various surfaces, sketches pinned to the walls. Her shoes stood by the door like they were waiting for permission to leave. Her kettle was in the sink, lid off. She answered the door as if I'd caught her in the middle of something—dark hair a little damp, the collar of a T-shirt poking past her crewneck, a star-shaped pimple patch on her jaw.

"Jesus Christ, Jo," she said as she closed the door behind me. The deadbolt slid home, and I flinched at the sound. The exhale she released let me know that it hadn't gone unnoticed. I shrugged my backpack off, let it hit the floor with a thud, and toed my dirty sneakers off. "Did something cut your cheek? Is there blood on your jeans?"

Yes, and yes. I touched my cheek gingerly and felt thin lacerations beneath my fingers. She pulled my fingers away, suddenly so close that I could smell her—the cool mint of having just brushed her teeth, something she did every time she ate. A faint wisp of weed clinging to her clothes. The clean apple of her cologne.

"You should have told me how bad it was," she muttered, dragging her thumb over my cheekbone, sliding all the way down to my jaw. I closed my eyes so I wouldn't reveal the way I wanted to lean into her grasp. "I hate when you lie."

"I'm fine."

"What did I just say? Give it up already, I'm not Caroline."

"I don't lie to Caroline."

"You lie to everyone. Caroline just lets you get away with it the most."

Finch slid her hand away and left me cold and missing it. I opened my eyes to find her surveying me again in that close, scrutinizing way. "You should shower. You can borrow something."

I didn't protest. I accepted the towel she thrust at me and the bundle of sweatpants and hoodie. In the bathroom I put them to my nose and shut my eyes again, breathed deep the familiar scent of her. The shower was a good idea—Rotham's water heaters were notoriously junky but I got about ten minutes before the spray went frigid.

I found her in the kitchen again as I toweled off my hair, cozy in her clothes. My pulse still hadn't slowed. She was smoking, the window over the sink cracked open a few inches. Blustery air blew in.

"Want a drink?" Finch asked me around the joint in her lips. She ashed it in the sink's basin. I hovered in the doorway, feeling vulnerable there in her clothes, too-big socks on my feet.

"What do you have?"

"Whiskey, beer, gin, some old wine, as long as you smell it first and make sure it hasn't turned into vinegar."

I wrinkled my nose. "I'll take the beer, thanks."

She bent to peer into the fridge and emerged with two of the pilsners she liked, opened both bottles and passed one over. I felt the heat in her palm as our hands brushed, immediately replaced with the cold bottle. Smoke curled around me like a beckoning arm.

Finch gestured to the living area with her drink and I obeyed, following her into the room. It was really just a ratty couch and a table propped up with more books. The pillows on the couch were flattened and imprinted with the shape of Finch's head.

"How are you feeling?"

I shrugged and tugged haplessly on the hoodie's strings at my neck. "Shitty."

Finch pointed the bottle at me. "Finally, honesty. I like it when you listen."

I blushed. The sound that left my mouth was meant to be a scoff, but it faltered. Either she pretended not to notice or didn't care. She flopped down on the couch and patted the seat beside her. I obeyed, sat and pulled my knees up to my chest, pressed my chin against the fabric of her sweatpants. The name of her high school stretched over one thigh. There was a little hole worn in the pocket.

"Are you gonna tell me what happened?"

It was already entombed somewhere unreachable. A mechanism for safety—erasing that unreality, a weak attempt at moving forward without losing myself in the process. What other option did I have? It was impossible to keep going with that scream in my ears.

I handed her my phone by way of answering. Finch turned it around and whistled at the shattered screen. "Damn, that sucks. You'll have to go into the city to get a new one. Maybe we can stop tomorrow, after we pick up Amrita." She looked at me from under her lashes, her eyes the same warm amber of the bottle in her hands. "Are you sure you're okay?"

"I'm fine, seriously. It was a deer in the road, I just swerved not to hit it." The lie was necessary. She'd clown me if I told the truth—the boar felt so ridiculous now, so obvious in its pointed hurt. I could not trust my eyes or my heart. I kept both trained on her throat as she swallowed.

"Not supposed to do that," she muttered, shaking her head, and for a moment I thought she was referring to my staring.

Irritation took over when I realized. "I had a lot on my mind. I didn't exactly remember the textbook walk-through of what to do when an animal is in the road."

"That's too long of a drive, especially by yourself. I would have picked you up from the airport."

"I wanted to be home now, on my terms."

Now she just shook her head. Clearly the word *home* had done something to her. I could see it in the way she wouldn't meet my eyes, her free hand squeezing her thigh, fingers curling in denim.

"It's hot in here," I said, mostly to run from that conversation.

"Want to sit on the fire escape?" Finch asked around a mouthful of beer. A drop clung to the corner of her mouth. I wanted to swipe my finger there like she had done to me, but I just nodded instead. She hefted our jackets off the hook by the door, and I followed as she crossed the room to where her bed was made up and hauled the window open. Feet first, she slid her body through the opening and out into the crisp evening.

I threw my coat on and repeated her process, awkwardly, throwing one leg over the sill and out onto the fire escape. I'd lived in this building last year and never felt sure of the fire escape's structural integrity, but either Finch trusted it or didn't seem to care. She slid to the left, and I filled the spot beside her. The metal was cold even through her borrowed clothes—December bit the air. I pulled my jacket tighter.

"Chilly now?" Finch asked. She threw her arm around me and pulled me into her. I rested my head on her shoulder and breathed deep. The scent of her deodorant, earthy and masculine, made me feel safe. One hand toyed with a damp strand of my hair. "You're going to catch a cold like this. Especially if you keep drinking that."

"It's alright," I answered, though I wasn't sure if I meant the cold or the beer as I took a pull from the bottle, folding in on myself to hold the warmth in. Finch's hand rubbed lazy circles against the fabric of my jacket.

"If I say something, promise me you won't get mad," Finch said. I kept my eyes shut. Whatever she said I didn't want to see it, bright and shapeless in front of me.

"I won't get mad," I answered.

"You will, but don't use it against me."

"I'm not going to use it against you," I insisted. Even heavy on my tongue, it tasted like the truth. I would have said anything to keep her hand on me.

Finch drank and I felt her head turn to watch the trees move in the wind. I cracked my eyes open and followed her gaze. It was nearly midnight, and I still held fast to the stories of Mother Crone coming out after dark. Anything could be imagined from the silhouettes of the humanoid topiaries. I wondered if we might be able to spot the Manor if we stood and peered down the promenade, wondered if it was still empty.

"I don't think it's good for you, being in that house," Finch said at last. "I think it's taking a toll on you."

I stiffened. "What does a car accident have to do with the Manor?"

"It's not just a car accident, Jo. You're distracted all the time. You have this distant look in your eyes like you're never fully there. Something's wrong, and you won't tell any of us what's happening."

Any of us. I knew she meant that I refused to tell her, that my silence got under her skin.

"I'm fine," I answered immediately. Finch sighed. "I swear. I've just been stressed over these last few weeks with Survey and my family and everything. Holidays always take a toll on me, and I don't want to let Moody down."

"You don't want to disappoint Moody or the rest of them in the Manor? I love them too, Jo, but painting isn't life or death. It's supposed to be something good, something that you do because you want to."

"Maybe for you," I snapped, sitting up. "If I don't have this, I don't have anything. I have to prove that I'm worth the time, the money, the effort. You're automatically good at everything you do. It's different."

Finch tilted her chin up at me. "Don't talk about things you don't understand."

I scoffed. "And don't talk to me like I'm Caroline. We have the same goals."

"I'm just trying to say that it's not the end of the world if you don't live up to whatever expectation Caroline has of us. We don't all have to be twenty-three and showing at the Whitney—you can make what you want and figure the rest out along the way. There's no time limit. Solo is Solo. Life will continue after it, regardless of the outcome."

Everything shook. I pressed my hands down into my lap to disguise the shiver. "But what if I want the same thing that she does? Is it so wrong for me to want to be good at what I love?"

Something passed in front of the lights lining the sidewalk. It cast us in a beat of dark as the trees rustled. Someone whooped, distant and joyful. I could almost picture Caroline with her head tipped back and her hands cupped around her mouth, delight spilling out into the dark.

Finch dragged a hand through my hair and let it linger. I kept my eyes trained on the divot above her top lip, the little scar beside her cupid's bow. "You're good already, Jo."

I shook my head, pushed it into her palm. I'd die if she took her hand away. It was like a third arm propelling me forward, keeping me upright.

"You don't belong to them," Finch said, under her breath. Her pupils were blown wide. I wanted to run my finger along the edge of her iris until my hand passed through her face. "You're your own person."

Maybe, once. But I hadn't belonged to myself since the Boar King. Since the stick-and-pokes in the kitchen branding me theirs. Since the first day I stepped onto campus, all those years ago, and found Amrita waiting in the room we shared.

I knew Finch could see that in me, and that was why she'd said anything at all. She could map out my indistinct edges, the places where I'd melted into the rest of them until our boundaries couldn't be deciphered. That was what proved it to me—that she'd been watching. That she'd been paying attention.

The lines between the two of us were more definitive. Clearer delineation to cross, if I wanted to cross.

Of course, I wanted to cross.

Everything about her was handsome: brows drawn up in the center with concern, the faintest pink to her cheeks, the soft parting of her mouth. Why not take that leap? What could I possibly have left to lose? There, with my face in Finch's hands, was one of the last places I felt safe.

"What if I want to be yours?" I said. There was a beat of quiet, and then Finch's head lolled to the side. She gave me a wry smile.

"You don't know what you're saying."

"I know exactly what I'm saying," I answered, trying to sound like it was the truth. "Everyone already thinks we're fucking. Why not prove them right?"

"You're ridiculous," Finch said. But she kept stroking her thumb across my jaw. Her hand was cold, her skin dry. She kept her fingers looped loosely around her beer bottle with the other hand. "Caroline would kill me. Amrita would put a stake through my heart. Saz—well, I guess Saz would love it."

"What about me?" I said indignantly. "Why would you be the only one who gets in trouble?"

Finch sighed. "Because you're theirs, Jo, in a way that I'm not. Don't roll your eyes, you know exactly what I'm trying to say. They always think that they're protecting you from me."

I wanted to tell her she was wrong, but I was afraid of sounding naive. They loved me, and they thought I could be weak. Those two ideas could exist simultaneously even if they took me apart in the process. Finch was somehow able to keep herself separate from that devouring. There was something about her that wouldn't lend itself to uniformity, and kept her just outside of our perfect circle.

But I was the combined effect of them. All their pieces and quirks and mannerisms were made anew on my face. I wore them all the time.

"I can make my own decisions," I whispered.

Her elbow brushed mine. I could feel the touch all the way through my body like her hot hands were already dragging their way up my thighs, fingertips digging into the skin.

"It would be a bad idea," she said, as if trying to convince herself. "I'm all bad ideas."

Finch laughed. "Yeah, you are."

She leaned into me. I stared at her mouth, willing her closer. Her hand cupped the base of my skull and her beer thumped against my knee and Finch pressed her lips to mine in an open-mouthed kiss that cooked me all the way down to my feet.

I drew in a sharp breath. The sound passed between us, shared. She kissed me like she'd been counting down the seconds. We moved, I leaning to make room and she following to press between my legs. I heard her beer tip and clatter against the rungs of the fire escape, spilling between the cracks.

"Fuck," she said against my cheek, laughing, and a laugh bubbled out of my chest too. I was giddy with the feeling of her so near me. The fire escape was a cold cage beneath my back. Her fingers twined in the bars beside my head as she kissed me again—there was the warm brush of her tongue against mine, the cave that her hair made around us, the shadows of her lashes against her cheek. My heart was pounding so hard I was sure she could taste it.

"Bad idea?" she asked when she finally pulled away. Her smile was big and shy. I loved her so much that it felt physical, like a stone that could be cut out of my chest. I couldn't speak. I just shook my head, trying to say *no, not at all, not one bit,* even though I felt ridiculous, like there was no way this moment could be mine.

She kissed me again, with finality. Just a warm press of her lips before she was rocking back to sit on her heels. I propped myself up to face her as Finch lit the joint again and inhaled before passing it to me. I put my lips where hers had just been and tried to calm my heart from ripping its way out of my body.

My head was fuzzy with the aftermath of her. The gentle buzz of our shared crossfaded high made the fuzziness warmer. I pulled my jacket closer around me again, cold without her pressed against me. I wanted to ask her if she was real.

"Should we talk about it?" I asked, shivering. The fire escape was so cold that I was afraid it would stick to me through my clothes. I hoped she believed my shaking was because of the cold and not because she made me unbearably nervous.

"What, do you regret it?" She fixed me with an anxious look, eyes dragging down to my mouth.

"No! No, of course not. It was great. Really good. Amazing."

"Amazing, huh?"

She stubbed the joint out as I raised my eyebrows at her. "What, you don't think so?"

"I've had better kisses," Finch teased, the corners of her mouth turning up as she exhaled smoke.

My mind went right to Thea, a poisonous, self-sabotaging image. "Oh, come on."

"What?" Finch asked, leaning closer, smiling the kind of smile that tried to contain itself the whole time. "Did I offend you?"

Our knees touched. I pushed mine against hers until I felt pressure down to bone, scoffing. "I'll kill you, I mean that."

She was grinning now. "Liar. You want to make up for it. I can see it in your face, you want to prove me wrong."

The face in question was hot with apprehension and the awareness that she was right. She took my jaw in her hand, thumb and forefinger pressing divots. I exhaled hard through my nose, lashes fluttering as she stared at my mouth.

"It's really fucking cold out here," she whispered, a breath away from my lips. "We could go inside if you want."

The implications of *inside* moved all the way through me, goose bumps prickling beneath my clothes. Her clothes, on me. The possession already determined.

I nodded in her grasp. Her smile became a beam.

I tried to leave myself out there, on that fire escape. In her room we shed our layers and pulled her blankets over us, still shivering and laughing, the kissing tentative at first until we found our footing and she pressed me down into the sheets. I tried not to think about the others. I tried not to think of myself as anyone but Finch's.

I laid my forehead against her shoulder as I touched her, our skin hot and cloying, and listened to her exhale against my ear as if it were words. Emotion prickled in my throat. If I never touched another person in all my life, that moment would have been enough. All I needed was her voice, cut out of the air in the shape of the moon. Just the unblemished surface of it glowing bright. Just the steady hum of us together in that bed. Taking each other apart. Dissecting what we found, pinning it in place like the sectioned halves of a butterfly, shadowboxing it until it was a memory preserved.

We stayed like that through the night, my cheek against her bare chest and my eyes half-shut in hopes of holding on to a dream. I brought her knuckles to my mouth—kissed that stained skin with color caught in the cracks. I felt her smile against my hair and she held my head to her as I took her heartbeat and made it mine.

22

COSMIC INTERFERENCE, COMET HEAT

Waking with Finch's nose pressed up against my throat was a new delight. It had been months since I'd slept so well. My eyes were sticky with sleep, skin overwarm where her thigh was thrown over mine, cold seeping past the inch of window we'd left open. She shifted and tightened her hold around my hips. That touch gave me new awareness—I was mostly naked in Finch's bed, hair a mess, teeth fuzzy in my mouth. I closed my eyes and savored it. The cottonmouth, her hair against my shoulder, her breath against my collarbone, the soft slide of sheets, the steady press of her fingertips.

Slipping out of the bed without ruining her sleep was impossible. I carefully lifted her arm and shuffled free. Found her hoodie on the floor and yanked it over my head, then her sweatpants. I thought I could still smell her on the clothes and then thought maybe that smell was on me, pressed into my skin.

"Are you leaving?" she asked, her voice coarse. I shouldn't have turned around. She looked so beautiful there, messy and dream-soaked, propped up on her elbows and watching me.

"Gotta change and shower again before we leave to get Amrita," I murmured. Now that our night had passed, I didn't know where to put my hands, what to say, how to move. She looked equally unsure.

We'd been naked around each other before, but only in short bursts—changing clothes, skinny-dipping after dark. I was newly aware of her body, unable to keep my eyes from dragging. She gave me a half smile. I could feel questions rising in her—a coming talk, an agreement, *we move past this, we pretend it didn't happen*—so I looked away. "Are we okay?" I asked.

"'Course," she said. I waited for more. She rolled over onto her back, dragged the blankets up to her chin and shut her eyes. "Always."

I swallowed. Everything I could've said felt insubstantial. There was an unspoken agreement in the air—last night would live with us in this room. The threat of implosion was too possible, neither of us willing to spark that fuse.

I pushed my hands deeper into the pockets of her hoodie. "I'll see you in a couple hours, okay?"

She nodded, holding on to that listless smile.

I knew I'd find the Manor waiting empty. But I was still nervous when I crept in the back door, turning the knob slowly and clicking the door shut with a careful hand on the jamb, as if someone might hear. The house was silent. The only sound was my footsteps, carrying me up to the third floor.

I stripped off Finch's things and stepped into the hot shower. Caroline's hair remained on the wall in swirls. I twisted my finger in one, watched it move against the tiles, water steaming up the room.

Part of me wanted to cry at the thought of washing off the memory of Finch's hands on me. The other part needed to scrub myself clean of all my desperate wanting—the need to know that we would all stay friends, the hope that maybe Finch and I could drift into something tenuously more. I closed my eyes and leaned into the heat.

Finch pulled around the front of the Manor around ten thirty. I was already waiting for her on the stoop with a hat pulled over my wet hair and an old parka of Caroline's zipped up to my chin. She stopped at the curb and I slid into the passenger seat. Finch turned her head just slightly as I closed the door behind me, eyes not quite meeting mine, as if afraid to show me the wrong face.

"Haven't seen you in ages," she teased, but I could hear an undercurrent of worry in her voice—the unspoken plea to know that we hadn't fucked things up. In my peripherals she was a cozy shape, all oversized jacket and hand-knitted scarf and hair slipping free from where she'd tucked it behind her ears. Looking at her felt like it would crack me open. A fracture in my resolve that couldn't be mended.

Overhead the sky opened like a slit throat, rain turning the car's roof into a staggered drumbeat. It was a thirty-minute ride between the Manor and the airport, the scenery mostly trees and roadside gas stations where only a pump or two worked at a time. The group chat kept pinging with notifications against my thigh as I kept my eyes on the trees. All I could think about was that dead boar in the road. I was so afraid that we'd pass it and find the body still there, equally terrified that it might be entirely gone. But Finch turned off the two-lane highway before the exit where I had wrecked. Instead, she took a detour past the cornfield.

My palms prickled. The corners of a headache thrummed at my temples. It was probably just a hangover from Finch's, still reeling from the beer and the weed and the tender way she had put her mouth to my hip bone. Finch hummed along to a playlist. Rain spat, and spat, and spat.

I leaned against the cool glass of the window, the heat puttering from Finch's vents too constricting. Corn blew by us, gray in the drizzle. The car wavered.

"Shit, sorry," Finch said, knuckles tightening around the wheel. "Road's slippery."

I jabbed a thumb against the window button and rolled mine down. Frigid air and droplets hit my face. I closed my eyes, let it wash over me.

"Can you roll that up? Your hair's still wet, and we're going to freeze half to death."

My tongue was heavy and dry. Tastebuds grated against the roof of my mouth.

"Pull over," I whispered. The car kept on. "Pull over, Finch, please, I'm gonna be sick."

The cold air coming through the window wasn't enough. I bent and let my head hang down between my knees and sucked serrated breaths down. Finch screeched to a stop on the shoulder. The car rocked as it hit the dead grass.

"Jesus, are you okay?"

I shoved the door open. Outside smelled like woodsmoke. The sky was so wet it nearly glowed purple where it touched the trees. Asphalt gave way to cornfield where I crouched, dry heaving, nothing coming up. Under my jacket I was damp with cold sweat. I couldn't get that burning scent out of my nostrils.

I kneeled there, breathing hard. The field went on and on. Her door slammed behind me, and the sound echoed forever. I flinched when Finch's hand landed on my shoulder. "What happened? Are you sick?"

There was so much concern in her voice. I shook my head hard. Her hand slid down my back, stroking the slick material of the parka. Fabric bunched around my neck, suffocating me. Spitting rain misted over us both.

"What do you need? Wanna stop at a grocery store, get you a ginger ale or something? You can lie down in the back seat for the rest of the drive."

I staggered to my feet, her hand falling away and her words drifting somewhere I couldn't reach. The corn rose over our heads. I hesitated at the edge of its boundary and took in the black smear against the sky. A crucified shape hung from a pole.

The resurrected scarecrow stood in the field, towering over the corn, covered head to toe in carrion birds.

"What the hell? Where are you going?" and then, "Jo, stop!"

I forced my way into the dead corn. Stalks crumbled beneath my grasp, brittle with frost and decay. Finch called after me again, voice growing smaller the farther I pushed on.

The flattened circle of stalks was the same as we'd left it that first time. Rotten growth and frozen dirt underfoot. That pole teetering above me. Most of the birds took to the sky as I interrupted their meal, only a few left to peck at this new scarecrow's body.

Someone had retrieved the Boar King's suit, but it was in a horrific state now, the tusks just gluey stumps, holes in the chest with straw poking out, empty pants hanging limp and shoeless. I'd assumed that the farmer who found the suit would have disposed of it or let St. Roche collect it. Who could have gotten their hands on it again? Who would know how to bring it back to life?

A dead smell permeated the air, cut past the clean cold of December. Grackles pecked at the stomach where snakes poured from the scarecrow's center.

No, not snakes—the twisted shapes were slack, hanging listless, fleshy and purpled and gnarled where the carrion had started to eat. The answer came to me like knuckles to the jaw—they were entrails. Something's intestines drooping from the cavern of the Boar King's abdomen.

"What the fuck?" Finch whispered. I spun to face her. Her eyes were wide with horror, her mouth hanging open. "Did you do this?"

I blinked once, twice, before I realized she was asking me, accusation in her voice. I paled and sputtered. "No, of course not."

We stood dwarfed beneath it, looking up at the strange picture the figure made against the sky. The meat appeared recent, or maybe just half-defrosted by the rain. The birds were unperturbed by the weather and starving for more, but they flitted away to the trees to wait for us to leave. Finch gestured to the entrails. "Are those—where do you think—are they real?"

They looked real. They had the old, browned hue of meat left exposed to air, but winter had done a decent job of keeping them intact.

"I think someone made a new offering," I whispered.

We stood in taut silence. I could feel Finch pulling away—there was so much distance between us, yesterday's warmth erased and her distrust taking its place.

"I'm done with this," she snapped. She turned and started to crash through the corn again, back to her car, calling over her shoulder, "I'm fucking done!"

"It wasn't me!" I called after her. Birds flocked back to the scarecrow and resumed their meal.

In the car, Finch shifted into drive and refused to look at me. But she left my window rolled down a crack. I drank in that air like a dog, with my eyes closed and my fingers pressed over my mouth.

We drove with the music turned off, the only sound the ping of ice on the windshield.

Amrita was so happy to see us. She launched into the back seat and yanked me into a hug smelling of her vanilla perfume. Finch was too quiet. I could feel the moment Amrita noticed we were uncomfortable— she stiffened slightly but hooked my hand in hers and held tight.

"I'm heading to Grainer," Finch said as we pulled back onto campus. Her tone was strained, her knuckles still white with tension. "I'll let you guys out in front of the Manor."

Amrita obeyed without question as Finch pulled to a stop at the front door. I stayed where I was in the passenger seat, and Amrita paused.

"Not gonna come inside and hang out with me?" she pushed.

"I'm going with Finch to get some work done. I'll be back this evening, promise."

Finch exhaled hard through her nose. Amrita just gave me a nod and closed the car door, turning into the Manor with her bags. The tires hissed as Finch pulled around into a parking lot centered in the hub of Rotham's campus, where Main Lawn led to Grainer. We didn't speak. She silently maneuvered into a spot and yanked the key from the ignition, then ran her hands down her face. When she finally hefted herself out of the car and started down the promenade, I hurried to follow, ducking beneath the rain.

Grainer was a flurry of activity, busy students passing us on the stairs and the studio itself filled with familiar faces—Mars in their cubicle with Cameron sitting by the doorway, Veda scrubbing brushes at the sink, Phoebe stapling canvas down to a frame. The greetings they called felt more cursory than friendly. Finch's responses were short. I had to nearly jog to keep up with her.

"Wait," I tried once we were out of earshot of the others. "We should talk."

Finch beelined for her studio and spoke without facing me. "What is there to say, Jo?"

I hesitated in her doorway. My stomach was still uneasy, head pounding with urgency. "It wasn't me. I didn't make that."

"Honestly, I don't really care, Jo. I don't care about any of this. But you clearly aren't okay. You came to my apartment looking like you saw a goddamn ghost or something, cut up and freaked out, and I'm just supposed to pretend everything is normal? Don't say some bullshit like 'I'm fine' to me because I know you. I know you really fucking well. And I'm tired of being lied to."

She was fuming. Papers and sketches fluttered as she rushed to pile materials, gathering them in her arms.

"What are you doing?" I asked, faltering.

"I'm going to work in my room," she snapped. "I want to be alone. Is that a problem?"

I rocked back as if hit. "No, of course not. I can just go," I said.

Finch gave me a scathing look. "Didn't you already leave once this morning?"

I flinched, eyes betraying me by welling immediately. Her expression softened a little. But she just shook her head before continuing, "I need some space, okay?"

My face must have fallen somewhere deep and irretrievable. She crumpled, fight drooping out of her shoulders and sketches wrinkling in her arms, smearing against her wet jacket.

"I'm sorry," I tried. I didn't know what else to say. I needed her to pull me into her again, to press her lips to my temple, to tell me she was sorry, too, that she didn't mean any of it, that we could figure this out and go somewhere where ritual and resentment couldn't touch us. I wanted to remember nothing else but the warm brush of her mouth. Her body aligned with mine. The comfort of her reaching for me in her sleep.

"I just need space," Finch whispered, and she brushed past me, paper fluttering out of her arms and landing on the studio floor.

I caught the hem of her jacket in my fingers. "Wait," I tried again. Finch's eyes met mine, shadowed with frustration. She stepped out of my reach.

"Gotta go," she muttered sadly, like she was sorry for saying it. But I let her leave. And the studio door swung shut behind her with an echoing bang.

I could tell that she wished she hadn't hurt me. I could tell that she would do it again.

Fuck the studio, and fuck painting. Fuck the rain and fuck my useless heart. In my cubicle I thrust my headphones on to block out Phoebe's music. Sleet hit the window, caked the sill, fogged the glass until the darkening sky and the lights across campus looked like a ghoulish recreation of a James McNeill Whistler *Nocturne*, all speckled dots of yellow against blue. Something passed behind me over and over again while I worked at my desk—each time the shape of its body blacked out the light behind me and cast a shadow over my sketches. But when I turned and snapped at it to leave me alone, one headphone pulled away from my ear to listen for feet, I found the doorway empty.

The sketches I made were horrifying things. Pencil lead dug so hard into paper that it tore lines down into the surface of my desk. Graphite smeared all over the side of my hand as I carved out terrible apparitions—the boar on its side, snout parted in a dying exhale. The creature in the glass case. The whorls of Caroline's hair on the shower wall. I hated them all. I could barely look at them; just finished a drawing before flipping the page and starting another.

The building rage was all-consuming. It took everything in me not to tear every painting I'd ever made into rags. Instead, I crumpled a sketch and ripped it into pieces, staring at the painting of us in the trees, my women hovering between the black trunks like apparitions in the dark.

I always thought they'd made me softer, kinder. Now I felt like a girl that would have killed for them. I wanted to fill with fury, or obsession, or some brutal intertwining of the two. I was afraid that my desire was different. That hunger came out of me like a transfigured heart.

I could see the cracks splintering between us—those awful tendrils spiking away from the dissolution of our perfect five. The poison had to be cut out.

But I was nearly sure that the poison was me.

23

Puddle-Eyed Vulgarity

Amrita bought me a lily our freshman year. It was the kind of present that made me feel incapable—I'd never been able to keep a plant alive on my own. That lily was the first. Fear bolstered me—the dread that its death would let Amrita down. She loved its white flowers and fat stamens and the way each bloom unfurled like a cupped hand. Loved how it would droop to tell us it was thirsty, as if saddened by my neglect. All that love made me love it too. We kept it just out of direct sunlight, and I watered it every Thursday.

It was New Year's Eve. I hadn't spoken to Finch in days, and Caroline had been silent in our group chat. Saz texted constantly, each message growing more excited about her flight back to Indiana in a few days. *Poltergeist* was on in the living room, and snow fell with wicked strength.

In the kitchen, the lily's leaves were black around the edges. The flowers hung and sulked, despite the still-damp soil from the last time I'd given them a drink. Pollen dusted the countertop as Amrita bent close and examined. I hovered at the foot of the stairs and scratched absently at my tattoo.

"We've kept her alive for three years," Amrita murmured, lifting one crispy leaf. It crumbled under her touch. "I don't understand what went wrong."

Everything I touched seemed to rot these days—my paintings, my body, Finch. The ruins of the lily gathered on the countertop like piles of razed ash. Amrita swiped the mess into her palms and emptied it into the sink. Instinct told me to blame the shadow trailing me. But I turned and found the stairs empty, only my body left to darken the doorway.

"You alright?" Amrita asked when she finally looked up at me. "Finch said you were sick the other day on the way to the airport. Why didn't you tell me?"

I kept my arms crossed over my chest and avoided the question. I contemplated a million different responses—*Why can't you let it go? Why didn't you know without me having to say it? How can I ever be expected to say it?*—and settled on a shy question of my own: "You talked to Finch?"

Amrita pulled out a chair at the table. She hesitated before sitting and said, "Want a cup of tea?"

I nodded and took the seat across from hers. She prepped two mugs with tea bags hooked over the handles. We still had a few hours before Finch was supposed to come over to watch the ball drop, and my mouth watered at the idea of caffeine. All that sleeplessness was catching up with me. I had a permanent headache and a lack of drive for anything other than sitting with them on the couch. Energy wouldn't have mattered regardless—if there was a party on campus, we hadn't been invited, and Rotham wasn't known for hosting any events for the New Year. It would just be the four of us and a quiet night inside.

Amrita slid my mug over. She'd made it just how I liked it—honey and lemon. I thanked her and said, "Did she tell you the rest?"

Amrita grimaced. "Yes, Finch told me what you saw in the field."

"It's not mine."

"I know that. It's not mine either."

"Okay."

She raised her eyebrows. "Just okay?"

I cupped my hands around the mug. "It's not yours, it's not mine, it's definitely not Finch's. Saz and Caroline have been gone since

Christmas, though we don't know how long it's been up. Someone else on campus could have made it. They all know about the Boar King."

Amrita shook her head. "It's too specific." By "too specific," I knew what she meant. There was too much intention behind it, in the organs hanging from its stomach and the purposeful propping up of the Boar King's tusked hood. "Only we would know to make it like that."

"We shouldn't have made it in the first place," I said.

"We didn't know it would be like this. It was supposed to be fun." Amrita held her scarred palm in the other hand and traced a finger over the faint line down the center. "I think you're making yourself sick over this whole thing. It's not real, Jo. You know that."

But even she sounded unsure. "Yeah," I said, mostly to wipe that regretful look off her face. I squeezed my left hand into a fist and felt my own wound strain at the edges. "What about Solo? Do you feel ready?"

"I don't want to think about Solo right now," she said. "Can't we talk about something else? Something exciting to take with us into the new year, like a resolution or goal?"

I took a long drink and felt citrus and sweetness coat my tongue. Finally, I cleared my throat and said, "I don't have any goals. I just missed you. I'm glad you're home."

Her smile crinkled the corners of her eyes. "Missed you too. My mom asked about you."

"Oh yeah? What'd she say?"

"She wanted to know when you're coming to see her again. Said she'd get the baklava you loved from that bakery in town."

"Fuck, don't remind me, now I need it."

Amrita's voice was gentle when she said, "That's your goal, then. Make it through the rest of this year and eat baklava with me."

I couldn't fight my own smile. It was such a simple dream, so nearly attainable that it almost broke my heart.

"You didn't drink your tea," I said finally, touching my fingertip to Amrita's cold mug. She looked at it and shrugged.

"Didn't want it," she answered. "I just wanted another reason to sit here with you."

The front door banged open and brought the wind with it. We both jumped at the sound and sight of a figure stumbling inside. Caroline unwound a scarf from her face. There was a suitcase in her hands, and her nose was red from the cold.

"Caroline!" Amrita called, grinning. "You're early!"

We went to her. It felt like a mirror of that first day on campus, pre-ritual and pre-Survey and pre-hysteria. She was just as bright as that day, elegant and imposing in an expensive winter coat and leather boots. But her eyes were such a dark and wild blue that when she hugged me close to her shoulder, I thought they might be black. I wondered if she was on something. If she was suffering the same creeping deterioration that I was. If we all were, and we just couldn't talk about it.

I once thought we could talk about anything. But the idea of any of them knowing what went on in my head was an impossibility. I was too afraid to be the only one. There was such a real, looming chance that they might come to believe there was something wrong with me.

I helped Caroline out of her coat, and Amrita got the kettle going again. Caroline kicked her shoes off by the door and called into the kitchen, asking Amrita if she had anything stronger than tea, if we planned on getting sloshed, if she was going to have to be the only one ringing in the New Year with any enthusiasm. Her presence sparked a new energy in the two of us. I accepted a shot from Amrita, who was a little giddy already with Caroline draped over her shoulders and laughing. Whiskey burned me all the way down to the bone. Antiseptic. Alive. Reinvigorated.

"I want to be drunk enough that you can't light a match next to me," Caroline said, immediately topping off our glasses with a second shot and clinking hers with mine. Amrita laughed into her glass. They drank again. I hesitated, stomach still tossing from the first drink—but when Caroline's black pupils fixed on me again, I knocked the shot back and grimaced.

This could be our way of coming together and banishing the near occult, Moody's ever-present gaze, Solo's eventual promise. We could get drunk and forget about it.

Caroline left her things by the door as we settled into the living room, freshly tipsy, everything warmer now. The movie was still playing but muted, its sound replaced by music on a speaker and the rising timbre of Caroline's voice.

She moved erratically, spoke with her hands. "I had to get out of there, my parents wanted me to stay until next Friday. I told them I'd rather bash my head in with their antiques than be in that house for one more day."

"Jesus," Amrita said, but she was laughing a little.

"Anyway, I wanted to tell all of you before you heard it from someone else," Caroline added casually, "but my parents donated a few hundred thousand dollars to Rotham this Christmas. They expect it to guarantee the Solo spot for me. I told them that wasn't how it works, but I can't stop them from wasting their money. So it's done."

We blinked back in stunned silence. Caroline swirled her drink in her hands. There was something deathly serious about the firm line of her shoulders and the half smile playing at the corners of her mouth.

"A few?" I asked. "How many is a few?"

"Five hundred thousand," she answered.

"Five hundred thousand dollars?" Amrita repeated.

"Caroline," I started. "That's—that's nearly double your entire Rotham tuition."

Caroline shrugged. "I wanted to tell you before Finch got here. You know how she'll be about it."

"She's going to know eventually," I said. "Like you said, people are going to talk. That stuff is public record, and Cameron already has it out for you. It looks like a bribe."

"Well," Caroline said brightly, teeth bared in a grin, "who says the spot is actually mine? All Moody talks about lately is how the work is shitty, how the work to come will still be shitty, how I need to apply myself if I hope to earn the spot. The only thing that might make me capable of a great body of thesis work would be if I sacrificed Finch next."

Amrita's throat bobbed with her swallow. "Caroline, fuck. Don't say that."

"I'm obviously kidding!"

But Caroline's voice was strained, her eyes still too dark, something piercing and endless about them beneath her fair lashes. There was a knock on the door, and then Finch emerged from the storm with an arm bent over her face, blocking out the worst of the wind.

"It's miserable out there. Sorry I'm late."

It felt like forever since we'd fought in Grainer. Since then, her studio had been empty, our shifts at the library canceled for the holidays, her window in Tuck House glowing without fail. On my walks to Grainer, I had stopped outside of it and contemplated doing something foolish, like tossing a stone at the glass until she emerged on the fire escape. I was such a coward. I wanted her like nothing else.

She was beautiful even now, with her hair dampened and skin chapped by the snow. The Manor's light illuminated her in shades of orange. The smile on her face was hesitant—her eyes bounced from Amrita to me, where that smile faltered a little, sheepish and private. Then she landed on Caroline, and the smile dropped away completely. "You're back," she said. It was a statement intended for exclamation that came out hollow.

"Come have a drink, Finch," Caroline said.

Finch hesitated and then shed her jacket, snaring it on a hook by the door before she claimed the spot beside me on the couch as if it were no problem. Maybe it wasn't for her. But I could feel every inch that we didn't touch, that fine line between us, the heat of Finch's hip so close to pressing against mine. My body recalled hers even when I wished it wouldn't.

Caroline sprawled on the floor and scrolled through her playlist, queuing songs that would only become more chaotic with her increasing drunkenness. Amrita started listing off requests as Finch's phone buzzed in her pocket. She touched it through the fabric but didn't check the notification.

"You've been working in your room," I said quietly, just for her.

She shifted uneasily. "Grainer is cold as fuck. I don't know how you bear it."

It was such a cop-out. I scoffed a little, tipsy enough to let how I really felt spill through the cracks. I could feel her looking at me but refused to turn my head. I didn't look up until she stood and beckoned for me to follow. "Come on, help me fix a drink."

"It takes two of you to make a drink?" Caroline drawled. It was a challenge. Her eyes flitted suspiciously between the two of us.

"Yeah, if you want a good one," I called over my shoulder, and followed Finch into the kitchen. She peered into the fridge and shook an old bottle of seltzer. I watched her unscrew the cap and taste it, grimacing.

"Flat," she declared. She grabbed a beer instead and closed the fridge, slid her phone out of her pocket to check it. I hefted myself up on the kitchen counter beside the dying lily as she set her phone down beside me and uncapped the bottle with the opener hooked to her keys. The music in the other room kicked off even louder now—Caroline's preferred brand of electronic clashing.

"We should talk about it," I whispered beneath the rumble of sound.

Finch looked at me. Really looked at me. Her eyes had a sad weight, that newborn-calf kind of gaze that made me soft for her every time. The Manor's warmth sapped the dampness from her hair, and now the strands around her forehead sweetly curled.

She cleared her throat and said, "You'll have to remind me what 'it' is referring to. If it's that gruesome display in the cornfield, I don't want to hear it."

I shook my head hard. "No, I—I mean us."

Some of the fight left her shoulders, replaced by a different directness. She set the beer down beside the sink and caged me with her hands on either side of my thighs, gripping the edge of the countertop. My pulse kicked. I was so aware of the two of them down the hall, their laughter carrying, the music loud enough to vibrate the room, skin humming with her nearness.

"Go ahead and talk," she murmured, looking at my mouth when I wet my lips with my tongue. Everything felt like a risk. Her T-shirt was loose around her shoulders. I reached up, hands trembling, and rested my fingers along the frayed neckline. Those two shots had sparked something in me. I needed her closer. I'd do anything to make it happen.

But my awful mouth went ahead and said, "Do you regret it?"

She shook her head and swallowed. "'Course not."

Her arms caged me. I dragged my thumb across her collarbone and tried to keep my voice from shaking. "Really?"

"Yeah," she breathed. There was a twinge of disbelief in her voice, thinly veiled frustration. "I want it to happen again."

Heat everywhere, in my head and my mouth, in the space between us. One of her hands slid up and brushed against my knee, just the barest flicker of touch. "Me too," I whispered when I finally realized she was waiting for me.

Finch smiled. She leaned closer and stopped a breath away. I could smell traces of her beer and the citrusy stain of linseed oil where she'd touched her T-shirt. Down the hall Caroline said something low and indistinct, and Amrita erupted into laughter.

"We can't do this here," Finch murmured, and I nodded immediately, but neither of us moved to pull away. Her palm slid up my knee. It was like her fingers were wired to my nerves—every touch lit me up, made me fight not to tremble. She stepped between my knees and rested her forehead on my shoulder, fingertips pressing into my thigh hard enough to promise a bruise. The image was invigorating; I imagined the outline of her hand marked on me, somewhere I could fit my hand to later in bed. I leaned my cheek against the top of her head and closed my eyes. Wrapped my arms around her shoulders and breathed in.

"Sorry about this week." Her voice was muffled against my neck. "I don't want to fight, I'm just scared."

She would have never said it if I could see her face. The admission tucked itself away in my throat instead where it could die unnoticed. I tightened my hold on her, as if she might float away without it.

"Forget it," I answered. I snared my fingers in the fine hair at the nape of her neck. She sighed beneath my touch. There was so much I wanted to say. That I was sorry, too, for scaring her. That I was fucking terrified. That if she could see what I saw, she'd never want to touch me again—she'd think me ruined beyond repair.

The softest press of her lips to my throat was my unraveling. I twined my fingers deeper into her hair and held fast.

"You scare me," she mumbled, the words dissolving into a second kiss. Then another. "Like, you really scare the shit out of me."

I laughed a little, dragged my nails over her scalp. "Why?"

"I don't know, you're just—" She hesitated. "It's like you see everything that we can't. You're smarter than us, and you're talented as fuck, and you get this look in your eyes when you're painting or when the rest of us are talking that makes me think you're somewhere else, far away."

Her teeth scraped across the soft skin at my shoulder. What would I say if she left a mark there? How would I explain it away? They always saw right through me. I could never get away with anything. I was barely hanging on to my concealed delusion, and clearly Finch had seen through it too.

"You make it so hard to know what to do with you," she said. Another kiss.

Her phone buzzed beside my thigh, loud against the countertop. My eyes slit open to look. Thea's name lit up on the screen above a message preview that read: wish u were at cameron's tonight so we . . .

I froze. Finch felt it and pulled away to give me a questioning look. Her hair was mussed, her lips red and damp, her pupils dilated with desire. She cocked her head askance. When I still didn't speak, her eyes darted to her phone, and she slackened as she flipped it face down against the counter.

"Jo, it's not—we're not—you know it's not like that, it's—"

"Three minutes until midnight! Hurry up, you're going to miss it!" Amrita poked her head out of the living room and peered at us from the end of the hallway. I could barely make out her face in the dim lighting, couldn't read what we looked like to her in the staggered action of pulling apart.

"Be right there," Finch called back. She turned to me, but I was already sliding off the countertop and away from her. The sound of my pulse in my ears was nearly loud enough to war with the music. "Jo, wait."

I left her behind in the kitchen. Amrita was stretched across half of the sofa, Caroline perched on the floor with her head against Amrita's legs. I hauled myself onto the empty cushion and watched the clock count down. Finch followed a second later, hovering in the doorway. I could only look at her out of the corner of my eye. I tried to focus on the back of Caroline's head instead, her hands in her lap, picking at the raw edge of a fingernail.

"I wish Saz were here," I said as the countdown glowed. "It's not the same without her."

Amrita hummed, one arm slung across my shoulders. "I wish *we* were there with Saz. Her dads probably took her somewhere beachy, I'm sure she's knocking back piña coladas by now."

"Oh, to be rich," Finch sighed.

"It's not all that great. Look where I ended up." Caroline gestured loosely around the room. Finch snorted a laugh.

"We are very fun," Amrita scoffed, "and you chose to be here, in case you forgot."

"Ten seconds," Finch reminded.

The numbers ticked off. I drew my knees up to my chest as if they could cage my pounding heart. Saz's absence was palpable, but the room still felt too full, as if there were another person in the room watching us unfold. Fireworks announced another year. Past the shut windows I could hear them echo across campus, brilliant pops of sound.

Caroline seized Amrita by the jaw and kissed her directly on the mouth. Amrita sputtered and laughed into it, until Caroline turned and snatched up my hand next, pressing her lips to my knuckles and smiling viciously. I didn't look at Finch. Lights bloomed on the TV screen, spark and spark and spark.

24

GORED AND ELATED

The first two weeks of January brought the mad crush of the studio again, critiques with Moody, Saz in her bedroom unfairly tan and sunny for a dead Indiana winter. Caroline declared that Saz's return to campus had to be celebrated, as if it were a surprise. I guessed in some ways it was—now that Saz had no chance of Soloing, the pressure had dissipated. I didn't consider that she didn't have to come back. She could leave Rotham behind forever.

The party became Caroline's baby. She invited anyone and everyone. There was a frenzied desperation to her, the need to be active clashing with the timelines dragging alongside us. The Solo selection would take place in early April. We had a little over two months to finalize at least twenty distinct pieces in addition to our completed thesis papers and artist statements. My paper was barely more than a rough outline. I hated everything I attempted to paint, scrapped and restarted four different pieces in a week. I was trying to capture Caroline sitting at the end of my bed in her lavender nightgown the morning the Boar King was found. But her face kept coming out wrong. The shadows wouldn't lie down.

I drank too much before the party could even begin. The evening was uncharacteristically warm—though warm at this time of year really meant just above freezing—and it made everyone giddy. Caroline took control of something synthesized over her speaker, and Amrita mixed juice and a cheap handle in a pitcher, shimmying around the kitchen with her cup sloshing over. Saz poured us all tequila shots with slices of lime. We clinked glasses, Saz's expression erratic as she seized my chin.

"Eye contact, Jo! We are not risking seven years of bad sex. The past twenty-two have been horrific enough."

The liquor burned all the way down to my belly and lay sterile on my tongue. Amrita made a twisted face, lipstick staining the rim where she'd drunk. "Yuck," Caroline declared, grinning and chasing the shot with a sip of Amrita's concoction. The grin crumpled into a grimace. "Extra yuck."

Amrita rolled her eyes and started to argue about the quality of ingredients she'd put into the drink—*love, grapefruit, simple syrup, chemical x.*

"Pour me some of Strega Amrita's potion," I said, laughing as Amrita blew me a kiss.

A sober start to the night wasn't an option. After New Year's Eve, I wanted everything to appear fuzzy enough to slip into unreliability. It was the only chance I had of dancing without soul-crushing humiliation, the only way I could pretend everything was fine and we were still the same people we'd always been, and the only hope I had of being able to stop fixating on the invented image of Finch naked in Thea's bed. Just the thought was enough to make me flush. I accepted a cup from Amrita and drank—it was actually kind of good.

That cup turned into three by the time Finch showed up. She came in the back door, knowing it would be unlocked, with a bag slung over her shoulder. She was wearing a shirt that used to be mine, cropped above the waist of her cargoes. The hesitant smile she gave me was such a present. The sight of it nearly made me forget all the ways things had gone wrong, all the foolishness that had calcified into a stone in my chest. I tucked my smile into my cup and took a long swallow.

"Can I leave this in one of your rooms?" she asked, hefting the strap of her bag up and off her shoulder. "I brought all my rolling stuff, and I don't want one of these kleptos to snatch it."

Amrita took the offered bag as Finch claimed the seat beside me and laid out her supplies. I was already tipsy enough to drag my eyes over her hands in front of everyone—memorizing her knuckles, silver rings, chipped green polish—and then her mouth as she slid her tongue along the paper and sealed it shut. Her eyes flicked up and met mine. I couldn't read what lived there. She held the joint up between us and gave me her soft smile, the one that made me think I might die if she didn't touch me again. "Want some?"

"Don't get her crossfaded already," Caroline said. She was swaying to the music, like she couldn't bear to stand still for even a second.

Finch told her that I could decide for myself. I nodded, swelling with pleasure at her defense and hating myself for it. She held the joint to my lips, her other hand coming up and lighting it, her rough voice telling me to inhale. Burned grassiness cooked my tongue and replaced all the acid of Amrita's potion. I turned and exhaled away from them, my head floating up, and up, and up, and away from me.

The Manor was bigger than any other on-campus housing, but it crowded quickly. Cameron, Phoebe, and Yejun were the first outside of our crew to arrive. Scattered faces from different fine arts majors came close behind. Veda arrived with someone I didn't recognize on her arm—a boyfriend who'd already graduated? A hometown friend?

Thea appeared an hour in with Mars at her side. I pretended to be caught up in conversation with Phoebe as the two of them melted into the crowd so I wouldn't have to witness Thea greet Finch.

"It's just so frustrating to not be chosen for Solo, because I don't think Moody like, gets what I'm trying to do here," Phoebe sighed. "I'm not claiming to be an outsider artist. I'm *inspired* by my anxiety. There's a huge difference, you know? You get me?"

I kept drinking.

Heat rose in the house as bodies packed into it. I recognized a few from my freshman year foundation classes—a girl I thought might be named Haeun smoked a cigarette inside, opaque smoke curling around the bottle blond of her hair, and beside her someone from graphic design fiddled with the window and tried to pry it open. The back door was propped ajar, and while a part of me was afraid of how loud we were being and how the sound might travel across campus, I was thankful for the cool air seeping into the living room. The music was just repetitive and familiar enough to get me bouncing. I started to bob my head, liquor sloshing pleasantly in my belly as Saz looped an arm around my waist.

"I told Caroline that some SOPHIE would get you going!" she cried, tugging me into her and turning the two of us around in a circle. "I was like, 'It's not a party without hyperpop,' and she told me to get the fuck out of her face when she's on aux, but look at you now!"

I laughed. I felt clumsy and wild as Saz drew me deeper into the crowd. My head kept turning and looking for the rest of them. It seemed impossible that they could have gone far from me without something in me knowing it instinctively. Saz flickered beneath the colorful lights. I blinked, or maybe my vision went away for a second, punctuated by blackness and the sluggish return of my mind. Her head rolled with a laugh. My hand went up as if I could hold her in place, but she melted past me, spinning and spinning and spinning. A near flutter picked up in my ear again. Louder this time, like a moth hovering too close to a bulb. I swatted around my head and turned into someone else's orbit, my foot catching, my hips stuttering.

Saz's hand slipped from mine as I twisted. I kept going, trying to right myself. Somehow in that blip of time she disappeared into the mix. I'd lost everyone. The faces I did find were just strange enough that I couldn't land on familiarity. I lingered too long. Eyes held mine as I moved, hands sticky around my drink, head too heavy to hold high. I let myself be swept up in thudding sound and the sweaty cling of my shirt against my chest. Movement was a new language. Our feet pounded the floor like a heart hooked to a machine. Caroline's party lights painted the living room in a million hues—she was purple when I finally caught her gaze across the crowd, her hands twisting above her head, her chin raised and the smile spreading there wide and knowing. The Manor was too full. It swelled and wheezed every time the front door opened, people pouring in and then spilling out onto the steps, floor creaking overhead where I imagined people in my room with their hands and their eyes on my things. Caroline's laugh carried. I scanned for her again and came up empty. That fluttering buzz continued, the endless whirring of a beehive or a blown speaker. I pressed a finger against my eardrum. It kept ringing. We were too loud. Probably going to face the wrath of administration soon. But I was the kind of drunk that couldn't be self-conscious. The kind of lost that couldn't connect neurons to limbs.

My fingers tingled when they bumped someone else's. I turned, trying to follow the touch, but none of the people pushing close belonged to me. Bodies kept writhing even when my own slowed. Why had Saz left? I wanted her back. I wanted Amrita's close comfort. I wanted Caroline, the white beacon of her head in that sea of color, the tall rise of her, mythic and mystical.

I wanted Finch. I didn't want to think about the consequences of that desire.

"Looking for the bathroom? I think it's upstairs, though someone's been in there for like twenty minutes."

I didn't recognize the voice. The eyes I met were heavy-lidded and pretty against tan skin, everything flickering blue now under the lights. I went to smooth a piece of hair behind my ear and snagged it on an earring, off-kilter. Water would be good. Water would be smart. My tongue wet my lips, numb with drunkenness. The girl in front of me was familiar in a discomfiting way. What was her name? Something like Amaya, or Azalea? Was her last name Prince? Or was that the music muddling my memory?

She smiled. "What's your name?"

I think I giggled. She'd read my mind. Or did I ask her first? Probably not. She kept staring, waiting for me to answer.

I shrugged. "You're in my house, you should know my name."

Her hands went up in defense, but her smile widened. "Your house, huh? Does that mean you have a room you could take me to?"

Agnes. That was her name. We had a class together when I was a sophomore—Fujioka's Intuitive Sculpture. There had been an odd number of students in the class, so I ended up paired off with Professor Fujioka for all the hours we spent soaking pieces of bread in resin and trying to make them stand on end around the classroom. I didn't think Agnes had met my eyes once in the whole time we'd been classmates. But now her gaze was heavy and hunting.

I considered the consequences. Fought the urge to search the crowd for Finch. She was probably off with Thea somewhere, tongues twisting down each other's throats. My stomach tossed.

"Yeah," I said finally, sweat pooling at the base of my spine. "Wanna go upstairs?"

I was kind of proud of myself for the drunken boldness, but she was the one that ended up taking my hand and leading me through the crowd to the dark staircase. I abandoned my drink on the kitchen table. We had to maneuver over people perched on the steps, something sticky nearly fixing my shoe to the wood. The second floor was dark with only a few people milling in the hall, waiting for the bathroom. The next staircase was empty as we ascended. I still hadn't seen any of the others. A tiny insecure voice whispered in the back of my head—what if Finch had left? What if she left with Thea?

But what did it really matter? We weren't exclusive. We were barely anything more than a night in her bed and her mouth on my neck.

Agnes asked which door was mine, and I nodded when she touched the knob on the left. Caroline's remained closed. Something thumped downstairs, too loud. A cheer went up among the crowd, and then the click of the latch muffled all sound to a dull drone echoing the one already digging into my ear.

As soon as we were closed inside together, she crowded me against the door and pressed her lips to mine. Her hands went to my waist, hooking in my belt loops, dragging our hips to meet in the middle. My brain took too long to catch up, and when it did, my lips parted in surprise and admitted her tongue. One hand rucked up the hem of my shirt and pressed to the soft skin of my abdomen. Her fingers grazed and made my stomach tighten in anticipation. I fumbled for something to hold on to and landed on her waist, touch light and unsure over her shirt. She sighed into my mouth.

I couldn't leave my own head. Everything was an awareness—the slick drag of her tongue against mine, the tension of her thumb rubbing circles against my belly, the clinging scent of weed in her hair. There were clothes all over my floor and three half-empty glasses of water on the bedside table, and I was a girl incapable of letting go. I couldn't remember how to play the part. Visions kept carrying me back to Finch's bed, her hands on me, her lips soft against mine, the tender way her hair slid through my fingers. But if Finch had wanted me all to herself, she could have said so. I had no one to answer to. Now I was somewhere outside of my body watching this girl want me like my life was just a secret I was privy to.

"You okay?" she mumbled against my lips, and I nodded. A kiss. And then, "You sure?" Another nod, more kissing. I pushed into her, let everything melt down to something messier, tried to claim ownership over this body and this moment and this girl in my room. She let me steer her to the bed, smiling against my mouth. We fell together. Her dark hair splayed against my pillow, my vision just hazy enough to make the planes of her face shift and morph. Her eyes were the amber of an old memory, something eerie that I couldn't place. I blinked her back to reality. A shrill whine picked up as her palms slid higher under my shirt and coaxed it over my head. I bent to kiss her again, fitting between her legs as she arched up into me.

This time the crash was so loud that I was sure that something important had collapsed.

I sat up, frozen. Agnes's hands clutched my hips. Downstairs some-one shouted, but the words were too muffled to decipher whose voice it was. Still—the intention behind them was filled with heat. Her fingers caught the nape of my neck to pull me closer again, but I pushed back.

"Wait," I pleaded, breathless. I hovered and listened.

There was a slam. The lilting rise of an argument among the shrill cry of a song. Then: "Are you fucking kidding me? Fuck you, Finch."

I slid off Agnes in a rush, nearly hitting the floor knees first when my ankle snared in the sheets. That was Caroline's voice. Agnes called after me, but I was already halfway back into my shirt, yanking it over my stomach and stumbling down the stairs. At the bottom, the sea of people jeered, the music too loud, the colors too bright. I grabbed the railing for support.

Caroline and Finch stood in the center of the disaster. Caroline was trashed or high on something—even from where I stood, I could see the hazy gleam of her eyes and the unconcerned way her hair fell into them. Her finger pressed into Finch's chest with a hard jab. I scanned the room for Amrita, Saz, anyone. One of us needed to rein this in.

"You think you're so much better than the rest of us," Caroline spat. "You think everyone worships the fucking ground you walk on. I'm sick of your attitude."

"If projecting your self-hate onto me makes you feel better, go ahead." Finch knocked Caroline's hand away from her chest. Caroline's face shifted. The shadow of moving lights made her unrecognizable. Her expression kept becoming a new person entirely. When her silence dragged on, Finch continued. "Oh come on, that can't be it. Say what you want to say to me, tell me to go fuck myself again. Clearly you need an outlet for whatever expectation you've put on yourself. Or was that your parents? Can't handle that you might lose out on your chance to Solo? That you might embarrass them and waste all the money they dropped on you?"

Caroline shoved her, hard, and Finch stumbled back, unprepared. The resulting grin that spread across Caroline's face was terrifying.

"I told you to shut the fuck up," Caroline snarled.

"Caroline!" That was Amrita, trying to shove her way down the hall with Saz following behind her, bodies pressed too close to breathe.

The buzz picked up higher now, like my hearing had faltered in one ear. A familiar dark figure stood at the edge of the packed room. I couldn't look.

"That would make everything easy for you, right? If I just shut up and got out of your way?"

"It would be easier if I never had to see you again in my life."

Laughter rose. The crowd was so tight that my ribs felt constricted. I sucked hard breaths down through my nose.

"Just let them knock each other out and give the rest of us a chance at Solo," someone called past a laugh.

"Hell yeah, get Prozac Kozak in there too."

It took me too long to realize that the voices belonged to Cameron and Yejun, and by "Prozac Kozak," they meant me. Someone shouldered me, hard. I kept trying to fight my way forward as a shout lobbed itself into the middle of things. "Hit her!"

"No," I breathed, but no one would let me through, no one would let me reach them.

Caroline was only a few inches taller than Finch, but she towered over her, her pupils too wide, everything cast in shadow. Finch didn't back down. She tilted her head back to take in the sight of Caroline's fury.

"I can't wait to watch you fail," Caroline said. "I can't wait until the rest of the world sees you for what you really are. I can't wait until they know how much time you spend fucking posturing. Until they see how deeply you despise yourself, and what a weak attempt at begging for praise your work really is."

Finch reared her hand back.

"Move," I said to the people in front of me, and then, louder, "Move!"

But the hit landed. Caroline's head snapped with the slap, Finch's palm a brutal connection with her cheekbone. A cry went up among the crowd—shock, delight, awe.

"Party's over! Everyone get the fuck out of my house!"

Amrita's shout carried over the careening noise. I couldn't remember ever hearing her yell before—it took my mind a moment to place her voice by the front door. She yanked it open, the world a black cutout beyond the jamb.

The noise just continued to rise. I was drowning in sound. I couldn't move, pinned in that writhing mess, watching Amrita finally body her way through to them as Caroline reached for Finch and mouthed *you're dead you're dead you're dead* over and over again.

"I said get the fuck out!" Amrita shouted again.

People poured onto the steps of the Manor. The house rocked with them as I pushed, trying to reach them in its center, the heart of my heart. Relief passed through me as soon as I saw Saz was with Caroline, cupping her face and examining. The lights flickered. Saz said something about taking Caroline upstairs, and I just kept asking, "What? What?" Trying to hear above the roar, trying to shove out that sickening buzz, trying to pretend all of this hadn't happened, that we were okay, that everything was going to be fine. But Saz's shoulder bumped mine as she called for me to follow, and together we helped Caroline start her ascent.

I turned back once. Amrita was a stern force as she guided people out. When Finch hesitated beside her, I watched Amrita shake her head hard and point to the door. It was too loud to hear, but I caught the shape of the words on her lips: *you too.*

Finch looked up. Our eyes locked. I wanted to snare her in place. I wanted to know what had gone wrong, wanted to pry her open and find the reason there, safe behind her ribs, in the place none of us were allowed to look. But Amrita's hand landed on her back and gently pushed, and we hefted Caroline up and out of the apocalypse.

She was a heavy weight on my shoulder. Saz's jaw clenched as she hoisted Caroline's right side, pinning Caroline between us.

"She was—" Caroline started, but she made an awful sound, like a cry had lodged inside her chest. "She can be so fucking mean."

Saz hushed and soothed her, telling Caroline we'd be in her room soon, that she could lie down and sleep.

"Bathroom," Caroline croaked. "I'm going to be sick."

Miraculously, she made it. Saz held blond hair away from Caroline's face as she clutched the toilet. I wobbled in the doorway. I was still too drunk.

"Go to bed, Jo. I got this," Saz said when she saw the look on my face.

My room felt different now that Agnes had been in it. The past hour had shifted something tectonic—there wasn't a space to get comfortable. Guilt made me shiver uncontrollably, teeth chattering. I perched on the bed and tried to obey Saz's command. But rest was impossible as I listened to them shuffle in the hall, Caroline's weak voice filtering under the door. Saz's answer was calm and comforting. They muttered back and forth for a while, and then things went quiet. I thought I heard someone go downstairs, or come up.

Somehow without my realizing, my eyes shut for a moment—or I blacked out—and when I came to again, it was dark and silent. I crept to the bathroom and emptied my stomach. Cold water on my face and swished between my teeth brought me closer to life.

Caroline's door hung open a crack, the space beyond it hot and dense as the interior of a mouth, red exit sign beaming down the hall and painting everything apocalyptic. Inside, it was silent—I hovered. I waited to hear her breathe. When I couldn't, I crept closer and found her on her back, mouth slack and eyelids fluttering along the restless boundary of near sleep.

"Who left you like this?" I murmured as I turned her over to her side. Caroline let out a weak sound. Something about it, that broken whimper and the clammy touch of her forehead under my hand, broke my heart.

I dragged the trash can over in case she might be sick, even though the sight of it made my stomach toss again, and crouched beside it.

"Jo," she said, voice cracking, eyes still squeezed shut. I could smell tequila and her shampoo mixing with body heat in the sheets. I reached for her hand, and my heart seized when her fingers twined with mine. Her eyes slit open. I couldn't tell what made them red—tears, or the drugs, or the exit sign's glow spilling past the doorway.

"Jo," she started again. Her lips were dry, and her tongue kept darting out to wet them. I started to stand to hunt for a glass of water, but her hand tugged me back to the bed, and I perched there beside her head. "I'm sorry, I'm so sorry, I didn't mean to—"

"Shh," I answered. I shook my head, though I doubted she'd even be able to register the action. "Forget about it. It's not a big deal."

What I really wanted to say was—we were supposed to love each other without limits. Without reservations, or holds, or weapons. Why did we insist on hurting one another in ways only we knew how to wield?

I thought she'd fallen asleep, but Caroline startled me by pushing her face into my lap, her damp cheek pillowed against my thigh. I stroked my fingers over her hair the way I knew she loved. The shuddering sigh she released hummed down to my bones.

"I'm sorry. Don't break up with me," Caroline pleaded.

It was something we'd said once in the first year of our friendship, commiserating about our inability to date, the impossibility of love. We'd made a promise. We'd never break it off.

"Don't be annoying," I said softly.

Eventually her ragged breaths lost their wet catch, and she drifted off there in my lap. I tilted my head back against the posters on her wall. A deep ache settled itself in my temples and worked its way down to my jaw. The slightest sound made me turn. There, in the doorway and silhouetted by red, Amrita stood with her hand on the jamb. The first time she spoke, the words were too quiet for me to process.

"What?" I whispered. Caroline stirred.

Amrita frowned at us. "I told you to get some rest. I'll watch over her now."

"She was alone," I said. I wasn't trying to accuse her, but it still came out sharp.

Amrita flinched as she stepped closer. "Sorry," she whispered, and I could tell that she meant it, that it hurt. "We were trying to clean up a bit, and I was on the phone with Finch." She shook her head. Her big eyes were wet. "It's fine, we'll talk about it tomorrow. Sleep."

My hand kept running over Caroline's hair. The headache pounded like a siren.

"I just want us all to be friends," I said quietly. "Now, forever."

"Jo," Amrita placated, and for a moment I believed she might cry. She was silent for a long time. Then she repeated, "Sleep."

Her tone said it all—there would be no more arguments. I lifted Caroline's head carefully from my lap, and I went to my room and slipped under the sheets. I waited to hear a voice through the wall. I never went to sleep.

Spring

IDEATION

25

The Inimitable Gift

"I don't think I need to remind you how important these final months are," Moody said from her perch on her stool. "By now, you're all aware of the limits of time. I suggest you plan accordingly and spend it wisely."

Time always, time forever. It was the burden we returned to without fail. February was an awful month that flickered into March like flashing slides—blink open to a world laden with gray mornings, blink again for black nights that came too quickly. The first sprigs of green began to push through the sluice, and I still couldn't let go of anything.

It was impossible to hold myself accountable for hope. I slept in desperate snatches and worked my body past its limits at all other hours. Every day it was canvas after canvas, painting after painting, depictions of dreamscape that fell into image like they'd been yanked out of my head through a muculent eye. I painted Saz in her bed with the duvet drawn to her chin and early-morning light coating her in pastels. Amrita on the couch, pulled into a New Year's kiss. The glowing lights of the Manor, Finch and Caroline illuminated in the throes of the crowd and leaning closer as if trying to hear what the other was saying. Every painted iteration felt more incorrect than the last: skin pallid and wrong, uncanny limbs akimbo, colors running muddy.

On the canvas, they were still friends suspended forever in the moments before violence. In reality, Finch and Caroline hadn't spoken more than a few words to each other in more than a month.

If I thought I knew the way tension could tear us apart before the party's unraveling, the studio environment that came after taught me new meaning. Even Moody could see the way we were fractured. Unless they involved her, Phoebe was densely unconcerned with studio politics. Veda and Yejun were impasses without much to offer other than a benign comment in critique, and Thea spouted off notes that appeared to be complimentary until further inspection. She always claimed the seat to Finch's right. Sometimes, if I was feeling brave, I claimed the one to the left. Amrita ran on the laser focus of obsessive perfectionism. Saz participated in discussions halfheartedly, more interested in scrolling house-hunting apps on her phone where Moody couldn't see in search of what she called "Saz's Dream House." Mars and Cameron existed in their own world—one where Cameron clung to the hope that Mars might be the one to Solo, leaving the rest of our collective in the dust. I thought that Mars just wanted their hard work to show for something.

We had three critiques left before Solo selection, and Moody wielded them like weapons. She wouldn't accept a lack of participation. We still showed our work as a class despite the Survey-narrowed list, so every Friday was a cycle through five or six sets of paintings where commentary was required. Most of us could barely look each other in the eye without dissolving into an argument. Caroline stood the whole time as she always did, preparing for war with her arms crossed over her chest.

We'd all been buried in our studios, even Saz, who took the lack of pressure as permission to explore. The paintings she hung before us were violent abstractions. She swung her brush with her whole body, emotion leaving marks. The pieces she created now felt entirely unconcerned with betterment. They were consumed with feeling, even if that feeling came out ugly.

"They're muddled and confusing and intense," Moody said to Saz in critique that Friday, "and that's why I enjoy them. You're no longer trying to make a 'good' abstract painting. You're letting us feel the same emotions I imagine you experienced while creating. It's a difficult thing to convey, and I think it's a direction you should continue to follow."

We could all see how impressive Saz's new paintings were. The understanding that only one or two of them would show in Grainer was disheartening. It seemed like such a crushing thing, to have spent her life working for one goal just to find it snatched away. Reality was too near and fragile. I was afraid to find myself on the other end of it.

"Finchard?" Moody called, tapping her rolled-up list against her knee. "Care to hang your work next?"

The paintings Finch hung on the wall looked like extensions of her body. She handled each canvas with confidence, hair pulled away from her face and a pencil tucked thoughtlessly behind an ear. On anyone else it would have been ridiculously affected. On Finch, it was a natural part of her operation—she would need the pencil. It would have to be accessible.

I thought about what Caroline had said at the party about Finch's posturing. About the way Caroline's head rocked back with the impact. Caroline weeping in my lap like she couldn't stop, reckoning with the aftermath of their resentment for one another. How it razed me to nothing to imagine that we'd never go back to our unified five.

I would have done anything. Snared any animal, stuffed any scarecrow, slit any palm open and drunk to the point of exsanguination if I thought it might knit us together again.

But Moody didn't let me dwell for long. Finch returned to her seat with two new paintings waiting on the wall, and Moody said, "Thoughts, everyone?"

One painting was a wash of light. It was rare for her to use such a pale palette—the surface was mostly thin golds and light yellows, paint applied in transparent layers until dimension began to build. Atop that faint color was a goose-like bird, lovingly rendered in near-black shades of deep brown. Surrounding the bird was the gentlest outline of a hairless head leading down to sloping shoulders. And emerging from beneath the bird's wings were two exquisitely rendered eyes in piercing shades of ultramarine. It reminded me, unwittingly, of Caroline's blown-out pupils and the way her eyes tore into you until you had to look away.

And the other painting was me.

I prickled with awareness. I felt the moment the others realized, too, a wave resounding through the room, Caroline stiffening until her spine could have rivaled iron. The portrait was a deep blue silhouetted bust. The hair was my hair, perfectly rendered in waves of brown terminating where it hit my bare shoulders. One eye was entirely gone—the other was a muddy hazel ring framed by a perfect circle of flesh and lash and sclera and pupil, like peering through the hole in a hagstone and finding a new world past its opening. Behind me was an expanse of field, this one darker, richer, fat strokes of paint applied with a palette knife.

Amrita hummed with appreciation, leaning forward with her elbows propped on her knees. Finch fidgeted with the ring around her middle finger. Moody circled each painting, spent time up close. The cloud of her hair blocked out most of my portrait. When she stepped aside, it was jarring all over again to find my eye glaring back.

"These certainly feel more personal," Moody said when she'd finally returned to her stool. "You've never painted anyone we could recognize before."

She smiled in my direction. I sank down in my seat as Caroline scoffed. Moody quirked her head at Caroline. "Want to chime in, Ms. Aster?"

Always Ms. Aster, as if the weight Caroline's name carried couldn't be ignored. Caroline remained still. She didn't even shake her head, just let the silence ring.

Mars raised their hand. "I might be wrong, but I think this is also the first time you've showed some of the flesh on the portrait's face. Typically, it's just the eyes that you give more detail to."

Moody nodded. "Great observation, that's right. You've allowed us to be privy to something concealed, Finchard. It's a good direction. It keeps the story of your painting speaking on, even when you're not around to tell it."

Her eyes dragged across the two paintings. I wondered if she could see what I saw in the bird portrait; Caroline's echo leaving feathers in its wake, like her Grotesque swan and the one in her burned painting. Finch shifted beneath the scrutiny.

"Now that I've seen what you're capable of imbuing in these paintings, I'd like to see you push your process in this direction," Moody said. "I want it to feel like something only you are capable of. I don't want to look at a painting and believe that the artist behind it could be an interchangeable entity. Show me why we should care that your hand was the one that crafted these."

Finch sat with her head held high, thigh bouncing beside mine. I wanted to touch her knee and still the shaking. But I didn't know how to breach the wall between us. I kept missing the right moment, kept forgetting the language.

"Alright, Ms. Aster, you're up next."

Caroline replaced Finch's paintings with one of her own. They still wouldn't look at each other—they moved as if the two of them were apparitions, flitting through the space, circumventing the boundaries of their bodies.

Caroline's painting was an autopsy. It was a canvas she'd shown before—the one with the damage right at its heart—but she shredded the outline of the burn, expanded and mutilated it, caked layers and layers of burgundy paint around its edges until it made a wound out of the piece. She'd painted a transparent image across the whole thing. It was another bird, one of her own, but the widened hole lived in its chest. She stood and stared it down until I expected the painting to blink and turn away, unable to meet her gaze.

"Wow," Moody said. "This is much more violent than your previous pieces."

Caroline's frown etched into her face. I could tell she was weighing the words, trying to decide if the intention behind them was positive or negative.

Cameron's laugh was dark. "If that's the kind of work you're hoping to Solo with, you must be thrilled that your dad gave Rotham a $500,000 Christmas gift."

Moody asked Cameron to be respectful. I felt Finch stiffen beside me.

"He's glad I'm actually taking risks with my work," Caroline said pleasantly, her eyes boring into the side of Cameron's head. "What do you have to show us? Let me guess. A guy on a horse. Toxic masculinity. We get it."

Cameron started to snap back, but Finch cut him off. "This isn't a risk, it's garish," she said. "Feels like you made it for shock value. It lacks all the nuance of your previous work and turns it into a spectacle."

Caroline wouldn't acknowledge her when she said, "I had to make use of someone else's attention-seeking destruction."

"Enough," Moody interrupted. "If you all can't be civil, then we're done for the day. Please take a break and use this time to consider the impact of constructive criticism. If you don't understand what *constructive* means, I encourage you to look it up. You're dismissed."

Caroline looked ready to lash out as she stalked forward and snatched the canvas off the wall. We milled away from the mess of critique, Veda and Yejun lingering in conversation in their seats. It was still early afternoon. I didn't want to go home yet.

Amrita stopped me before I could step into my studio. "Saz and I are going to grab coffee. Want to come?"

I shook my head. "No thanks, I'm going to try to do some work. I'll meet you guys later."

The look she fixed me with was disappointed, but I didn't have the heart to tell her that I needed to be alone. I was exhausted and entirely unprepared for my critique next week. There was always something new to complete. Another opportunity for me to let Moody down.

She let me go, but I only had a moment of isolation in my studio before Finch darkened the doorway.

"Did you know?" she asked.

"Know what?"

I opened my laptop and scrolled through my thesis document as she stepped closer. She leaned against my desk and crossed her arms over her chest, making herself impossible to ignore. I was eye level with her hip. I wanted to lean forward and press my forehead there, feel the heat of her through the fabric. But we hadn't touched more than cursory hellos in the past few weeks. We were strangers again, with far too much knowledge of one another.

"Did you know about the donation?"

My pulse picked up. "Of course, it's the Asters. They drop money on Rotham all the time."

Finch scoffed. "Yeah, sure, but this is $500,000, Jo. Right before Solo selections. You think administration is going to ignore that?"

"Is that why you tried to tear her apart in crit today?"

She rolled her eyes. "It's a bad painting. It's too obvious, and she knows that."

She wouldn't quite look at me. I knew we were both thinking about the painting Finch had shown the class, and the way my eye had looked out of it.

"Why didn't you tell me you were painting me?" I asked softly. Finch stuffed her hands in her pockets and stared at the floor.

"Dunno, didn't want to make it weird."

"I paint you all the time."

Finch shrugged. "Yeah but . . . yours are different. I don't know. Sorry, I should have warned you."

This time I did touch her. I couldn't help it. Index and thumb encircling her wrist, tugging the hand out of her pocket. Fitting our palms together. Fingers interlocking. She sighed, a low exhale out of her nose. Voices carried in the background, studio life continuing behind us.

"I liked it," I whispered. "You made me look brave."

Now she shook her head and smiled, that beacon I loved. "Oh, come on," she said, and that was how I knew I had pleased her. I imagined Thea stumbling upon the image of us. I hoped she would appear, that I could make myself evident.

But beyond that, I wanted a chance to set things straight and stop the endless back-and-forth of Finch and Caroline's war. So I said, "I wish you two would work it out."

Finch didn't have to ask who I meant. She immediately slid her hand out of mine and leaned back on my desk again, as if preparing to snap something scathing. Her hand went down behind her and landed directly on my uncapped X-Acto knife.

"Oh shit," I exclaimed as she gasped, lifting her hand to her mouth. "I'm sorry about that, shit shit shit. Are you okay? Let me see it."

There was a slice all the way down her ring finger. It twisted from tip to knuckle in the soft bends of her joint. She hissed with pain as I felt around the wound. The sound devolved into cursing as I scrambled for a rag, settling on the paint-stained one I kept in my apron pocket.

"You're probably introducing a million new toxins to my bloodstream," she joked faintly, her face going white as the blood stained the few places of the cloth that weren't yet oiled and colorful. The irrational part of me wanted to bring her finger to my lips, to taste it clean too. Instead, I just squeezed the rag harder. Watched her blood spread and spread.

We hovered like that, in the silence. There was so much to say, nowhere to begin. When the bleeding finally slowed, she dropped the rag beside my laptop and stepped out of my reach, injured hand cupped in the one she'd once purposefully cut open. "I'm gonna go wash this," she said. "I'll find you later."

I let her go with my questions unanswered, my mouth unkissed and her blood stiffening the rag on my desk.

The studio was nearly empty that night, mostly everyone packed up and gone, with only me and someone else unseen shuffling around in the background past midnight. I kept my headphones on to block out the sound—half of me wanted to explore and see which one of them it might be, but I was terrified to go looking and find something inhuman dragging itself around Grainer's sixth floor. Fear was teaching me how to finally mind my business.

The critique of Caroline's work instilled new insecurities. The latest painting pinned to my studio wall was the portrait of Caroline and Finch at the party. Neither of them had acknowledged it—by now it seemed they were content to pretend it had never happened, that they had never been friends in the first place, that they would never be friends again. I thought it would take time. Amrita said that maybe they were just too similar to let it go. Saz said they were both embarrassing, and that it could have been a great party if everyone just chilled out.

I lifted the painting from the wall. In its place I tacked up a fresh canvas. Despite how frustrating painting had become, there would never be another sensation in the world like this one—the blank belly of new potential, clean fabric under my hands. I began to sketch a new image with a hunk of terracotta charcoal. The earth tone marked out a faded depiction, like an old photograph buried beneath the bed: Finch sitting on her fire escape with the woods behind her, jacket pulled close and her eyes on my mouth just out of frame. I wondered if the others would look at this and know—the same way they must have known the moment she hung that painting of me, the two of us claiming each other's image.

I rubbed my hands across my jeans and left smears of earth. Stared into that monochrome replication of her face. Felt it brand me some-where evident, skin prickling with awareness. My satisfied angle of her mouth, the same one that set me alight every time I saw it. Self-control was a fable meant to warn me away from the edge of her.

Would it have been better to be warned?

Under my music, I heard the studio door swing shut. The resounding bang froze me in place, and I listened for feet. I couldn't tell if I was alone or if someone new had joined me.

"Hello?" I called. Silence answered.

It would be embarrassing if it were Cameron or Thea coming in to work, to have them hear me call out like a child. But I couldn't help it. Midnight had long since come and gone. Anxiety prickled along the nape of my neck.

I ran my fingers over the edge of the canvas, a shiver prickling up my spine. I scratched my tattoo through my sweatshirt. The skin slid in an awful way, like a newly forming scab.

I reached for the back of my sweatshirt and yanked it over my head. Without it I was left in a thin tank top, cold raising the hair on my arms. The tattoo still oozed along Finch's carefully inked lines, the skin around it wrinkled in a state of forever wound. The slice on my palm was the same way. Always scabbed halfway over, incapable of righting itself. I didn't understand my body's failure—how the others had healed just fine and yet my skin wouldn't stitch back together. I dragged my fingers across the tattoo's rippled edge. The crusted flake of blood and serous fluid slid away with my touch. A corner of my skin went with it.

Corner wasn't the right word. It was the tattoo's boundary, the place where redness and rot had spread across my arm, the skin simply falling away from my body. I dragged in a horrible breath. Sucked it down over and over again and pulled my hand away, looking at my fingers as if they had the capability to separate muscle from bone.

I could feel my heartbeat in my teeth and the hot, swollen wound. My hand dragged back up to it and pressed over the tattoo, pain prickling through the soft tissue. Skin slipped under my touch. Flesh sloughed off in one ruined piece. The hyacinth fell away.

Instinct was to scream, but the sound came out more like a gasp, constricted in my throat and pushed through clenched teeth. I dug jagged nails desperately into the ditch of my elbow, and the ache brought me back into my body.

"Oh fuck," I breathed, "fuck, what do I do? What the fuck do I do?"

My shouts echoed in dead air. Grainer creaked quietly, the moan of an old building shifting in the wind.

I expected blood to pour down my arm. But beneath the wound was just the raw red of exposed interior, rippled pink and veined white, the marble of meat. Saliva filled my mouth. I was going to be sick. I needed to get out of here. I needed to do something. I needed to—

I scrabbled at the materials on my desk. The knife that had cut Finch rolled away, the rag already stiff with her blood. A pincushion perched among the mess with a needle poking out of its center, red thread trailing from the head, the same red we'd sewn the Boar King into life with.

I could put myself back together.

I tried to hold the skin in place. The needle's first puncture flashed white-hot—I cried out, the sound carrying throughout the room. I pulled thread to its knotted end and made another stitch, teeth clenched against the sting.

Now the blood ran. Fat drops fell from the new wounds I'd made within the first. Somehow, that was what destroyed me: that red, weeping line. I grabbed the rag with shaking hands and pressed it over the tattoo, watching my blood soak into Finch's.

"I can't," I whispered to the air, head dropping down between my knees and the rag falling to the ground as my trembling grip loosened. "It hurts."

My whole body pulsed. With one hand still gripping my arm I staggered to the sinks and ran the water, slipping my arm beneath it and crumpling at the basin, eyes closed and forehead digging into the metal curl of the faucet. The water erased the pain for a moment and brought me back to my skin and my awareness of it, of the way my bones fit beneath the muscle.

When I opened my eyes, the tattoo rippled beneath the spitting water. The skin was right again. The wound was nothing more than irritated black lines, pink around the edges. Flesh fitted back where it belonged, and a single stitch of red thread punctured through the inside of my bicep. I let out a sob and scrabbled for something to hold on to. I landed on a cup of brushes at the sinks' edge. A long pair of shears poked out of the cup among all the oily brushes—I yanked them out and snipped the thread, needle clattering to the bottom of the sink. I pulled the rest of the thread out. Now the only sign of the wound was two perfect punctures.

The studio's door remained shut. The room was silent. I rocked back on my heels and stumbled back to my studio in dazed shock. Endless white cubicles, dirty wood floor, pale lights overhead. Shadows moving with my footsteps. The empty cutout of my doorway, the sign beside my studio that said *Joanna Kozak, Studio 11*. Inside, Caroline, sitting on my stool.

I didn't question where she'd come from. Part of me believed she wasn't really there. The rest tried weak excuses—that she'd been here the whole time, that she had been the one to slip in with the door's slam, that she had come to finish me off, that she was the only merciful thing I had left in the world. I just waited there in the doorway, staring, afraid to speak and hear her answer with a voice that didn't belong to her.

"What happened?" she finally asked.

I started to cry. I couldn't stop the flow once it began.

"I'm falling apart," I said thickly, the words sticking to the roof of my mouth. "I'm going fucking crazy, Caroline. I'm so scared. I don't know what to do."

The look she gave me was unreadable. Her pupils were the heavy black of a sated snake, the irises a thin band of blue. Dark circles beneath them dragged me down, down, down. "I know," she said at last. "Me too."

She reached for me. I went to her, let her pull me into her solid arms, my blood-spattered shirt pressed between us. I wondered if she thought the stain was just paint. If she knew the truth and let me get away with it unsaid.

"I'm going to fix it," she whispered against my head. "You won't have to worry about anything anymore, I'm going to make it all better. We should go away, don't you think? Let's get off campus for a while, go somewhere different." Her fingers stroked over my head. I'd made the shoulder of her shirt wet. "My parents are going out of the country during our spring break. We can go to their place, spend some time by the water. All of us. I'll even ask Finch."

I let my eyes shut and breathed in her close warmth. She gave me a squeeze. "Let's go home and you can sleep. In the morning we'll tell the others. I'll work out all the details, and we'll plan to leave for the week. How does that sound?"

I nodded. She fixed me upright, led the way out of my cubicle. At the last second, I turned back for my laptop, still waiting on my desk with the cursor blinking on my thesis paper.

The desk was a disaster: papers and brushes and fabric and tubes of oil paint and empty bottles of solvent and the half-closed glow of the laptop screen. Red thread lay across my mess like a vein. Beside it, there was a blank space in the calamity signaling where Finch's blood-soaked rag had been. My eyes dropped down to the empty floor. The rag was gone.

26

Mark the Spot Where We Buried It

We spent our days of break on that short stretch of beach, taking turns reading from a book about Ana Mendieta's life. Saz wanted to be topless, so she lay between us and we read over her bare belly. The pages cast shadows where the sun couldn't reach. It wasn't quite warm enough to tan, but the ice had finally given way to true spring weather, and the sun made everything freshly pleasant. Faint goose bumps peppered over Saz's stomach. I kept my shorts on and threw a bandaged arm over my eyes, tattoo obscured beneath it. Amrita read the most often out of all of us, her voice a gentle lull, fingers leaving wet circles on the pages. Caroline produced beers and shandies and endives in hummus, sandwiches Finch had made slick with mustard and cold from the cooler, strawberries halved and red in our sandy fingers. Sometimes I'd bite down, and that sand would crunch between my teeth. It made everything a little more delicious.

Our isolation made escapism easier. Caroline's parents had a whole segment of steep sand dunes sloping down into private beach, and March was hardly peak season in Michigan, typically still cold and impenetrable. But we were lucky. The sun was warm overhead. The house itself was a dream, all pale blues and whites in a cottage-meets-craftsman style that was likely meant to emulate the other shoddy cabins along the shore but had far too much money invested in it to come across as anything other than opulent.

Despite all the comforts of staying in a nice house, I still awoke from nightmares most nights. But we didn't sleep enough for it to be much of a problem. We drank all the time, or smoked Finch's pre-rolls. We built bonfires on the beach. Skinny-dipped in the frigid water to the point of near hypothermia, raced each other down the dunes, drank coffee on the porch before the sun could rise past the conifers. We played bastardized croquet in the yard and read tarot in the sand. Slept in each other's clothes. Brushed our teeth in one scrabbling cluster, spitting into the sink, foaming together there in the basin. There was only one rule—no Solo talk, no Rotham reminders. I was being so good. I'd almost forgotten I could paint at all.

Now Caroline had her hair up in a claw clip, sun bleaching it white. The thin straps of her bikini top slipped down her shoulders. Her skin glowed gold all the way down to her unbuttoned jean shorts. I shivered when the breeze picked up again.

"You're missing an earring," I said, gesturing to Caroline's head.

She felt around her ears with a frown. "Fuck, really? It's probably at the bottom of the lake by now."

I grimaced. "You should embrace it. It's very Moody-esque."

"Dear diary," Caroline said around the mouth of her beer bottle. "Today, Jo told me I looked like Moody. Maybe I should tie cinder blocks to my ankles and Virginia Woolf myself in Lake Michigan."

"Oh, come on, that is not what I said." My cheeks were hot, and I crossed both arms over my head to hide the color. Past the X of my forearms, I saw Saz fix her sunglasses and clear her throat. Amrita held her spot in the book with a thumb. Beneath her baseball cap, Finch's eyes were flat and shadowed as she rummaged in the cooler beside her.

I regretted saying anything. We hadn't spoken of any topics beyond immediate desires: swimming, drinking, eating. I'd been content to erase the moment shared with Caroline in the studio, my skin still whole and connected and my hyacinth resuming its typical itching, and she had been doing well the past few days now that we were away from Rotham—no strange disappearances or bouts of anger, no cryptic claims or fights provoked with Finch. They even had a few civil conversations about what to cook for dinner. Need outweighed their anger and fit us all into a comfortable rhythm. Everyone seemed to be happy to pretend the events of the last few months hadn't happened. We were perfectly fine without a reminder of Solo, even one as innocent as Moody's earring.

But still, in the echo of lake water lapping at stones and sand, all I could think about was Moody's roster and the status of our names at the top of that list—what kind of notes she had made, where we stood as Soloists, which of us would be venerated above the rest by this time in two weeks.

Caroline pressed her head to my shoulder. I closed my eyes. Everything was soft and grainy—the sand under my back and sifting through the blanket, the sun's white beam overhead, the brush of Caroline's hair against my cheek. Her scalp was warm as I ran my fingers over it and twisted a lock around a knuckle. She hummed. I breathed her in, lotion smelling of grass and honeysuckle, the promising summer of her. For a beat, I let myself imagine the years to come. A line of houses on a street with our names on the doors. Five apartments in a high-rise, taking the elevator to coffee at their dining tables, falling asleep in the same beds, a movie playing on a projector. Nights on a beach like this one. A home where we each had a room.

The thought almost made me sick. I was so afraid of a timeline where it did not exist. I would have to take this moment—I would have to hold it and be happy with it.

"I want to be high," Caroline said. She gave her thighs a perfunctory swipe with her palms as she pulled away from me and stood, sand scattering in her wake. "Let's drink some tea."

"Hear! Hear!" Saz said, raising a hand in triumph.

Inside, we found that the "tea" was a little jar of mushrooms that Caroline produced from her bag, steeped in hot water and squeezed with lemon to disguise most of the earthy taste. We stood around her in the kitchen as she tipped the fungi out into her palm, and I was immediately apprehensive. Behind my eyes I kept seeing the wide black of her pupils at the Manor party, the feral snarl of her mouth, her hands scrambling for a violent grasp on Finch.

Saz boiled water in a kettle until it screamed. Caroline weighed the mushrooms and dropped them into mugs.

"None for me, thanks," Amrita said. I wondered if she was thinking about the same thing—how Caroline had been so unlike herself, how we wished she would stop pushing her own limits and putting the rest of us in the path of her destruction. I supposed, if I stepped outside of myself, I could see them all saying the same about me. I hadn't exactly given anyone a reason to believe that I was fine.

Afternoon light turned the kitchen that burnt-gold kind of color that never failed to make me want to paint. The smell of coffee lingered. Crumbs littered the counter where we'd crafted our sandwiches. The recycling bin was full of bottles, yeasty and sour. Half of a severed and sweating watermelon sat on the table, not yet right for the season, a product of the bougie supermarkets Caroline's parents frequented. Caroline drained her tea and set the mug down beside it. Saz followed suit, smacking her lips thoughtfully with each sip. We were a divide all over again.

Caroline smiled. "You sure you don't want any, Amrita? Jo?"

She didn't ask Finch, and Finch didn't move or look at any of us, anxiously adolescent in her cuffed sweatshirt and basketball shorts, her feet bare on the rug before the kitchen sink, hair loose around her face.

Amrita shook her head no. I hesitated, and Caroline's smile widened. She started to fix another cup without prompting me again. Finch made a sound under her breath, something disapproving.

The liquid in the mug Caroline handed me was the pale brown of lake water. I tipped it back until about half of the tea was gone—then turned and handed the rest to Finch. The look she gave me from beneath her eyelids was doubtful, but she put her lips where mine had just been and drank until the mug was empty. Caroline sighed.

"Well, you might have just fucked your trip. With the amount we added, you'll barely experience more than a microdose," she said, slinging an arm around my shoulders. "But I guess it's a good place to start."

Caroline wanted to walk up the dunes. Amrita said it was foolish to do so when we were already high, but Saz just ruffled her hair and laughed, told her not to be a stick-in-the-mud. Amrita went quiet for a while, and I could tell she was fretting in silence.

By the time we reached the foot of the dune, craggy with driftwood and half-concealed rocks, I was a little lightheaded, unsure what percentage of my deep breathing and loud heartbeat could be contributed to the drugs as opposed to paranoia. Sun beat off the water like a mirror, wind whipping sand around our legs. Caroline jogged ahead of us and spun in a circle with her arms outstretched as she whooped with delight. The dune rose eternal as she pushed forward, climbing the slope with Saz close behind her, sand slipping away from every foothold.

"Wait up!" Saz called, her dress blowing and tangling around her. "Your legs are too fucking long."

We reached the summit, out of breath from the climb. The lapping sound of water amplified as I closed my eyes and let the glow cook my cheeks. Light pushed past my eyelids in pale shades of red. We were so close to the sky. It felt possible to reach out and touch it.

"Is it working?" Saz asked.

"I feel fucking fantastic," Caroline sighed. "I haven't felt this good since the sacrifice."

My eyes slit open. Finch and Amrita were quiet. Caroline stared at the water, a pensive look on her face as she watched the water toil.

"Thought we were leaving that at Rotham?" Finch asked wryly.

Caroline ignored her in favor of turning to me. The look on Saz's face was distant—she was smiling, but it felt like a defense, like trying to imbue the rest of us with an easy happiness, hoping the moment would pass without incident.

"Acting like we didn't do what we did will never let us move forward. I'm not finished growing yet. I think we deserve the world." Caroline turned to me and smiled, lazy and catlike. "Jo knows. Don't you?"

I thought about Caroline's arms around me, her mouth against my hair, her low voice saying, "I'm going to make it all better." My bicep still throbbing with imagined pain. The misalignment between what I saw and what was true and what I was capable of believing.

"What do I know?" I asked.

But she lurched forward and took off without answering me. We watched her run, then throw herself to the sand and slide the rest of the way down the dune.

"Caroline!" Amrita called. "Wait!"

Finch started after her, sliding downward along the slope. Jagged pieces of old fencing and sharp brush marked their path. Then it was Saz, dress seized in her fists, steps unsteady along the decline. Caroline's shrieks of joy continued as she got to her feet again and hit the ground running. She darted forward, stumbling, screaming, the water stretching out before her. Distant sailboats speckled the surface. Birds swooped past swollen white clouds.

"Fuck," Amrita sighed, and then she picked her way down. I started to follow and lost my footing, debris cutting up the bare skin along my calves. I hissed with pain.

Caroline refused to slow. Sand flew up around her steps. She crashed forward into the water, spray rising like a storm.

"You shouldn't swim like that!" Saz called, the desperate rise of her voice caught by the breeze and tossed away. At the bottom of the dune, I staggered to my feet beside her. One hand shielded her eyes. "The ground is moving," she whispered. "It's not safe. Can you see the colors rippling with the water?"

"Stay here," I commanded. Finch waded into the lake. I couldn't see Caroline anywhere. It was hard to drag air into my chest, each breath short and shallow, my lungs refusing to properly expand.

Waves crested and crashed. I watched for the rise of her head. Finch pushed through the lake and screamed Caroline's name.

"I don't see her," Amrita panted beside me. "Can you see her?"

Saz splashed forward. Finch went under. She disappeared for a beat and then surfaced again.

Finally, Caroline bobbed back above the water, yards away from the rest of us. Finch called for her to come back. Caroline's head was a blip among all the blue. I kicked off my shoes and plunged in, the water so fucking cold, the kind of chill that sank immediately down to the core.

In a flash she was under again. Finch was deep enough to swim, her arms cutting hard lines through the water. Coins of light refracted along the surface of the lake. Numbness crept from my waist down to my feet, shivering hard enough for my teeth to chatter, clothes wet and heavy enough to make it feel as if I were walking in a dream. I could see Saz's colors now—tendrils of gold and green, just the faintest lines in the distance.

Finally, Caroline surfaced again, even farther. Finch pushed closer and snatched her arm. I stopped and watched them, Caroline lifted by Finch's grasp like a siren come to devour, her laughter swelling and taking flight. She barely acknowledged Finch. Just threw her arms up in the air and tipped her head back. The two of them blue silhouettes against the white sky. Opposing duplicates, too alike in their differences. A reluctant pair.

Amrita swam past me. Her hair fanned around her, red shirt bright in the water. Together, she and Finch ferried Caroline back to the shore. We gathered on the sand again. Caroline was still laughing though she shook with cold, her lips a dead periwinkle and her skin a colorless white like Laura Palmer come back to life.

"That was amazing," she sighed, her voice somewhere far and dreamy. "I could breathe under that water if you'd given me the chance."

"You could have killed yourself," Amrita said sharply.

"I could think of worse ways to die," Caroline answered. Saz turned away. Finch stayed silent as she wrung water out of her shirt. Amrita led us down the beach with her eyes on the white house and never turned back. To our left, the sun began to set over the water. With its absence came a more brutal chill.

We took turns showering. Saz brushed and braided Caroline's wet hair silently on the couch, frowning all the while. Amrita instructed everyone to sleep their trips off before retreating to the room she shared with Saz. I lay awake in mine and Finch's, staring at the ceiling fan. She turned her back to me and drew the quilt up to her chin. I watched the fan turn until I could no longer keep my eyes open.

◆ ◆ ◆

In the morning, I woke to find most of the house already empty. Barefoot and half-dressed, I poked around in the kitchen for sustenance—someone had already made coffee, and I found a bowl of washed raspberries in the fridge. Tomorrow we'd go back to campus. Back to bland Banemast food, the Manor, and the promise of Solo.

Finch sat in the living room with her sketchbook in her lap. I brought the raspberries to her and perched on the arm of the couch, looking over her shoulder at the open page. I listened to her pencil scratch the paper as she sketched Caroline through the gauzy kitchen curtains. Caroline stood past the glass with her eyes on the water again.

"How is she?" I asked.

"Fucking unhinged, as per usual. It was a bad idea to drink that tea."

Shame made me shiver. The bowl of berries was cold against my thigh. Outside it was overcast, all the warmth of yesterday sapped away, spring banished once again.

"Thanks for getting her," I said under my breath. We weren't touching, but I could feel how warm Finch was through her clothes. She wouldn't meet my eyes—just looked at my thigh, and the bowl resting on it, and the place where my thumb cupped blue-and-white china. She ate a berry. When she touched the paper again, it left a red smear.

"Don't worry about it," she said.

I worried. Now she looked up at me through her lashes, like she could feel it. "I don't know what you assume, but I don't want her to be unhappy either. I think she's selfish and cruel and violent and smart and I love her to a fault. But you let her think she can get away with shit like this. You let her believe that it's always going to be this way, that nothing can ever go wrong, that it's all going to work out in her favor no matter how awful she acts. And I can't let her do that. She doesn't see the toll it takes on the rest of us."

Finch was right—Caroline always got away with everything. *Everything* meaning the inevitable. She was so impossible to criticize. She made a joke out of every jab, and when she was wrong, she had you halfway convinced her answer was the better option. I loved that about her. I was so afraid of the lengths I would go to if I needed to explain away her actions.

A distant flutter behind my ear, thumping against the glass of the French doors that led to the porch. There were no bugs in sight. I swiped at the hair curling against the nape of my neck, as if that might make it better.

Finally, I whispered, "You can love someone and still wish them dead."

"Don't say that," Finch snapped. "You know it's not like that. I went out in that fucking water for her. I could have let her drown."

The screen door banged in the breeze. My bare feet were numb against the floorboards; I kept looking at the beach and forgetting it wasn't yet summer. The cold found us, no matter where we hid.

I swallowed past the lump in my throat. "What if she really does something awful to herself?"

Finch's hands stilled against the paper. Her shoulder finally pressed against my thigh. Just that simple heat and I wanted her to drop it, to pull me into her lap, to kiss me on the corner of my mouth. But the dip in her voice paired perfectly with the plunge of my stomach. "You can't love her back to life."

I would only ever try.

For our last night, we made a bonfire down the shore. The sky awoke with stars, and the fire at our feet made its bed in the sand. We sat in a circle around it. The glow turned their faces into lively coals. Saz slid her knees forward and propped her chin atop them, looking at the flames.

"I don't want to go back," she said, pulling the sleeves of her sweatshirt over her exposed hands.

Music played from a speaker. Finch held a beer between her knees. Amrita toyed with the frayed hem of her sweatshirt, a string coiled around her finger. Caroline had barely spoken all day. She just stared into the fire and dug her toes down into the sand, shoes abandoned somewhere closer to the path that led back to the house. I wondered if she regretted yesterday's swim—if she was crashing, or if she felt guilty for scaring us. The woods loomed against my back, but near the fire everything felt safe and warm. If I never turned around, I had nothing to fear.

"We could stay here forever?" Amrita tried.

"I wouldn't mind that," I answered.

The warm, delusional image of the five of us in that eternal house. The light in the kitchen left on all night. Snowy winters with firewood stacked by the back door and hot summers spent exactly like this—sitting around the fire, swimming naked and unashamed, shrieking at the sand spiders and eating dinner on the porch and letting the sun burn me just enough to remind me it had the power to.

We'd come to Rotham in search of more. But I liked good and simple. I couldn't trust my eyes, but I could trust theirs. Now I was trying my hardest not to waste time, but it seemed impossible. Where was the delineation between wasted and treasured? Wasn't time spent with the people you loved worth it enough?

I loved them. And it was a huge word, one my mom might have laughed at, one that plenty of people would tell me wouldn't last. But if I said it was true love between the five of us, would anyone believe me?

We had a marriage of minds—a selection made by dedicated time, by remembrance, by experiencing our hurts and hopes and honest delight in the same room. Love on purpose and love beyond kiss. Their hands on my shoulders or their heads in my lap and comfort in silence, in booming sound, in the rocking of waves against Caroline's childhood home where we watched the sun go down.

If I told you it was forever love between the five of us, would you believe me? Finch's eternal drive and passion, Saz's belief in the unreality of magic, Amrita's authoritative comfort, Caroline's Midas touch and all the gold she gave us, the Manor and the way it held us as one.

If I told you it was a hurting love between the five of us, would you believe me?

I don't know. I hardly believed myself.

That night, I woke to the sensation of the bed dipping beneath weight. I smelled her before I saw her hand on the pillow—smoke from the bonfire, her expensive shampoo, the faintest cling of salt.

"Are you asleep?" Caroline asked, beside my ear.

"Yes," I said into the pillow. I shut my eyes again, so I wouldn't lie to her.

"Good," she answered. Her hand came up and held the back of my skull, stroking patterns against my scalp. "Stay like that."

I remained still, the scent of her continuing to wash over me, mixing with the day's sunscreen and something earthy and cool. Her nails gently raked over the skin at the nape of my neck.

"You're so tense," she whispered. "You're scared of something. You wear it all over you, Jo. What's got you so terrified? It's not me, is it? Would you tell me if it was me?"

The way she spoke—languidly, thoughtfully, a ragged drag to her words—made me think that she wasn't looking for an answer. She hooked an ankle over mine and settled closer, an exhale fluttering across my ear. One arm rested in the dip of my waist and pulled me back into her until we were two slotted spoons. Finch shifted in the bed on the other side of the room.

I considered pretending to be asleep again as she sighed against my shoulder. Finally, heart pounding like a drum in my ears, I said, "I've been seeing something. It follows me."

Caroline nodded immediately. Her hair swished against the pillow as she tightened her hold on me. "Yeah," she said. "Me too."

It should have terrified me, to hear her say it. But the comfort that came over me was a rush of relief. My voice was muffled in the pillowcase as I said, "I think that ritual fucked us all up."

She laughed a little, cloying. "Don't be so negative," she murmured. "I told you I was going to fix it, didn't I?"

She had. And I liked to trust her, even when I thought she was keeping something from me, even when I was afraid of where she would go next.

"Keep sleeping," she said. "I won't go."

I buried my cheek in the pillow. She held me for a long time, but in the end, her promise fell flat.

I felt her roll off the bed. Through the narrow slits of my eyes, I watched her pad across the room to the dresser where Finch and I spread our things—necklaces and rings, bottles of perfume and sunscreen, hair ties and brushes. Caroline picked up Finch's brush. Her fingers worked through the bristles until they plucked a clump of hair free. She kept it there, balled in her fist. And when she finally left the room, turning the doorknob so its click wouldn't alert me, I listened to her leave, her footsteps growing quieter and quieter until the house was nothing but a silent tomb.

27

POSSESS AND DEVASTATE

Our final critique as Rotham students unfolded with the mournful quiet of a vigil.

Amrita went first. She had only one new painting to show—but it was a massive stretch of good, thick paper, the kind that made me marvel when I touched it, heavy and creamy and made for marking. She smoothed it across the critique wall and clipped it into place, taking care not to mar the edges.

The composition writhed with bizarre animals, legs and teeth and snouts all wrong like they'd been drawn by someone who'd never seen the real thing. Invented plants wove between them. It was mythical and entrancing, a garden of earthly delights that existed only within Amrita's mythology, the stories she'd tell on her deathbed with her family gathered around to listen. She'd painted it all in pale washes of watercolor and the thinnest outlines, shades of orange and gold and a blue so deep it was nearly black. There was a woman on horseback, the horse's eyes oddly human. Tigers coiled behind prey until their bodies were a spineless spiral. Stars hung in a pink sky, fire burst from a lantern, snakes wrapped around the branches of an imagined tree with bells hanging instead of leaves. Figs and apples and melons patterned the spaces in between, so vivid and detailed that I wanted to pull them from the paint and taste them.

"It's so *rich*," Phoebe said.

Moody had her hands clasped beneath her chin, delight all over her face. "What a scale you've managed to accomplish, Ms. Balakrishnan. This painting is immersive. It's exactly what I hoped you might accomplish since our first day together."

Amrita fidgeted with the weight of the rest of our gazes on her back.

"The details really are amazing," Veda added. "You could show me this and tell me it had been painted a thousand years ago and I'd believe you."

"Is that a compliment?" Cameron asked. "I'd assume you were telling her it looks tired and ancient, in that case. It doesn't really fit through a contemporary lens."

"And how do we define contemporary, Cameron?" Moody cocked her head in question. "Isn't it just work made by the artists of today? Aren't we all contemporary? Art itself is inherently undefinable, a statement made by the artist regardless of depiction. A work is contemporary when it exists in context with the world we live in today. So Amrita's piece can be considered a direct response to her interaction with the world."

Cameron didn't answer, just leaned forward in his seat and peered closer at the painting.

"Now, I do have questions for you," Moody said, turning to meet Amrita's eyes. Amrita straightened in her seat. I watched Saz shift with discomfort, as if anticipating a fight. She kept twirling a strand of hair around a finger and punctuating the twist with a hard tug.

"It's impressive. Incredible, really. But as you're preparing for a Solo exhibition, I want you to consider how the entire scope of your work will appear when it's hung. How will your smaller pieces relate to this big one? What do they say to one another when displayed side by side? Are there gaps that need filling with additional larger pieces? These are all questions I want you to ask yourself."

"Of course," Amrita answered quietly.

"You know that my purpose is to lead you all to your best possible work. And I can see it here, in this painting," Moody continued, her voice a little softer. "You've worked hard. Don't do the pieces you've created an injustice."

Amrita tried to smile. I watched it flicker over her, unsure and unsteady.

Mars was up next. I helped Amrita take her painting down, and Cameron took my place to prop up Mars's three massive canvases, all self-portraits against intricate patterning with sections of cloth sewn into the canvas. Mars's face stared back at us past dense fields of green, orange, and blue, the colors vibrating against the warm umbers of their cheek and shoulder and outstretched hands. They were beautiful paintings—technically well done and rich with emotion in the contortions of Mars's body. Moody thought so, too, and said so without much critique apart from encouragements to vary the position of their body in each of the portraits to provide us with more of a story within the paintings. There was no question of quality or dedication or passion. Mars was good. The paintings were good. The work deserved to Solo.

"I want the gallery to feel like a hall of mirrors," Mars said. "I want everyone in that room to see these paintings and feel as if they're a part of me, like they're seeing my face instead of their own."

Cameron nodded sagely. Yejun got up to get a closer look at the way the fabric became a part of the painted patterns of Mars's clothes. I didn't envy Moody's choice. That room was so full of desperation—each of us pushing ourselves beyond the limits of our bodies to try and make our lasting impact. Four years of work. What was it all for, if it would only be one of us hanging in that gallery? What did we have to prove to anyone other than ourselves?

"Jo?"

I looked up, surprised, and Moody's eyes narrowed with a flicker of concern. "I said, are you ready to go next?"

Finch's hand brushed my elbow, her voice suddenly beside my ear. "Come on, I'll help you set up."

I collected my work—five paintings, smaller than my usual work, all rolled up in one stack of unstretched canvas. I gave some to Finch and kept a few for myself. She spared them a glance and frowned, something changing in her face. But she went where I pointed her to and began to hang them without question.

Two of the paintings were exactly as I had left them: the piece with Caroline and Finch in the Manor, and the one of Amrita on the couch. They were packed with color and invented atmospheres, their figures illuminated by hundreds of invented candles with the same chiaroscuro of a Renaissance painting. But the other three were new, even to me. I hadn't painted them.

Except, I had. They carried the same loose brushwork and dark palettes I always painted with, shades of blue and green and brown interspersed with light. But the images were unfamiliar. One was just a pair of hands in an otherwise entirely black space. The fingertips were lovingly rendered, palms turned to the viewer, nails rising beyond the ridges of flesh. A fresh wound marked the hand on the right. That was what told me they were Caroline's hands—the only one of us that hadn't slit the left.

Beside that painting was another flat expanse of blue-black. The only shift in image was the glimpse of a head peering out from a slash in the canvas, like Caroline's rising above the surface of Lake Michigan. Her exposed eyes stared back at the viewer. Challenged us to reach for her and pull her free of that descent.

The final piece depicted an animal curled on its side, something indistinctly mammalian and wounded. There was no detail in the creature itself, but the area surrounding it was so dense with texture that it emphasized a flat black outline of the animal's body. Burgundy paint marked out the keening shape of its head and the tusks affixed to its jaw. In its stomach sat a pale white house; just like Caroline's on the shore. Its windows were full of gold light. I imagined we were safe inside of it, sleeping in the belly of that beast.

Moody didn't say anything for a long time. The only sounds were Grainer's ominous creaking, the shuffle of someone's shoes against the floor, and my own too fast, panicking inhale.

"These are a departure," Moody started. Then she faltered. "They're . . . frightening."

Someone snickered. The memory of "Prozac Kozak" made me flush, and I swallowed around my dry tongue. Time felt liquid and far away from me. How had my life continued without my noticing? When could I have created these?

"I don't mean to say *frightening* in a way that discourages you," Moody continued. "Plenty of painters have depicted scenes of horror and violence throughout time, and these paintings evoke some of those darker masters: Caravaggio, Francis Bacon, Hieronymus Bosch, Francisco Goya, Henry Fuseli. They've all painted variations on nightmare. And that's really what I'm getting from this work, Joanna. I feel that you've entrenched us in your own nightmares."

Maybe no one else could see what followed me, but I still brought it into every room. I didn't know if the Boar King was Kolesnik or the devil or some other manifestation we'd raised from the ritual. That shadow was omnipresent. The paintings said so too.

"Are you trying to scare the viewer?" Phoebe asked politely. "It's working, by the way. You scared me."

Moody smiled. "Fear is as palpable as beauty or adoration. Sometimes, even more so. If your goal is to strike fear, Joanna, then I think you've succeeded. But I'd like to see how you discuss the work in your thesis paper, and how these newer paintings tie in with your previous portraiture."

Moody got to her feet and turned her back on my paintings, facing our circle.

"Between today and next week's Solo selection, there will be no further public critiques. After the choice is made, we will begin curation for the Grainer Gallery show, so please consider two pieces you would be interested in sharing with the public. I think you are a talented group, and it will be incredibly difficult to decide which student will represent us as our Soloist."

Her smile was genuine, but her eyes were a little sad. "We've endured some tough obstacles this year. I'm very sorry you all have had to navigate your final months at Rotham under the weight of grief. But I hope your time here has imbued you with new passion and the lasting drive to create."

We were a chorus of nods back at her. Caroline stood like a statue and stared into my dark depiction of her wounded hands. Finch bounced her knee relentlessly. Saz kept twisting that piece of hair between her fingertips, and Amrita sat still and straight, as if she'd even slowed her breath.

Moody clapped her hands together. "Have a good weekend. I'll see you bright and early on Monday."

◆　◆　◆

We gathered around the Manor's dining table that night with our laptops a glowing circle before us, the screens touching like points on a star. Half-empty bottles of wine made our centerpiece. Saz stood and poured another glass and raised hers over her head.

We'd barely spoken after that final critique. What was there to say? We were all so aware of one another and that power we held between us. So conscious of the ways we had hurt each other and the ways we would go on to keep swinging the blade.

"Regardless of what happens," Saz started. She cleared her throat and tried again. "Regardless of what happens with Solo next week, and regardless of how weird and awful this year has been, I just want you guys to know that I love you. All of you. Like, I'm fucking obsessed with you."

Caroline's distant eyes were painted pale blue by her laptop. Finch sat across from her at the table, hands behind her head and elbows splayed wide.

"You say that like we're never going to see each other again," I said.

Amrita closed her laptop halfway. "I mean, of course we'll see each other, but things are going to be different after this year. We won't live together like this. No more school and no more assignments and no more studio space."

"Okay, vibe killer," Saz sighed.

"We're at our prime," Caroline said, low in her throat. "Have we peaked? Is this it?"

"No way. I've heard thirty is your hottest year," Finch said.

Saz smiled. "I don't know. If this is our prime, then I can be happy with that. I think we made the best of it."

"This can't be it," Amrita said. "There has to be something better."

What else? What could possibly be better than this, than sitting in the room with them and listening to the music we loved, warm with wine and adoration?

I kept my mouth shut. I didn't want to be the only one satisfied by what I had.

"I'm going to bed," Caroline announced with the click of her laptop shutting. "We can be sappy in the morning. It's our last weekend before the end of the world, so let's make it count."

Saz dumped the rest of her wine out in the sink and trailed after Caroline up the stairs, their voices trickling down to where Finch and I still sat at the table. Amrita pushed her chair in and turned to head up to her room but gave me one last glance over her shoulder.

"You two alright?"

I nodded. "We're fine, get some rest."

She accepted the answer and ascended after the others. Finch started to gather her things.

"Can I walk back with you?" I asked.

Finch looked up, surprised. "You don't have to do that. It's not that late."

"It's dark. I don't like the idea of you walking alone."

"I've done it hundreds of times. Besides, if you walk me home, then you just have to turn back alone. Unless you plan on staying." Her last words were soft, a little unsure of themselves.

"Haven't made up my mind yet," I answered, trying not to smile and failing. "But I'm brave. I'll be just fine."

Finch rolled her eyes. "Yeah, sure, whatever you say." She inclined her head toward the door. "You coming?"

28

Toiling and Waking Hour

We walked the promenade side by side. Spring air simmered, buds unfurling on the sycamore branches, and everything smelled like new growth and rain. Night made it all a silhouette with Grainer's façade behind it, like a stage where our play had been set.

Our hands brushed. I jerked, involuntarily—but Finch's fingers found mine again and hooked. We'd been friends for so long. She'd kissed me into a slackened mess. Yet somehow that tentative touch was enough to turn me shy, like this was a first date and I was still learning the steps.

"You working at the library on Sunday?" she asked lightly, as if holding my hand were something she did every day.

I answered just as casually. "I think so, gotta check the schedule again."

She squeezed my hand. Our shoulders were near enough that I could feel the heat of her through her hoodie's thin sleeve. She led us out of the night and into Tuck House, up the stairs and down her hall, only dropping my hand when she had to fish out her keys.

Inside, we kicked our shoes off at the door, and she dropped her bag beside them. I followed her to the couch. The scent of incense lingered—I imagined her in this room alone, burning something with her eyes shut, the kind of meditative state she indulged in when the rest of us weren't around. She reached for me. I let her pull me down until she was on her back with my head tucked against her shoulder. Our legs tangled together. Ankle to ankle. Her bare calf peeking out of the cuff of her pants. I couldn't remember the last time we'd been alone like this, but my heart recalled. It was pounding like we'd been running. We lay in that silence for a while, her fingers stroking over my back, one of mine snaking beneath her hoodie and resting against her ribs. She smelled like a good dream. Like finally falling asleep.

"I wanted to do this in Michigan," she murmured against my hair. "It was just weird, with everyone else there."

"Me too," I whispered. "But, I mean, Michigan was weird in general. Everything's been weird for a long time."

"Is this weird?"

Finch's hand gestured loosely between us. Her cheeks were flushed, her lips dampened by her tongue. I wondered if she could feel my heartbeat in all the places we touched. Instead of answering, I leaned up and caught her smile—kissed her openly, hesitation falling away and simple comfort taking its place. It was so right, to be there with her, held against her chest, her hand sliding up to cup my cheek and fix me in place. Like something I'd waited all my life to earn.

"Not weird," I whispered when we finally parted. The smile on her mouth made me want to kiss her again, so I did. Her fingers twined in my hair and held fast. I watched her map my face, gaze darting from eye to eye to nose to mouth and back up.

"Would you have been—" She stopped, hesitated. "If the others found out, would it embarrass you?"

"Of course not," I answered honestly, even as my pulse picked up. "But it's kind of nice like this, isn't it? Not having to worry what the rest of them might think or say?"

She must have seen something anxious in my face, because she frowned.

"I just know they would give us shit for it," I tried again. "And it's not like either of us really know what we're doing. So why try to justify it? Why not just . . . enjoy the time we have?"

I turned my head so I could bury it against her throat and felt her chest rise and fall with a sigh. Her blunt nails scratched softly against my scalp. "You say that like there's an expiration date. Do you want an expiration date, Jo?"

There was something buried beneath the question—the quiet uncertainty that characterized her insecurities, the fear that we were out of alignment. What did I want? To kiss her again. To leave it all unsaid. To paint her over and over and over. To go home to a house that I loved and find the people I loved in it. For the people I loved to love one another. To mend our rifts, to fill the cracks with gold, to watch it all glow.

"No," I said. "I want everything good to last forever."

She laughed. "You're such a romantic."

"And you're not? You're a painter, you love idealization."

"Exactly, idealization. I'm not afraid to hope, but I also know where my expectations should lie."

I tried to focus on the way her fingers locked in the short strands of hair at the nape of my neck, the warmth of her skin against my nose.

"I don't know, I think it's nice to dream," I admitted. "Things don't always have to change. We could all get a house somewhere out in South Bend or in the country. They're always auctioning off old places for cheap. We could fix it up, build a studio."

Finch exhaled. "Be realistic."

"What's so unrealistic about that? Why do your plans always leave us out?"

She sat up a little, forcing me up with her. "I'm not leaving you out, I'm trying to prevent you from getting hurt when these dreams don't pan out. People have to move on with their lives, Jo. Caroline's parents will get her some bougie apartment in Chicago or wherever else she wants to go. Amrita will probably end up with an internship in New

York and Saz's trust fund will give her her choice of the world. They can go anywhere, Jo. I don't have any real money, and if I don't Solo, my options are limited. I'll try to get a job in the city. Hopefully I'll find a cheap place to rent. And if I don't, I'll go home for a little while. It's reality, Jo. Places like the Manor don't exist outside of Rotham. It's not worth pretending otherwise."

"You don't even try!" I said as I pulled away from her. "You don't even want to imagine a world where we all might want to stay together because you can't bear the thought that people might care about you, that we might want to spend time with you because we *like* spending time with you. And I know you and Caroline have your fights, and I know you're your own person, but we take care of each other. Why would you want to isolate yourself from that? Why can't you let someone else love you without trying to figure out what they want from you?" I hesitated, avoiding her eyes. "We've talked about it before. Caroline has said a million times that she and Saz could pool their savings and get an old place for us to fix up. You said it sounded nice."

"Of course it sounds nice, Jo," she murmured, one hand circling my ankle and squeezing. "You know it would be great. But do you really think Caroline's parents would let her use their money to live with a bunch of lesbians in the countryside? I'm sorry, but it's not going to happen."

"Saz is bisexual," I snapped pointlessly.

"Fine, one bisexual and four lesbians. You need to accept that Caroline will Solo and some gallery will love her work, and they'll offer to represent her as a professional painter. She'll go on to make amazing things, and she'll be hanging in a museum by the time the rest of us are still finding our footing at a coffee shop, barely making rent."

I yanked my foot out of her grasp and slid off the couch. The sigh she let out was fed up and exhausted. "You can go ahead and admit it," I said, shrugging my coat back on. "You're jealous of her. She has what you want and you can't bear it."

"Jesus Christ, Jo. You just need to get it through your head that it's not going to be like this forever," Finch snapped. "We leave. People move on. It all fucking changes."

"I'm jealous too," I admitted, as if she hadn't spoken at all. "It's impossible not to be. But you always think the worst of them. You never give us a chance."

Finch shook her head, her voice softening. "You're not listening to me. It doesn't matter how I feel about any of you if that feeling isn't rooted in reality. And I know it's scary to think about, but you're not a failure if you have to go home for a little while. You can take time to figure out where you want to go, and what you want to do, and who you want to become."

There was no life if I left this one behind. The person I'd been before Rotham no longer existed. There was no home to go back to where I could find myself reflected unless they were there, filling its halls.

"I can't," I whispered. My eyes welled with tears. I didn't want her to see me cry—somehow it was the most pathetic thing in the world. "I can't go back there. I'm different now."

Finch got to her feet and reached tentatively for my hand. When I let her take it, she pulled me into her again, wrapped her arms around my neck, pressed her cheek to mine. I closed my eyes and let her hold me.

"I'm sorry," she murmured. "Forget I said anything. You don't have to go anywhere you don't want to go. You know I love you." *Love*, said like that, like it was so easy, like it still meant the same thing it had when we'd just been infatuated friends. "I'm just trying to keep you from getting hurt. I don't want you to pin your hopes on Caroline."

I nodded.

"We can go to sleep," she whispered. "You don't have to leave."

I shook my head.

"Are you sure? It's late. You shouldn't walk home right now."

She was so solid beneath me. Her fingers pressed down into my shoulders as if rooting me in place, fusing me with her.

"I'll text you when I'm home," I said against her throat, my hands drifting at the base of her spine. She hesitated—I could feel her pushing back, wanting to tell me that she was sorry again. But we let the silence live on. I pulled out of her grasp and laced my shoes back on.

"Wait," she said finally. I watched her disappear into her room, heard her rummage somewhere unseen. When she finally reemerged, she took my hand and unfurled my fingers to press something into my palm. It was a little white pill, pale against my angry scar.

"Take this and get some rest tonight," she murmured. "You look like you haven't slept since last month."

I scoffed a laugh, but her face remained serious. Her only goodbye was a tug on my arm and a kiss pressed to my temple, the kind of tender action that made me almost regret going.

But I wanted to be home with them in the Manor. I wanted to prove Finch wrong and to show her that we could figure things out, that we would choose each other with intention. We wanted to be artists. But what good was art when made alone? What reason would I have left to paint if it wasn't about them, if they wouldn't see it in completion?

Campus was barren during my walk home. The promenade wove past the woods, trees shaking in the dark, the breeze cool enough to raise chills along my arms beneath my jacket. I tried not to look into the black pockets of night. I was so afraid of my mind's potential for invention—all the ways it could and would hurt me, all its opportunities for destruction.

But I caught the flicker of movement anyway. It was impossible not to; the shift was so stark against all that shadow that my eyes went right to it. Sight dissolved until the shape was a girl stepping into the woods, shrouded in a white dress, underdressed for the spring night. My first thought was *Mother Crone*. All those Rotham stories proving themselves to be true.

I stood and watched and waited. When my brain caught up to my body, my feet kicked into gear before I could fully realize what I'd seen.

It was Caroline making her way into the woods.

I shivered, already afraid, and I followed her to the trees.

29

OBLITERATE, INSENSATE, OFFENSIVE

I lost Caroline immediately. Part of me was afraid that she hadn't really been there at all—that I was seeing shit again, my mind no longer mine.

Still, I hurried down the path where she'd disappeared. There were no lights out this way—they didn't want to encourage us to leave at night. I went anyway, to the place where Rotham's property line devolved into woods. Lysander Gate was covered in dead ivy. I ducked as I passed under it, though it wasn't nearly short enough to warrant the action—something about it made me want to shrink.

The path went from stone to dirt and the moon reflected off the pond. Even this close to the water, I could hear music carrying across campus from one of the dorms—I wondered if somewhere a party was happening. If Finch could hear it too. If she was waiting for my text to announce I'd gotten home. I touched my phone in my pocket and considered lying. But crashing footsteps drew my eyes back up. I pushed between the trees and let my ears be my guide.

Against all efforts to be quiet, my shoes crunched over winter debris. She flitted through the trees without looking back, a distant flash of white, like a camera snapping shots in the dark. I wondered if she could hear me and just didn't care. If her goal far outweighed the consequences of my following. Branches whipped my cheeks. I could hear something panting behind me, like an animal coming too close—I glanced for it over my shoulder and turned back to find Caroline gone again.

"Fuck." I pushed on in the direction I thought I'd last seen her. Something trampled behind me, recklessly loud. There were deer out in these woods. Bears had been spotted before, but rarely—though I'd thought the same about that boar I'd hit with my car. I grabbed a branch and felt thorns rip into my palm. Let out another hissed curse. Stumbled forward, nearly lost my footing.

Brush gave way to dirt as the sound of trickling water came close— the ground dipped down into the belly of a creek.

Caroline stood in the water, clutching something against her chest. I opened my mouth to call to her. But she stepped forward onto the dirt beside the stream and fell to her knees, the bundle tumbling from her arms to the ground.

She clicked on a flashlight and aimed it at her work, one hand sifting through the materials. Now the beam of light showed me what she'd been carrying—the clothes Finch had let me borrow after that night I slept over and the weighty tome of *ANTHROPOMANCY*, the letters on its cover gleaming gold beneath the glow. She set the flashlight down beside her leg and got to work, ripping up grass and dead leaves to stuff the arms and legs of the sweatpants and hoodie, filling out a Finch-shaped doll. The light rolled across the ground with her movement and illuminated my paint rag, hardened a dull reddish brown with the blood from Finch's cut.

She'd stolen from my room. She had taken the rag from my studio. Now it made sense—Caroline in that Michigan room, her fingers working Finch's hair out of the brush.

I took an uncertain step forward, and the hill's slope sent me slipping closer to the water. I swung for a grasp on one of the trunks surrounding me, but my nails just scraped over bark as I cried out. Rocks clattered into the stream and I skidded to the bottom of the hill.

She spun with the book in her arms and turned her flashlight on me. All I could see was its white eye, the searing beam turning everything else to haze.

"Hey," she said casually.

"*Hey?* What the fuck, Caroline?" I panted as I got to my feet, one hand up to block her light. "What are you doing with that?" I gestured to *ANTHROPOMANCY* and the mess in front of her, then took a wobbling step across the stream of water. She turned back to the effigy without a word and continued to stuff it with new fervor. The body became so plush with her work that I expected it to sit up and speak to us.

That vision sparked urgency in me. I bent and snatched up the bloody rag. Caroline finally acknowledged me again. In the dark, she made such a ghoul, her face ghostly and colorless, her eyes two black caverns.

"Jo," she said, languid, serpentine, "come on."

"Did you take this from me?"

"Don't be annoying, of course I did. Give it back." She held her hand out. I shook my head hard. "Did you follow me out here?"

I thought about what she might say if she knew I'd seen her after leaving Finch's apartment. "Get up. This is done," I said, ignoring her question.

Caroline sighed. "You're impossible."

"I'm impossible? Caroline. Get the fuck up."

"Go home."

"I'm not going anywhere until you stand up and leave this alone. This is what you meant by *fixing it*? Are you out of your mind? You saw what happened to Kolesnik. How could you . . . what could you possibly—" I faltered, sickness rising in me.

Brush crackled again. I spun in search of what could have made the sound, but Caroline ignored it, her deft hands ripping an opening in the chest cavity of the hoodie. I took hold of her shoulder and pulled her off it—she shoved me hard enough to knock me back into the dirt.

"I said *go home*," she snapped with vicious heat, index finger jabbing hard in my direction. "You have no idea what you're fucking with, Jo. You came to me and you told me you were afraid, that something needed to change. So I'm changing it. I'm protecting us. Don't be upset just because you got what you asked for."

"I didn't ask for *this*," I cried. Caroline loomed effervescent above me—something reincarnated, summoned with a spell, an entity haunting the wood.

Her voice dropped to a rough hush. "There's never been another option. We fucked the first ritual, and that's on us. We never should have left it somewhere so volatile."

"But—" I stopped, uncertain. "You can't do that to her. Not Finch."

"Then who, Jo? Who else stands in our way other than *her*? You want to pick someone else we should murder?"

"Stop," I whispered. "Please, just stop, I need to think."

"We're out of time. We'll bury the scarecrow so deep no one will ever find it. It will live on forever, and leave us alone, and we can go on to create beautiful things. Don't you want to make something beautiful?"

Of course I did. She knew that. But if I couldn't make something beautiful on my own, what right did I have to claim exaltation? What had I ever worked for and earned? I would do anything to keep her, to keep all of them. I would not do this.

Caroline was still speaking without waiting for me to answer in the same rush of emotion I could hear her spew past the walls of our Manor bedrooms. Her eyes had the wild look of a hunted animal. I looked at her and thought about that feral pig bleeding out on the road, screaming in the voice of a man we'd murdered.

It was a struggle to stagger upright. Her head snapped to meet me. We watched each other like we were preparing to circle, to stalk and lunge—I was afraid that I'd never seen this side of her, that she had shown me a new face. A deeper, sharper part of me assumed this was her in entirety.

"You asked me to fix it," she said. The words dragged out of her like she had winched them from her chest. "You. Asked. *Me.*"

Another flurry of movement in the woods. Too close. The trees bent and whistled in the wind, *ANTHROPOMANCY*'s pages fluttering through a succession of gruesome images like an invisible hand was turning them. I stepped away from Caroline and the effigy, still sprawled on the ground before her feet.

"Let's just go home," I pleaded.

Something groaned in the brush. I fought to keep my eyes off the dark, but it was pervasive, everywhere and everything. The rag felt like an omen in my hands—as if just by holding it, I'd made an offering to something terrible. I dug my nails into the bloodstain.

Caroline fixed me with a look devoid of feeling. One foot prodded the Finch doll on the ground, and the belly spilled rotten grass. The sound of heavy breathing surrounded us.

"Do you hear that?" I whispered, rag held to my chest.

"I told you what I saw. I know you saw it too," Caroline said flatly. "If you refuse to let me keep us safe and we walk away now, this mess is on you."

I wasn't good. I considered. I imagined what it would be like to watch Caroline continue the ritual, to let someone else bear that fear, to release myself from Kolesnik's shadow. It would have been so simple. So necessary. I didn't know how much longer I could last without another option. But what was safety anyway, if choosing it meant hurting them?

I loved Finch, even when I hated her. I closed my eyes so Caroline's couldn't convince me otherwise.

"We can't do that to her," I said finally.

Caroline kicked *ANTHROPOMANCY* away in disgust. I snatched it up and held it to my chest as she stalked past me into the woods, and I hurried to follow.

Everything was dark and damp between the trees, like walking down a throat with its tongue roiling underfoot. She moved so quickly—I jogged to keep up, branches tearing welts across my arms. By the time

I broke out into the garden again, Caroline was a speck of white in the distance.

She let the Manor's door slam before I could catch up. I fumbled with the knob in a rush. When I shut it and locked it behind me again, I heard her footsteps thumping overhead against the last stairs before her bedroom door slammed too. The rest of the house remained still, everyone else likely in bed, used to Caroline's ways.

I didn't look behind me to see what might have followed us. I was sure that whatever it was had already made itself at home inside the Manor, inside of me.

Caroline's voice was low and angry on the other side of the wall as I shut my door, shed my dirty clothes, and perched on the edge of my bed. I set *ANTHROPOMANCY* down beside me on the quilt, fingers grazing over the cover like it might be able to give me an answer through the thin leather. It had the warm, fleshy sensation of a limb. Like something cut from skin and called to life.

I knew the answer I craved and its simultaneous impossibility. I wanted a break from myself. I wanted to wake and find the fear erased.

There was a place to begin, at least—in the morning I could tell Saz that I knew what we had done and where the ritual had come from. I'd share my concerns for Caroline and the influence this horrible book held over us. If the ritual stemmed from it, then there had to be something else in its pages: a way to go back to how things were before.

I shed my clothes and slid into bed, yanked the blankets nearly over my head, shivering there between the sheets with Finch's pill melting beneath my tongue. The coating slickened everything. I shut my eyes as the floor outside my bedroom door creaked beneath Caroline's weight. Movement hesitated, as if she was standing outside with a hand raised to knock. But the sound never came. Lights flickered until the glow beneath my door was nothing but the faint red of the exit sign.

For the first time in months, tongue still candied by Finch's pill, I hurtled into black.

30

BUILD A BLUE HEARTH AND KNEEL BESIDE IT

When I woke, the house was eerily dark and silent. Sweat slicked my body. I sat up in a rush, T-shirt contorted around my torso.

The door to my bedroom sat open. Its rectangular cutout was completely black, the kind of darkness so thick you couldn't make out your hand before your face. It took a moment for my mind to register its wrongness—the exit sign's light was out. No more red.

I hesitated, perched at the end of the bed, listening. Something thumped far away in the house.

I scrabbled over the bed, hands seeking a weapon, and landed on the heavy tome of *ANTHROPOMANCY*. I pulled it onto my lap. It pulsed with heat, like the book itself had a heartbeat.

There were options. If morning hadn't come yet, I could turn over and try to will myself back to sleep. But if the exit sign was out, then maybe the rest of the power was too. Amrita would be scared. She hated to be alone in the dark.

My first step out of bed emitted a low creak. I listened. Waited. Watched. The flashlight on my phone would have been an enormous help, but I had no idea where it was and couldn't remember seeing it since I'd found Caroline. The fear that it might be sitting out in the woods next to Finch's half-formed doll was all-consuming. Now the hall's lightlessness was so heavy that some part of me believed I would look down at my clothes and find them stained with shadow. Even with the curtains drawn back, no moon poured past the glass. The night was too new.

I felt for Caroline's door and found it shut. If I wanted to, I could go in. Rouse her from a restless sleep. But I was scared of who she might be upon waking. I pressed my ear up to the door. The Manor remained silent. Maybe she wasn't in there at all. Maybe the darkness had summoned her from her rest too.

Someone's footsteps fluttered at the bottom of the stairs. I turned and waited.

"Saz?" I called.

ANTHROPOMANCY was an uneasy weight in my arms. I kept it clutched to my chest with one arm as if it could form a shield between me and whatever was in the house. The other hand gripped the stair railing for stability, each step cautious in the dark.

"Amrita?" I tried again. And then, against my better judgment, "Caroline?"

The sleeping pill had left my mouth dry, my head stuffed with cotton. I kept swallowing around nothing. It would have been smarter to stay at Finch's for the night. We could have talked things through, moved on and pretended none of it ever happened. But in that universe where I stayed, would Caroline have completed the ritual? Would I have woken to find her body in her bed with my arms still locked around it? Would the two of us have gone down together?

Saz's bedroom door sat open. I peered inside, unable to decipher movement or shape in the lumps of her blankets. I tried whisper-calling her name again. Something clicked distantly, like a lock sliding into place. This time I didn't stop to listen. I just pushed on until I was outside Amrita's room, one fist raised and knocking.

I waited. My pulse was a white roar in my ears. "Amrita!" I called, voice trembling. "Are you awake?"

Nothing. I could hear something sigh past the door, so I knocked harder. Still no answer. I turned the knob and felt something resist, as if a hand was holding it shut on the other side. I could taste copper. I threw my shoulder against the door and shoved.

The door slammed open to show me an empty room. Amrita wasn't in bed. The sighing stopped immediately, all sound ceasing as if I'd been sucked into a vacuum.

And then the screaming began—a disembodied wail rising around me in every room and on every floor of the house. I tried to cover my ears but couldn't find it in me to drop the book. Instead, I fell into a crouch with *ANTHROPOMANCY* pressed between my chest and my knees, as if protecting it might keep me safe too. I shouted my throat raw, calling their names into the empty Manor as the shrieking just went on and on. I staggered to my feet and hurried down the stairs. I had to get out of the house and find where everyone had gone.

Outside rain spat and soaked everything like a dewy spiderweb, until it felt as if I could walk right through the world and find it tangled in my hair. The promenade's path to Grainer was pocked with puddles—past the film of rain, I could see the illuminated studio windows and silhouettes moving behind them.

Without my phone, I had no concept of what time it was or who might be in the studio to witness me as a barefoot, underdressed mess. The chilly night racked me down to the bone. Chattering teeth were the only sound. Inside Grainer I could escape the rain but not the fear that something was following me—and the recognition that I'd never be able to banish it.

Faint voices carried as I climbed the endless stairs. I was numb with cold and sick from sleeplessness. Finch's pill's effects wouldn't leave me, a fuzziness that clung to everything.

I could hear Caroline's voice warring with another as I neared Grainer's summit.

"What, you don't want me to hit you now? You were so ready to let me last time."

Someone's response was muffled and wet—they sniffled as I nudged away the brick propping the studio door open and let it quietly close behind me. "Stop it," Saz pleaded. "You don't know what you're saying."

"I'll break your nose and black your eyes again," Caroline called. "All you have to do is ask!"

They were gathered in a triangle where our critiques unfolded. Amrita stood between Caroline and Saz. One of Caroline's paintings hung on the wall—that piece from our first days with the swans and its pulsing heart in the center. There was a jagged cut down the middle of the painting and a pair of scissors in Caroline's hand. The floorboards creaked beneath my feet and announced me—three sets of eyes turned to look.

"Nice of you to join us," Caroline said. "Here to fuck me over again?"

"What?" I said, at the same time Amrita commanded, "Go home, Jo."

I balked. Saz looked at the book in my arms and the color drained from her face. "Where did you get that?"

"What's going on?" I asked, avoiding her question.

Amrita's eyes flickered between me and Caroline. She seemed reluctant to take her gaze off the scissors in Caroline's hand. "I said go home, you should be asleep. What are you doing up?"

"You left me alone," I said, voice small. "The power went out. I was—"

I was afraid, I wanted to say. *I went looking for you.*

"Why did you all leave?"

"That's my fault," Caroline sighed. Her hair was a mess, strands slicked to her forehead, her body still cloaked in that same pale nightgown. Now it was smeared with mud. "It's like you all have a fucking nanny cam on me or something. I wanted to work in the studio for a bit, and everyone just *had* to join me."

"You were slamming doors and screaming loud enough to wake the dead," Amrita snapped. "We wanted to make sure you were okay."

"Well, I'm fine, aren't I?" Caroline made a wild gesture in the air, pointing loosely at her shredded painting. Her eyes were wide and feral, her mouth red. Her tongue kept darting out to wet her lips.

"Caroline, you destroyed them." Saz's voice wavered. As she spoke, my eyes wandered across the room and landed on the *them* she was referencing—Caroline's paintings. She had shredded them down to rags. Now they were piles of smashed canvas, strips ripped from their frames.

"They weren't good enough," she said simply. "I was going to create something better, something suited for Solo. But Jo interrupted me."

The eyes trained on me again. I dug my fingers down in the warm leather of *ANTHROPOMANCY*.

"What's she talking about?" Saz whispered.

I swallowed around my pounding heart, afraid that speaking Caroline's intentions aloud might manifest them into reality.

"You didn't tell us the ritual came from the book," I said shakily.

Amrita turned to Saz. "Is that true?"

Saz's already weepy expression fell. "It's just a book," she started. "How is that any worse than the internet? It's not real. None of it is real."

"We killed him," I said.

"Jo. Enough." Amrita said, deathly serious. "Don't say shit like that."

Fury bubbled up inside of me. "We killed him, we killed him, we killed him! And Caroline planned to do the exact same thing to Finch, I saw her in the woods. We killed him and we raised something awful and it's coming after every last one of us until we kill each other, too."

Caroline rolled her head in my direction and grinned. She brought the scissors an inch from her throat and pretended to draw them across. "Snitch," she sang. "I was just trying to help. I could cut my belly open now if you want. You could use my entrails and tell the future. Is that better for you, Jo? You want the real thing offered to you, so you don't have to get your hands dirty?"

"Caroline, please," I said, fighting the sting in my throat.

"Where's Finch now?" Amrita asked. "Is she okay?"

"I texted her, but she never replied," Saz answered.

"Oh right, run to Finchard, she'll save us all," Caroline said. "You're delusional if you think she could do anything. I'm the one who's helping us. I'm giving us a chance at Solo, and I'm taking out the trash in the process."

"Your chance at Soloing relies on killing Finch? That must make your work pretty worthless," I snapped, leering closer to Caroline. "I thought you had more talent than that."

The smile slipped from her face, and her knuckles tightened around the scissors.

"It's rude to assume. Didn't your mother ever teach you that?" Caroline said, her eyes needling down to the core of me. "Or was she too busy reminding you how to hate yourself?"

"Enough," Amrita declared, but I was already lunging forward, my face hot with unbearable fury. This Caroline was no longer mine. She was a creature wearing her skin. She was a shadow walking upright. She was—

"Go ahead and hit me," Caroline coaxed with her arms thrown wide, coming closer and closer and closer. "Go ahead, Jo, I dare you, go for it, swing, don't be afraid! Hit me! Hit me! Hit me!"

Saz barreled forward and shoved Caroline. They went sprawling together—and Caroline's head slammed into the corner of a metal easel. The scissors skidded across the room.

I stood, frozen, as Saz crumpled to a heap on the ground, tears streaming down her cheeks. Caroline pulled her hand away from the back of her head. Her fingers were slicked with blood so dark it was nearly black—it stained strands of her hair and ran down her wrist. A smile claimed her face, faint but still present.

"That's more like it," she said lightly, struggling to pull herself up to her knees. One hand slid across the studio floor, leaving a sanguine smear. "Blood sacrifice. Sexy. I knew you had it in you, Saz."

"That's enough," Amrita said again, but her voice was full of more horror than insistence. Caroline dragged herself up until she was kneeling on all fours and spat once, twice, three times on the floor.

"Fuck. I think I'm gonna be sick." Her chest heaved, and she spat again. "Do you hear that ringing?"

"I'm sorry, I didn't mean to—I—" Saz whispered. "Caroline, we need to get you to a doctor. You're probably—you might have a concussion."

Caroline turned her eyes on me. Spit trailed down her chin and pieces of hair hung in her eyes. "Your turn, Jo. I said, hit me. You want a fight? Let's fight. Let's see who Solos after all."

I raised the book. I was still trembling, so hard I could barely keep my grasp on it. But instead of swinging *ANTHROPOMANCY* at her, I just held it out in front of me. "I'm not—I'm not going to hit you, I just want to fix it, there has to be a way to fix it. The ritual came from this book. It worked once. There has to be something else in here that tells us how to cancel it out, or how to close the spell of what we did to Kolesnik."

I splayed the book open and thumbed through until I landed on the ritual's bookmarked page. Text across the top read "Resurrection Exchange of Godly Creation." Beside the blurb of text was a picture of a person spread out on the ground, entrails spilling from the belly. I tore the page from the book and held it up for the others to look at.

"See?" I said.

ANTHROPOMANCY erupted in flames.

Grainer was a tinderbox of solvent and wood and cloth and accelerator. I dropped the book with a shriek, and Saz scrambled away from it, screaming the whole time. As soon as it hit the floor beside the mess of Caroline's paintings, the pile caught, flames licking across the paint, erupting in a cloud of fire.

"It's not real," I stuttered, rocking back. "It's a hallucination, it's not real, it's not real—"

But Caroline, kneeling on the floor with her head hanging low on her shoulders, began to laugh. She laughed, and laughed, and laughed. Amrita pulled Saz to her feet. "We need to get out of here!" Amrita shouted, and just as she turned to leave, the studio door burst open to reveal Finch.

The fire painted her in a million shades of gold as Finch leaned away from the rising flames. "What the fuck is going on?" she cried.

The book's pages fluttered and crackled as the flames spread. From the spine of *ANTHROPOMANCY* a black figure rose—a tusked creature lifting itself from the devastation, head rearing back, limbs snapping and expanding and tearing itself out of the book. It let out a horrible cry, that pained death wail that had clung to me for so many months. That plea sounded like *HELP ME HELP ME HELP ME HELP ME HELP ME* except now I didn't know where it was coming from, who to go to, how to keep the world from ending.

"Caroline, get up!" I screamed, arms coming up to block my face as another whoosh of heat rose like a wall between us.

The fire devoured, the creature heaving and gasping and swinging its body through the burn. I tried to plunge forward to reach Caroline but had to duck away as a crumbling section of Grainer's roof came crashing into the burning debris. The figure roared, sparks alighting off its body as it rippled like an oily mirage.

"What the fuck is that?" Amrita cried.

"The Boar King," Finch answered, awestruck, her fingers closing around my wrist.

The oil drum of disposed solvent sat beside the sinks, half-full. If the flames reached it, there was no chance of survival—the whole place would go up like lighter fluid on a bonfire. Fire worked its way across the room, crawling up the walls, blackening everything in its wake. The heat was unbearable. I felt as if my skin would melt away and leave only bone. The creature stood tall in the blaze, its roaring head tipped back and rippling with heat. Caroline's delighted gasp was nearly buried beneath the crackle of fire as she took in the sight.

"Get up. We need to go," Amrita begged Caroline, keeping Saz on her feet with an arm beneath her shoulders. "Please, Caroline. We can't reach you, you're going to get hurt, you have to try to step across—"

Fire engulfed the painting hanging on the wall. It curled in on itself as smoke and fumes tangled in the air. Saz stumbled toward the door. Amrita tried again, pleading for Caroline. Her pile of paintings had created an impasse between them—it stood like a burning hill.

Through the blazing light, I could see the perfect frame of her face. Her eyes circled with purple and her hair slicked with blood. Caroline looked back at me. There was so much feeling there, in the twist of her smile and the pleased glimmer of her eyes. Between us stood the Boar King's figure and the echo of its roar as the fire devoured it.

"No," I said, "no no no no no."

Amrita pushed Saz out the door, her eyes never leaving the Boar King as it grew with the fed fire.

Caroline raised her hand to me—the right one, with her heartline cut in two—and I went for her. Finch's grasp yanked me in the opposite direction.

"Let me go!" I shouted, "I need to get to her!"

Everything was enveloped by the blaze. I couldn't see Caroline anymore. Finch's hand was a vise around my wrist.

"Jo," Finch said raggedly, "I'm sorry. We can't."

The ceiling—that high white ceiling with its ever-spinning fans, those brilliant windows, that cathedral of a room—buckled further, pressing close, threatening to smother us all. I watched the Boar King expand until it was a plume of smoke, the heart of the fire itself, a massive ember pulsing with heat.

Finch dragged me past the studio door. The fire flashed and oxidized. I couldn't see the flames catch the solvent tank, but from the first floor I heard the resulting boom of gallons of accelerant bursting into the air. The sound shook all of Grainer. Glass shattered, raining down on Main Lawn. We fled into the night as the sound of sirens picked up, carrying toward us, Caroline left behind in a burst of white light.

Saz collapsed on the promenade with her head between her knees. Amrita crouched beside her and gripped Saz's shoulders. She had her phone pressed to her ear, saying, "We need help now! Should I go back in? Should I try to get her? Do you think I can bring her out?"

Glass rained and rained. Grainer melted in on itself. The building groaned beneath the weight of the collapsing burn.

Finch held me to her and looked me over, hunting for wounds. If I was hurt, I was too numb to feel pain. I just stared back at her and buzzed with adrenaline as I finally said—

"We let her die." And then—"You saw it too."

Finch's face fell open, like I'd let her down, like she'd hoped to find someone better inside of me. Her fingertips dug down into the meat of my arms. Left bruising impressions of her grasp.

"Yeah, I saw it too," she whispered.

31

SCATTER THE CLOUDS

For the second time in less than six months we lined up outside of St. Roche's office. Everything smelled of smoke—it clung to my hair, my clothes, under my nails. Amrita sat to my right and Saz to my left, with Finch closest to St. Roche's door. Two tracks of pristine skin ran down Amrita's cheeks where her tears had wiped away the ash. The rest of her was grimy with disaster.

Now there was an empty chair in our row. Saz hadn't stopped crying for hours. She kept drawing in horrible, broken breaths. Finch was vigilant at the end of our row, one knee bouncing relentlessly. I wore a pair of slippers that St. Roche had pulled from beneath her desk and offered me. They were thin enough that I could feel the floor press back against me.

It had been six hours since the fire department finally got Grainer's fire under control. The three floors at the top were gone. The entire body of thesis work was destroyed. There would be no Solo. There wouldn't even be a group presentation. All we had to show for our time at Rotham was ash and blackened beams, and to everyone's surprise, a faint slush of snow over everything. We were back where we started, frost coating the wet remnants of Grainer and turning the world into a tomb.

St. Roche emerged from her office, looking haggard. Her questions were surprisingly resigned, mostly asking us where we had been, what time we noticed that Caroline was gone, and what exactly we had seen. Amrita instructed us to keep our answers vague. She did the talking. The story she spun made me nauseous: Caroline had been pulling all-nighters and sleeping in short bursts in the studio, caught up in the stress of Solo. She liked to smoke when she worked. She must have drifted off with a cigarette in her mouth. There was never a chance of getting out alive with that much solvent surrounding her. It was a part of her, seeping out of her pores.

Amrita had been the one to wake and find Caroline's bed empty. We'd gone looking for her in the only place we expected her to be, to bring her home and back to bed. We arrived to find Grainer's alarms already blaring. The fire consuming everything in its wake.

"The police will want to talk with you all again," St. Roche said finally. Amrita ran her hand up and down Saz's back as she sniffled. "For now, you may return to the Manor. The Asters will likely stop by this evening to retrieve their daughter's things. They're with—" St. Roche paused. "They're speaking with the coroner."

"Oh fuck," Saz wept.

Reality hadn't quite landed yet—the insensible part of my brain kept thinking that we'd return to the Manor to find her waiting there. I kept trying to anticipate my devastation, but I was too numb.

St. Roche held the door for us. We walked the promenade to the Manor. There was a crowd gathered around Grainer. Someone had already laid candles and flowers beside photos of her pulled from Rotham's website, sickly sweet promotional stuff where Caroline stood beside a canvas with a brilliant smile on her younger face. All I could think about was the snow snuffing it out, falling heavy over her monument.

"They're still looking for pieces of her," Finch sneered. "Who the fuck do these people think they're grieving?"

"Finch, please," Amrita whispered hoarsely. I shivered in my thin pajamas.

"I need a shower," Saz said wetly.

When we finally reached the Manor, it was dark, daylight barely permeating the halls. I went in last, still afraid—I expected to find the bulbs shattered, every door hanging open on its hinges, the stairs creaking beneath invisible feet. But it was just as we'd left it before I went to sleep the night before. Caroline's half-empty glass of water sat unfinished on the table.

The sight set Saz off into a wave of fresh tears. She pushed past the rest of us and up the stairs into the bathroom on the second floor. The door shut and the lock clicked.

"We need to talk before the police get here," Finch said.

"Thirty minutes. Just give us thirty minutes, please. I need to change these awful clothes," Amrita pleaded.

Finch relented and went to the living room. I heard her kick her shoes off and sit. The room was quiet as I hesitated by the dining table; if I really wanted to, I could have gone to her, pushed my way into her arms. But there was a barrier between us. She had seen the Boar King. She had pulled me away from Caroline and let her die.

I ascended to the third floor. In the bathroom, I stripped off my smoky clothes and stuffed them right into the trash can. I pressed my forehead to the shower and let the spray soak my scalp and my back, hot enough to sear. The arrival of grief was a sedative more powerful than Finch's sleeping pills—it sent me down to the cave of myself where I resented being touched, where I could stew in my own hurt. Time passed, or it didn't. When I slitted my eyes open, they landed on a swirl of Caroline's hair still clinging to the wall. I reached for it immediately but stopped an inch away. My eyes stung with tears until I finally snared it with my fingers and pulled it free.

When the water went frigid, I dried off and shoved the towel against my mouth to release a horrible scream, until the sound left my throat raw. I panted. Listened for a sound in Caroline's room that would never come. In my bedroom, I placed the lock of hair reverently atop my desk where it made a blond crescent moon.

Downstairs they gathered in the living room. It seemed impossible that it might be nearly noon—outside, the sky was the pale gray of a sunless day.

Finch bent near the fireplace. She started a fire in the hearth with newsprint and a box of matches, and Saz was crying all over again, saying, "Really? You're really going to do that now?" as Finch snapped back, "It's fucking cold." She poked at forming embers and wouldn't meet my eyes.

"You have to tell me what happened before I got there," I said from the doorway. Even with my arms wrapped around myself and my sweatshirt pulled over my hands, I still couldn't regain sensation in my fingertips.

I stood in the far corner of the room. Saz sat on the couch with her knees pulled up to her chin. Finch squatted by the fire. Amrita's feet were bare against the floor. I found myself wondering if she was cold too.

"Well? Is anyone going to speak up?" I tried.

You left me behind, I wanted to say. *You left and I slept here and you let me think everything was going to be alright.*

Past the Manor's windows, the snow fell harder, flakes fattening and blanketing everything. Late March never looked so untouched by sun.

"It wasn't on purpose," Amrita said, her voice hoarse. "It happened so quickly. She was making so much noise and saying all this stuff about new beginnings and destruction before she slammed the door and took off. And you—you were asleep for the first time in forever." She spoke from behind her fingers, as if she might crumble if she pulled them away. It hurt me to look at her. I trained my eyes on Saz instead as anger began to boil its way back up my throat.

"You should have woken me up. Maybe I could have helped," I snapped. I tugged my sweatshirt tighter around me. "I saw her last night, before we went to bed. She wasn't okay." The anger slipped, replacing itself with hot panic. "I should have—oh, fuck, oh my god—I should have called her parents, or St. Roche. I should have told someone she was going to do something reckless, or hurt herself, or hurt one of you. Caroline was in the woods last night and she—she was creating a new ritual. She had Finch's hair. She was going to repeat the steps."

"Fucking hell," Finch said, paling. The fire poker clattered to the floor. Amrita slid her hands up her face until her eyes were hidden behind them too, and Saz let out a whimper.

"I stopped her," I said immediately. "I didn't let her finish it."

"Jesus Christ," Finch continued, as if I hadn't spoken. One hand pressed down around her knee, her knuckles white with strain. "She was fucking crazy."

"Don't say that."

Finch frowned against my defense. "It's not your fault that she lost her mind, Jo."

"You're right," I snapped. "We're all at fault. We let her die."

Amrita got to her feet and paced closer to the fire. "I feel like I'm going to be sick," Saz whispered, watching the flames. "Please don't fight anymore. Please, I can't take it."

"You should have thought of that before you—" I started, but I couldn't finish. Saz looked so small, like she was folding in on herself. We hovered in the silence instead, until I couldn't take it anymore.

"What do we do?" I asked. "When the police come knocking, we need a unified story, don't we? An alibi?"

"You have one," Amrita said. "You were here, asleep in your bed. Finch gave you a sleeping pill. We woke you when it was time to look for her."

My stomach bottomed out. I sank down and sat on my heels, holding myself together with shaking limbs.

Some of Amrita's fierceness melted away as she scooted closer to me. I flinched when she touched me, but I let her ease my head onto her shoulder, sank into the gentle combing of her fingers through my hair. I felt myself start to cry, just silent tears that slid from the corners of my eyes.

What was I supposed to do? In that moment, could I have done anything but let her hold me, let them watch me, listen to them instruct me on exactly how we were going to walk through this situation?

"It's alright," Amrita murmured.

But it wasn't. Above the rough fabric of my sweatshirt, I slid my hand up and started to feel for the scabbed-over patch of my tattoo, those peeling petals poked in place by Finch's hand. But my fingertips found flat, healthy skin.

"It's my fault," Saz said. "We could—we should just tell the police the truth."

My eyes met Amrita's. Her mouth quivered like she might cry too; in all the years I'd known her, I'd never seen her composure break.

"There's nothing we could tell the police that they would believe," Amrita said at last.

Finch's eyes were dark, eyeliner shadowed and smudged across her lids like they'd been freshly bruised. She scrubbed the heel of her hand over one, smearing a black line down her cheek, a tear of her own. "What, you think they won't go for the whole 'shadow manifestation of the old man we cursed' story? Or how about the haunted ritual book that spontaneously combusted in Jo's hands? I think they'd love that story."

I shifted uncomfortably, looking away from her. I hated how small she made it all appear.

"We tell them—" Amrita started. "We say exactly what we told St. Roche. Caroline had been sleeping in the studio. She was cracking under the pressure of Solo, smoking too much, getting lazy about disposing her old solvent. It's not a lie."

My stomach turned. I could see Caroline in that invented image, jacket pillowed beneath her head, golden hair falling across the dirty studio floor. I wanted to lie down beside her, pull her into my arms, breathe into the nape of her neck until the rise and fall of our chests fell into place.

"But that's not what happened," I said from underneath Amrita, whose fingers stilled against my head.

"No," Amrita agreed finally. Her hand slowly picked up its pace again and scratched along my scalp. "That's not what happened."

We were all silent, as if afraid to be the first to acknowledge what we'd collectively seen. "Caroline and I," I started, then faltered. I imagined telling them all of it—how that ritual had burrowed down to the core of me, all the ways it had ruined me in its wake—the boar in the road and the creature behind glass and my mother's voice warping into something unfamiliar. Saz wrapped her cardigan tighter around herself. I could feel Amrita's eyes on me, urging me on. But it all felt so worthless. Telling them wouldn't bring her back. Instead, I said, "Do you think they'll know that we hurt her? She was bleeding a lot."

"She fell," Amrita said at the same time as Finch said, "There's nothing left."

"I pushed her," Saz wept, the words coming out like a moan.

"You didn't mean to hurt her," Amrita said, then continued, as if trying to convince the rest of us, "she was about to attack Jo."

In my head Caroline rose, wheat pale and sickly, mouth painted like Saturn devouring his son, swallowing every last bite.

"I pushed her, I pushed her, I pushed her," Saz wailed.

"She was going to kill you, because she was sick in the fucking head from all that ritual shit you started," Finch snapped, jabbing a finger at Saz.

"Watch yourself," Amrita said to Finch. "It was an accident. We all know that. Saz had to defend herself, and Caroline was egging everyone on."

I whispered, "You didn't let me help her."

Silence answered. I wanted to push Amrita off me but couldn't bring myself to do it.

"You know we couldn't have done that," Amrita said at last, her voice soft as the fingertips grazing my scalp. "She was already so far gone."

I pressed my mouth to my knee, trying to do anything but picture Caroline's skin, cooked and seared. I could still feel her hands ghosting over me.

I slid out of Amrita's grasp and pressed a palm to the Manor's floor as if the house might swallow me whole, take me through the studs and the insulation and the fitted wooden slats down into the basement where I'd be safe from the truth I voiced. "The police will know we were involved. She was ours."

"You didn't do anything," Finch said. "This is not on your hands, and we are not saying a goddamn word."

"Of course it's on my hands!" I cried. "If something happens to one of us, it happens to all of us. They'll never believe it if we deny being involved." Above us, I thought I heard the creak of the floorboards and fought to keep myself from looking up. There was no one up there. Caroline was gone, always would be, burned up into nothing but ash and the melted remnants of her jewelry on the studio floor.

"I need a fucking smoke," Finch said as she tore the front door open and slammed it behind her. Saz sniffled thickly, her eyes red.

"Jo," Amrita said, crouching beside me again. She pushed her hair behind her ear and smiled sadly. "You know that there's nothing to say, right? Caroline was sick and high, and she fell, and she shouldn't have been smoking around her paints. And we love her, and it was an accident, and if there was any way that we could have stopped it, we would have."

She cupped my face and leaned in until we were just a breath apart. I let myself feel it—the warmth of her hands, the comfort in her touch, the way each breath she exhaled operated in time with my inhales.

"Tell me you understand," she said.

"I understand," I answered through my tears.

"Good." Her smile was the same loving one she'd shown me for years. "Help me make some tea, okay? Saz could use something warm, couldn't you?"

Saz nodded. Her sweater bunched up around her face, obscuring one of her eyes. She looked like one of her own paintings, mottled and greening and frantic.

Amrita helped me to my feet and pulled me into the kitchen. Caroline's dish still sat in the sink, crusted and sticky with the jam-covered toast she'd had for breakfast two days ago. The scene set itself like a memento mori version of Tracey Emin's *My Bed*, soap scud clinging to white bowls, bite marks still in the crust.

I stood with my arms crossed over my chest. Amrita hummed as she filled the kettle and set up the mugs, dropping a tea bag in each one. I watched her hands shake as she tore open the last bag and I moved to take over.

"Let me," I said, and Amrita turned back to the kettle, her face angled away from mine. Her shoulders were drawn up near her ears. She looked so tired—all this time, Amrita had felt solid and sure and radiant. Now she was diminished.

I couldn't look at her. Instead, I spooned honey and sliced lemon. I filled each mug. Amrita wavered next to me and pressed her forehead to my shoulder. I closed my eyes and sucked a painful breath in through my nose until I was crying raggedly. I wanted Caroline. Where was I supposed to put all the love I had for her? Where could I lay its flowers down?

"Shh," Amrita mumbled, turning until her cheek was against my shoulder. I kept my eyes squeezed shut. "Don't cry, Jo. If you cry again, I will too."

But I couldn't stop. The Manor suddenly felt so big and empty. I wanted to go running to the charred remains of the studio. I wanted my paintings back, and I wanted to hear Caroline's voice, even slurred, even aching. I hadn't even had time to mourn all the things we had made. All the work we'd devoted ourselves to melted down to nothing.

And my mind began to betray me, already sketching the painting of this moment—a new Gathering, the hazy outline of Caroline standing on the shore of Lake Michigan, water so cold it could rip your breath right out of your mouth. The rest of us waiting in the distant horizon. The rocks by the water's edge, breeze whipping reeds hard enough to leave stinging welts on our ankles. Dunes rising high. Caroline's hair glowing beneath the sun. The gold shape of her, like a ghost, like a dream. If I'd had a brush in my hand, I wouldn't have been able to stop myself. I would have recorded her on the first surface I could have made contact with.

I don't know why I stood there so long, Amrita holding me together. There are times when I think that I should have walked away from the Manor in that moment, or from Rotham entirely. I have to believe that it would have been easier that way. But who would I have turned to? No one had ever known me so well.

It was awful, to be seen like that. There was nothing to hide. Every direction I turned, someone would have caught me in the act. But I knew then that I would let them get away with anything. I would always forgive them for hurting me.

"There's someone at the door," Amrita said. I opened my eyes. I watched steam sift through gray light, the tea in my hands scorching my palms pink.

On cue, a knock sounded. The door opened before any of us could reach for it, Finch stepping inside with her cigarette still hanging from her lips.

"Don't bother, I have a key," she said over her shoulder, and then the police stepped into our living room.

They were so out of place among our decor—posters and pride flags and string lights and nude paintings and torn-up bits of paper from a game we used to play, where we'd rank our favorite foods by rearranging the order. The two officers took it all in. I couldn't move.

"How can we help you?" Amrita called, her hands slipping away from me.

"I'm Detective Adriana Piccioni, and this is Officer Steven Hirsch," one of the officers stated, a short woman with her hair slicked back into a low bun, hands on her hips. "You all lived here together?" As Amrita and I joined the others in the living room again, passing out hot mugs, I watched Detective Piccioni's eyes trace over our walls. They bounced from the collages to our horror movie list beside the TV. Her taller partner, a broad man with a buzzed head, remained silent at her left.

"It's on-campus housing," I said. "Finch lives in Tuck House, though. It's another dorm building."

"Finch?" The woman asked. Finch raised her hand, petulance written across her face.

"Jodie Finchard."

The woman nodded. "Understood. So you're Jodie. I assume the rest of you are Amrita Balakrishnan, Sarah Murphy-Choi, and Joanna Kozak?"

Her eyes flickered around the room, landing on each of us. We raised our hands in unison with her words until she seemed satisfied with who was who. Saz blew her nose noisily into a tissue Amrita produced for her.

"I'm very sorry for your loss. I regret that we have to be here under the circumstances, but with the unfortunate events of last night and the extensive damage to Rotham's campus, I'm sure you understand why we need to speak to you. Your friend Caroline Aster lived here as well, correct?"

Finch scoffed at *unfortunate* while Saz nodded. "On the third floor, with Jo."

This time, the man—Officer Hirsch—spoke up. His eyes were such a washed-out blue that they appeared nearly milky. I met them once and made it a point to never look in his direction again. "I've heard Rotham's a tough institution," he said. "Pretty competitive."

"Of course," Amrita answered.

"We work hard," I added.

"And your friend? Was there a lot of pressure on her?"

"There was tremendous pressure on all of us," Finch said, her tone sharp. "Painting seniors at Rotham have to compete for a Solo Show, and only one student gets it."

The woman whistled. "Sounds intense. Was she struggling with that pressure?"

Saz swallowed. "Everyone was. Doesn't matter now, though. The work's all gone."

The man hummed thoughtfully. "Sorry to hear that. I'm sure that's a huge loss for your class."

"It's everything we made in our time at Rotham," Finch said. "Anything worthwhile, at least. There won't be a thesis. We're done."

Amrita gave her a look that begged her to shut the fuck up. Detective Piccioni glanced between them, a frown on her face. "Can you tell me exactly what happened last night?"

Amrita walked through our agreed-upon details. I sank deeper into the couch as she spoke. I thought about Caroline crouching over that effigy of Finch with her hands splitting the chest, grassy innards bursting free. The vicious intent on her face. Commitment to an end. Her sure grasp on that bloody rag, on the yet unburned copy of *ANTHROPOMANCY*. How would she have finished the ritual if I hadn't followed? And how would she have gotten away with it? Because the question wasn't *if*—Caroline would always get away with everything. The fire was the first time she'd ever been snared in a mess of our making without a neat exit waiting on the other end. Even now, I had a close, sinking feeling, the kind of thought that suggested maybe she'd meant for it to happen this way. That if she couldn't be free of the violent haunt at our backs, she'd find another way out.

"Ms. Kozak?"

The woman detective was crouching before me. I wondered how many times she had called my name, what had made her think she needed to get down on my level. She had her elbows resting against the navy slacks stretching across her knees, thick brows arching down toward the bridge of her nose. I blinked back at her. It took me too long to realize that Amrita was pinching my thigh where the others couldn't see, trying to call me back to myself.

"Can you corroborate that account? Ms. Aster was sleeping in the studio, and you hadn't seen her alive since early yesterday afternoon?"

I pushed into the feeling of Amrita's nails digging into my skin. "Yes, after critique. That was the last time I saw her. She wanted to stay late and start a few pieces over. They choose a Soloist next week. She wanted it to be her."

The look Detective Piccioni gave me was closed off. Finally, she cleared her throat and got to her feet again. She gave the other officer a little wave, and he angled toward the front door. "Right. Well, if you don't want that position, I can't imagine why you'd put yourself through a school like this. Seems like a tough gig."

"Like Jo said, we work hard," Amrita finished.

"Right, right. I have to ask you all not to leave the campus. There are tapes to review, and details to understand about the extent of damage. It's a tragedy, truly. I've never heard of anything like it." The detective turned to go, then hesitated by the door. "As I said, Ms. Aster's parents will be by to pick up her things. They are . . . distraught. I recommend giving them space."

Saz thanked them, and Finch saw them out. When she closed the door, we listened to them descend the stairs, their shoes crunching over ice, car doors slamming.

"Fuck," Finch said, "I'd bet anything that they think we had something to do with it."

"You know as well as the rest of us do that the Grainer cameras are props," Amrita argued. "And even if they could have recorded something, the cameras on the top three floors are melted by now. I think they seemed perfectly reasonable, and we gave them no reason to doubt us. Just . . . be cool."

"Easy for you to say," Saz said. "I'm going to fucking prison for fucking murder."

"Don't," Amrita hissed, rounding on Saz. We all froze. The wild terror in her eyes was all-consuming. "Do not say shit like that. None of us are going to prison, and none of us are murderers. She was just as complicit in this disaster. That's all it is, okay? I'm sorry. It's an awful, tragic, miserable disaster. But we will have to carry that and move forward. Do you understand?"

We sat in collective silence. "Tell me you understand!" Amrita snapped again.

We mumbled our affirmative responses. She straightened. Fidgeted with the hem of her sweater. Looked at the closed front door and said, "Alright. Good."

I ran my thumb over the cut on my left hand. It was the smooth, puckered pink of a heal. That reassuring closed line. I shut my eyes and felt the raised ridge of skin and said, "I think we sacrificed something big enough to close the ritual. I think it's finally done."

Finch turned and left, slamming the door behind her hard enough to rattle the Manor's teeth.

32

Every Last One a Temple

That night they held a vigil outside of Grainer. Caroline's parents stood entangled beside St. Roche. Her mother wept loudly and profusely. The detective and officer were half-obscured by the crowd of Rotham students and faculty, but my eyes kept snaring on them anyway. The pile of grocery store flowers and photos of Caroline had grown. Candles kept snuffing out. The wreckage rose high above us, Grainer roped off and blackened, the top three floors entirely gone save for some of the staircase's skeleton. St. Roche's megaphone blared across campus.

"THIS HAS BEEN A YEAR MARKED BY TRAGEDY," she boomed. "A TERRIBLE TIME IN ROTHAM HISTORY. TONIGHT, WE MOURN THE LIFE OF AN INCREDIBLE STUDENT AND A BRILLIANT MIND, ROTHAM'S VERY BEST, CAROLINE ASTER."

"She would have died if she saw they used that picture," Saz said past her tears, gesturing at a photo of Caroline sitting on Main Lawn with her head tossed back in a laugh, some more of the high-quality promotional shots Rotham had used for catalogs.

"Poor choice of words, Saz," Amrita muttered.

"She meant, Caroline would have died *again*," Finch said.

I elbowed her. She refused to look at me. Her chin was angled high, cheeks pink with the cold, hair mostly hidden beneath a baseball hat. I couldn't tell if her lashes were damp from the misty rain or from emotion.

Saz was holding Amrita's hand. I heard her say something like, *When can we go home?* to Amrita but never caught the answer.

"Are you really going to ignore me?" I whispered to Finch.

Finch kept her eyes trained on St. Roche. We were a few rows back from the front—Phoebe, of all people, had arrived before us. I saw Thea to her right. Then, a few rows down, Mars and Cameron. I couldn't spot Veda or Yejun, but I imagined they were somewhere among the crowd; it seemed that every Rotham student had come out for the gruesome spectacle. I wondered what they had done when they learned their work was gone. Which of us they blamed—our remaining four, or Caroline's immortalized memory.

I was full of hate with nowhere to put it. St. Roche continued to spout meaningless adjectives about who Caroline had been while her mother cried and her father remained rigid, his silver hair wet with rain and the high collar of a coat brushing his jaw. I wanted to seize St. Roche and shut her up. I wanted to tell Caroline's parents all the ways they'd driven her to this frenzied point, wanted to raise Kolesnik from the dead again and spit in his face for Caroline's sake. I longed to hit a past version of myself for thinking our theses were worth it in the first place, to shake Finch until she had to look me in the eyes and say something, until she could no longer blame me for all the ways we had failed one another.

But I remained frozen in place. The cold climbed down into my bones. Someone began to wail, someone who wasn't one of us or Caroline's parents—and I thought about Caroline at the Masquerade Grotesque, disgust in her voice as she said, "*Someone's crying?*"

By the time the crowd disbanded, it was just the four of us and the administration. St. Roche led the Asters away. I could feel eyes on me—I was afraid to look up, terrified that they might belong to the detective. Instead, I stared at the devotionals: a trove of gifts and paintings and sculptures and printed photos. It was like an installation, an art project someone had been assigned, homework left outside too long and sodden with storm.

Finch left first. Finally, Amrita turned and called for us to follow.

I wanted to go back in time. It was all I could think about. *I want to go back. Give her back to me. I want her to live.*

Those words, said aloud, could have been a spell. I could dig my thumbnail into that old, healed wound on my hand and rip it open again. I could bite down on my cheek until I drew blood. I could spit three times onto the promenade, tear out a hank of my hair, pluck eyelashes from their raw lids. There was possibility in ritual. The hopeless idea of forever.

But I kept my mouth shut and followed them home.

The sound of slowly ascending footsteps came later than we expected. I was on my side in Amrita's bed with my head in her lap, terrified to be alone on the third floor again, listening to the stairs creak in frozen fear. I closed my eyes as if sightlessness might help me believe that there was no creature lurking beyond Amrita's door, that it was just Caroline's parents on their way to empty her room. But both ideas were almost equally terrifying.

I shifted, and Amrita stilled me with a hand on my shoulder.

"The detective said to give them space," she whispered.

How much space could there be? I already felt as if Caroline were drifting away from us, miles between her and me. But maybe we'd been that way since the beginning of this terrible year. Maybe we'd never had a chance.

"Do you love me?" I asked Amrita, tugging at the strings of her hoodie.

"Of course."

"Will you love me forever? Even if I'm worse one day?"

Amrita smiled. "Even then."

"Would you find me in the next life?"

Her palm was hot against my scalp as she leaned closer. "Anywhere," she said. "Anytime."

I could smell her shampoo and her toothpaste. A gold bracelet slid down her brown wrist. There was a cut on her thumb—a spot where she had nicked herself at some forgotten point, likely with her X-Acto. It was a wonder to see that mar and know that it would heal. That a wound could be a wound.

"Go to sleep," she murmured. "I'll still be here when you wake up."

She brushed that hand over my hair again, soothing me.

"I miss her," I said finally, and I felt her startle; she was probably thinking I'd fallen asleep.

I waited. But Amrita didn't say anything. The only sounds were the floor shifting over our heads as the Asters carted the remnants of Caroline away from us, and Amrita's low, ragged inhale as she tried her hardest not to cry.

33

LEAVE THE LIGHT ON ALL NIGHT

The last time I saw Moody was at *Posthumous: A Celebration of Life*. With the absence of thesis work, Caroline's parents had donated every painting of hers that they still owned, and Rotham filled the atrium with it to host a show in her honor. Painting students were encouraged to create a commemorative piece for Caroline that would be displayed along with her work in place of a Solo exhibition.

The only materials I had left that hadn't burned were a pad of sketchbook paper and a set of charcoal. They had been safe on my bedroom desk, far from Grainer's fire. I wanted to draw Caroline, but I tried a million times, couldn't get the eyes right, her face always emerging incorrectly. Instead, I tried to capture something meaningful. A place we could go, before things had unraveled.

Of course, there was the summer before senior year, what I now thought of as our last truly peaceful time together. On the last day we all lay on the beach under hot light, spread out in a star with our heads in the center. I picked out a meditation and put it on Saz's speaker. Amrita folded her arms behind her head. I could feel my sunburn under my clothes as we listened to the woman's voice tell us how to manifest. Above us the clouds were wispy, a daytime moon directly overhead and a slice of rainbow beneath it. We'd chosen that spot without knowing; it marked us in place.

I couldn't think of anything to manifest, but I looked at that piece of sky from behind my sunglasses and teared up with the love I had for them.

We walked down to the water after and linked our arms until we were an interconnected row. Upon Caroline's instruction we howled at the surf like dogs, laughing, stumbling. Even Finch did it. I couldn't remember ever being so happy. When we turned back to our blanket, seagulls flocking overhead and hoping to snatch up the food we had abandoned, we found an elderly woman watching us. "I'm not a creep," she said, laughing. "I just took your picture."

It took forever to teach her how to text us the image. But we got it after a while, and there we were, an intertwined line caught forever in her lens.

With my first painting now ash, I drew that photo again for Caroline. The five of us at the edge of the water with our arms linked together, heads tipped back in our howl. I thought that maybe she might like the memory, too, if she could see it somewhere, if she was in the room with me, if she'd never left at all.

It hung beside a painting Caroline had made our junior year before she'd leaned into abstraction—a portrait of her mother sitting on their porch in Michigan, little white dog bundled in a blanket in her arms. But the sky and lake were loose approximations. She'd outlined them with a dry brush, coaxing color from the background with a wash of burnt orange until the scene felt like an earthy memory. It was strange to see a painting like that from Caroline's hand. Like looking at a past version of her, one still seeking a way to make her parents proud.

The room was laden with paintings like that. Someone had carefully arranged vinyl lettering on the glass beside the doors that read *Posthumous*. It seemed like such a crass name for a memorial show—but Caroline's parents stood beside the entrance and greeted students, faculty, and the public with smiles on their faces. Caroline's death made national news, and now there were cameras flashing in every direction. She'd given her parents the legend they wanted out of Rotham.

"It's lovely," Moody said as she took in my drawing. She had her hair down and was dressed in a tight black turtleneck, one that made her appear like a floating head. Her single earring was a bell this time—it chimed when she moved.

She didn't wait for me to respond, just kept on: "You always have such a wonderful way of showing your viewer exactly who and what you love. Your pieces are like time capsules. You take me with you, and you let me live in that moment. It's something to treasure."

I fought tears, but they rose anyway, burning high in my nose. When I didn't speak, Moody touched my shoulder gently.

"I'm so sorry about what happened to Caroline," she continued. "And I'm sorry that the work you did is gone, but I hope you continue to paint. It would be a shame if this awful year discouraged you from sharing your gift with the world. I think you would have made a fine Soloist, Joanna."

I thanked her hollowly—it was a compliment, sure, but one that only made me feel more alone. Caroline was gone. Finch wanted nothing to do with me. Saz was broken beyond repair, Amrita trying to hold the rest of us together and watching us slip through her fingers.

"You're so young. You have nothing but time. Rest now, and grieve. But don't let the world pass you by." Moody gave me a knowing smile and squeezed my shoulder before she turned back into the crowd, stopping beside Mars's piece—a gorgeous, intricate houndstooth pattern that resembled one Caroline had often worn as a quilted jacket.

I went walking in search of Amrita. Everyone, regardless of the fact that St. Roche's email hadn't stressed a dress code, had arrived in black, accessorized by gaudy jewelry and fancy little scarves. It made the atrium feel like a trendy German club as opposed to a memorial. And it made it much harder to find anyone I knew when everyone was a carbon copy of each other.

Finally, I spotted Amrita by the fountain, sitting next to Saz with plastic cups of wine in their hands. Amrita leaned her cheek against my hip when I reached them. I wrapped an arm around her and held fast, looking past the crowd at their pieces hanging side by side. Saz's was the most tender painting I'd ever seen her make: it was Caroline's torso, the thin fabric of her shirt barely concealing her chest, the pale wash of her stomach and belly button exposed. Her arms were full of limp flowers. The whole thing was made up of thick blue brushstrokes, so swollen with color that I imagined I could eat it. Even without Caroline's face in the image, you could tell it was her—the knuckles were so perfect, the wrists delicate and freckled, fine gold bracelets outlined with a narrow brush. To its right hung Amrita's piece—a finely rendered illustration of Caroline made to look like a doll in a box, with exact copies of her favorite clothes twist-tied to the packaging, so vivid and lush with color that I felt I could reach into the painting and pull that little Caroline free. And between the two paintings was another Caroline original, this time from our sophomore year. It was the painting she had made in the class where we met, an abstract layering of all the different hues we had mulled and mixed. I could see a place where her thumb had left a print.

"Seen Finch yet?" Amrita asked.

"She probably went outside to smoke," Saz said, shrugging. Her dark hair bounced with the movement. She hadn't cried yet today, but there were blue circles beneath her eyes, and her cheeks were flushed as if she might start at any moment.

Amrita gave me a pointed look. I grimaced down at her. "Finch wants nothing to do with me."

"Oh, come on. We all know there was something going on with you two. We promised we'd never date each other and ruin the friend group, in case you forgot."

I paled. "Well, something a little more drastic ruined us, wouldn't you say?"

Amrita looked away again, back to her painting. Saz's lip trembled. "I should have never opened that disgusting book," she whispered feverishly. "I should have never even brought it up."

Amrita's smile was sad. "It's not your fault. We would have done something foolish eventually. You just sped up the process."

I saw a head bob through the crowd. Finch melded and warped with the packed room. Every time I turned, I expected to find another creature in a corner. But the room remained unburdened by the dead— beyond Caroline everywhere, imprinted on everything.

"I'm going to do another lap," I said, pulling away. "Let me know if you need me?"

"Don't wander too far," Amrita answered. "Caroline's mom wants to take a picture of all of us, and she told me to wrangle you."

Saz scrubbed a hand over her face. "A picture? What is this, the fucking prom?"

Amrita shrugged. "I'm not going to argue with a woman who just lost her daughter."

I sighed and slipped back into the wave, passing Phoebe's sculpture of burned wood and rubble piled atop a marble stand—jarring to see, and even more jarring to contemplate if she'd pulled remnants from Grainer or burned the wood herself. Cameron's perfectly captured hyperrealist portrait of Caroline was so accurate that it had lost all its soul; her eyes were a cold, piercing blue staring back at me.

I passed those pieces by and went to Finch's.

It was a faceless silhouette, featureless, hairless, just a deep red shape that I recognized from a photo Saz had taken of Caroline lying on the grass our junior year, hands crossed over her head like the wrists had been knotted together. Beneath that silhouette was a warm sea of sand—the slope of the dunes sliding down to meet the shore, everything glowing with imbued light. The only mark made in the body was a bright and humanoid eye peering out of the skull. It was so alive, so opposite from Cameron's, yet equally well rendered. This one had captured something imperfect and beautiful. It was as if Finch had plucked the eye from Caroline's head and set it into the recess of the canvas.

I finally spotted Finch again. She was standing beside Thea with her arms crossed over her chest, nodding along to something the other girl was saying. I balked, considered turning away—and then forced myself forward.

"And I talked to this gallerist, but he said I'd have to intern for a while in the city, and I said I couldn't do that without a stipend, and he said I should be thankful for the opportunity at all, but I tried to tell him that—oh, hi, Joanna."

The look Thea gave me was pitying. I didn't want to think about what she was looking at—my sallow, sleepless appearance, or the way I couldn't stop myself from fidgeting with a ring around my middle finger.

"Can we talk?" I asked Finch, ignoring Thea's greeting entirely.

Finch finally looked at my mouth. She still wouldn't drag her eyes up to meet mine. "Now?" she asked.

"Yeah, now," I said, fighting to keep the irritation out of my voice. "You busy?"

Thea narrowed her eyes at me. "No," Finch said finally. And then to Thea, "I'll catch up with you later."

I led her outside. The world was finally beginning to hold on to its light; it was after five, and the sun was just starting to set. Still, I wanted real spring. I wanted everything green and good to come and stay forever. I thought if it never snowed again, I would be the happiest girl alive—that the snow would always remind me of that day, the sirens, the rising flame.

"I can't do this with you," Finch said.

"Do what?"

"You know what," she snapped. "I'm not going to feed into this ritual bullshit. Caroline is dead because of it, and you might as well be. You've been a walking corpse for six months, Jo. It's taken everything from you. That ritual was the biggest mistake we've ever made and we can't take that back, but we can move on and let it go. I need you to let it go."

"You *saw* it," I whispered. "You cannot tell me that I'm crazy."

Frustration built in her face. I could tell she wanted to lash out, to hit something, to implode, but she just ran her fingers through her hair.

"Doesn't that scare the shit out of you?" she asked. "I don't care if I saw it, because it doesn't change anything. I never want to see it again. I want to get as far away from that thing as I possibly can. We can do that. We can lock up that night somewhere and never think about it again."

She took my hands—her fingers were so warm and mine so cold, the heat of her wicking into me, seeping like blood on cloth. "Please, Jo," she begged. Then, heartbreakingly, "You know I love you so fucking much. I love all of you. That's why I'm asking you to drop it."

I wondered if Caroline had felt as alone as I did all this time, even surrounded by them. If she had also lived in the joy of seeing the creature rise and finding everyone else in awe of it too, that haunt and its capacity for power, in all that it asked of us, in all that it fed on.

"I can't," I said. "It's with me forever."

Her face fell. I thought maybe I'd see her cry for the very first time.

"Finch! Jo!" Saz called. "Photo-op time!"

Finch dropped my hand, and the absence set in immediately. She twisted away from me and obeyed Saz's call. I followed and joined the line of them as Mrs. Aster arranged us with new determination on her face.

"Perfect," she said with Caroline's mouth, "that's just right. That will be beautiful. Right side, don't look so dour."

"Smile, or she'll make us take another hundred of these," Amrita muttered through her teeth.

I obeyed Mrs. Aster's demands and forced a smile on one end of our four. Finch stood at the other. The world stretched between us in the shape of my women. I felt that eternal chain and the gaps we would never cross, all the ways we had become necessary for survival for one another. Who else would ever understand this moment? Who could ever comprehend what we had done, and where we would go, and how we would continue to go on? How would we continue on?

Amrita hooked her arm with mine. I held fast.

Summer

SUBJECTION

Epilogue

Old Friends

Most mornings, Amrita wakes me at dawn.

There are chores to be done. There are beds to make and breakfast to cook. Fields to mow and fences to mend and an old mailbox in need of a coat of linseed oil to repel the termites. There's laundry to hang out on the line. Floors to sweep. Walls to sledgehammer. Paint to coat.

This far out of town, the earth is a quilt of felled trees and overgrown grass. The property—I still feel unstable when I call it that, acutely aware of how adult it makes me feel to term the land we own *the property*—stretches for a little under twenty acres, spotted with the old buildings that are now ours. The house reminds me of the Manor with its tall ceilings and pointed windows, the glass peppered with flecked paint and bird shit. The barn is a stranger thing, closer to the charred remnants of Grainer than anything else. We'll make studios there if the grant money comes in. For now, its second floor is a tarp-covered loft where my studio sits. I burn a candle there by the curtains and ask fate to be tempted by me.

The summers are hot, the winters frigid. Time moves like a heart beating behind glass. Amrita's hair falls to her waist, and each night I sit in her room and I braid it, often falling asleep in her bed afterward with my head pillowed on her wrist. There are strands of gray along her scalp, early just like her mother. I wonder if I'm the one who put them there. If I weigh on her.

Two years of our pair sequestered in the woods, that pale isolation. Do you know how lonely two can taste?

The money was Saz's, so the house and the land are technically hers too. But it was her gift to us. In the first days of that final summer, she drove me and Amrita to the property—took us an hour outside of Rotham into the heart of Indiana where the world was just grass and sky, the house sprawling across the field.

"What is this dump?" Amrita had asked as Saz shut the driver's side door and beckoned us forward. We followed. I thought about a cornfield stretching on forever. About the five of us pushing past stalks and Kolesnik's constructed body waiting at the center.

"This," Saz said, throwing her hands wide, "is your house."

It was a farmhouse. Gabled and massive and rotten in places. The lawn hadn't been mown in what looked like years. The white paint was weathered away, sun bleaching everything a bony gray. I could smell honeysuckle and my own sweat. Saz shook her hand—a pair of keys jangled with the movement.

"What do you mean?" I asked, breathless.

"Well, it's technically *my* house. It was Amrita's idea, but I paid for it. Don't tell my dads. That money was supposed to go to grad school, and they're going to kick my ass the moment I see them."

"Saz," Amrita whispered, incredulous.

Saz gestured wildly in Amrita's direction. "I mean, you've said it a thousand times. We should open an artist residency, it would be fun as fuck, we could host artists from around the world and they could live here with us for a few weeks, making whatever work they want. We'll charge enough to get by and just have a good time. And I know the place looks condemned. It'll be a lot of work, but I think it's worth the effort."

My Saz. Her hair the longest I'd seen in the short years we'd been friends, brushing past the shoulders of a blue button-down as the wind whipped it open around her denim dress. Her hands still splayed in offering and the left one marked with a scar. Eyes gleaming with sad delight. "Don't we deserve something nice?"

"I said it could be cool," Amrita said in a rush. "*Cool*, Saz. I didn't tell you to buy an entire house. And you're—you're leaving. In a week! For god knows how long."

Saz shrugged. The smile on her face was a brilliant white beam, all straight teeth. "You two fix it up and I'll foot the bill, and someday soon I'll be back to critique all your design choices. How does that sound?"

It sounded like the end of the world. Like the only option I'd ever get. Like losing them all over again. Like waking up in the middle of a good dream. I thought about a life in that house with Amrita and the eventual promise of Saz's return. The closest proper town was a twenty-minute drive, but we could look for work there. I knew nothing about renovating. I wanted it more than anything.

"By the way, you can't say no," Saz insisted. "I forbid it."

Amrita shook her head. But I could see that she was smiling too. Her eyes caught mine and passed a question. I answered it with a smile of my own.

"Thank you, Saz," I said finally, and Saz threw her arms around me. Amrita wrapped hers around us both. I tried not to cry, but the emotion came anyway, stinging in my throat.

Finch wasn't there because Finch wanted nothing to do with us.

Graduation meant the end of Saz's student visa. She left the house in our hands and flew back to London a few months after *Posthumous* and the burial and the last time I spoke to Finch. We called all the time. We still do, spending hours discussing the future, renovations, business ventures, exhibitions, marriages of convenience, a night like all the ones we'd loved before, full of horror movies and drunken babbling and pining. We talk about the day she'll come back and all the ways our life could still change. Never Caroline. Never Rotham.

Now Amrita's still the one with the vision. We'll have cabins for the artists to stay in throughout the year. A ceramics studio with a proper kiln, plenty of easels, woodworking tools, blowtorches for welding. Home-cooked meals and enough room to share a space with other creators. There will be conversation and critique all the time, art in every room. We'll call it Aster Park. It's the closest we can come to Rotham, after its end.

Amrita handles the organizing too—she balances our finances, hosts our website, creates a newsletter. I stick to physicality and work with my hands. I cook us meals and do the washing up, particular about the way the pans get scrubbed. Feeding two is nearly impossible. I always make too much food. The kitchen isn't much, but I keep it stocked, take care of all the runs to the grocery store. The trips are nice—they give me time to consider who I am on my own.

It's a shopping day. Another with Amrita waking me just past the frayed pink of morning. She goes downstairs to start the water for her tea and my coffee, and I lean into routine—face splashed with water, summer heat weighing heavy even before the sun rises completely, sweat prickling along my hairline and the waistband of my jeans. I dry my hands and face with a towel and keep it pressed against my eyes, breathing past terry cloth.

Then she calls my name with so much panic in her voice that I nearly fall down the stairs trying to reach her.

Amrita is the one who taught me to shoot. She took a class with a man named something like Splinter or Twister or Skinner. He showed her how to handle the pawnshop bolt-action rifle we keep in the "office" in case of emergency, and in turn, she shared the knowledge with me— stock straining against the muscle between my shoulder and my throat, one of her hands dragging the bolt home, her finger coaxing mine on the trigger, a Coke can pinging with my bullet cutting it in two.

I seize the gun off its hook. She's standing by the back door—the one that faces the garden by the barn where we planted rows of cantaloupe and lettuce. There, with its head down and its tusks rooting in the crop, a boar snorts up a storm. We stand in the doorway and watch. I planned on working in the barn that evening. I'd have to walk through the garden, knowing the boar might still be nearby, waiting to gore.

"It's dangerous," I say. "We have to take care of it."

"Are you sure?"

"Google it."

Her phone takes a while to load. Amrita reports that the internet says feral pigs are aggressive, that they can't be outrun. I can only think about Caroline.

"Leave it be," Amrita says, but I step out onto the porch and bring the rifle out.

All that death on my hands. What's one more?

Rotham gave me everything that mattered: most importantly, my ability to get the work done. Two shots bring it down. Together we roll it up in a tarp, crushing half-grown melons beneath the weight of its body. On three we lift it into a wheelbarrow.

"Feels like an omen," she says. I don't say anything at all, because I'm getting a little tired of her being right.

In the house, I put the rifle safely back onto its hook, gather what I need, and tell her I'll drive it out to the edge of the property and bury it.

I wheel the boar around to the driveway and dump it into the trunk. The car is already packed. I did it last night in the dark, everything most important to me loaded into a suitcase and tucked beneath a blanket beside the boar's body. In the driver's seat, I hesitate with my hands on the keys before I twist the engine to life and take off down the dirt road.

I've thought about leaving for a while. When I'm in the car we share, it's instinct to want to steer it down a two-lane highway deeper into rural Indiana and let that wasteland swallow me whole. I could go anywhere. I could be anyone. I could shed Jo Kozak and blend into the shadows between the trees. The dream was easy enough—the commitment impossible. Where could I go that hadn't been touched by them? How could I hope for something more than the promise that Amrita would be there in the morning, and that Saz might one day come home?

I don't hope for Finch. I live in a loop of mistakes and all I want is a break.

The boar is an enormous, malignant mistake.

The car putters. Guilt roils in my stomach. By going without a word, I leave Amrita alone without a car. She'll have to figure out some other way to get into town. We're low on groceries, and she'll be hungry. The thought razes me down to the bone. I pull off the road into a familiar embankment where the trees gather, sun beating on the hood and making coins of light along the pavement. Stars bloom behind my eyelids when I press my knuckles too hard. I drag in a painful breath, and I get out of the car with my bag looped over a shoulder.

With heaving effort, I lift the tarp from the trunk and begin to drag it to the edge of the trees.

The path through the woods is worn down from my past hikes, and I follow the trampled greenery. The dense old growth is where I wander when I need to be alone, when the house is too massive and Amrita too close and Saz and Finch too far. It's the kind of place that made a myth like Mother Crone possible to us Rotham students. The origin of a cryptid makes sense when I can imagine myself standing on Rotham's campus again, staring into the dark pockets of trees. I picture myself a few years older, crushing foliage beneath my feet. Somewhere along the line, I transform from a frightened kid to the crone herself. I haunt my own forest.

In a way, that boar's appearance is the permission I've waited for.

The copse always arrives quicker than I think it will, and the forest's growth peters out until the sudden cluster of dark trees. In my own mythology, I invent a hundred reasons for it to exist—maybe a house once stood where these trees grow, their trunks marking out its boundary, notating a life once spent far from the rest of humanity. It makes a perfect spot for my reliquary. I'm grateful to see it, panting with exhaustion—the boar is heavy and the tarp slippery.

The blood all over that blue plastic is a sanguine black, and the boar's fur is coarsely matted where the wound has dried over. I clear away most of the dead foliage with a boot and roll the animal out onto the dirt, trees leaning over my shoulder as if watching me work. It's been a while since I painted anything, but now I itch for a brush. I want to leave myself and watch me work from somewhere high in the sky.

I arrange it into a simulacrum of a human body. Flies alight on its tusks as they jut toward the leaves overhead, the eyes pockets of rolled-back white. My bag hits the dirt with a thud, and from it I pull the necessary materials: the button-down I'd stolen from Caroline's closet, a little plastic baggie, a bowie knife Amrita gave me last Christmas, a folded sheet of paper long since yellowed with age. Holding my breath, I fit the shirt around the boar and roll it back into place, the head staring up at the trees and the tusks brown with old blood.

When does the body become capable of violence? What crucial thing failed in me that made this so necessary? I thought I could do anything if it meant resurrection. It all seemed to trace back to Caroline and the ways we should have kept her safe, or the times we could have let each other go before it was too late. And it's too late now, those chances long gone—all I have left is the need to see her again. The desire for her to live on, deathless.

The gash in the boar's stomach appears to bubble with an inhale. I close my eyes, blood under my nails, drag in the kind of breath you take when struggling not to cry. The baggie is difficult to pry open with my slick hands. The clump saved within it is a perfect coil of her hair—the same swirl she used to draw with on the Manor's shower walls. My fingers stain the hair when I touch it, and the sight makes my heart seize, but I tuck the blond hank into the boar's belly anyway. Next comes the creased paper. I unfold it for a final glance. It's the page Saz bookmarked in *ANTHROPOMANCY*, ripped from its binding and put away for safekeeping. I'd never been able to throw anything away. The flaw is fatal in a thousand different ways.

The scar across my palm is pink with time. I make a new cut right above it—the blood welling red and immediate. It drips over the folded paper, the curl of hair, the boar's open belly.

"I'm supposed to speak my intention," I say into the forest's lush quiet. "That's what you and I did once. That's what set us apart, isn't it? We wished it upon ourselves."

I wait, as if expecting Caroline to answer. What did she say to the Boar King we created? *May you fester?*

I look at the horror I've made, and I say, "May you wake." And then, a beat later, "Don't break up with me, asshole."

Simple, like she would have liked.

It seems reductive to think of anything related to Caroline Aster as simple. I could live a million lives and still find her somewhere along an invisible thread strung between us. In the next one we'd end up sitting beside each other in the same train car, rain plastering our hair on our foreheads, mascara painting wet spiders under our eyes. I'd wake up as her loyal dog with a collar around my neck stamped with her new name. She'd be a child on my doorstep, asking me to purchase her cookies. We'd become two men standing in a field. I would hit the ball she pitched, shade my eyes, and watch it soar. If it never landed, we never had to move on from our suspended awe.

In this life, I'm sitting on my heels in the dead green of an Indiana summer under the cover of maple leaves. The only thing in the sky is the hard white circle of the sun, too bright to look directly at, but I let it sting my eyes until the light starts to fade. The car is still waiting on the shoulder when I walk back.

There's no way for me to turn up empty handed. So I get behind the wheel again and I drive to the grocery store to pick up the things Amrita left for me on her list. I pull over at a gas station on the way back—the kind of place meant for stopping by with cash in your pocket and buying a pack of cigarettes and a Coke—and I get one of each, perched on the hood of the car and smoking three in a row, thinking of sitting beside Finch on a Rotham fire escape.

When I park the car in front of the farmhouse again and see the fireflies blinking around it, summer heat heavier than the worst winter snow, the lights on in Amrita's bedroom, I know there are no alternate universes. There is only this field, this distant whistling bird, this flickering lamp in the window.

Amrita meets me in the driveway and asks me to go for a walk.

We traipse through the grass. Amrita's not wearing the right shoes. I worry, thinking ticks. I offer to turn around, but she just shakes her head and loops her arm through mine.

There's a bonfire in the field across from ours. The farmer who lives there likes to burn their trash, and when the flames get too high, the sky turns a bruise color. As dusk falls, the pyre builds. I keep my gaze trained on its flicker. I stand there, unable to pull myself away, until Amrita digs a thumb into my pulse and turns my head to hers.

She kisses my forehead. It's just a press of the lips, a gentle reminder of our bodies.

"It won't be this way forever," she says softly. "Grieving her will weigh less one day."

I don't answer because I'm not sure if it's the truth. I feel Caroline compounding. Growing heavier and closer and sharper.

"You know you can talk to me if you need to. Haven't I told you that a million times?"

"I know," I say.

She smooths her hand down my arm and turns back to the fire. "I have something to show you."

I let Amrita take me back into the house. I drink from the cup she fills for me and eat from the plate she offers. I tip my head back when she washes my hair in the bath. And I follow when she leads me to the office, the scent of smoke banished from my body.

There's a spreadsheet pulled up on her laptop, cleverly outlined with Amrita's handiwork. She gestures for me to sit. I obey as she clicks around and scrolls through schedules and budgets, highlighting a name at the bottom of the mailing list.

"Don't be mean," I say immediately. My tongue is thick with rising tears.

"She emailed me an hour ago."

Jodie Finchard's name is lit up in green, along a column with her included note: *Are you accepting applicants yet?*

There's a bedroom in the main house's attic that we remodeled before anything else, insisting that we save it for a guest. But the room remains empty. And in the unspoken space of my heart, I've come to think of it as Caroline's.

I found Amrita in there once, asleep on her side like a child in a cot, a piece of fabric bundled up in her hands and pressed beneath her nose. One of Caroline's shirts, a piece that I recognized from where it used to hang in her Manor closet beside the one I'd claimed. We'd each gone through her room before her parents came to clean it out. Silently and with intention, we took what we wanted from her.

She was ours. We were hers. Even now I see her in dreams, in the warped original glass of the farmhouse's windows, between blades of wheatgrass in the far-off fields, hunching in the black corners of the house.

I want to go home, but maybe home was years ago; maybe it would always be the Manor with them all at my side; maybe home was unreachable; maybe home was a daydream I'd never stop having; maybe home was our youth and our belief and our power in succession. There is a piece of me in that Manor, under the floorboards. I visit it in hallucinations—water shimmering somewhere far and unreachable down the road. There's no going back. My heart still remembers theirs.

For now, I sit in Amrita's room while she showers and look at the ceiling until I imagine that my eye could peel back the wood and see into the attic where Caroline's empty bed waits, a bed that might soon hold Finch. My hands make a pleading knot beneath my chin as I expose my throat to the dark.

Finch, my solid girl with the combustible heart. What will she look like now? Just the same or brand new? Her hair still long and in her way or shorn down to the scalp? Clothes baggy and paint-stained or tailored and clean? Cheeks freckled by the sun or makeup smeared along her waterline?

"Thank you for bringing her home," I say to the apparition in the corner of Amrita's room. The shape is thin and starved and long, a blot of black beneath the soft glow of a lamp. All her golden edges sanded down. Her memory become a specter conjured by my penance. Caroline stands in the dark. The wan pocket of her face looks back at me, charred around the edges but altogether present.

Can you blame me for my belief in magic?

I think I can hear her final, wheezing cry, an echo of the day Grainer burned. Beneath the sound there's the clink of Amrita shutting the shower off, then the tapered drip.

"Did you hear something?" Amrita comes in half-dressed, toweling off her hair as she peers past her window. Caroline flickers and fizzes indistinctly. Amrita either doesn't see her or doesn't acknowledge her, but I look, I look, I look. "Must be coyotes out there again," Amrita murmurs.

With the promise of Saz's return, there could come a day when we all live in the same house again. The realization feels fated—summoned out of sacrifice.

When dawn arrives with the sound of new tires crunching over gravel, Amrita doesn't need to wake me. I'm already up and perched on the end of the bed, staring at the corner where Caroline stands. Waiting to welcome Finch home.

Acknowledgments

I lived in my own Manor once—an old brownstone on a Brooklyn art school campus, packed with my dearest friends in the world. It was haunted and the hot water rarely worked and we had to kill a legion of roaches, but I spent nearly every night overcome with gratitude. I knew what we had was rare. That the two years I spent living down the hall from people I loved were an outlier. That the moment we left, the work would start—love not influenced by proximity, but by the effort we put into making it last.

Alex, Amy, Lucy, Monica, Nico, and Nina: we work hard, and we've made it last.

Voice Like a Hyacinth is (thankfully!) not a true story, but the love written into it is real. To be eighteen and queer, afraid of everything, living in a big city for the first time and unsure of how my identity would come to grow and change left me in over my head. I am eternally lucky to have found people who would become lifelong friends and family in the process. Sorry for stealing all the cool things about y'all and writing them into this devotional of a book.

A book about art isn't possible without the incredible team who supported it. To my agent, Bailey Tamayo—your encouragement, kindness, and brilliant mind are gifts in my life. To my excellent editors, Tegan Tigani, who never fails to make me laugh mid-edit, and Liz Pearsons, who embraced this book wholeheartedly.

My time as an art school student was made possible by a menagerie of people. Truly incredible peers and equally inspiring professors made all the long studio days and nights beautiful.

To my fellow painters: a million thank-yous for the critiques, the companionship, the encouragement, the understanding, the ideation, the appreciation, and the camaraderie.

To my family, who paved the way for me to dream: I'll be putting my love for you into words until the end of time. This book, just like the first one and all the rest to come, is for my parents, my grandparents, Taylor, Ella, and Jenny. I'm proud to be yours.

And as always, to all the friends who make me a better writer and a better person—to Erin, for loving me regardless of distance and time, and for always being a home away from home. To Emma, for late-night conversations that have made each book a million times better and for being my family. To Cecilia, for your unwavering friendship and for being down for truly anything. To Aly, for a lifetime of love and for hating horror and still reading everything I write.

Finally, to all the queer girls. You're the most important thing in this world. Make art and make magic and love each other beyond words.

About the Author

Photo © 2022 Justin Borucki

Mallory Pearson is the author of *We Ate the Dark*. She is a writer and artist portraying themes of folklore, queer identity, loss, and the interaction of these elements with the southern United States. She studied painting and bookbinding, and now spends her time translating visual art into prose. She is an avid fan of horror movies and elaborate stews cooked in big witchy pots, and her work has appeared in *Electric Literature*, *Capsule Stories*, and *Haverthorn Press*. Mallory was raised in Virginia and now lives in Brooklyn, New York, with her dearest friends. For more information, visit http://mallorypearson.com.